BANSHEE   1
MOM   0

"You're not human," Mom said, rather unnecessarily. "You're a monster."

The banshee laughed. "Monster is it?" She waved her hand languidly. Six-foot-two of snarling, furry, taloned, fire-eyed rage materialized between us and the sofa. It stood on its hind legs and raised its paws to the ceiling. Thick gouts of brackish ooze dripped from the tips of its claws . . . Its breath was unspeakable, but I wasn't going to be the one to tell it about Listerine.

I caught sight of that same slim white hand making a second pass, and the beast was gone.

"Now *that* was a monster," the lady said. "I am a banshee; ye'd do well to mark the difference."

Gnome Man's Land

Don't miss the outrageous sequel . . .

Harpy High

. . . coming soon from Ace Books!

GNOME MAN'S LAND

ESTHER FRIESNER

ACE BOOKS, NEW YORK

This book is an Ace original edition,
and has never been previously published.

GNOME MAN'S LAND

An Ace Book / published by arrangement with
the author

PRINTING HISTORY
Ace edition / January 1991

ISBN: 0-441-08122-3

Ace Books are published by The Berkley Publishing Group,
200 Madison Avenue, New York, New York 10016.
The name "ACE" and the "A" logo
are trademarks belonging to Charter Communications, Inc.

PRINTED IN THE UNITED STATES OF AMERICA

10 9 8 7 6 5 4 3 2 1

Prologue

It was the smallest of holes. Neither one of the Guardians noticed it. Of course they were having one of their more hectic days, orders coming thick and fast. It was quite understandable, really, for them to overlook an accidental hole of so inconspicuous a size.

He was the smallest of sprites. His eyes were no bigger than poppy seeds, and in the Good Old Days he had taken a size XXXS in acorn caps. Even on the Leeside he was virtually undetectable, and on the Outside—? Unless the ancient vices took him over again—a puff of the pipe, a *wee drap o' the craythur*, a sip or so of Type A-Negative—he was the most discreet of midnight horrors.

He touched the edges of the hole with long, wondering fingers, unable to believe his good fortune. The rim was smooth, as if the fabric separating the Leeside from the Outside had somehow melted through. There was no sign of foul play or violence, though there had been times enough when his folk had fought desperately to break through to the Outside. They had been caught at it and stopped every time.

It was not that they loved humankind so much, or longed so dearly to return to their forfeited Outside territories, but rather that their own skins fell into peril from the unseemly habits of the neighbors. On the Leeside, you could choose your friends *and* your relatives, but neighbors were another story. He wanted Out. He was not alone.

He poked a nose long and white as a parsnip out the hole by way of experiment. If something large and fierce snapped it off, he could always grow another. Nothing did. Instead, a most delectable air of steaming meats and pungent spices wafted up the unholy length of his nostrils, setting them aquiver with ecstatic anticipation. He wiped a trail of saliva from the corner of his mouth. He had not smelled such wonderful viands in well over a century.

He was the picture of circumspection as he let the rest of his face follow his nose out the hole. A warm breeze stirred his ginger whiskers. He leaned his elbows on the circular rim of the hole much as a washerwoman might take her ease between loads to watch the passing scene from her open window. A sleek expanse of black and white linoleum tiles rolled away before him, a giant's game-board. Farther off stood a forest of massive trunks, vast distances separating them. The angle was all wrong for him to cock his head and see where each of these limbless trees ended, but it was unnecessary. He was no changeling pup to gasp in awe or shake in ignorance. He knew a table leg when he saw one.

He couldn't help himself. He *had* to see whether the hole would pass him. With many a scrabble and silent curse on the Leeside, he put his petal-slippered feet to good use, boosting himself across the sill until he hung with his rump on the Leeside and his reason on the Outside. It was rather a tight fit. If one of the Guardians had noticed, she would have compared it to trying to pry the first pickle out of a packed jar. The wall was rougher on the Outside, allowing small and clever hands purchase to pull and tug and haul until, with a moist *pop*, he was through.

He lit on his head and tumbled across the floor, landing splay-limbed on a white tile. He was on his feet and running long before he took the time to curse his injuries. As he ran, he cast one backward look at the miniscule hole that had afforded him this happy chance at freedom.

It was still the smallest of holes. Only . . . now that he had forced his way through, not quite so small as formerly. Stretched, a bit. Only a little. Probably just temporary. It was hardly worth noticing, or thinking of. He had bigger fish to fry. Without another glance, he sprinted off into the night. A world was waiting.

On the Leeside, Julia Caldaria and Torquatus Frigidarium were taking their postprandial stroll with as much dignity as their more aggressive neighbors permitted. Julia was the first to remark upon the draft. Peevishly she settled her *palla* more snugly about her head and shoulders, but Torquatus was not paying her discomfort any heed. His fine, aquiline nose twitched. He cast about to left and right like a bird dog sifting meadow air for the betraying scent of a lone, doomed partridge. It was only a matter of time before he found the hole and brought it to Julia's attention.

It was a tight squeeze, but afterwards they agreed that their passage could not have done *too* much damage. After all, they were the smallest of *lares* and *penates*, and it was still the smallest of holes.

1

Tarzan of the Yard-Apes

I WAS STANDING next to the window when I heard it: *Woe, wurra-wurra and woe to the Desmond! Death runs round the high seat of Desmond's lord! Death and dolor to the Desmond, for ye shall surely die!*

I thought it was just the radiator.

I've got to be honest, the first time I heard that spooky voice gurgling and wailing just this side of understandable, I had plenty of other stuff to listen to. Like Mrs. Mandel shrieking in my other ear that she was going to have me up on a kidnapping charge unless she killed me first. Personally I always half believed that the inch-long gel nails she wore were tipped with curare, but I never thought I'd get the chance to prove that theory in the flesh. *My* flesh.

"What have you done with my baby?" she screeched, her talons clawing the air between us. "Where's my little Blake, you pervert?"

"Now Emmeline . . ." Mr. Mandel stood with his back to the far wall, trying to call off his wife long-distance. The whole length of the Mandel living room was between him and her, and his voice wasn't made for grand opera. Even if he'd had a bull-horn, he'd need a backup mike to be heard. Provided that his wife wanted to hear him, which I doubt she did.

Mr. Mandel kept his distance. It was safer for him that way, but what about me? I never planned on dying this young, at least not until after I'd gone through the Preliminary Scholastic Aptitude Tests. In my wildest dreams (which I *thought* were pretty wild up until I learned the real meaning of the word) if I had to

die young it was going to be from a bad case of *Love Story*
disease. There I'd lie in the middle of the Sheep Meadow in
Central Park, apple blossoms drifting down over me, while the
lovely and unattainable T'ing Hau Kaplan pillowed my head in
her lap and begged me not to die. I did, though. It wouldn't
have been fair otherwise. Then my ghost hung around long
enough to make sure T'ing went into whatever's the Jewish
equivalent of a convent (Head Counselor at an all-girls Catskill
Mountains camp? Acting in Woody Allen movies?) where she
devoted the rest of her days to writing *The Life of Saint Timothy
Desmond*. If you've got to go anyway, that's the way to do it:
classy.

I sure as hell never planned on cashing it in at *chez* Mandel,
with a crimson gel nail through my heart. I just worked there,
and not that often if I could help it. Baby-sitting's a dirty job
that gets absolutely foul when you've got to mind the Mandel
Mafia, three of the loudest, meanest, most convincing argu-
ments for birth control in all Brooklyn.

Which was what I'd been doing with my Friday evenings for
most of freshman, sophomore, and this, my junior year at Glenwood High; and which I would continue to do through senior
year as well, unless Princeton got institutionally smashed and
decided to drop the whole silly idea of charging me tuition to
attend.

You know what *fat chance* means?

Tuition or not, right then Fate didn't look much in favor of
the name Timothy Alfred Desmond showing up on the Freshman
class list at old Nassau. In the *New York Post* obituary column,
yes.

"What happened to my baby?" Mrs. Mandel demanded. "His
bed is *empty*! The child is *gone*!" She stopped shrilling and let
her voice drop to the low and ominous depths of a well-gloomed
dungeon. "You were smoking dope, weren't you?" Her expen-
sively revamped nostrils twitched. Even my mother, who's not
much for gossip, had her piece to say about Emmeline Mandel's
Cybill Shepherd sniffer on an Oliver Hardy face.

"Mrs. Mandel, what you're smelling is what happened when
Colby locked himself in the bathroom and Blake jammed a pea-
nut butter-and-jelly sandwich in the toaster while I was trying to
get his brother out."

"A likely story!" Mrs. Mandel decided to ignore the corrob-
orating evidence, namely the thick wad of ashy smoke still hov-

ering captive in her windowless kitchenette. The whole apartment smelled like burnt sugar and incinerated bread. "I know dope when I smell it. I'm an educated woman, I went to City College. You were stoned out of your mind, and my Blake—my baby— he could've just fallen out the window for all you'd have cared!"

Well, she was half right.

"Now, Emmeline," Mr. Mandel said again. "We don't have any proof. We mustn't go around making unfounded accusations. Timothy is a good boy." It wasn't that Mr. Mandel was so calm or even-handed when it was a case of coming up one kid short; it was just the fact that he was a paralegal. Too much daily exposure to the blessings of the United States legal system had taken its toll. I once saw him jump when I introduced him to my cousin. Her name's Sue.

"What proof?" Mrs. Mandel snarled. "We leave this—this *punk*—with our precious children and when we come back, one of them is missing!" Her claws kept curling in on themselves, getting closer and closer to my eyes. I didn't know how much longer her husband was going to be able to restrain her. I slued my eyes discreetly around to check on whether the window behind me was open. I had visions of me leaping through the gap to freedom, vaulting over the fire escape, dropping lithely from one set of peeling steel railings to the next, rebounding gracefully when I hit the open awning of Mr. Vasquez' *bodega* below, and sprinting away to freedom.

Or I could just go splat on the concrete. Either way, I escaped Mrs. Mandel. One problem: The window was closed.

Woe! Alas and alack and woe betide the Desmond, root and branch, stock and scion! O vile despair and desolation, wrack and ruin, death and dole!

The caterwauling behind me was louder. I could hear it more clearly, especially since Mrs. Mandel had switched from howls to growls. The words were *very* clear; too clear. There was no way I could blame the shaky heating system in our building for this. No radiator around here was ever this articulate, or this depressing.

Great. First I lose Blake Mandel, then I lose my mind.

And right on cue, I heard a tinkly tapping behind me, a delicate rat-a-tat-tat on the windowpane. If this was a burglar, he was a damned *chutzpadik* one, as T'ing would say. He also had no sense of timing. I turned my head to see who this idiot at the window was, exposed my jugular, and Mrs. Mandel leaped.

"Don't you dare look away when I'm talking to you, young man!"

"Now, Emmeline . . ."

"Oh, shut *up*, Raymond. It's your son he lost, too." She pointed the Fingernail of Death at the closed door behind which lay the No Man's Land of the Mandel brothers' room. "Or don't you believe your eyes? Didn't you see our baby's bed empty? Our darling Blake *vanished*?"

Right then two things happened: The cage—I mean the door to the boys' bedroom—opened and five-year-old Blake Mandel emerged, looking like a wayward angel. He scuffed into the living room, rubbing sleepy eyes and cradling an incredibly mauled teddy bear. "Mommy?" he piped. His voice was so ungodly sweet he could've made Christopher Robin sound like the demon in *The Exorcist* by comparison. He reached up his chubby little arms and said, "I need a kiss night-night."

This is all fine, unless you know that Blake Mandel normally has a voice that sounds like someone feeding ferrets through a Cuisineart, always refers to his mother as "Hey!" and has never in remembered history asked for anything that wasn't advertised on TV as only $39.99, plus tax. A kiss night-night? For *free*? Right.

Mrs. Mandel stared. Mr. Mandel tried to burrow his way backwards into the peach- and blue-flowered wallpaper. Blake toddled closer, blue eyes full of the pure light of innocence. He was wearing blue Dr. Denton pj's with feet. (The last I'd seen of him, he'd been sporting a Ninja suit with a rabid dragon on the back.) Tenderly he handed the bear to his mother. "Would you please fix him for me, Mommy?" he asked. "I think Teddy's got a boo-boo."

This was the same bear whose belly the kid had slit open with a pair of Romper Room safety scissors that very evening. Next he had ripped out the stuffing, refilled the cavity with torn comic books, a rubber gecko, and a Jell-O chocolate pudding pop, and stapled it shut. I know, because I was the one who stopped him during Phase Two, which included gouging out the poor beast's right eye and trying to stuff it up his younger brother's nose.

His mother mumbled a promise to put Teddy through boo-boo triage right away. He kissed her and told her she was the best mommy in the whole, wide world. He gave his father the same treatment, which Mr. Mandel accepted in just the same shell-shocked way as his wife. And then . . .

Then he came over, grabbed me around the knees, and said he thought I was the neatest, bestest, swellest babysitter he'd ever had, cross his heart and hope to die!

From that same wonderful kid who'd called me "Dead meat" earlier that same evening when I wouldn't let him stab his big brother J.R. with a fork.

Something was rotten in the state of Flatbush.

That was when I smelled it. It was like someone had unloaded a dump truck full of dead halibut on the fire escape behind me. Right through the glass came the smell, and the tap-tappy-tap noise got louder.

The Mandels didn't smell it any more than they heard the rapping. I don't know how they could ignore it. I have smelled ripe gym socks, their special bouquet brought to full perfection by proper aging in my good buddy Scott Harper's locker. This was worse. This was a stench you could build time-share vacation homes on. This was a smell that not even the dead could ignore. In spite of that, the Mandels acted like nothing was going on. Together they walked their precious middle son back into his bedroom. I heard them ask him where he'd been hiding when they'd done bed-check just a few minutes earlier. I didn't hear his answer.

What I heard was: *Death flies low on the Morrigan's dark wing, circles the heir of Desmond! Woe, out, alas, and evil tidings! Horror on horror piled, and horrors more to drink the Desmond blood!*

More tapping in back of me, and then: *Listen, lad, would ye be kind enough to open up the window? A body could catch a mort o' chill out here.*

I turned around. There she was. Gorgeous and golden-haired, skin so white it shone like a star. Even all hunched up on the fire escape, knees and elbows drawn in tight, I could tell she had the kind of long, graceful limbs high-fashion models starve and study to get. I couldn't say whether her most fascinating feature was a pair of huge, glowing, tip-tilted green eyes or lips so red they looked as if she'd been raised on a diet of candy apples. I wondered whether her mouth would taste like a candy apple if I kissed it.

Did I mention she was naked? She was. That slipped my mind for a while. As I said, she had *very* fascinating eyes.

Lad, are ye deaf to me? Her voice didn't come to me through my ears, but rather seemed to rise up my spine. She banged on the window some more, harder. *Open up, I said. There's words I'd have with ye before ye perish. Come on, step lively, ye've not got all that precious long to live, and it's a busy banshee I am!*

Not long to live? Me? But what about Princeton?

I opened the window and handed her into the room. "Want to tell me more?" I asked.

If she did, she was suddenly no longer in a hurry to do it. *Ah, isn't this the fine place, then,* she breathed.

She clasped her hands behind her back and began a leisurely ramble around the Mandel living room. Fortunately for my peace of mind, once she was vertical, her gossamer hair was long enough and lush enough to put Lady Godiva to shame. It covered an awkward situation just fine.

Barefoot, bare everywhere else, she gave the place the once-over. The painting of a purple Persian cat on black velvet enthralled her. The row of *Reader's Digest* Condensed Novels in the bookcase got the briefest glance. She stopped dead when she found the pink ceramic planter on the coffee table. It was shaped like a castle, with an iridescent white unicorn besieging it. He had only half a gold-leafed horn left, thanks to one or all of the Mandel boys. The princess in the castle turret had a bunch of Scotch ivy growing out of the top of her head in lieu of hair.

"Mercy on us." My friend from the fire escape spoke in hushed tones, covering her mouth with her fingertips. That planter *was* pretty stunning.

"Hey, you're speaking normally," I said. It was true. It was the first time I heard her utter a sound that didn't scrape flakes off my shinbones.

"Sure and why shouldn't I?" she replied. She looked miffed. "Isn't it enough and to spare of a warning I've brought ye? Or is it thick as bog oak ye be, and needs must have the message spelled out further?" She took a deep breath—*Doom and undoing to the Desmond! Mourn ye the fall that shall be! Death and the dark house rising o'er the bones of Desmond! Woe, woe for the final fall in blood battle!*—and once more I felt as if mice were gnawing my nerves.

"Have ye got it now, Timmy lad?" she asked pleasantly.

I didn't know whether to question her first about who she was, *what* she was, why she was predicting such depressing things as doom and death for my future, or where she got off calling me

"Timmy." I never got the chance to choose; that decision was made for me.

The boys' bedroom door opened again. The Mandels came out, looked right at her, then at me. This time I didn't have to worry about being the only one aware of an alien presence. The seafood smell was even stronger since she'd come inside. Mrs. Mandel's expensive nose wiggled. Mr. Mandel's bargain model wrinkled expressively.

"*Who* is *this*?" Mrs. Mandel's deadly digit was now leveled at the lady's barely veiled heart.

"And—if you don't mind my asking, miss, absolutely no sexism implied, just ask my wife, I fully supported the ERA—why are you naked?" Mr. Mandel inquired.

If Timmy lad hadn't gotten it now, I was sure going to get it real soon.

2

Generation Gap

MY MOTHER HAS her own problems. That's what she always says whenever she hears someone else complaining about those little things that go wrong every day: the repairman who doesn't show up, the secretary who puts you on "hold" and forgets you're there, the hairstylist who saw *The Texas Chainsaw Massacre* right before you sat down in his chair. The thing with Mom is, she really does have her own problems. She calls them the three M's: Money, McDonald's, and Me.

Money's been a problem ever since Dad decided to go out for a Sunday *Times* and didn't bother to come back. That was six years ago. Checks never came, or letters. There were never any phone calls. Once I asked Mom why she didn't do something like track him down through a good, cheap detective agency. She just gave me a funny look, went into her bedroom, and came out with a bundle of letters. She took them down the hall to the incinerator and tossed them into the chute. It didn't take a rocket scientist to figure out that those letters contained every last trace connected with my father, every clue that might allow me to follow him. Gone was gone. Now that I was playing Sam Spade Jr. she was going to make very sure I didn't unearth something best left buried.

I guess I can't blame her. Sometimes I still wonder, though.

McDonald's is where Mom works. Starting at the counter the week after my father left, she made her way up to being a manager, and she's a good one. The only trouble is, she hates her job because it leaves her too tired to work seriously on what gives her real pleasure: painting. She's turned out some mighty impressive work, all self-taught. I may be prejudiced, but I think that an objective observer would agree with me about how much raw talent she's got. The walls of our apartment are covered with her canvases. If she could quit the day job, or even cut back on the hours, she'd be happier, but a cutback in hours means a cutback in pay, and that takes us right back to the Money problem.

Then there's Me. When Mom used to talk about the three M's, she always laughed when she mentioned me. My inclusion was just a joke, done strictly for the sake of alliteration, and she did everything but spell that out with alphabet blocks to make sure I knew it.

After Mrs. Mandel got through talking to her, I wondered whether she'd laugh about Me as M Number Three ever again.

I never thought I'd equate the sound of our front door locking with the crack of doom, but that's just what it sounded like after Mom herded Mrs. Mandel out and shot the bolt home. Then she turned to me.

It was like that old Abbot and Costello routine. "Niagara Falls." Costello's trapped in a jail cell with a man who's all right until he hears the words "Niagara Falls." Once that happens . . . slooooooowly he turns, step by step, inch by inch, until he lets out an insane yowl and leaps for Costello's throat.

And there stood my mother, looking at me like I'd just said "Niagara Falls." Slooooooowly she turned, step by step, inch by inch—except that's where it stopped. Mom did not leap. She just . . . looked. What a look. I wish she'd have gone for my throat instead.

I was sitting on the Castro convertible sofa in our living room, which is also my bedroom. We live in the dinkiest of three-room apartments in the Lyndhurst, a sixties construct not noted for generous floor space, high ceilings, or soundproof walls. You can hear it when the people next door count their money; paper money. If you practice long enough, you can even tell the different denominations apart. Maybe it was the tissue-paper walls that kept Mom from letting out the insane yowl, but I doubted that. She didn't scream and go for my gizzard, because she didn't have the heart for it. I'd taken that right out of her.

"Oh, Tim," was all she said. Then she shook her head and went into her bedroom, shutting the door behind her.

I stayed on the sofa, miserable. Mom has given me heart-to-hearts, lectures, sermons, and full-blooded Little Big Horn dressing downs. She's not afraid to raise her voice to me for fear of bruising my psyche or turning me off strong women. When I make a total jackass of myself, she cares enough to let me know it. When she sees me tap-dancing on the lip of a volcano in margarine shoes, she'll haul me back by the scruff of the neck and ask my psyche's permission afterwards.

When she couldn't drum up enough ginger for more than one anemic *Oh, Tim*, I knew I'd really done it this time. What was worse, I wasn't even sure of what I'd done. I felt like someone had sneaked in and snapped a pair of lead shackles on my ankles. Even with the extra weight dragging me down, I managed to get up and shuffle across the room to Mom's door. When I knocked, she didn't tell me to come in, but she didn't tell me to stay out either.

It was light and bright in Mom's bedroom. She had every bulb blazing. She isn't the kind of mother who holes up in the dark for effect. They're never going to make her Prom Queen of the Martyrs, either. I found her the way I knew I would, sitting on the edge of her bed in front of her easel, working ferociously on a new picture. When what's inside can't come out any other way, she paints.

"Mom?" I said. She kept lashing on the acrylics. "Mom, I swear to God, I don't know who that lady was in the Mandel's apartment."

"That was no lady, that was your wife, right?" Mom replied, jabbing in a bunch of blue flowers with a blunt-tipped brush. "Tim, if you don't want me to tell Mrs. Mandel about her, fine. But *I* want to know who she is. I have the right to know."

"Look, if *I* knew, I'd tell you. I've got nothing to hide."

"Neither did she, apparently." Mom's mouth twisted into a sardonic smile. "Mrs. Mandel told me that they couldn't find a stitch of her clothing in the apartment after she left. Mr. Mandel looked very carefully as soon as he got his fingers bandaged."

I regarded my shoes. "I don't know who she was and I sure as hell never told her to bite Mr. Mandel."

"Don't use that kind of language in front of me, Tim," Mom said automatically. Ever since the recess gang in the P.S. 269 started expanding my vocabulary, she's been waging a long, losing war against even my mildest curses. It hasn't worked completely, but I do tone it down around her.

"Well, I didn't," I maintained.

Mom cleaned off the blunt brush and picked up a pointed one.

She started tracing in the features of the person in her picture. Mom never uses live models, except when she does practice sketches in the park. Her style is what they call Superrealism; she works from photos mostly, and sometimes just from whatever springs into her head. This painting I'd driven her to was one such flight of pure fancy. Everything was still just roughed in, but it looked like a balcony scene to me, maybe her idea of how Juliet must have looked while waiting for Romeo to show. I squinted my eyes at the lone lady in the picture. Even this early on, Mom's Juliet looked peeved.

"You know, Tim," she said, "if it weren't for the physical evidence—Mr. Mandel's bitten fingers—I'd assume that the strain of raising those three mini-thugs had finally gotten to our neighbors. Catching you with a naked woman is one thing, but one that apparently materialized in a seventh-floor apartment with no clothing to call her own? Not even a robe?"

"I'll pay for Mrs. Mandel's housecoat," I said.

"You're missing the point—and anyway, since they didn't pay you for tonight's stint with the Brattish Inquisition, I'd say you're even." Mom leaned forward to do some detail work and a strand of coppery hair fell across one eye. She's got the kind of hair that's a spiritual barometer: It doesn't like being kept tied up in a tight, businesslike twist any more than Mom likes being trapped in her job. It keeps trying to escape, even if she can't. She tucked it back in place and went on. "Mrs. Mandel said that this person called you by your *full name* within her hearing. What's more, she said that when she questioned the woman, she made several comments that revealed she knew much more about you, me, the Mandels, and several other people in this building than she ought to know, under ordinary circumstances."

Mom popped her brush into the water jar, planted her hands on her hips and leaned back to look at me. "Tim, this could be serious. The Mandels have three children—trainee Creatures from the Black Lagoon, every one, but still just kids. There are a lot of other children in this building, too. When a total stranger who acts—so bizarrely—just shows up and speaks about those kids as if she's been *spying* on them, knowing their comings and goings, like she's been *watching* them for some reason . . . "

I felt sick. I knew what Mom was getting at. It hadn't happened so long ago, but everyone in the building, on the block, in the whole neighborhood, had done their best to forget it as soon as possible.

Somebody stole a child. It was in the papers. It was a little girl, just about eight years old, who lived right down the street from us in the next apartment building over. Her mother went to pick her up from Brownies, and the den leader told her that the child never showed up. The Brownie troop met right after school, in the same building where she'd been all day—her teacher said she was in class. Somewhere, somehow, between school dismissal and Brownies, between her classroom and the lunchroom where the troop met, she disappeared. They never found her, dead or alive.

"Darling, this—friend of yours—may be perfectly harmless. She might be just a bit eccentric, like Aunt Mariah, but I have to know. I have to have something to tell the Mandels. Thank heaven, we haven't had any other—incidents—but if God forbid another child vanishes and someone *that* strange has been seen in the neighborhood, knowing so much about everyone in this building—"

La! The cheek of herself, to go slinging mud on a poor, defenseless banshee's reputation! And when did these hands ever soil themselves with the stealing of mortal children, I'd be knowing?

I stiffened like an unwashed paintbrush. The voice was back. So was the Fulton Fish Market smell. Once more, both were coming from the window: the window behind Mom, the window giving on our fire escape. It was deep night outside, and all the track-lights and occasional lamps Mom used to brighten her bedroom were on full blast. The glare off the window made it pretty hard to see outside, but I had a feeling. . . .

Feeling, hell. I *knew*!

Mom saw me tense up and asked, "What's wrong, baby?"

I couldn't say. I couldn't hear the question. My ears were too full of another voice, a voice that rode up the inside of my spine and bored right through my brain.

Is it the elf-lord's lap-dog she'd make me? No better than ouphe or pucklet, to be rattling round the Midrealm with a basket o' babies under one arm and a clutch o' snot-nosed changelings tagging at me skirts?

My eyes adjusted. I saw a familiar face pressed against the glass, scowling at me. Her original nakedness was safely hidden by Mrs. Mandel's stolen housecoat, but something about her wild beauty made that tatty rayon wrap look like silk robes fit for royalty. I couldn't help staring.

"Tim, what is it? What *are* you looking at?" Mom asked. She turned her head and glanced over one shoulder, out the window, right into the banshee's irate face. The banshee put her tongue out and made a gesture I'd never thought of as Irish. Mom turned back to me and shrugged. She hadn't seen a thing.

I heard an indignant snort that rattled the windowpane. *And this is the thanks I get for coming to keen over her only son's grim doom! It's not as if I haven't better things to do. Nary a reverence she makes me, but looks me full in the eyes, the brazen slut. 'Tis not merely a graceless wench she is, but a purblind bitch in the bargain!*

"You can't talk about my mother that way!"

"What did you say?" Mom gaped at me.

"There!" I shouted, pointing madly out the window. "There, on the fire escape! She's there!"

"Who is?"

"Her! The lady who bit Mr. Mandel! The banshee!" I lunged for the window, but Mom and her easel were in the way. I managed to upset the water jar, knock the canvas over, smear wet paint down the left side of my denim jacket, and skin my right ankle on the bed caster. Mom let out a cry like a tail-trodden Yorkie; I ignored it. The window was latched. I pulled one fingernail halfway out of its bed as I jerked around with the lock. With a loud, inarticulate shout of triumph, I flung the window open.

On nothing. The fire escape was empty. The banshee was gone.

"Young man . . ." When Mom says those words in that tone of voice, it's all over but the reading of the Will.

"She was there," I protested weakly. "I saw her."

"Young man, if you think that was funny—" Mom stopped. She stood up. She sniffed the air.

"*What* is that atrocious stench?" she asked.

"Stench, is it?" came a high, unhappily familiar voice from the living room. "From one who hasn't a whiff of breeding to her name, and fancies herself a garden of roses in the bargain! The curse of Cumhail on ye and all yer high, persnickety ways."

Mom and I almost wedged ourselves in the doorway as we rushed back into the living room together. The banshee sat on the sofa, her long, bare feet curled under her. She was eating the last of the bowl of fruit Aunt Mariah had brought us, and obviously enjoying it.

It was wax fruit. This didn't seem to make much difference to the banshee, but it sure made an impression on my mother.

"You're—you're—you're eating—"

The banshee popped one last bite of fake pear into her mouth. It looked like a glob of melted yellow birthday candle, but she smacked her lips anyway. "Sure, and it's a tasty larder ye stock, even for a charmless harridan such as yerself," she told Mom.

"You're not human," Mom said, rather unnecessarily. She was doing a pretty fine imitation of a stranded goldfish, gasping and goggling, but she still managed to add, "You're a monster."

The banshee laughed. It was like music; music of the John Cage variety. This time Mom winced just as much as I did at the grating sound of that otherworldly voice.

"Monster, is it?" She waved her hand languidly.

Six-foot-two of snarling, furry, taloned, fire-eyed rage materialized between us and the sofa. It stood on its hind legs and raised its paws to the ceiling. Thick gouts of brackish ooze dripped from the tips of its claws. It opened its orange maw wide enough to accommodate a whole watermelon and roared until all the pictures hung crooked on their hooks. Its breath was unspeakable, but I wasn't going to be the one to tell it about Listerine.

I caught sight of that same slim white hand making a second pass, and the beast was gone.

"Now *that* was a monster," the lady said. "*I* am a banshee; ye'd do well to mark the difference. Teleri of Limerick, as I'll be thanking you to call me, at yer service." She yawned and stretched, causing her borrowed housecoat to fall open. Mom was still too dumbstruck to order me to cover my eyes, or the banshee to cover her options. "And it's a weary one I am at that." She drew herself into a rayon-wrapped ball on the sofa and began to snore.

Mom recovered a bit and started for our unanticipated guest. I grabbed her arm before she could reach the sofa. "What do you think you're doing?" I hissed.

"Well, I'm—I'm going to wake her. She can't sleep there; it's your bed. Where will you sleep?"

"Mom, if we annoy her, we might not have to worry about where either one of us sleeps ever again." I tried to ape the vanished monster and probably looked like an idiot. "Look, I don't mind, I can drag out my old sleeping bag, I'll be fine. You go to bed. Maybe when we both wake up in the morning, it'll all have a turned out to be a bad dream.''

If it was, it had more endurance than a Hollywood divorce lawyer. When I woke up the next day I had a stiff back, an apartment that smelled like cat food, and Teleri of Limerick, who'd moved off the sofa and right into my sleeping bag. For a nightmare, she took up an awful lot of room.

3

Ain't Mama Happy,
Ain't Nobody Happy

"OUT," I SAID. It emerged from my throat as a croak, but I was afraid that if I said anything too loud, Mom would hear. When Mom hears something, she comes to investigate, and this was one situation I didn't think I'd be able to handle with my natural boyish charm.

Teleri made a purring noise and threw one arm over my chest. Her golden hair was tickling the right side of my face and the dead dolphin smell was gone, banished by the gentle scent of spring lilacs.

"Is it awake ye are, love?" She shifted some. In a sleeping bag that size every shift had a meaning all its own. I groped for the zipper, really wanting out more than I'd ever wanted anything in my life, including the lovely and aloof T'ing Hau Kaplan. Anyone who's ever done any hard time in a cut-rate sleeping bag knows that finding the zipper, let alone manipulating it, is not easy even without company. So let's just say I really, truly, honest-to-God swear I *meant* to reach for the zipper. I did.

What I wound up getting . . .

"Ooohh, 'tis a bold-faced rogue ye are, my lovesome lord, and no mistake!" Teleri went kittenish, her pale cheeks tinted a delicate shade of pink oddly tinged with green. "Death hovers nigh, and all that, but it's dearly glad I am to see that the last of the Desmonds knows how to live what's left him to the full."

"I *do not*!" I shouted, and found the zipper. I wish Mr. Ambrogio, my Phys. Ed. Teacher, could have been there to see how fast I slithered out of the bag and scrambled to my feet. He'd never bawl me out for slacking again.

Panting for breath, I gazed down at Teleri. The lady—er, banshee—was miffed. Her little chin rested pugnaciously on one
fist, and the fingers of her other hand were drumming out a dead
march on the carpet.

"Is it monstrous ye find me, then?" she asked. Her voice was
too sweet, like chocolate-covered caramels. Anyone who's ever
put in a session with the family dentist knows that *too* sweet is
always the prelude to really intense pain. The way she said *monstrous*, too, made me recall the toxic horror she'd summoned up
the night before.

A woman scorned can make you wish you were dead. A banshee scorned can deliver the goods.

I never talked so fast since third grade, when I had to explain
the live gerbil on rye that *somehow* got into Billy Klauser's lunch
box. (Not fast enough, though; Billy grew up to be two hundred
ten pounds of grain-fed beef, the prize halfback of the Glenwood
High Gargoyles, and the chief reason I don't loiter in the locker
room. A halfback never forgets.)

"Oh, you're not monstrous at all, ma'am—uh—miss—I mean,
Ms. Teleri." (Hey, play it safe!) "You're a very beautiful woman.
It's just that I'm—I'm not good enough for you. It wouldn't work
out between us. I need some space. I'm not ready for a com-
mitment. You deserve better. Someone special will come along
for you, you'll see. But I hope we can still be friends."

All right, so I'm not Mr. Originality. I was banking on the
fact that a creature fresh from Fantasy Land was not going to be
up on all the clichés of Splitsville-speak.

There was a yellow flash all around me, and when I blinked
away the after-spots, I was staring at the ceiling from way down
low near the floor. Huge waves of cloth, a familiar color, were
looming over me from all sides. I felt very cold.

"Ribbit?" I said.

Teleri picked me up and balanced me on her palm. Her face
looked different when viewed through a frog's eyes, but my brain
quickly compensated everything back to human terms. I wish it
hadn't. Being turned into a frog is bad, having to *know* you're a
frog is worse.

And that sly, smug, gloating expression on Teleri's face as she
looked at me? The worst.

I said a quick prayer that her knowledge of this world didn't
include garbage disposals or microwave ovens.

"Now, me dearie, there'll be no more o' that blarney with

yer Teleri, will there? Sure, with the black wings o'erspreading the sky before ye, it's naught but natural for a man to play the fool. Play it with someone else than me, yer lordship, and while it's no longer ye'll live, at least it's a pleasanter few days of life ye'll pass.''

She motioned with her index finger and I was back among the non-amphibious. "So in other words, no more bullshit. Right?'' I asked sheepishly.

Her smile was bright and cold. "Not the smallest spadeful. If ye've no wish to dally, 'tis a poor banshee's lot to accept her lord's desires in all—almost all—things. Ye cannot hold a girl to blame for trying, though.'' She sighed. "A pity. A dreadful shame. So finely made a lad as ye be, too. Well, perhaps it's but the thought o' death has put ye off frolics . . . for a time. Could be ye'll mend. I'll bide.'' Her eyes lowered slowly. I could almost feel them sliding down my skin.

Which was about when I realized that skin and air were the only things Teleri and I were wearing. When she'd whomped me into a frog's body, she hadn't taken my pajamas along for the ride. They lay in a heap on the living room rug, next to the tousled sleeping bag. I gave a loud squawk and dived for them.

Too loud, too late. The bedroom door opened. Mom came out. She had her mouth all set to demand *what* was going on out here, but when she got a good look at the players, she didn't need a scorecard. Her mouth snapped shut. She didn't want to know what was going on; she knew. She was wrong, but try telling her that.

She just stared, shook her head, shrugged her shoulders, and went back into the bedroom, closing the door behind her.

I turned to Teleri. "Now see what you've done!" The look in Mom's eyes was one I'd never seen before. It was the distillation of all past disappointments she'd suffered on my account, and it cut scalpel-sharp and deep. I didn't care if the banshee turned me back into a frog and dropped me in Bio. 109 (OUR AMPHIB-IOUS FRIENDS, IN PIECES), I was mad.

Teleri crossed her hands on her chest and opened her eyes wide. "Me?" Her magical voice slammed me right in the stomach with a dose of offended innocence. I knew it wasn't rational, but I felt as if I'd just kicked a cocker spaniel puppy, or a Muppet.

She turned from me with a sweeping gesture that ended up as a hand limply pressed to her brow. She strode back and forth the length of the room, as if our apartment were the stage for a third-rate melodrama. She wrung her hands, rolled her eyes at the ceiling, beat her breast, did everything except wail *But I can't pay the rent!* and struck several alas-poor-Yorick poses while declaiming:

"Ah, woe, alack, and false accusation fly readily from the ungrateful sprout of Desmond's own! Alas and weep ye now for the poor banshee that was only seeking to comfort the graceless lad with what few humble gifts the Powers have dowered her. Out, out on it, and dreary dole be all my lot, that ever I should live to see the day when—"

Meryl Streep she was not.

"Shut up," I said. I didn't mean to snarl it that way, but I was trying to get my pajama bottoms back on, hopping around the room, and Teleri kept jostling me with her posturings.

"What?" The word came out crisp and cross.

Uh-oh. Curtains. Asbestos ones.

Since I was slated to die anyway, I decided to do it like a man. It crossed my mind that most of the men I'd seen die were in movies and comic books, which meant there was going to be an awful lot of blood splattering around the apartment real soon, flesh melting from bones, vital organs popping like over-inflated party balloons, kiss your security deposit goodbye, but what could I do?

I had nothing left to lose, so I was honest.

"I said—I *asked* you to shut up. Please."

"Oh," Teleri said. "All right, milord." And she went into the kitchen. That was that. She didn't summon up any extras from Nightmare Central, she didn't leap out brandishing any sharp objects, she didn't even holler at me. Nothing.

Well, not precisely nothing. She hadn't ducked into the kitchen to sulk. Soon the smell of frying bacon and percolating coffee came drifting out. Take my word for it, the first cosmetics manufacturer who can bottle that aroma is going to have the Number One unisex lure of all time. I started counting to ten on my fingers, and before I hit six, Mom was out of the bedroom, nostrils twitching and the love-light in her eyes.

"Ah, it's there ye are, mum!" Teleri bent over the breakfast table, pert and pretty in a gingham apron that demanded *who invited all these tacky people*? Her smile was so welcoming that you had to look really close before you realized that under the *tacky people*, our banshee was still in the buff.

Setting down a plate of perfectly crisped bacon and a mug of coffee at Mom's place, Teleri said, "Now just feast ye awhile on this, and drink deep, and we'll settle the sorry misunderstanding that's come between us, milady. Aye, that we will, and to yer full satisfaction, curse me for a *cluricaune* else."

I didn't go to the table right then. I took the opportunity to get dressed for school. I did it in the bathroom, with the door locked, and I put on more layers of clothing than the weather called for. Suddenly I was a great believer in defensive dressing.

You see, there's nothing . . . *wrong* with me. I mean, Teleri was beautiful, and desirable, and probably I'm going to wake up ten years from now and break my back trying to kick myself for passing up a chance like that (if I've got ten years, or even ten days!), but I just—couldn't. And I wasn't even sure why not. It could've been Mom's presence in the next room, or my own sorry lack of Boy Scout training (Be Prepared!), or maybe just plain old stage fright—how old, and how experienced was Teleri, after all?—I just knew it was out of the question.

I came out of the bathroom to find Mom and Teleri chatting away as if they'd been college roommates. Both beckoned me to breakfast, and Teleri even chided me for not drinking all my orange juice.

"It's all right, Tim," Mom said. "Teleri's been explaining a few things about being a banshee to me, and I've been letting her in on how we do things a little differently over on this side of the Atlantic. It's a family thing you inherited from your father. I'm supposed to give her a saucer of milk for her troubles, but she prefers Maxwell House. She's promised me she won't bother you out in public again, where people can see her."

"Nor smell me, what's more," the beaming banshee added. That bizarre pink-and-green blush rose to her cheeks. " 'Tis a fool I've been to blame ye for noticing what's as much a part o' me as breathing. Accustomed as I am to living with it, it slipped me mind. A touch o' the nixie blood as runs in my veins, is all."

"Water spirits," Mom put in for my benefit. "On her mother's side. Sort of like your Aunt Mariah, only with gills and without gurus."

"Aye, 'tis a tossbrained lot the seafolk be." And Teleri and Mom fell back to trading blood-relative horror stories.

I pushed away my plate and cleared my throat as loudly as I

could without tearing it silly. "Aren't you forgetting something?" I asked Mom.

She paused midway through the saga of Aunt Mariah's past-life bout with being both a Montague *and* a Capulet. "Why, I don't think so, dear. Was there some permission slip I had to sign for you? Tim, I've told you and told you, don't wait until the last moment to let me know when you need me to do something for you for school or—"

"The last moment," I said, "is just what's on my mind. *My* last moment, if you don't mind." I pointed at Teleri. "She didn't just show up here to serve breakfast. She came to announce that I'm going to die! You mind if I get a lit-tle concerned about just *when* that's going to be?"

Mom's bright expression turned dark at once. Only then did I realize that she'd been using the mental tricks so many people turn to in tough binds: If I act as if everything's just the way it was before, maybe the bad thing will go away. In this case, the bad thing was bringing out a fresh pot of coffee and asking whether Mom would like some toast.

Mom started to cry.

"Whisht! It's English muffins I could make ye instead, curse the name o' them, if ye feel that strongly," Teleri said. She laid a comforting hand on Mom's shoulder, and had it shrugged off violently. Thoroughly confused, the banshee turned to me for guidance. (MORTAL WOMEN IOI: UNDERSTANDING THE HUMAN MOTHER. This class canceled pending further notice, until we can find someone smart enough or dumb enough to believe it can be taught.)

Very slowly I said, "I think she's upset because I'm going to die." I got a blank stare back from Teleri, and louder sobs by way of confirmation from Mom. "You *do* know about sorrow? Bereavement? Mourning?"

Teleri scowled. "The cheek! And what manner o' banshee would I be did I not? Mourning's me business, so it is! And sorrow me second nature. Faith, this is as poor a reception as any I've had. Die? And so ye must, as must we all, even the Fair Folk in their season. 'Tis grateful ye should be for the convenience of knowing aforetime, that death not catch ye with yer breeches a-sag. What's tainted the fine blood o' the Desmonds on this barbaric soil? Time was, on the old sod, that I'd come round keening to beat the band, and soon as the family knew who it was I meant, they got on with the funeral arrangements and no more said until the death itself. Then there was weeping, right enough, but none o' this''—she dismissed Mom's grief with a wave of her hand—"anticipation, like. To wail after a dead man, that's fit conduct for mortal lasses. To keen for him before he's proper dead, that's banshees only!"

Mom gulped down the next sob and sat up straight. "In other words, I'm poaching." Her eyes got small as she stared at Teleri. "Out," she said.

I wondered whether Mom would have better luck than I did when it came to ejecting banshees.

I should've known.

The banshee turned up her tiny nose, wadded up the apron and tossed it aside. I looked down at the floor really fast, but I heard her say, "So be it. And by the Powers, may ye never more hear my voice, if that's how ye'll be about it. Aye, only the Desmond may hark and hear, save that his lordship desires it otherwise, and none but the Desmond sight and see me. Moreover, may all knowing of me be as a dream to ye, mortal mole, and a sorry harvest be all yer reaping."

She snatched another strip of bacon from the plate and vanished, munching.

Mom blinked. Her face was that funny, empty mask of someone who *knows* there is something important to remember but hasn't a clue as to what.

Nature hates a vacuum. Mom filled hers by saying, "Tim, if you don't get a move on, you're going to be late for school."

It was nice weather out, for early spring. A few lumps of dirty packed snow still hung on at the curb, gray speckled with black, and spattered yellow from you can guess what. The leaf buds on the one lousy tree on our block were still curled tight. This wasn't the *Tree Grows in Brooklyn* variety; it was an elm. A raggedy, soot-coated, moth-eaten elm that had somehow cheated vandals, runaway trucks, and Dutch elm disease to hang on in its little circle of sour city earth cut out of the pavement. For an elm to last this long in a place where experts agree it wasn't supposed to, it had to be very lucky or very tough. I gave it a pat on the bàrk, hoping that maybe some of the luck or strength would rub off on me.

The branch just over my head trembled and burst into purple flowers. I froze, but you can't turn off your nose: Lilacs.

And fish.

4

A Little Knowledge

GLENWOOD HIGH IS what you call a good New York City public school. Every time I tell that to my cousins from Indiana, they ask if that means that the weekly body count stays under twenty. Very funny. As if the Hudson River were some kind of magical border where the drug problem and teen pregnancy and in-school violence and Ms. Alexinsky's *Hamlet* lecture stop dead.

Well, okay, maybe they don't have to put up with Ms. Alexinsky's hour-long yawner out in Terre Haute—the undead cannot cross running water, and the Hudson's mucky seep comes close enough for jazz—but they've got all the rest. Broasted chicken and regular patronization of your local Stuckey's are no guarantee of virtue. And I don't know for sure, but I don't *think* the local chapter of the KKK has been too active in Brooklyn. For one thing, their sheets wouldn't stay white.

So why do I call it a good school? Let's just say that no one at Glenwood High has been dragged in for packing serious weapons. Not yet. Certainly not me. It's not *Leave It To Beaver*, but it isn't *Flatbush Chainsaw Massacre* either. All in all, it's a pretty nice place to rack up four years' credit towards a ticket out of Brooklyn, and that was all I asked of life; that, and somewhat more of the unattainable affections of the lovely and aloof T'ing Hau Kaplan.

Or did I already mention that?

This, of course, was the situation pre-Teleri.

Wurra, wurra, and woe to the Desmond! Dark the raven's wing that shades the brow of Desmond! Sorrow shall surge up like the sea, and tears flow like the Shannon. Aye, many the moan that shall be made round the rath, and all for the passing of the Desmond!

Not exactly the kind of pep talk you need cramming your ears when you are desperately trying to remember both forms of the past subjunctive of *tener* during one of Mr. Richter's alternate-Friday pop quizzes in Spanish.

I got a forty. This was not good. This was bad. This was seriously undesirable. Face it, this bit dead puppies.

"I'm never going to get into Princeton!" I shouted, slamming a fist against my locker. The crumpled quiz was in my hand, the big four-oh blazing like a beacon. I don't know where he gets it, but Mr. Richter manages to use incandescent ink to mark all of my tests that fall below eighty. You can read the miserable digits clear across the cafeteria, even if I wad the stupid paper up into a ball the size of a Chicken McNugget.

"Hey, Tim, calm down. It's not that bad." Larry Perlmutter lounged against the locker next to mine and observed my tantrum with the cool, emotionless eye of a man whose golden future is a foregone conclusion. Straight A's followed him home all the time, like stray cats, and he got to keep them.

On the other hand, females were not so cooperative, which might be why we've stayed friends this long.

Larry isn't that bad-looking, but his perpetual unflappability can get on a person's nerves. The problem is, he doesn't *look* unflappable. He looks ready to panic over everything, anything, and nothing, all at the same time. It wears you out, waiting for the crisis that never comes.

There's nothing about his outer looks to warn you about his inner sang-froid, either. Here's this borderline-babyfat guy with these big, brown, nervous eyes and a yes-ma'am-please-ma'am smile on his face, and the minute a girl starts trying to kid around with him, maybe break the ice, taking it really slow and easy so she doesn't spook the poor little guy, she gets an in-depth psychosociological analysis of every word out of her mouth. If she's like most, she doesn't like it, and she's gone.

I like to think of him as Mr. Spock caught in the body of the Poky Little Puppy. I also like to while away the lonely winter nights imagining what would've happened if just once someone had rigged the original Mr. Spock's belt so that his pants did an unscheduled beam-down on the bridge. It might've done him—and his Glenwood High incarnation—worlds of good. In my head I was always screaming, *Loosen up, Larry! It's okay to lose your*

head once in a while. These are the best years of our lives; we're
supposed *to be scared shitless!* In the real world, I just let him
go his own way.

"Not that bad," I repeated. "Right." I jammed the paper
into my notebook. "You don't have to get your quiz signed at
home. You don't have to face a grounding. Maybe," I added. I
have to be honest. Mom is never thrilled by bad grades, but
mostly all she does is yank TV privileges and ask why-aren't-
you-in-the-library every time she finds me somewhere non-
library, including the bathroom. The sheer nuisance value
generally gets my average back up where she's happy, and the
bathroom is my own again.

Larry looked wistful. "Lot of difference it makes, whether I
get grounded or not." He sighed. "So, if your mom doesn't
lower the boom, you want to go catch a movie tonight? If you
don't have a date, I mean," he added.

*Late the hour and cold the wind that are but warp and woof
of the winding sheet to wrap the heir of Desmond!*

I winced. Larry thought it was because I, like he, had another
Friday night of male-bonding staring me in the face, oh-joy-oh-
rapture. For an instant I wondered whether I should tell him
about Teleri and the sleeping bag. Either he'd take it as a warped
joke, a symptom of incipient hormone-induced insanity, a really
juicy Jung-yard dog of a dream or else . . .

He might believe it.

Naaaah!

"No, no date," I said. Larry relaxed. The status quo of the
Glenwood High jet-set remained, well, status quo.

And then the ceiling shattered, the lockers groaned and gave
birth to penguins, the floor dropped out from underfoot and
slammed sideways right into my face, and the structure of reality
in general assumed the stable qualities of molten pizza cheese.

Or in other words, the lovely and aloof T'ing Hau Kaplan
appeared at the end of the locker row, spied me, made an end-
zone rush an NFL scout would kill for, and flung herself into
my arms like the finale of a really good old Bogart-Bacall movie.

"Oh, Tim, thank God I've found you!" she gasped.

Larry stared. Vulcan logic didn't cover lunacy. My eyes
needed roping in some, too. Was I dreaming? She smelled real
enough. T'ing's personal fragrance was a blend of Breck sham-
poo, Johnson & Johnson baby powder, and Jean Naté after-bath
splash cologne. I know, because I put in enough time doing

clandestine deep-breathing exercises in the lady's general vicinity while pretending to copy her notes on Ms. Alexinsky's *Hamlet* lecture.

"Uh, T'ing," I said. (God, I'm masterful.) "What's up?"

"Are you doing anything tonight?"

"Well, I—" I darted my eyes at Larry. He rolled his to Heaven. Clearly T'ing had lost her marbles, and if I didn't grab them all while the grabbing was good, I was nuttier than she was. "I mean, Larry and I—"

"—was just telling Tim that I already saw that movie, and it was too bad, because Tim really, really, *really* wants to see it." Larry's eyes radiated heavy honesty. All he needed was a chestful of gold chains and a used car awaiting sale in the wings. "I don't suppose you'd be willing to go see it with him?" He projected Artlessness about as well as he handled Sincerity. If he batted his eyelashes at her, I was going to knock his block off.

"Yes! Oh, yes!" T'ing's normally sleek black hair was a storm of wisps around her face. Her skin was too pale for health, and her eyes kept darting sharply from side to side, as if she were being followed by IRS agents. Her hands clutched mine. And I thought *my* palms were sweaty! "Please come get me right after dinner. We're done by six-thirty. Don't be late, *please*!"

A bell rang down the hall. She startled like a dawn-caught ghost and raced away. I told the empty air that yes, sure, I'd be there right on time.

So much for aloof. Was this the same T'ing Hau Kaplan whose usual sum total of conversation with me was, "Oh, hi, Tom—I mean, Tim: 'djou get all of what Ms. Alexinsky said about Ophelia being a precursor of the Industrial Revolution?"

I turned to ask Larry whether we'd entered the *Twilight Zone* and no one had bothered announcing it over the P.A. system, but Larry was gone. Promptness was his watchword. The day a class bell rang and didn't find Larry neat in his seat, ready to suck up knowledge, the world as we know it would be *terminado*.

I'm no slacker either, I just didn't happen to have a real class right then. If you sashay into study hall late, the most you'll get is a low-key growl from the teacher on duty. Generally they only have a teacher's aide minding the store. Most of these are nice local housewives built like a fleet of sofas. They actually *like* kids, which puts them at a real disadvantage when it comes to maintaining anything like discipline in study hall.

Things were about as usual when I came into the room. In the back row a couple of suspicious contrails were creeping up towards the ceiling from behind open textbooks. Nearly all of the undercover smokers sit in there and bring looseleafs the size of elephant ears to cover up their nasty habit. The middle rows are taken up by Glenwood High's urban answer to preppies, most of them female, all of them heavily into student government, social committees, and pompoms.

I had to climb over eight sets of elegantly pantyhosed legs to get to an empty seat. "Hi, Brooke; 'scuse me, Ashley; howzit going, Heather? h'lo, Megan; sorry, Summer; hey, Kirsten; wanna move that bag, Jennifer? pardon me, Tiffany." They pouted at me. It was better than when they giggled.

Just in case anyone thinks that I grabbed a midsection seat because deep in my heart-of-hearts I nourish a secret yen for alligator shirts, forget it. I don't sit in the back with the smokers because I'm allergic, but try convincing Mom of that when she comes home, takes a sniff, and declares that my clothes reek of tobacco.

Sit in the front, then? No, thanks. That's a good way to die young, with or without a banshee on your case.

Solid leather. Heavy metal. Wall to wall meatloaf between the ears and a *bad* attitude problem. There are only five of them, but when they decide to come to study hall—or school, for that matter—they like to sit right up front. That way they can whisper words that would make a Marine blush, *just* loud enough for the monitor to wonder if she heard right. They take bets on how she'll react, highest prize if you can make her send for the assistant principal, extra points if you can bully an innocent bystander into taking the rap for you when he shows up. If the words don't work, they can make little paper balls and flick them at the other kids. No one says anything. No one wants trouble. When they really get the wind up, and the monitor's a teacher's aide who made the mistake of wearing anything less than a turtleneck, they try shooting cleavage baskets.

Ladies and gentlemen, the Rawbone Kings.

Could be it was the phase of the moon, or maybe something besides the usual dose of plutonium in the drinking water—the same mysterious element that had turned T'ing from the Ice Queen into someone about as aloof as a game-show host—but today of all days, the Rawbone Kings were bonzo. They didn't bother whispering the S, F, B, and C- words; they yelled them

top volume and even improvised the Y, N, G, and W- words on
the spot. They *chewed up* the little paper balls before flicking
them at Mrs. Fiorelli's ample target. Neil Fitzsimmons, alleged
head of the Kings (if slime-molds have heads), went so far as to
tear the top off a pack of Camels and light one up in full view.

That did it. Mrs. Fiorelli was the one school aide at Glenwood
who did *not* like kids. She had four of her own, all of whom she
loved with an intense, maternal passion and for whose sake she
would commit murder, but damned if she *liked* any of them. I
overheard her on hall duty once. She'd captured this poor geek
who was trying to exit the school via a side door where she
played Cerberus. She got very philosophical:

"Look, you, you try to pull any of your little shenanigans
around me, you'll wish you never got born, got that? You-are-
going-to-*hell*, you hear me? You and all the rest of these morons
with cork for brains. Listen all day to that trash music, sit all
night in front of those lousy TVs, burn your stupid eyeballs out
playing video games, wouldn't pick up a book if it came and sat
in your *lap*, and the whole rotten world could go to the devil for
all you ever care. You ever help your mama around the house?
No! You ever pick up one lousy rag of your dirty clothes? *No!*
You even care that your mama spends all day slaving over a hot
stove making *your* meals, going blind from darning *your* stinking socks, working her fingers to the bone keeping *your* room
clean? *NO!*" She folded her arms across her bosom—no easy
call. *"And you want to go out my door?"*

Like I said, a regular Aristotle. What made the incident perfect was the fact that Mrs. F. is four feet five inches high by
four feet two inches wide and her victim was my old pal Billy
"No Neck" Klauser. Of course he never went home and tattled
about that dressing-down.

Now, Billy is a basically okay guy, even if he does want to
snap my spine between his teeth. So if that was how Mrs. F.
reacted to a "good" kid trying to bend a minor school rule, you
can imagine the impression Neil "No Parole" Fitzsimmons
made when he lit one up under her nose.

After she screamed her face a nice, uniform eggplant shade,
she sent him to the vice-principal's office. Only she didn't trust
him to go there on his own, and she wasn't about to leave her
post until the bell rang.

Three guesses who got tapped to ride shotgun on the suicide
run?

"Look, Desmond, you're not stupid," Neil told me when we were well down the corridor from study hall.

I had to agree with him on that one.

"You know there's no way I'm going down to have Jarhead Jared rag on me." (This was Neil's quaint way of referring to our imposing vice-principal, Mr. Jared Alden. Yes, descended from *that* Alden who was told to speak for himself. Our Mr. A. never had any trouble speaking for himself, plus playing mouthpiece for God Almighty, Who always agreed with every word Mr. A. ever said. Nine out of ten Glenwood high students would rather do time in Mrs. Fiorelli's idea of Hell than in Mr. A.'s Puritan Heaven.) "So let's go."

"Huh?" I suggested.

"You know, let's get outa here." Neil thumbed down the hall in the direction of the big green front doors, where the security guard sometimes lurked between cups of coffee. "Catch a slice of 'za, play some Double Dragon, you got any quarters?"

While he patted me down expertly for small change and separated me from same, I asked what had to be my most intelligent question of the day: "You mean, cut school?"

Neil had to take his hand out of my pocket to straighten up and look me in the eye on that one. "Yeah. What else?"

"I can't do that."

"Yeah?" He shrugged. "So okay. See ya." He started away, my change jingling in his jacket pocket.

Plutonium. It had to be plutonium in the water that had mutated my brain. Neural controls that once screamed SURVIVE! were now urging SELF-DESTRUCT!

I ran after him and grabbed his arm.

"You can't go either," I said. "I've got to take you to the V.P.'s office. You know the kind of trouble you'll get if I show up and tell them you cut out?"

"Hm," Neil said, giving me the once-over. I'm no shrimp, but if you want to make a pasta-schematic of me and Neil side by side, you'd use ziti for his arms, vermicelli for mine, and if Billy Klauser gets in the picture, his are canneloni. So when Neil said, "You're right, we can't split up," I should have worried. "That's why you're coming with me."

"Look, I said I can't cut school—"

"See, if you don't come with me, I'm gonna get shit here and more shit at home. I don't need this no more. My old man gave me plenty last time I was just having a little fun, and he puts the beef behind it when he's not happy with me." That was true. Neil had shown up in school a number of times sporting facial bruises and never mentioned the other guy's funeral. Mr. Fitzsimmons was no Mr. Rogers.

In this same cold, psychotically *reasonable* voice, Neil told me that I was going to be the one to suggest our mutual exit, so that when we got caught—as we eventually would—the royal hooraw surrounding a "good" kid gone bad would provide welcome distraction from the more ordinary event of a "bad" kid just doing what everyone expected of him. I'd take major heat, Neil would get a slap on the wrist, and everybody would be happy.

"I won't," I told him. And I wouldn't. If Mom didn't ground me for the Spanish test *el stinko grande* grade, she'd have to be dead not to do it for this. In light of what now awaited me this very evening, damned if I was going to risk losing a date with T'ing (even if she had lost her mind) just to oblige Neil. For one thing, T'ing smelled better.

"Okay." Neil's gang-jacket creaked when he shrugged. "You don't want to walk out of here on your own, that's fine by me." The leather fairly groaned as he pulled his right fist back. I watched him go into his wind-up with all the autonomy of a small furry animal hypnotized by headlights. How appropriate: I was going to be a Parkway Pizza too. Neil was clearly determined that I was leaving school with him one way or another— as co-conspirator or carry-out hamburger.

I closed my eyes and wondered if T'ing had any silly old prejudices about dating dead men.

5

Our Little Secret

THE IMPACT OF the blow echoed through the school hall.

I opened my eyes. Something was wrong. I was still vertical. I wasn't supposed to be the one left standing. And what was Neil doing flat on his back on the floor, taking up *my* place?

Why was I so upset about still being conscious? Good question.

Better question: Why was there a small albacore tuna fish flopping its last across Neil's face?

Sure, and what's the madness of the Desmond line, that they're forever courtin' their own dooms? Teleri's long-suffering words bloomed in my brain just as she materialized cross-legged on the black linoleum by Neil's head, wearing about as usual. *Whisht, that's a chill welcome!* She winced and promptly levitated, legs still tailor-style, until she reached my eye level. *Can't ye at least wait until I've cried the final keening o'er ye proper before ye have this great spalpeen perish ye? 'Tis a fine keening, and many's the long hour I've spent on the poetical refining of it. The curse o' the* lhiannan sidhe *on ye, is it bone ignorant ye be, else mere ill bred that ye'd so scorn a lady's artistic endeavors?*

While I searched for some adequate reply to the banshee's accusations, Neil stirred. He groped across his face and got a tail-hold on the tuna, which he pulled aside. Mouth hanging slack (ditto the tuna), he sat up to a brave new world.

"Holy shit," he said. "A fucking banshee."

I started talking fast first, listening second. "Look, Neil, I'm sorry about the fish. I should've warned you, I'm taking this new martial arts class, *Sushi-No-Ginza*, the art of low-cholesterol self-defense and—'' You could almost hear the sound of brakes skidding over my tongue as his words finally registered. *"What did you say?"*

"Her," Neil replied, pointing up at Teleri. He wiped a few stray scales from his eyes. "The banshee." While I had been paddling like hell to explain away the ad-libbed tuna fish, he'd been looking at my banshee as if he saw one every day.

When I didn't respond, his eyes and mouth narrowed. "You *do* see her, don't you? I mean, she's talking to you and you're, you know, talking back."

"Well, and to whom else should I be talkin', ye great ugly brute?" Teleri gave Neil a glower of chill disdain that the (still) lovely and (formerly) aloof T'ing Hau Kaplan might have envied. "Nor what business be it of yours that the last of the Desmonds has harmless commerce with meself, as is his family's own proper *bean sidhe*?"

I grabbed Teleri's elbow and hissed, "Hey! You said no one else but me was going to be able to see or hear you! How come he can? What gives?"

Before she could answer, I felt a meaty paw wrap itself around my elbow. It was Neil. He'd dropped the fish, which now lay glazing over nicely on the hall floor, and he was back on his feet. "You got no brains at all, Desmond? Jesus Christ, don't you know *nothing*? You treat the Good Folk with respect or, man, you are *fucked*. You want that?"

I allowed that I didn't. Then I decided to play it sly. "So, uh, Neil, you really see her?"

"What's not to see?" Neil's severe expression melted back into his normal doggy leer. "Pair of tits like she got, man, I'd still see 'em in the fucking dark!"

Teleri folded her arms across the points under discussion and scowled. "And be this the respect ye preach, ye young mouse-turd?" She floated the tuna up from the floor and caused it to swing back and forth before Neil's face in a threatening manner.

Neil gave the albacore pendulum a good shove that turned it into a finny pinwheel. Obviously the menace of further ichthyic assault didn't faze him. "Hey, what is it with you women, can't take a simple compliment?"

Teleri rolled her eyes., "Lug's arm, is it that incorrigible a barbarian ye be? And where's the grave of all sweet Irish speech to a lady, if that's the best ye offer me?" She vanished the spinning fish. "It'll take more than a tunny to beat courtesy through yer thick skull, I vow."

Neil shrugged. "Who ain't courteous? I'm courteouser'n hell. Just said I liked the merchandise. Anyway, you're *his* family banshee. He's the one gotta watch his ass around you; not me."

"Watch his ass, is it?" Molten caramel oozed into Teleri's voice. I'd heard that high-calorie tone before, and being a quick study I knew it was the prelude to something really vicious, possibly with fangs. I could have warned Neil that now was the time for all smart men to start making with the apologies.

I could have done that. I really should have. It would have been the right thing to do. Maybe I don't eat enough oatmeal. Guess I'm just not going to get anything but coal in my stocking for Christmas.

"Yeah, what I said, baby." Neil winked at Teleri. "He watches his ass and I watch yours."

"Watch yer own," Teleri remarked softly, twitched a finger, and instantly made poor Neil physically able to comply with her directive.

"Oh my *GOD*!" Neil grabbed two dark and curly handfuls of his hair and tried to yank them out, don't ask me why. Maybe he thought the pain would be enough to rotate his lower body back to where his feet once more pointed in the direction he was facing. It didn't work. His knees buckled with shock. Now that they were 180 degrees around from where they used to be, their weakness pitched the poor guy forward—er—backward-uh—right onto his face. *And* his butt. Now, that was an impressive maneuver.

"What's all this?"

Thunder broke over Brooklyn. Very well-bred, well-modulated, Harvard-educated thunder. With a ghostly glide any Renaissance assassin might covet, Mr. Jared Alden had manifested in our midst without word or sound of warning. He is the only adult I know who can turn a pair of slick, squeaky new oxblood wingtips into Stealth sneakers.

"M—Mr. Alden. Sir," I said.

The V.P. skewered me with a gimlet eye until I knew how a fishworm feels when the hook goes in. "Desmond, isn't it?" His voice had the power to turn my name into a list of criminal charges. It's a point of pride with him to know the name of every Glenwood High student by heart, the way doctors keep mental lists of noxious bacteria. Mr. A. stands about six feet four inches tall and a hefty one hundred forty pounds. I know it sounds negligible, but imagine a WASP python with the same measurements. It's all muscle and it's all mean.

"Yes, sir," I said, admitting my shame. "Timothy Desmond. Ms. Lenotre's homeroom."

"*Miss* Lenotre." One long, white, shiny-nailed index finger flicked up an inch from my nose as he corrected me. The same finger began to tap his lips, which wasn't easy because he doesn't have lips. Almost every feature on his face, from ice-blue eyes to intermittently flaring nostrils, can be described as a series of slits and slashes.

"And tell me, Timothy Desmond, why a young man who doubtless should be somewhere else, pursuing his education, is instead making loud the welkin ring in company of *this* living proof of Darwin's theory?" He twitched a nostril in Neil's direction.

Not for one second did he acknowledge the presence of Teleri (which I guess was understandable) or the fact that good old Darwinian Neil was back-to-front from the belt down (which was not).

Neil groaned again, then started to gibber. It was fascinating. I thought the only things that gibbered were nameless abominations in H.P. Lovecraft stories.

"Be quiet, Fitzsimmons," Mr. Alden snapped, still trying to bore holes in my skull with his eyes. "You'll be dealt with in turn."

"But Mr. Alden—" Neil's whine shrilled up to touch a note he hadn't hit since his voice changed, back in fourth grade. "Mr. Alden, *looka* me!"

Mr. A. sighed. "Must I?"

"Aw, c'mon, I mean, just *look*, woudja?" He gestured insistently at his subequatorial turnabout.

Mr. Alden did look. His expression remained unchanged, his comments came as close-clipped as a draftee's scalp. "Very good, Fitzsimmons. Ingenious. Anything to get a laugh, as if your grade-point average weren't enough."

"Mr. Alden, this ain't no *joke*!" Neil tried to take a step closer to the V.P., but forgot one little detail. Thrown off-balance, he windmilled his arms and did a crazy cross-town stagger. Mr. Alden made one neat sidestep and permitted Neil's face to intercept the wall. Rubbing his cheek, Neil muttered, "This is for real."

"No, Fitzsimmons, this is another of your mindless, childish pranks. It is also a needless visual reminder of your entire ass-backwards career here at Glenwood. While I admire the effort and expense you've gone to, I can't say as I see the place of all this in a reputable high school. Rest assured, your exploits will receive my full, personal attention. I no longer have to get your home phone number from your personal file, did you know that? I put it on my automatic dialer just to save time. In a way, I should thank you for this opportunity. I've been meaning to ask your father whether this early chill we've been having is affecting that war injury of his. Such an interesting man. So ready to understand the importance of proper discipline."

I watched Neil's face go white when Mr. A. mentioned his father. But you don't get to be the head of the Rawbone Kings without an inner wellspring of reserve gumption. He swallowed his fear and declared, "Mr. Alden, I'll prove this ain't no joke." He reached for his fly.

Fortunately, he'd forgotten that it was now around back. Teleri tittered as Neil fumbled for the zipper that wasn't there. Mr. Alden's slitty blue eyes got down to razor-blade thinness, and his mouth followed suit.

"Fitzsimmons, expose one millimeter of illicit epidermis within my ken on school property, and expulsion shall be the least of it."

"Huh?" said Neil, frazzled by the V.P.'s vocabulary and frustrated by his recent reversal. I wondered what the poor geek was going to do when Nature called.

"Moon me and die," came the translation.

The bell rang, saving us all—or so I thought. Mr. Alden's cold grin flashed on and off like a neon Budweiser sign. "Well, well. Time for your next class, gentlemen. Don't let me keep you."

I could hardly believe my luck. Mr. A. was so ticked with Neil over what he thought was just some mighty good, mighty stupid costuming that he was going to let us off on the loitering-and-disturbing-the-hall-peace charge. "Yes, sir. Thank you, sir," I said. If God had given me a tail, I'd have wagged it. I started back to the study hall to recapture my books.

"Yes, no need for me to keep you now," Mr. Alden drawled. "But I'll want the two of you in my office directly after your last class. One hour's detention. *After* I make a few phone calls."

The hall was already building up its between-classes roar as the doors opened and students came rushing out, most of them in more of a hurry to escape their previous class than to get to their next one. I felt the last inch of Mr. A.'s needle slip into my spine just as the noise-level surged around us. Detention! *After* some phone calls, and I knew who he was going to call. At work. Add disturbing Mom while she was on the job to the news that I'd pulled an hour's detention, *plus* the forty in Spanish, and the other end of the equation would have to read: NO DATES. Not tonight. Not Saturday. Not next week. Not until a week after you're dead.

Very quietly, very thoroughly, I cursed Mr. Alden. It was a classic—I guess you'd call it a cliché—but it came from my heart.

There was no way he could hear it, not with the distance between us and the racket around us. I only did it to let off some steam.

Someone did hear it, though.

Arrah, not so poor a saying fer a tender lad like yerself. It could use a mite o' refinement, but have it just as ye would, milord. I obey.

Way down the hall, Mr. Alden suddenly let rip a maniacal yell and took off running. Startled students exchanged glances of mixed terror and delight. No one found the personal initiative to jog after the V.P. in his mad race, but the Glenwood High jungle telegraph of rustling whispers tore alongside him in a parallel course.

Less than three minutes later the riptide of rumor washed back up the hall to where I still stood. "—into the *pool*?" hissed Scott to Brooke to Larry to Tiffany to Tinker to Evers to Chance to me. "Jarhead jumped right in the pool with *all his clothes on*?" I never even had to move a step.

Not quite the lake ye requested he jump in, milord, but a good banshee makes do. Without further by-your-leave, Teleri planted a quick kiss on my lips and vanished.

I was left to give solitary thanks that I hadn't uttered a wish that Mr. Alden drop dead, go choke, or kiss my—

"—associate with a great guy like you, Des." Neil clapped me on the back, partly to top off the load of heavy friendship he was trying to forklift onto me, partly to hold himself steady. "Yeah, like I always told the Kings, you got something." Sure I did: a banshee. "It's, like, a real honor to kinda hang out with a take-charge, kick-ass guy like you, you know what I'm saying?"

"Yeah, Neil, I know." I was feeling drained, but Mom always taught me to tidy up after most major disasters. I closed my eyes and mumbled another request into the void.

From somewhere both as far away as the moon and as near as my own skin, came a peeved response: *Oh, very well, milord. If ye'll insist on it. 'Tis a fortune ye caught me still near enough to hear ye.* There was a *ping*, or possibly a squeee-*pop!* Whatever the sound effects, Neil was again able to face north and sit south.

I tried fending off Neil's gratitude by pleading a class to get to. That worked only until dismissal time. Dutifully, dumbly, I headed for Mr. Alden's office. Neil and part of his gang met me at the door.

"Hey, Des, no sweat, okay? I was just in, and old Jarhead's secretary didn't have nothing down about no detention for us." He showed me a fine set of teeth. "Looks like Jarhead's got his own troubles, after that dunking you gave him. He's down in Doc Ox's office right now, trying to explain."

I felt sorry for Mr. A. Our beloved principal, Dr. Clark Oxenstierna, is as hard a man to deal with as to spell.

The other Rawbone Kings didn't take it too well when Neil informed them that from now on, I was theirs to protect, defend, and cherish, though it cost them their lives, their sacred honor, and their British Knights hightops.

"Des is gonna be the man to fear at Glenwood High," he told them, with a wink to me. Being wise, he didn't try explaining to his minions that the reason I had suddenly acquired so much juice was supernatural. He must have figured that as their leader, *Because I say so* should be reason enough for his men. "Yeah, Des is gonna *rule*. We want in on it, we're his."

"Bullshit," they replied, with all the harmony and unity of the Vienna Boys' Choir.

It took a few high-level management-personnel arbitration sessions out on the basketball court after school, but he made them see his point. Also the blacktop, up close and personal.

Which was how I came to call on the lovely and aloof T'ing Hau Kaplan in company of Brendan Macray and Ibrahim Carter. The latter bears an imposing similarity to a young Walter "Refrigerator" Perry. True to his leader's directives, he rang the doorbell *chez* Kaplan for me. I don't know, maybe he'd seen *The Godfather* one time too many.

Mrs. Kaplan opened the door.

Mrs. Kaplan is a Democrat, supports the ACLU, and stood up to her mother-in-law when she and Mr. Kaplan decided both to adopt T'ing Hau through a Taiwanese liaison agency and let the baby keep her given name. She will not wear fur, saves the whales, recycles, defends to the death uncensored rock 'n' roll lyrics, and permits her children to read science fiction.

Ibrahim smiled. "H'lo, Mrs. Kaplan, we're here for your daughter."

Mrs. Kaplan slammed the door.

I wound up baby-sitting that night, a last-minute call from the Mandels. Mrs. Mandel had decided to forgive me for the naked lady—out of the goodness of her heart and the realization that no one else in the immediate neighborhood was desperate enough to mind her trio of juvenile werewolves at any price. I tried to get Ibrahim and Brendan to come along, but they folded. Even a Rawbone King knows some fear.

Though Blake was still as unnervingly adorable as that weird night a week ago when I'd first met Teleri, his brothers were normal. Read: rabid slugs. I called down one picturesque *sotto voce* curse after another onto their curly heads; in vain. My banshee was not on the job. Hey, maybe she had a date.

By the time I dragged home, a little before midnight, all I wanted was bed and a childless marriage.

The phone rang. I flung myself on the living room extension at the first ring, afraid it was some crank who'd bother Mom.

"Tim, where *were* you?" T'ing sounded farther past the end of her rope than when she'd first accosted me in the hall. "Why did you have to come get me with those *people*?" Even if I could have explained, T'ing didn't give me the chance. "Never mind. Come over here now. My parents don't have to know. I'll sneak downstairs and meet you in the convenience store on the corner. You've got to come. I have to see you."

"T'ing, it's too late at night. You should just—"

"Please!" And she hung up.

Fifteen minutes later I was pretending to study the dirty magazines at Bradley's News 'n' Chews while being eyed by three types who'd give the Rawbone Kings *and* the Mandel boys pause.

Sixteen minutes later T'ing showed up and dragged me out. She wanted me to come with her, somewhere she could tell me what it was that had her so upset.

Sixteen and a half minutes later, by my best hindsight guess, we'd picked up something nasty, and I don't mean on our shoes.

Three of them. Two of us.

I hate math.

6

Who Was That Masked Lunatic?

PATIENCE IS A virtue. That must have made those three bits of bad news behind us the most virtuous muggers in Brooklyn.

Of course I didn't know that they were behind us at the time. They didn't make their move right away; they couldn't. T'ing lives in an apartment building much like mine, on a pretty busy street. Friday around midnight things are just getting started, even in Flatbush. Couples are getting out of the movies, heading for restaurants, going home or just looking for someplace else to be. T'ing and I looked like just another couple, and our three prehensile tails looked like just a bunch of guys—you know, kinda hangin' out, not hasslin' nobody, sorta messin' around, not doing nothin', you got a problem with that, mister?

"Can we go get a Coke somewhere, Tim?" T'ing asked. She was hunched up inside a Glenwood Gargoyles pep squad jacket, her hands jammed into the pockets of her jeans. I swear, she was shaking as if it were midwinter, though the October night wasn't all that cold.

"Yeah, sure, whatever you want. Only let's make it somewhere quick. We've got to get you home." *And me, too, before Mom finds out,* I thought.

"There's McDonald's—"

"No way!" Utter panic hit me right between the eyes. I didn't need one of Mom's fellow managers on the late shift spotting me and bouncing back the news that Mrs. Desmond's little boy was out when he should have been in. "I mean"—I downshifted fast from *heebie-jeebies* to *God, I'm suave,* and nearly stripped gears—''I mean, why settle for McD's? We can do a little better. I just pulled a stint with the Mandel menagerie. I've got money.''

I've also got a good, loud, carrying voice. It was a sucker bet whether the threesome from the News 'n' Chews overheard or not. They couldn't help it. One punk kid and one little girl, and the punk kid's got money on him for sure. No wonder they didn't veer off in search of other game. When a bunch of lions have a crippled zebra under their noses, they don't go off looking for a healthy bull elephant.

Were they in the Napoli Pizzarama with us while we got Cokes and slices, or did they lurk outside, waiting? I don't know. I was too caught up with T'ing to notice anything else. Billy Klauser missed his big chance. If he'd have sneaked up behind me that night and put a lizard in my shorts, I'd never have known.

Come to think of it, being around T'ing always makes me feel like I'm harboring reptilia in my Jockeys, but I try to think about baseball, so no harm done.

This night was different. I was too worried about her to feel anything stirring but my heart. T'ing looked rough. Even when we were inside the Pizzarama, she still trembled. All sorts of worst-case scenarios flashed through my head. Was she in some kind of major trouble? Drugs? Sex? Money? Sickness? Something wrong with her family? She didn't give me a clue. I hung suspended on a filament of cold dread, on the one hand terrified that she was never going to tell me what was wrong, on the other scared to death that she would tell me, and I wouldn't know the first damn thing to do about it.

She wasn't making it any easier. Not a word, not one beyond saying she wanted a diet Coke instead of a regular one and a plain slice instead of pepperoni. She sat with her hands still anchored in her pockets. If you're wondering how she managed to eat and drink like that, I'll let you in on a secret: She didn't. She bent her head over the food and stared at it, but that was all.

I couldn't take it anymore. I mean, she didn't just ask me out at this hour, that desperate, to watch her watch olive oil congeal over a layer of mozzarella. Being a woman of mystery is not like her at all. T'ing was born in Taiwan, and despite the fact that she was barely three months old when she came over here, she's still had to deal with a lot of that inscrutable-Oriental and ineffable-mysterious-East crap. She has always been direct, honest, and unafraid to say exactly what's on her mind. What was so big to make her hold back now? Time to go fishing, before I cracked under the suspense.

"So, T'ing . . ." I fiddled with my straw. "You feeling all right?"

"Mmgph."

Oh-kay. That didn't sound like a *mmgph* of severe distress. Nothing major wrong with T'ing Hau per se.

"You as antsy as I am about the PSATs next week?"

She shrugged. If that was all the reaction I got for mentioning the Preliminary Scholastic Aptitude Tests (insidious instruments of mental torture that exist solely to keep me out of Princeton, with ulcer-inducing capabilities second only to the for-real Scholastic Aptitude Tests we'd be taking next year), then T'ing wasn't having any sort of academic troubles worth the name.

"Uh . . . So how's your family doing?"

She shrugged once more, but this time it was a pretty fraught shrug. I can tell the difference. I decided I was on the right track and dug deeper.

"Everyone OK?"

She nodded her head, *then* shrugged. Mixed signals on the family front. Not good.

"No one's . . . sick or anything?"

Again the shrug, this time with a negative shake of the head for backup. I took a bite of 'za and pondered the philosophical implications of T'ing's big silence. The pepperoni tasted like a vintage Property of the Board of Education pencil eraser. It's impossible not to wax philosophical while chewing on a hunk of pseudofood like that. Philosophy takes time, and so does grinding down a mouthful of truly awful 'za.

I decided I might try another tack. "I heard your sister Daniela was supposed to be getting married at Rosemont Manor in two months," I said. This bought me another nod. Too bad T'ing didn't look up right then, because the smug and knowledgeable supersleuth smirk I put on would've made a dog laugh. *"But"*—swear to God, I laid a finger aside of my nose—"I haven't heard any more about it lately. *Is the wedding off?"* Sam Spade had nothing on me.

She looked up. Ah-ha! I *knew* there was just one occurrence, short of personal disaster, that would undo a nice, steady girl like T'ing, and that was having to live under the same roof with Mrs. Kaplan, Daniela, and a wedding that had crash-dumped *after* the bridal gown was altered and the deposit was down at Rosemont Manor.

I awaited a full confession. What I got was:

"No."

A tiny vertical line formed between T'ing's eyebrows, and her mouth twisted up in plain puzzlement. "Why should the wedding be off? I got my maid-of-honor dress and everything." I got two seconds more of that cancel-a-wedding-at-*Rosemont Manor*-are-you-nuts? stare before she went back to contemplating the bubbles in her diet Coke.

All right, so I wouldn't be solving the case of *The Maltese Falcon* any time real soon. If she had something to tell me, I'd have to wait for it.

She did. "Never mind, Tim. I'm being silly. I never should've bothered you. It's nothing. Could you take me home now?" She sighed and laid her hands on the table.

She jumped in her seat when I lunged across the red Formica and grabbed them. "T'ing, listen, you can't just sit there like a lump all this time, *after* you go calling me up this late at night because you've *got* to see me, and then tell me nothing's wrong. If it's a joke, it's not funny."

She pulled away her hands and sat up straight for the first time all night. The old, cold T'ing was back. "It's no joke." You could see cartoon icicles hanging from every word. "It was just a mistake." She rose from the table. "If you won't walk me home, I'll go alone."

I tried to grab her hands again. I guess I figured that if I got a physical hold on her, she'd have to let me get a grip on what was bugging her, too. She evaded me easily, still with that austere frown. The cold front pushed me back in my place at the table.

Now I was the desperate one. I pleaded reason: "T'ing, look, I'll take you home, no problem. But for God's sake, *what* is the matter? I'm your friend. I want to help you. If I can. If you'll let me."

Her shoulders stiffened. "If you want to help me, take me home." And that was that.

So we left the Napoli Pizzarama and walked back the same way we'd come. This time I had my fists driven deep into my pockets too, doing my best to clout the ungrateful wench over the head with the body language message that two could play the game I've-Got-A-Bad-Attitude-Secret.

"Hold it," said the first man, whipping around the corner to block our way.

"Keep 'em there," said the second when I started to pull my hands out of my pockets. He was right behind me. I could smell the stale beer on his breath as it blew hot and sour over my left shoulder. Something sharp pricked right through my jacket.

My first thought was, *Oh, shit.* My second was:

"Teleri . . . " My banshee's name came out no louder than if I'd said it in my sleep, but too loud for some people's taste.

"Shut the fuck up," the third man said, coming around the same corner as his buddy and quickly stepping in to fence T'ing and me against the storefront of a darkened beauty parlor.

We were about a block from T'ing's apartment building, one short block, but a bad one to walk on if you have something against being a victim. Discount the traffic signals at the corners plus the few lonely lights burning in a couple of upstairs windows, and the grand total of public illumination for the whole street is two lampposts. Only one of these was anywhere near us. A few score yards behind us lay the junction of Nostrand and Flatbush Avenues, lit up like Christmas with the neon of late-night movies, restaurants, fast-food places, all bustling with people. It might as well have been the moon.

This block is strictly residential, and the little street-level tax-payer stores propping up the old apartment buildings are Mom-and-Pop concerns that close for the day at five, six the latest. The families living upstairs go to bed at nine. The nearest place with any people still up at this hour is Shannon's Bar, all the way at the far end of the next block. Few lights, little traffic, no witnesses. Like I said, a great place for a mugging.

"Come *on*, man." The guy behind me was nervous. He jabbed me a little with his blade, which calmed him right down. "Give."

I set my teeth firmly in my lower lip, to keep it from trembling. *Scared* didn't start to describe how I felt. As I slowly pulled my wallet out of my pants, I focused every wish of heart and soul on my absent banshee. She'd saved me from a minor bruising in the school hallway without even being asked. Now that I needed her worse than air, she was nowhere.

Oh boy, did I ever need her now. You see, even crime's got its standards. When you get mugged in the Greater Metropolitan New York area, you had precious well better be ready to fork over what the (alleged) perpetrator considers to be his fair value minimum wage.

The trio of overachievers who'd cornered us were obviously planning on splitting whatever they got from me. They knew I had *something*, because I'd mentioned it. What they didn't know was how much; or how little. They couldn't know that Mrs. Emmeline Mandel is a firm believer in prorating a sitter's wages to the minute, with the corollary that if you give a high-school kid a tip, he'll only spend it on cocaine and hula girls.

When these three guys discovered the pittance they were going to get for their trouble, they'd take out the difference on my face.

That was frightening enough. What they might do to T'ing, just for being with a loser like me, was worse. My stomach churned as I passed over my wallet and watched the first man open it.

"Teleri . . . " I called to her through gritted teeth, her name rising sharply as panic refused to stay tamped down inside me. I didn't care if the guy behind me heard and made another pointed objection. I was dead meat anyway, but if T'ing could just get away—"*Tele—*"

"I said *shut up*!" And the third guy landed one across my jaw that brought out the stars.

I slid down the storefront window. I wasn't out—a human jaw can take plenty—but I was dazed and hurting. If I stayed vertical he'd probably try belting me again; no, thanks. Possums live longer than panthers. T'ing started to scream. The guy with the knife grabbed her arm and snarled at her to be silent. Through a haze I saw light from the distant street lamp glimmer on the blade.

I was hit harder than I thought. I saw *two* blades shine in the lamplight. One was pretty big. And if that was T'ing screaming again, she was getting creative. Most women leave it at *Eeek!* She was rumbling through a roll call of yips, *ki-yis*, and bizarre ululations you don't usually hear outside of the less disciplined dog shows.

T'ing had also become a bass-baritone and a ventriloquist. The barbaric yammerings weren't coming from her lips after all.

The second blade whirled like an electric fan in the semidarkness. Its crazy spin sent a gust of pure stink right up my nostrils. This was a stench that went beyond beer. This was serious, organic, holistic sweat, cold lamb fat, and warm animal manure.

Wet dog, too, and a reek like a rainy-day locker room full of Billy Klauser clones all wearing hundred percent wool sweaters.

I blinked, sure that I'd had something vital jarred loose by that jab to the jaw. Now I was seeing *four* genetic mistakes surrounding T'ing and me, and the fourth man was a sight fit to give King Kong the collywobbles. Nearly every short, stocky inch of him was covered in fur and leather from the neck down, even to a pair of bloodstained rawhide trousers. From the neck up he had a whirl of long, black braids matched with the bottom-weirdest set of razor tracks down the sides of his head and a *square* bald spot high up. A tuft of bangs stood alone, like a Hitler moustache that took a wrong turn at the nose.

No question at all why he was waving around a sword the length of my arm: He was hunting the hairstylist who'd done this to him.

They didn't see him. They didn't hear him. Not one of the three guys closing in on T'ing seemed to catch a whisper of the hoarse howls this wild man was launching at the moon. Hey, they didn't even act like they could *smell* him, which was flat-out impossible. If he touched them, would they feel it?

He seemed to think it was worth a try. *"Yagha!"* he roared and his sword came cleaving down right for the head of Bachelor Number One.

"Yang! *Bu*!" T'ing shrieked.

Boo? My brain was still kind of scrambled, but I had the sense left to wonder why T'ing was doing cut-rate ghost impressions this far before Halloween.

The swordsman scowled. His blade swerved, swung away from the mugger's skull, then swept back in flat-side-to a lot lower. It happened so fast that the first guy was still telling T'ing how he was going to kill her if she shouted again, when a slab of tempered steel thwacked him hard across the rump. He fell forward, yowling. Two more backhand smashes whomped his brother muggers aside. They tumbled with the blows, scrambling to their feet quickly. Their eyes darted everywhere, rolling with terror.

The swordsman's grin was gappy and golden beneath a trailing black moustache. He gave them each a second helping, knocking all three down again as soon as they got up. This time two of them stayed down. I could see them shuddering. Why? Sure, it was a big blade, but they had him outnumbered. Were they *that* big cowards?

Not my pal with the pig-sticker. He was down, but not defeated. Crouched like a cat, he twitched his knife this way and that, stabbing shadows.

"C'mon out, man!" he hissed. "You wanna fight, you come *out* an' do it. I ain't afraid of you, you hear me?" The whine in his voice was unconvincing. "Where you hiding, you muffu—?"

Hiding?

The swordsman picked his nose and flicked all that he found right in his challenger's face. The guy jerked his head. He'd *felt* something. "Who done that?" He forgot all about T'ing and me, all about discretion being the better part of armed robbery. *"Who done it?"* His companions got into runners' starting positions and bolted. The swordsman yawned, belched, and took a bandy-legged golfer's stance before giving the malingerer one last swipe. He sailed across the sidewalk like a shuffleboard disc, his knife clattering from his hand. He didn't bother retrieving it when he stopped skidding; he just up and ran.

So did T'ing. She was crying bitterly.

I got up and slowly approached the swordsman from behind. He was watching T'ing's retreat, unaware of me. "Yang, *bu*, Yang, *bu*, all the time it's Yang, *bu*," he grumbled. "What's the damn matter, she doesn't want me to have any damn fun? *There's* filial fucking piety for you! And what makes that little mare so damn sure I *want* to be talked to in sodding Mandarin? Miserable gaggle of silk-assed pottery-painting, poem-puking . . . " He groused on, making noises like bad plumbing.

I opened my mouth, though I'm not sure whether I was going to thank him for saving us or to ask him whose little nightmare he was. Whichever, I missed my chance. I forgot that you have to inhale before you talk. Half of my olfactory nerves died, quick-fried on the spot. I was still doubled over, choking, when he vanished.

7

A Little Chat

IF T'ING AVOIDED me on purpose for all of the school week following our adventure, I never noticed. Like the solitary storm cloud that seeks out luckless characters in comic strips, gloom and doom hovered over my head, leaving me with ceiling zero for any glint of hope.

My only recreation was listless doodling of pie-charts during study hall, trying to assign a relative share to all factors in my life currently infuriating Mom. Let's see, there was the abysmal Spanish pop-quiz grade (a clean fifteen percent right there); the fact that my new buddies, the Rawbone Kings, kept coming by the apartment after school to harangue her into giving me a reprieve from grounding so that I could "come out and, like, have some *real* fun" (twenty percent, twenty-five if they called her "Yo, lady"); Mrs. Kaplan's phone call, blaming me for her younger daughter's return home at an ungodly hour Friday night/ Saturday morning (twenty-five percent, even with the Fellow Aggravated Mother of an Ungrateful Adolescent Scuzz discount reckoned in); and of course my own bruised and bleeding return from that night of mad and glorious delight, at which point the pie-chart went to hell because you can't add ninety-five percent to all the rest and come up with a real-world math solution.

Oh yes, I was in doo-doo deep enough to require bathysphere assistance. I was grounded so thoroughly, so explicitly, so eternally, that I would be lucky if Mom let me out of the house for my honeymoon.

"Which is no more than ye deserve, bad cess to ye fer a

wanton rascal!'' Teleri knelt astraddle my stomach, her golden hair crackling with anger.

I rubbed sleep from my eyes. It was Wednesday morning. Five A.M. Wednesday morning. I had been having a dream about the upcoming PSAT exams, now less than four days away. I won't go into details beyond saying that the nightmare involved the Gobi Desert, Donald Trump, marshmallow linoleum, partial nudity, and a Number Two pencil *unsharpened and with no eraser.*

Given the above, my reaction to the lady's chosen place of materialization was not hormonal, just *huh*? (For any situation to be suggestive, it helps if both parties are fully awake.) I could even say I was comparatively pleased, in a muzzy sort of way, to have a banshee on my breadbasket. Teleri of Limerick didn't weigh half as much as PSAT anxiety.

''Where've you been?'' I mumbled. I hadn't seen her since the tuna incident with Neil Fitzsimmons.

Teleri pursed her lips and vaulted gracefully to the floor beside my sofa-bed. ''The impertinence! Never ye mind what's no concern of yers. I've better things to do with me time than play constant wet-nurse to a big broth of a lad like yerself.'' Primly she tugged down the hem of her lime Spandex miniskirt and fluffed the ruffles on her pink-and-purple tube top. Then she archly added, ''Missed me, did ye?''

I was groggy with sleep, but alert enough to notice that the banshee was not used to playing it coy. Flirting embarrassed her, and I saw a deep blush rise and ebb on her cheeks. Teleri had been up to something; *what* was anybody's guess. However, my carborundum-honed powers of observation turned keen as warm butter when it came to picking up on the fact that for once my banshee wasn't buck naked. Oh, my eyes *registered* the new wardrobe, all right; I just didn't *see* it, if you know what I mean.

''Okay, okay, so keep your little secrets,'' I told her, grudgingly. ''You're entitled to your privacy, even if you don't seem to think I am.'' I got out of bed and yawned widely; too widely. My battered jaw still hurt, and I'm not one to suffer in silence.

''Aagh!'' I cupped a hand over the big black-and-blue mark.

''Mercy on us!'' Teleri plucked my hand away and stared at the bruise. ''In Anu's name, who's done this to me darling lord?'' I told her about all the fun she'd missed on Friday night, without mentioning any details of my smelly savior. Prudence made me fudge him into a stray passer-by who had inadvertently spooked the muggers into flight.

My recitation had a staggering effect. Every tint of healthy color drained from Teleri's face. The banshee was devastated. Multihued tears like rainwashed oil-slicks flooded her cheeks. For all that, she never uttered sigh or sob, which made her grief that much more dramatic to see. Silent sorrow is not a banshee's usual mode of self-expression.

I couldn't help wanting to comfort her. "Teleri, don't cry. It's okay, honest. All I got was the one right to the jaw, and it'll heal soon enough. Please, stop; it's not that bad." My arm went around her shoulders and she pressed her head against my chest, but she didn't stop crying. Warm tears soaked through my pajama tops, leaving a tingly feeling on my skin.

At last she raised her chin and gulped for air. "Oh, milord, it's worse! Woe, 'tis a wicked, selfish, vain and foolish wench I be, and me skull as empty of sense as a warrior's breasts of milk!" The iridescent tears poured down as she wrung her hands and wailed, "What'd become of me this day had the villains killed ye, and me nowhere in sight to keen the dirge o' the Desmonds over yer poor, pale corse? After I worked on it so long, too."

"Is *that* the only reason you're crying?" I shouted, jerking my arm away as if Teleri's soft shoulder were the third rail. "Because you nearly missed your chance to show off your song at my funeral?"

" 'Tis a fine one, milord," she said, looking meek. "All lyric-like, and most passin' poetical."

"Why, you—!"

I had a lot more I wanted to say, but a sleepy voice from the bedroom called, "Tim? Tim, you'd better not be playing the television at this hour."

"I'm not, Mom, honest," I called back at a more moderate volume.

"Then what's all the racket?"

"Nothing; I'm just talking to myself."

"Oh. On top of everything else, you're crazy. That's nice." I could hear the creaking of her bed frame through the closed door and assumed she'd gone back to sleep. With luck, she'd recall nothing of our conversation when she woke up. Like I said, she had enough to be mad at me about without my adding to it by daring to go insane.

I got back down to cases with my banshee. Teleri had stopped crying, which was fine, but she didn't look in the least repentant, which was not.

"Whisht, I see that it's half a care more I'll have to take from now on with ye, milord. Nay, not from my sight a minute will I let ye stray." She shook her head slowly. "Faith, it's a wicked, savage land I've come to, for me ill deeds. In the old country, when it came to the deaths of lads so young as yerself, a banshee might live her own afterlife all during the week with never a worry. She'd only to linger near her fellow of a fine Saturday night when a wicked cruel thirst lured him to the shebeen. Then a wee drop o' the craythur, a word missaid, a quarrel picked, an unfortunate quick temper on both sides but a hearty skull-rap o' the shillelagh on only one, and she could wail him over the border and still have time for a frolic with the Gentry before the moon was down."

"Well, you won't get that from me," I said half under my breath. "The drinking age in New York State is twenty-one."

"More's the pity." She sighed. "If the lads didn't die in a fight, more times than not they'd pitch themselves dead drunk into a flooded ditch and drown. I don't suppose—?" She raised her huge eyes to me and looked hopeful.

"No."

"Not all of 'em drank. Some was kicked in the head by cattle," she pursued, still optimistic. "Else took with the measles."

I explained about inoculations and how the nearest I got to cattle in Flatbush were two all-beef patties, special sauce, lettuce, cheese, etcetera. Teleri sagged under the weight of knowing how safe it was to live in Brooklyn.

"Ah, 'tis an evil hour has befallen me, linked to a land that hasn't the faintest notion of how to do a lad to death proper. All higgledy-piggledy ye Yanks be in yer dying, with no whit of respect for the old, traditional deaths, nor the common decency to think it shameful."

"If you can't stand us Yanks that much, why did you come over here in the first place?" I sneered. Only the thought of what my Social Studies teacher, Mr. Kaiser, would say kept me from telling her to go back where she came from. (Mr. Kaiser went to Woodstock and hasn't come home yet. He thinks President Carter was too right-wing.)

Teleri met my question with haughtiness. "Is it deaf ye be as well as ungracious? 'Tis the Desmond banshee I be, to yer line o' the family alone. Seamus Desmond was the last of ye to perish on Eire's sweet soil, so wasn't I just condemned to fly after them as yet lived?''

That name, Seamus Desmond, struck a funny kind of chord with me. A memory came, warm and painful at the same time. I was only about six or seven years old. Mom and Dad were still together and we drove out to visit Dad's grandma in a nursing home on Long Island. I remember her very well. I may have been young, but the thought of anyone human getting to be that *old* had some kind of fixative effect on my memory. I couldn't forget Katherine Desmond if I tried.

She was in a big, sunny room, sitting up in a wheelchair. A brightly crocheted afghan lay over her legs, and on her knees was a book that looked at least as old as she was. I forgot about being afraid of her wrinkles and the funny, sweet, old-person smell clinging to her like a halo. I *had* to see that book.

Dad tried to stop me. "Let the lad be, Tim," she told him. Her voice was surprisingly low and steady. To me she said, "Come near, Timmy lad. Wouldn't ye like to see what yer old granny has here? 'Tis a wonder, child. 'Tis a tale writ large and grand, and all for ye."

I went closer. "Like a fairy tale?" I asked.

Her blue eyes danced when she laughed. "Mercy on us, that well may be. There's more than a hint o' the Gentry having had doings with the Desmonds. Some o' them stories they'd tell in our village o' Seamus Desmond's midnight rambles made me say three rosaries in gratitude that I'd accepted his brother's proposal, and not his. A lass can't bide with a man that's forever haring himself off to the raths with the Good Folk!"

I wanted to know who the Good Folk were.

"And didn't I just tell ye? Why, the Gentry, the People of Peace, the Fairies as ye'd call 'em, God shield us from all their wanton mischief." She let me look into the book, which was an ancient, wood-covered photograph album. "There he is, Timmy. There's Seamus himself. 'Tis a miracle the camera might still capture him, for everyone swore he'd sold his soul to the Good Neighbors years agone."

The memory faded. "Seamus Desmond," I said slowly, "was my great-grandfather's brother."

"So he was, and a merry man," Teleri agreed. "And when his hour'd struck, *he* knew better than to discommode a lady," she added meaningly.

"Now, wait a minute. You said that Seamus was the last of your private herd of Desmonds to die in Ireland, right?"

"That's so."

"Then what kept you from America so long? Why didn't you show up to wail over my great-grandfather's death? He had four sons; where were you for any of them? And my dad had six brothers, so when Uncle Gil died in Korea and Uncle Kevin had that heart attack, where—?"

My indignation was not making any impression on Teleri. My grandparents' fertility was. "La, seven boys is it? Well, begging yer lordship's pardon, but after such a fine lot of good Irish lads born, how is it that the noble Desmond line's come down to be no more than yourself?"

I was going to rattle through the simple math that seven sons minus two dead, minus Uncle Quinn gone for a priest, minus Uncle Donald (who saved blue yarn) never married, minus Uncle Sloan and Uncle Paul fathering only daughters, left just my dad to produce the only male Desmond of the latest generation. Then something occurred to me.

"Why should I be telling you?" I demanded. "You knew right where to look me up when you wanted. You *knew*! Why don't you know anything about the rest of my family? Why weren't you there when any of them died?"

Teleri basket-wove her fingers and refused to look me in the eye. "I've been busy."

"Busy, huh? Busy since my *great-grandfather's* generation? I think *sloppy* is more like it! A fine thing, here all along the Desmonds have had a family banshee and she's a freaking incompetent!"

"Ye haven't the right!" Teleri shouted right back at me. " 'Tis a better banshee I've been to the Desmonds than any o' ye deserve. Aye, how many o' me sisters took the pains I did to fulfill their proper calling? Snug back in Eire they be, not gallivanting across a great, chill, nasty ocean, and what thanks does a faithful heart have from ye? None! A murrain on all yer cattle, and may the spavin take yer horses!"

For some reason, this curse didn't get me too bent.

"Look, faithful heart, I want a straight answer, not a tantrum."

The banshee's brow darkened ominously. *Uh-oh*, I thought. *Toad time again.* But instead of turning me warty, she just said, "Very well. I know I'm not guiltless, but if I failed yer kin, 'twas but that I erred overmuch on the side o' common courtesy. 'Twas the very day that Seamus passed over that me natural lord among the Gentry told me as how Ireland was fresh out o' me sprig o' the Desmond tree. If I liked, I might retire to the shadows 'neath the rath till Judgment Day. Retire? And me little more than a slip o' three hundred summers, or thereabouts!''

I assured her that she didn't look a summer over two hundred.

"Ah, there's a touch o' the Desmond blarney to ye yet, milord." She did look pleased. "Well, as I've said, I couldn't retire—not at my age, and with that poxy hoyden of a Fitzgerald banshee in the same rath, forever twitting me about what a *busy* lass she was, and how *she* knew the difference between a banshee's duty and a barnacle's. Proud as a purple pig, the clapjawed wench tells me that with naught to be me occupation, I'd soon let me looks run to seed." Teleri's voice and eyebrows lowered and lifted, respectively, as she confided the dark secret, "And a fine one to talk o' looks is Badb o' Kildare. The weeest suckling *phouka* knows she tints her hair with cabbage stalks and lye!''

"Tsk," I remarked.

"Well, I couldn't bide under the same mound with *that*! So it's down to the port I went, and 'twas there I met the kindest mortal lass, with such a gift o' the gab. Going to America too, she was, and graced with enough o' the Sight to see me, for all she wasn't a Desmond but a Murphy, born and bred. Oh, we talked and we talked—a fine one fer talking was Bridey!—and what became o' the time we neither one of us knew until it had passed. Last that I saw of her was the lass shaking a wee bit o' dust from her bundle and saying as how she'd changed her mind, for certain she was that no one in America could offer a lass a proper little Irish chat. I got on the next boat out, after that, and crossed over as quick as ever I could." Teleri tilted her head to one side. "I wonder what did become o' Bridey Murphy, though.''

"Judge Crater married her to Ambrose Bierce and they honeymooned in the Bermuda Triangle." I can be glib.

"*What?*" Teleri scowled so darkly that I was afraid I'd glibbed myself one over the line. "Married by a *judge*? A fine Catholic girl like herself? Pull the other one, it's got bells on it.''

Rather than pulling anything remotely connected to Teleri, I decided to change the subject before I got myself any deeper in her bad graces. "What I don't get is why you couldn't keep your career going back in the old country. I mean, so what if you ran out of my flavor Desmonds? Couldn't you branch out? Go scare the succotash out of an off-brand Desmond? Especially since you're so unhappy here.''

"Oh, I'm happy enough," Teleri said in a way that led me to believe she was happier than that, but was too fond of being able to complain about us Yanks to admit it. "But haunt another sept o' the Desmond clan? Badb would never let me hear the last o' that!''

I was starting to dislike the Fitzgerald banshee. You see, I'd gotten this weird idea into my head that if somehow I could persuade my banshee to take a hike, she'd take my imminent death along with her. I know it sounds like I was confusing the disaster with its messenger, but I'm not the only one. Or why do so many people hate TV anchormen?

"Then I guess we're stuck with each other, huh?" I wasn't what you'd call thrilled.

"As is only fitting." Teleri struck a resolute pose. " 'Twas a wild young Desmond o' yer line alone as caused me own death in the evil days of the devil Cromwell, may he burn in his bones. Cromwell, not the Desmond.''

"Then you were once . . . human?"

"Oh, aye, human enough. But dying by yer own hand's a tricksy business, most especially in Erin. Take but a step outside the Church and—whisht!—'tis the Gentry themselves standing ready to welcome ye into their company.''

"You *killed* yourself?" I was shocked.

Teleri treated the whole thing lightly, having had over three hundred years to get used to the idea. "And what choice was mine, dishonored as he left me? All the town knowing it, what's more! I might have gone for a common trull, else lived no better than a slave in me brother's house, and him with that great, ham-handed slattern of a wife to tyrannize me days. Better a short death and done with than spinning out a long misery, I say!''

My banshee's spirit deserted her without warning. The rainbowed tears welled up again in her eyes. Her sweet voice quivered and broke. "Better dead, and with me darling once more in Paradise, I thought." She looked at me. "If he'd been less the hero, he'd have wed me and made me honest. But it's ever a foolhardy lot ye Desmonds be. He died in the Boyne, rest his sweet soul, fighting fer Ireland. I died too, but Heaven nor Hell won't have me, and there's no rest fer mine.''

I put my arms around her again and she hid her tears against my shoulder. Nothing outside my dreams felt half so silky as her hair. Her skin was warm, yet touching it left me with the uncanny sensation of being wrapped head to foot in the cool comfort of a mountain lake at the height of burning summer. Whoever he was, that long-gone ancestor of mine whom Teleri had loved so dearly, I envied him.

I lifted her face, wanting to tell her not to cry. Somehow the words turned into a kiss. She didn't mind. I don't know how long we would have stood there like that.

"Oh, my God." Mom stood in the bedroom doorway, staring at us.

Staring at me. Teleri had removed herself from human ken (which might be why Neil Fitzsimmons could see her). Not even six A.M. of a frosty fall morning and my mother comes out in her bathrobe to see her only child in a clinch with—nothing.

"That does it. Those teachers of yours have been working you children too hard. No wonder you've been acting so weird. Even if I get docked, I'm going to talk to your guidance counselor today." Having fired off this pronouncement of militant motherhood, Mom slammed back into the bedroom.

My guidance counselor, Richard Izanagi: Adolescent Development's answer to *Plan 9 From Outer Space*.

I was doomed.

8

Use a Number Two Pencil

"BRITTANY, DEAR, DADDY likes the song about the little fishies very much. Daddy thinks you sing the song about the little fishies very well. Daddy is very happy with Brittany when she sings the fishy song, but only when it's time for the fishy song. This is not a fishy song time. Daddy has to be there for Timothy. Daddy can't be there for Timothy if Daddy can't hear what Timothy is saying. Daddy wants to be a good listener. Daddy knows that Brittany can be a good listener, too. Why doesn't Brittany try being a good listener for just a *little* while, and after Timothy goes away Daddy will listen to Brittany sing the song about the little fishies just as much as Brittany wants him to. Okay?" Mr. Izanagi gave his daughter a molasses-sweet smile.

"No," said Brittany. She stuck out her tongue and went back to singing the song about the little fishies. This was a melodic masterpiece based on the "A Hundred Bottles of Beer on the Wall" principle, the Death of a Thousand Cuts set to music. It was a gem she'd picked up at the Ananda Panda Wholly Child Nursery School, so of course all the little fishies felt very, very good about who they were.

"Brittany, darling, please." Mr. Izanagi's smile grew rigid. "Daddy is sorry you can't be in nursery school today. Daddy is *very* sorry that Starchild fell in the toilet and drowned."

He must have caught a sideways glimpse of my reaction, because he was quick to tell me that Starchild was a hamster, tribal bride of Moonfree.

"What happened?" I asked. "She get out of the cage?"

"*Cage?*" Mr. Izanagi was aghast. "Do you really believe in

keeping animals in *cages*, Timothy? Don't you feel that any intelligent, mentally healthy person must in good conscience refuse to place another living being under any sort of restraint? Timothy''—his hands described an invisible globe—''we have a planet to share.''

A planet, okay, I thought. *But a toilet?*

I stifled my words before I said anything unholistic. At the same time, Mr. Izanagi kept trying to stifle Brittany. ''Now Brittany, you know they had to close the school for a day so that Moonfree can work through his grief in privacy. Also so the nice plumber can fix the toilet. We all respect Moonfree's needs, don't we?''

Brittany stopped singing long enough to blow a loud raspberry, which I guess was her editorial comment on the widower Moonfree's needs. Mr. Izanagi ignored it.

''Daddy knows you feel sad about this, too. Daddy wants you to share how sad you feel with him and Mommy, but you can't do that until tonight, when Mommy comes home. When Mommy comes home is sharing time. Daddy knows you're singing the song about the little fishies because you feel so sad, but if you keep singing it when you're sad, soon you're going to feel sad when you sing it. I don't think it would make your teacher, Five Bear, very happy for you to be sad when you sing the little fishy song.''

Can you guess whether any of this was working on Brittany? I think you can.

From her place up on top of the Freshman file cabinet, Teleri's eyes shot blackest ruin at the little fish-singer. ''May she warble a different tune to the horrors that ring Scathach! Hasn't the man the sense to know when to go cut a hazel switch?''

I covered my mouth with my hand and hoped Teleri could hear me mutter, ''Uh-uh. No spank. Child abuse.''

''Abuse, is it? And what of the abuse to a poor, captive banshee's patience, I want to know? I've a mind to snatch the tongue from her head and turn it into a stoat.''

Still keeping my mouth hidden, I all but whispered, ''Don't. No stoats in school.''

Some voices just aren't meant to whisper. ''What did you say, Timothy?'' Mr. Izanagi's narrow, high-boned face reminded me of a hunting hound, keen on the scent. ''Something about a boat? Did your father have a boat?''

''He didn't say *nothing*!'' Brittany's face reddened with rage.

She kicked the hell out of her daddy's desk. "He's a big stupid moron *idjit*! He wasn't even listening to me *sing*! You didn't listen *either*! I *hate* you, Daddy! I hate you and I hope you swell up and die and fall in the toilet and drown and get flushed and the plumbing 'splodes and we gotta move out of the house for *three whole days* until they fix it and you're dead, *dead*, DEAD!"

Did I have a boy for this kid. But would the Mandels thank me for it?

Mr. Izanagi folded his hands on his desk blotter. "Brittany, Daddy is very disappointed in what he is hearing you say."

For answer, Brittany threw herself backwards onto the floor and demonstrated Primal Scream Therapy. Somewhere back in the sane world, a bell rang.

"I've got to get to class, Mr. Izanagi," I said, springing to my feet so fast that my chair shot backwards across the floor.

"Yes, yes, of course, Timothy." Mr. Izanagi slapped my manila file shut. Now he resembled one of El Greco's taffy-pulled martyrs. "We can get back to this tomorrow. We really ought to work through what's troubling you. My theory is that it's just a little pre-examination tension, but we mustn't jump to conclusions." On the floor, Brittany was trying to jump to the moon from a supine starting position. She looked like she might make it.

"Yes, sir," I said, edging around the thrashing child in the direction of the door.

"I'll expect you at seven, then."

"Yes, sir. Seven it is."

"And try to see how much you can remember about your feelings for your father. If we can just get to that, I'm sure we can—"

"I'll remember or die trying, sir," I called from the hall. I shut the door just as Brittany started her air-raid siren impression.

Teleri took the shortcut, right through the wall. She was waiting for me in the corridor and had a number of things to say about Mr. Izanagi's qualifications as a molder of young persons, mostly on the lines of the blind leading the blind. The hall was jammed with kids heading for their next classes, so I couldn't say a word.

My banshee was a spirit of unyielding honor. Stick by me she'd sworn to do and stick by me she did. She wasn't about to be caught with her dirge down, not when death in America was so haphazard and poorly regulated. I told her I wasn't going to meet poor Starchild's fate, but that didn't stop her from accompanying me into the Boys' Room. Her only concession was staying on the outside of the stall, ready to burst into wails of bereavement at my first gurgle.

Wednesday was bad. Thursday was worse, although it started out pretty good. Mr. Izanagi called in to say he had to postpone our appointment. Starchild was being cremated and he wanted to be there, to make sure Brittany verbalized all her feelings before they torched the rodent.

The good start didn't last. Thursdays I had Speech class with T'ing. I kept trying to catch her eye; she kept trying to avoid mine. I passed her a note; she crumpled it up unread and let it drop to the floor. I made so many urgent faces at her that the teacher asked me whether I wanted to go to the nurse's office.

Teleri noticed my one-sided efforts. She wasn't happy with all the attention I was giving—or trying to give—T'ing. Mr. Izanagi would have told her about counterproductive hostility and sharing the planet and aggressive thoughts being as ergot upon the greening soul. Teleri would have changed him into a mold spore. I hoped she didn't have any similar transformations in store for T'ing.

Besides, T'ing seemed to have enough troubles eating at her without getting zapped into the lower vegetable kingdom by a jealous banshee. She didn't look angry at me; she looked frightened. The one glance she gave me pleaded, *Go away. Leave me alone.*

The hell I would.

Friday played fair. It started rotten and kept it up until dismissal. Starchild and the Ananda Panda plumbing having both been settled in their proper ecological niches, Mr. Izanagi was free to concentrate on me.

"So what did you tell him?" Scott asked me over lunch.

"Nothing."

"*Right.*" Scott Harper's my best friend after Larry, but he's a third-degree black-belt master of sarcasm. "You clam up in Izanagi's office and he goes into Rorschach overload. Nothing wilds that man up worse than a student who won't talk. Right away he's sure you're hiding some deep, dark secret that'll make him famous once he writes it up for *Mental Case Monthly.*"

"Tim." Larry put on his I-am-so-sincere-it-hurts face. "Tim, my boy, I'm your friend. You can tell me about the black lace underwear.''

''Sorry, Larry, it's not your size.'' I gave him a hard shot to the arm and glommed the brownie off his lunch tray.

Scott pondered the relentless Mr. Izanagi's tenacity. ''The Gestapo could've used a couple guys like him.''

''Only if the Gestapo felt very, very good about their personhood,'' I said, stabbing a piece of school cafeteria codfish to death with my fork. The fish under attack did not go gentle into that good night. Teleri watched my molars fight a losing battle with the rubbery morsel, her eyes a-shine. I cast a quick, nervous look to see if the Heimlich Maneuver poster was still up on the wall, then dared to swallow. The fish and Teleri's hopes both went down hard.

Larry leaned across the table. ''So, talk, Tim. What *did* you tell him?''

''Oh, you know, the usual stuff. I have a lot of work, the PSATs are coming up, next year the SATs, I want to get into Princeton, Mom doesn't know where the money's coming from—'' I pushed away the remains of what some clown in administration called a well-balanced meal and ate Larry's brownie. ''Didn't matter what I said, he kept wanting me to talk about my dad.''

''Oh.'' Both Scott and Larry didn't pursue it. They know how I feel about Mr. T. Ahern Desmond. They're my friends, unlike Mr. Izanagi. He chased my father down more cold psychological trails than a paperback detective. Did I hate him for leaving us? Did I resent the fact that he'd never sent Mom one penny of support? Did I feel hostile toward him for not once, not one single time, *never* having gotten back in touch with us to see if we were alive or dead?

Do I need stupid questions? Do I need old hurts made new?

Of *course* I hated him. You damn well bet I resented the way he just took off one morning and never came back, never tried to learn how we were doing without him. The only thing I didn't give a shit about was the money. Even if Mom and I needed money, we'd never need his. But not to send a word of explanation? Not even a lousy goodbye?

I could still see his face. *Be right back, Timmy. I'm just going down to the corner, get me the Sunday paper, maybe some cold cuts. We can all go on a picnic. Would you like that? Wanna go on a picnic, Timmy?* And he ruffled my hair as he went out the door, because I'd told him that I was too big for kisses.

Yeah, Mr. Izanagi, I hate my father. Now play Freud.

But who I hate is my own business, just as much as why I hate them and who I love and why. So I told Mr. Izanagi that I'd worked through all my hostility years ago, but that I was having a lot of trouble with Geometry.

"Timothy, do you perceive your Geometry teacher as a father-figure, perhaps?" he asked.

"My Geometry teacher is Ms. Fine, sir." That's Ms. Cecelia "Sine Curve" Fine, otherwise known as Swimsuit Issue.

"Ah, but according to recent studies on the blurring of sexual imagery in our culture—" He would have gone on to explain how a woman built like a comic book heroine was subliminally a Rambo symbol, except he got a phone call from Ananda Panda to pick up Brittany. The sensitive darling had made the unilateral decision to send Moonfree on an Orphic voyage in search of his dearly departed Starchild, via the same lead-pipe route. Saved by the hamster!

He said he wanted me back on Monday. For the first time all year I had something besides the PSATs to dread.

Saturday. The PSATs at last. *El momento de la verdad,* for all you Hemingway buffs. How can a school that's been the dull gray backdrop for the past three years of your life suddenly turn into a house of horrors?

The windows squinted at me malevolently as I walked up the front steps with cement in my shoes. The doors groaned on their hinges, and I thought I saw the worm-eaten face of a hideous corpse where the door knocker had been, until I remembered that Glenwood High doesn't have door knockers.

It's got its share of corpses, though. Everyone I passed in the hall on the way to the auditorium looked like a recent graduate from one of those *He Scarfs Your Spleen* zombie flicks. I saw T'ing, but with all the other long faces surrounding her, she didn't look as purely miserable as before. No one said two words to anyone else, unless you count prayers.

"La! Why all the dole and dread?" Teleri had gotten used to the minimum daily requirement of chaos at Glenwood High. All this gloomy silence weighed on her nerves. "Is it that there's some wicked sacrifice to be made? Some sweet youth to pass into the shadows?" She considered this. "If 'tis so and the unfortunate lacks a family banshee, d'ye think I might pinch-hit? To warm up some, y'see.''

I was too far gone to latch onto Teleri's sudden sports literacy. I explained to her about the PSATs, and their big brother ghouls, the SATs. "Yer joking." I wasn't. "Then it's daft ye be, and the lot o' them with ye. Faith! Such faces pulled, and for what? A whisper o' paper and an hour or two o' chicken-scratching! Fill in the wee spaces wi' pencil and send the lot to dance wi' the Devil, I say!''

I tried to make her understand about how important these few wee spaces were to my future. To do this, though, I had to spirit her off to the Boys' Room before I got barred from the exams talking to lockers. I wanted to make it a short, sweet lecture on Education: Your Key to Never Having to Become a Quiz-Show Host, and for that I wanted privacy.

I didn't get it. Neil Fitzsimmons was in the Boys' Room, doing what came naturally.

He turned seven shades of red when he saw Teleri, and almost suffered a major mishap in his haste to rezip his jeans. "Milady, I—I didn't expect to see you here.''

Which aside from the ''milady'' (*Milady?* Neil Fitzsimmons calling a female something more respectful than ''love-weasel''?) just about summed up my reaction to finding Neil in school on PSAT Saturday.

"Hey, Neil, you know what day this is?'' I demanded.

"Yeah, we got a calendar from O'Toole's Funeral Home last Christmas. Why?''

"What the heck are you doing here, then?''

"Arranging my, y'know, attitude before I take the Pee-Sats, okay?'' He looked sheepish. "I get a little nervous taking exams, and then I gotta go real bad. Hey, we better get going. I think they're gonna start giving the test real soon.'' He pushed back his gang-jacket cuff and studied a watch; no, let's be frank and call a spade a Rolex. "Wow, I'll say it'll be soon. You coming, Tim?''

My hand shook as I waved him out the bathroom door. "No, no. You go ahead. I'll be along. I've just got to—adjust my own attitude some.''

"Well, for gosh sakes, hurry. You wouldn't want to be late for a test.''

"Milord, are you well?'' Teleri hovered near me, deeply concerned. Well she might be.

I had gone into shock. Over the course of three years at Glenwood High my pal Neil had done his bit to induce that state in a number of individuals, but he'd never accomplished it previously without the aid of a baseball bat. My mouth, with no directive whatsoever from my brain, stupidly repeated, " 'For gosh sakes'? *'For gosh sakes'?* This, from the guy who once used dirty words *Billy Klauser* had to look up! And he's here."

Teleri was giving me the chary eye. "So he was, milord. Right here, certain as yer born." Beneath the soothing tone in her voice were unspoken promises of rubber rooms and jackets that buckle up the back.

"No, you don't understand: He was *here*! Here in school when he doesn't have to be, taking a test he doesn't have to take! The PSATs are only if you're planning to apply for college admission. Fitzsimmons *hates* school. He hates tests worse than he hates school, and the only thing he wants to do after he gets out of Glenwood High is illegal in Texas. And did you *see* that watch? A Rolex costs a fortune; where'd *he* get one?"

"Perhaps, milord, doing that wee thingie as is illegal in Texas?" Teleri suggested.

"Trust me, he doesn't have the strength, yet." I shook my head. "Something is wrong. Something is dreadfully rotten in Flatbush. Oh well, I've got enough worries of my own. I'd better get to the auditorium."

I sprinted down the corridor and bolted through the auditorium doors just as Ms. Alexinsky began the invocation. I slipped into a back row vacant seat on the aisle while she intoned the holy obligation of having two sharpened Number Two pencils, the blessed necessity of breaking the seal on our examination booklets with the *eraser end only* of one of our pencils, and the awesome and inviolable prohibition against going on to the next section of the test before she had consulted the sacrificial entrails and the gods gave us the big thumbs-up. If God would have sent Ms. Alexinsky to explain the ground rules to Adam and Eve, we'd all still be in Eden; sound asleep.

I swung up the write-on arm of my seat and received my test booklet and blank answer-sheet from one of Alexinsky's acolytes. I've been to Holy Communion services that were less solemn. I looked around the room while my English teacher continued to expound on the hallowed doctrine, "Blessed are they who do erase incorrect answers completely and neatly." The test candidates were seated in the checkerboard pattern sanctified by Holy Writ, with two empty seats flanking each one occupied. There were three proctors manning one side of the room and three more on the other, all faculty members. I recognized Ms. Lenotre, Mr. Richter, and Mr. Kaiser. Mr. Kaiser recognized me and flashed me the peace sign, but I wasn't feeling too peaceful. I'd spotted T'ing.

She was seated in the same row as me, right in the middle. She kept looking all around her, like a fugitive from the law. There wasn't even a snowflake's worth of her old cool left. Teleri shimmied down into the vacant seat beside me and deliberately angled her head to block my view.

"Hmph. So that's the proud slut that's got ye spoilt fer good women, is it? The tallow-faced trull."

I started a hot defense of T'ing's honor, but snapped my mouth shut without a word said. Mr. Richter was watching. My Spanish teacher was an old Glenwood hand whose beverage of choice was the blood of cheaters. He knew all the tricks, plus a few he'd developed to stymie future generations. It didn't matter to him that the test had not yet begun: Martial law was on. If I made one sound not necessary to simple respiration, he'd use my larynx for a handball. I was silenced, shut up, skunked.

Not so Teleri. She leaped into a spate of invective against poor T'ing, an ever-flowing stream of name-calling plain and fancy that would sear the graffiti from a subway car. She wasn't just coarse, she was loud. I had to strain my hearing to pick up when Ms. Alexinsky finally said, "Do not begin until I say 'Begin.' When I say 'Begin,' you may begin. Begin." I tried to stuff my ears with spiritual cotton, but banshees are notorious for the piercing quality of their voices. If the Verbal part of the PSATs had a section on profanity, I'd ace it on the spot. Too bad it didn't. I gritted my teeth and forced my mind to focus on the exam booklet instead of on Teleri's bile.

It worked, after a while. City people can get used to ignoring anything. But soon something else crept through my defenses, an almost imperceptible sound that subtly insinuated itself between Teleri's tirade and my fragile concentration. I looked up from my paper.

T'ing was crying.

The test wasn't *that* hard. Still, I saw her sitting crumpled over her booklet, sniveling. Teleri caught me at it and shifted herself so that I lost sight of T'ing for an instant. I made a countershift, and entered the Outer Limits.

He was there. He, who? *Him!* The short, smelly swordsman from last Friday night's dream date. Just like Teleri with me, he was seated beside T'ing. He had his thick boots up on the seat in front of him and a strand of T'ing's long black hair twined through his fingers.

Very distinctly I heard him say, "Hey! How come we gotta sit here? It's nice weather out. You gotta horse? You don't, don't worry; I'll steal you one. We can go out, mount up, put a couple villages to the sword, catch lunch. You sure you're still a virgin, beloved granddaughter? We find any village man looks good to you, he's gotta strong back, you can keep him, have babies. When Yang pillages, *everybody* pillages!"

Teleri turned her head and saw him. "Why, the brass o' the filthy great lob!" she exclaimed. Yang blew her a kiss, then improved on it with an obscene gesture that went into great detail. My banshee clouded over, storms ahead.

Then T'ing covered her face with her hands and sobbed loud enough to get Mr. Richter's attention. My Spanish teacher scowled and started from his post against the wall. I didn't need a banshee to presage the tragedy coming up. T'ing would be asked to leave the test room. It didn't bear thinking about what would hit the fan when she got home with that news. The Kaplans were Liberals, but they practiced remorseless results-oriented parenting. Once T'ing's sister Daniela idly announced that she wanted to go to beauty school, and Mrs. Kaplan came down with a case of shingles that lasted until Daniela said Sarah Lawrence and meant it.

I'd been blamed for getting T'ing into trouble at home before. I wasn't about to stand by and let this Yang—whoever or whatever he was—get her into more. I slapped down my Number Two pencil. I stood up tall. I looked old Yang right in his glittering black eyes and declared, "You get the hell away from her, you son of a bitch!"

Yang heard me, all right. The surprise on his face lasted only long enough for him to rev up a canine snarl. The big blade I'd last seen on the street glittered in his hand. T'ing gasped.

"First thing I'm gonna do," Yang growled, "I'm gonna sever your brainless head from your stinking shoulders. Second thing I'm gonna do, you won't like. Beloved granddaughter! You know where I can steal a good catapult, cheap? Ah, never mind. First things first. *Yaaaarrrraaaagggghhhaaaa—!*" He sprang from his seat, his sword whirling.

Teleri leaped from her place, shrieking something in a language I couldn't understand. I understood the shortsword in her grasp, though. Its leaf-shaped blade licked through the air as she flung herself at Yang's head. Banshee and barbarian met in midflight. Teleri grabbed one of Yang's black braids, he seized a hank of her golden hair, and with wonderful coordination and harmony, both swords sliced across both throats simultaneously.

Of course no one died.

"Hey!" Yang looked cheated and resentful.

"Mercy on us!" Teleri cried, very peeved. They made a second murderous slash at each other with as little effect as the first.

Yang spat, then grinned. "So all right, forget about killing. You want some lunch and sex, woman?"

Teleri pursed her lips and sheathed her sword. "I might." To me she said, "Don't ye dare die while I'm gone, Tim, or it'll go the worse for ye." She threaded her arm through Yang's elbow and the pair vanished.

T'ing and I locked eyes. *Did you see what—?* We couldn't deny the bond now linking us. Her tears dried at once; an invisible burden fell from her shoulders. Her joyous relief was so immediate and intense that it transfigured her. I had to smile, too. The crisis was over. Fortunately, no one else seemed to have noticed a damned thing.

Or so I thought.

"Mr. Desmond, may I have a word with you?" Mr. Richter's hand fell heavily on my shoulder. "Outside."

9

Friends of the Family

"I KNOW I'M going to be sorry for this," Mom said. She shut the door, leaving T'ing and me alone together in her bedroom.

"Jesus, what did you say to her?" I asked T'ing as she sat on one corner of the mattress, hugging her schoolbooks protectively close to her chest.

"That, my friend, is one of the ineffable mysteries of the Orient." T'ing giggled. "Actually, it wasn't me. I enlisted my mother. She can talk an aluminum-siding salesman honest, *and* make him feel guilty about not having called home enough." She put down the books and got serious. "I owe you, Tim. You saved my life."

"Yeah, sure I did."

"Okay, my sanity, then. You *saw* him! For the first time since he showed up, I realized that someone else besides me could see him. I wasn't losing my mind!"

"Well, you picked yourself a great character witness for a sanity hearing." My corner of the bed was right near Mom's easel. She was working on a landscape, but the colors were as puddled and dingy and mucked up as the atmosphere in our home. They'd sent for her on Saturday and told her that I'd yelled at one of the PSAT proctors, calling him a son of a bitch. I was not to be allowed to retake the test; my score would be based entirely on how much of the exam I had completed. They suggested drug-testing. Mom didn't even wait until we were out of the school to burst into tears.

"Tim, you know you're not crazy either," T'ing said. "I saw

what's been following you. I even''—she wrinkled her nose—''I even think I *smelled* her. Whatever she is, she stinks.''

''Yeah, well, your friend isn't any flower-show himself.''

''He's not my friend. Friends you get to choose, relatives you're stuck with.'' T'ing tucked up her legs Indian style. ''He's my honorable ancestor.''

If life was a sitcom, this would have been when I did a hammy double-take, bugging my eyes out and squealing: ''He's your *what*?!'' But life doesn't take diddly off of Norman Lear, Grant Tinker, or some dead dog named Ubu.

''Your ancestor, huh?'' I thought it over. ''And Teleri's my ancestral banshee. Family connections; it jibes.''

''What's a banshee?'' T'ing asked.

''A banshee, ye miserable chit, is a better woman than ever ye'll make of yerself, do I permit ye to live that long!''

Guess who was back, *poinking* herself slap in the middle of the mattress between T'ing and me. She looked cranky enough to chaperone a parochial school dance.

She wasn't alone. Yang appeared behind her, muddy boots splayed wide on my mother's ivory bedspread. He was picking out the ample spaces between his teeth with a splintered bone, varying the task by occasionally using it to dig wax out of his ears or explore a bristly nostril before sticking it back in his mouth. I gagged.

''Oh, you must be Teleri!'' T'ing let her books slide to the floor. She grasped my banshee's hands warmly, giving Teleri no chance to pull away. ''I'm so glad to meet you. You have no idea what you've done for me.''

''Fer ye? If there's aught that's good I've brought ye, 'twas inadvertent and bitterly repented.''

T'ing tilted her head, confused. ''What have you got against me? What have I done to you?''

''Done, is it? Hark to the curd-brained slut! Bold as a landlord's thrice-cursed agent, she is.''

Yang whonked Teleri one in the back with his kneecap. ''Hey! I bought you lunch, you didn't have sex with me, so you don't call my beloved granddaughter names. Got that?''

My banshee gave him the gimlet eye. ''And if I'd been daft enough to take ye fer me lover, *then* might I call her the hoyden trollop she is?''

Yang bit the bone pick in two and sucked out the marrow. ''That'd depend on how good the sex was.''

"Look, everyone," I said. "I don't mean to break up the party, but my mom is standing on the other side of that door, against her better judgment, and I don't need to have her come barging in here until we get a few things settled. All the racket you two are making, she might not even bother opening the door to get in."

Teleri draped her arm around my neck. "There, now, milord, and didn't I tell ye that none but yerself might see or hear me?"

Yang grunted. "Same goes for me. Only those in whose veins flow the blood of Yang the Despoiler of Cities, Yang the Bane of Movable Property, Yang the Borrower of Virgins, are fit to behold me in all my unspeakable magnificence!" He flung his arms high and almost emptied the bedroom. His deodorant was *not* working.

I saw my duty. "I hate to break this to you, Teleri, but you're pretty darn audible and visible to Neil Fitzsimmons. Okay, he's got a little Irish in him, maybe that's why, but as for T'ing—" I threw up my hands. "Unless Saint Brendan took a wrong turn when he shipped out from Ireland and ended up in the South China Sea, you aren't going to find any shamrocks growing under her family tree."

"Hmmm. There's the truth in that," my banshee admitted.

"And as for you, Yang—"

"—the Despoiler of Cities," he prompted. "But you can call me just plain Dread and Fearsomely Omnipotent Lord."

"As for you," I reiterated, "I can guarantee we don't have one lousy red corpuscle in common, but I can still see you, hear you, and sme—"

"Watch it." His sword scraped an inch out of its scabbard.

"So how come?"

"Hmm," said Yang.

"Hmm," said Teleri. Both slipped into deep, silent meditation, although for Yang going into any kind of thought-mode was a visible strain. At last the banshee spoke up, framing each word with care. "Milord, would ye be in the way o' knowing what a *luchorpan* might be?"

"If I guess it's something you cook in, I'd be wrong, wouldn't I?"

"Or a goblin, then?"

"Oh, yeah, well *that* one any kid worth his Halloween candy would know. It's some kind of imaginary monster. You know, like ogres, trolls, gremlins—"

T'ing discreetly cleared her throat and leaned across the bed to murmur, "Banshees?"

I caught on to what wasn't being said. "Teleri, is there something—some*one* you want me to meet?"

My banshee beamed. "La, the wisdom o' the lad! Sharp as a fishwife's tongue, so he is, and just as quick. 'Tis even as ye've said it, milord: There's two fine fellows whose acquaintance I'd be proud t' have ye make. And ye can't imagine the power o' good it's done me t' learn that the line o' gab Master Runyon's been handing me is more than mere blarney."

"Who is Master Run—?"

She didn't even give me the chance to finish uttering his name. Teleri pounced on my hand, seized it tightly, and the bedroom spun itself into a candy-colored mist. The brilliant, twirling colors gave way to darkness, absolute and unrelieved. A wet, whining wind blew over me, wrenching shudders from my bones. It wasn't that the gust was so chill but that it seemed to be heavy with an ill, evil feeling the way healthy winds can carry a burden of rain. Then color came back, and warmth, and I was standing beside Teleri under the marquee of a movie theater showing *Leather Weekend*, *Moist Whipmistress*, and *Vincent's Vassar Vixens*. I figured we weren't anywhere near Disneyland.

"Begging yer pardon, milord, fer any discomfort ye may have endured in our passage." Teleri fussed with the lacy flounces of her cobalt blue skirt. Suddenly I found myself noticing and wondering why my banshee was dressed for the dance-club scene.

"Yeah, getting here wasn't exactly half the fun. What *was* that?"

Teleri's face was drawn, her continued twiddling with her clothes a device to cover how badly our trip had shaken her. "The Leeside's no genial land t' cross, even fer such as me. There's too much as was human yet clinging to me nature fer the dole and dread o' that uncanny realm not to leave me a-tremble. Me natural lord, back home under the rath in Erin, he often warned us as were too close kin to mortals: *'Don't step across the bounds that mark the grim Leeside lands, me darlins. What's fey in ye might be caught, and what's mortal in ye might perish o' the gloom.'*" She forced up a smile. "But it is the only good shortcut we could use to get ye here, milord, and that's what matters. Come on."

I slammed on the brakes when she tried to drag me along the sidewalk. "Whoa! Wait up a minute! Where is this? Times

Square?'' Her proud-mama look told me I'd scored. ''Are you nuts? What are you doing, jerking me across the city just like that? What if my mom goes into the bedroom? What's she going to think when she finds T'ing in there alone?''

With a small, malicious smile Teleri said, ''That'd be a problem fer those as we've left behind to handle with what wit they might possess. If any. Come along, I say. 'Tis high time that we find him and tell him all we know.''

''Find who? Tell who what?'' I kept up a steady squawk of questions while my banshee bodily hauled me the length of the block. The few passers-by who weren't Personal Entertainment Professionals quickly averted their eyes and got real interested in the shopwindow displays. They probably thought she was a P.E.P. and I her reluctant client.

I was still kicking up a fuss when Teleri swung me through the narrow doorway between an obscene T-shirt shop and a Vermin Nuggets franchise. I smelled leather. In this neighborhood, somehow I wasn't surprised.

In the dim light my groping hand closed around something large, firm, and rounded. I looked down. It was a shoe. This time I *was* surprised.

The shoes were everywhere. As my eyes grew used to the dingy interior, I saw shoes crowding the shelves on every wall, shoes piled on the counter, shoes filling the lone, cracked glass display case, shoes without number and shoes without recognizable style or mates spilling from cardboard boxes, strewing the floor. It was very serene, there among the shoes. You could almost say that the atmosphere was worshipful, if you wanted to stretch a point or if you happened to be Imelda Marcos.

''Milord, will ye join us?'' Teleri's sweet voice simpered prettily from farther down the Valley of the Schoon. She had dropped my hand the minute we crossed the threshold. Things unlikely had been part of my life long enough for me to know that a banshee never drops her guard or her prey unless she's got the home-court advantage and knows it. Like I said, it was quiet in the shop, even though all Times Square lay just a few yards behind me. I looked over my shoulder. The shop door had disappeared.

I heard the tinny sound of hammering, which grew louder as I made my way to the rear of the shop. The light had a warm, brown, well-used quality to it, like the worn spines of old books. The jumbled shoes seemed to glow with their own secrets. The straight path from the vanished front door to the source of the hammering began to twist and turn under my feet. One moment I could see Teleri, waving for me to come nearer, and the next she was out of sight, hidden by a pile of shoes that had bubbled up out of nothing, right in front of my eyes. Then, just as suddenly, they were gone and I could see my banshee again. She was miffed.

"Master Runyon," I heard her say in ruler-wielding schoolmarm tones. "I'll be thanking ye t' lay off yer tricks with milord of Desmond."

A second voice, whiskey-rough and whiskey-genial, replied: "Miss Teleri, I am most shockingly perturbed by such unfounded accusations. Nay, I would even go so far as to say that your erroneous imputations have wounded me to the ticker. Upon what firm basis of fact do you so cavalierly attempt to lay a chicanery rap on me?"

"Away with yer jabber, ye wicked imp! I'll stand surety fer milord, if 'tis yer piddling pinch o' gold as has ye so far sunk in black discourtesy."

"Seeing as you are willing to stand up for the gentleman, it would be a grave breach of hospitality on my part not to glad-hand him with all dispatch. Hobson, my good associate, would you see fit to do the honors?"

A third voice, cavernous and solemn as a cathedral, responded. "Certainly, sir. At once, sir."

I heard footsteps on the far side of a miniature mountain of mismatched footwear. A speck of light materialized at the heart of the shoe pile. This quickly irised open into a tunnel a yard in diameter, and through it came a small, brown-skinned, hairy, long-faced little man dressed in the rumpled uniform of an old-fashioned butler.

He raised his huge, watery red eyes to me and looked as if he didn't think too much of what he saw. A sigh riffled the trailing moustaches that dribbled halfway down his chest from beneath a beaky nose. "Walk this way, sir."

He turned and went back the way he'd come, which meant I had to get down and *crawl* that way, sir, right through the pile of shoes. As I came out on the other side I saw Teleri standing beside a cobbler's bench. Straddling it, hunched over the half-finished shoe on the last, was a jockey-sized fellow. He was to hairless what his butler pal was to hairy. The skin atop his skull looked as smooth and polished as the tip of an expensive oxford, but laugh lines had dug in permanent quotation marks around his broadly grinning mouth. When he saw me, he set aside his hammer and rolled down the sleeves of his *Phantom of the Opera* T-shirt over massively corded biceps. The hammer glittered; gold. He laughed at the way my eyes widened when I saw it.

"It would appear, Miss Teleri, that our young visitor might stand in need of some slight moral memorandum on your part while he is occupying these premises." To me he said, "I would heartily advise you to refrain from appropriating any items not specifically presented for your express use, young man. Much as it would pain me, I would otherwise be compelled to violate your cranial integrity. I hope that I have made myself clear in this matter?"

"I touch it, you break my head," I translated.

He beamed and turned to the hirsute butler. "What did I tell you, Hobson? Did I not only moments previous impart to you my opinion that the lovely and talented Miss Teleri, a banshee of the most impeccable breeding, would never associate herself with ruffians of any stripe, even were they part of the obligations of her current employment?"

"I believe, sir, that you might have made some comment to that effect," Hobson intoned.

The little cobbler stuck out a hand calloused and browned from much acquaintance with labor. "Master Runyon at your service. It is truly an honor and a signal privilege finally to press the flesh of that person of whom the divinely talented and toothsome Miss Teleri has spoken so warmly." He pumped my hand with vigor, then dropped it and slapped himself across the brow. "But where have my manners gone, deserting me to my humiliation? Hobson, my blithesome comrade, pray step forward that you might likewise cozy up to this veritable compendium of juvenile virtues!"

I don't know why, but I got the feeling I was being insulted.

Hobson came forward, as bidden, with that impossible gait peculiar only to Renaissance Spanish infantas and the best old English butlers—you know, as if they're moving around on ball bearings instead of legs. He bowed smoothly from the waist, but didn't offer his hand. "The pleasure is entirely mine, sir." He didn't sound as if any pleasure—outside of the occasional funeral—was entirely his.

Satisfied that the protocols had been taken care of, Master Runyon dug into the pocket of his leather apron and produced a small white clay pipe which he stuck in his mouth. Immediately a tickle of violet smoke rose from the bowl, without benefit of tobacco or matches.

"Well, Miss Teleri," he said. "You have obviously come to grace my unworthy footgear establishment for some excellent reason. Pray be kind enough to illuminate me."

"Away wi' yer long-winded blather!" My banshee waved her hand impatiently. "I've brought the young lord for no more than to bear witness to the great undoing as is upon us all! 'Tis even as ye said when first we met at the Automat, Master Runyon, when ye'd be explaining whence yerself and Hobson here sprang. I'll be asking yer pardon fer not believing ye then, but ye must admit than the luchorpans do suffer perilous dear from the palterer's reputation."

Master Runyon blew shamrock-shaped smoke rings at the ceiling. "Through no fault of our own, dear female, but through the vast malevolence of those footpads and grifters as would desire to part us from our lawful property." He tipped me a wink and added, "The pot of gold, young sir; the legendary pot of gold. Though to eschew all prevarication, I confess I put my own meager assets into T-bills, mutual funds, and CDs."

"Pot of gold?" I repeated. Came the dawn. "You're a leprechaun!"

Master Runyon shifted the pipe from one corner of his mouth to the other. "Give the gentleman from Flatbush his pick of this lovely washer-dryer combination in your choice of decorator shades, or what lurks behind Curtain Number Two." He knocked invisible dottle from the bowl and puffed out pink smoke this time. "The term you use, in what I will be charitable enough to term ignorance, is a sorry British corruption of the proper manner by which to name myself and any kinfolk to whom I might yet not owe serious simoleons. Be instructed, young man, that I am a *luchorpan*. And in passing, kindly note that I do not wear green buckled shoes, a yellow waistcoat, emerald knee-breeches, a Kelly derby studded with shamrocks, nor a swallow-tailed cutaway in any bilious hue. I also do not hawk pre-sweetened cold cereal, with or without marshmallow fetishes."

Teleri laid her hand on my shoulder. "The luchorpans are an ancient kindred, milord, and much respected in Erin. They are cobblers to the Fair Folk, and marvelous fine work they do."

Hobson cleared his throat, discreetly but loudly. Teleri gave the hairy brown butler a dazzling smile.

"Faith, Hobson, me love, I shan't neglect ye. Milord Timothy, Hobson here's in a constant pother lest folk believe he's a luchorpan as well, simply because he associates with Master Runyon. Truth to tell, he's—"

"—a goblin," I finished for her. To her startled stare I said, "Simple deduction. You asked me whether I knew what a goblin was, remember? Back in Mom's bedroom? *Back in my house, where I really think we ought to go right now?*"

"His young lordship is possessed of a most healthy color," Master Runyon commented. "I find it difficult to believe that a person capable of turning that intense shade of scarlet as to the face is destined to push up the daisies any time in the foreseeable future."

"Ye tend t' yer shoes and leave the bansheeing t' me." Teleri didn't like being second-guessed as to my demise. She gave Master Runyon the cold shoulder and was all the more ingratiating to me. "We'll be on our way just as soon as ever I tell Master Runyon about that arrant rogue of a Yang as is presently cluttering up the world with his vileness." And she did.

The lepre—pardon me, *luchorpan*—grew more and more thoughtful as Teleri outlined her first-contact experience with Yang the Unpoised. "Then it appears to be as I assumed," he said. "My dear Hobson, would you be willing to corroborate?"

The saturnine goblin's moustaches drooped a whole bunch of degrees lower. "Without the slightest reservation, sir. We are obviously in the grip of a leakage."

"A what?" I asked.

"A leakage of extraordinary magnitude," Hobson went on, growing more funereal with every word. "A breachment of the boundaries that may give us all just cause to regret our present freedom." His sigh rattled the upturned points of his starched white collar. "I, myself, have often voiced the opinion that no good would come of it. What though the hole was there? We did not need to traverse it. Act in haste, repent at leisure; if we are vouchsafed any leisure time within which to repent. I doubt it."

"*What* is leaking?" I demanded.

Teleri looked as crestfallen as Hobson, which wasn't an easy gambit to play. "The Leeside," she said, and shivered.

I remembered the wicked crawly feeling I'd gotten when she and I passed through that place. An unhealthy memory of despair and darkness still clung to me. Sometimes you just *know* that you'll be happier staying ignorant; sometimes you realize that happier or not, you can't hide from the truth.

"What's the Leeside?" I asked.

"Milord, wasn't that wee taste of it enough for—?"

"Going through it isn't the same as knowing what it *is*, what it *means*. Especially now that you tell me it's leaking. *What* is it leaking?"

Master Runyon spread his hands. "Us."

10

Oops

T'ING BENT DOWN one of the aluminum slats in the Venetian blinds. "Did you know there's a black horse on your fire escape?" she asked.

"Phouka," I said.

"Hey!"

"He's a phouka. His given name is Donahue, and I rode him all the way from Times Square."

"So that's where you've been. Why didn't you come in through the window, then?"

"Maybe I should've. It would've beat tippy-toeing through my own living room the minute Teleri said Mom was in the bathroom and the coast was clear."

T'ing looked skeptical. "Your banshee friend poofs you to Times Square in the blink of an eye, but she can't return you the same way? Not even from out in the hall into this room?"

"She could do it, all right." I was grim. "I told her not to." *Begged* her not to was more like it. If I never saw the Leeside again, I'd die happy. If I did pay it a return visit, I'd just die, period.

"Weird. Why not?"

I was getting a little tired of the object of my affection's snoopiness. No wonder Sherlock Holmes never had a date. "Look, I just figured that maybe a little normalcy—like me walking into a room through the door instead of the wall—might be a real treat, for a change. We all did."

T'ing peered intently through the blinds. "What *we*? Where's Teleri?"

Yang belched and smacked his lips. "Gone to make herself worthy of having sex with me," he volunteered. "Or else she's taking a crap."

I tried pretending he wasn't there. "Teleri's around. She rode Donahue with me, and she put a run in her pantyhose. Master Runyon and Hobson are treating her to a couple of new pairs down at Park Lane Hosiery."

T'ing folded her arms. "You *have* been making new friends. Want to tell me about it?"

"Actually, no," I said. "But I think I'd better."

Yang had taken over the bed, lolling lazily with his boots on the pillows, so T'ing and I had to stay standing while I brought her up to date on my ever-widening circle of unearthly acquaintance. "—and as far as any of us know, all of them except Teleri are here because there's a leakage in the boundaries of the Lee—"

"*Shut your mouth or I'll cut you a new one under your chin!*" Yang did a backwards somersault that landed him on his feet, between T'ing and me. His sword cleared the scabbard in mid-tumble and lined itself up across my windpipe. Droplets of rancid spittle pattered over my face as he snarled, "Speak the name of that damned place in my presence again, and I'll feed your spleen to the dogs."

This was not the time to tell him that our apartment building had a strict NO PETS policy.

"Yang! *Bu!*" T'ing shoved her way between us and gave her honorable ancestor a genuine Flatbush noogie on his sword arm.

Yang's eyes narrowed. "Again? Again with this 'Yang, *bu*' shit?"

T'ing did not shrink or falter under her ancestor's evil eye. Glare for glare she matched him. "Listen, my mother pays plenty for me to learn Mandarin so I won't lose touch with where I came from. If you're any ancestor of mine, you might pay more attention to someone yelling at you in your native tongue."

"The only thing native tongues are good for is stringing on a rawhide thong and smoking over the campfire." Yang's mood jollied right up with memories of the Good Old Days. "Beloved granddaughter, it may be that somewhere in the dunghill of your ancestry there were plenty of worthless maggots who spoke Mandarin. I am not one of them. The only reason I learned that goat-buggering language was so no one could keep secrets from me at tax-gathering time." He batted his eyelashes coyly, doing an impression of Great Moments from Yang's Past. " 'Oh, look, Zhou. Here comes that big, stupid Mongol. You tell him we don't have the money, I'll go check on the twenty-three pigs we hid behind the temple.' " Yang howled with laughter. "Did *they* ever lose face! Heads, too.''

T'ing was not amused. It was frightening to see how closely her scowl twinned Yang's own, family resemblance with a vengeance. "Okay, Gramps, no more Mandarin. And no more nonsense out of you with that pig-sticker, either!" She gave the blade a flick with her fingers.

Yang took umbrage. "Is that how you talk to your honorable ancestor?" He appealed to me. "You use that kinda language to your domestic spirits?"

"No, but—"

"There, you see?" In his jubilation, Yang resheathed his sword and decided I was his good buddy. United we stood against his beloved though testy granddaughter. "You listen to Tim. Not much meat on his bones, got kinda camel-face, but he knows about respect. Bear his children, if you get the chance."

"Respect this," said T'ing, and she hooked an ankle behind Yang's foot, then gave him a hearty shove to the chest. He toppled, taking the easel down with him.

"Tim? Tim, what's going on in there?" Mom opened the door. She surveyed the room, paying special attention to the relative positions of me, T'ing, the bed, and the easel, in that order.

At least I thought she was staring at the easel.

"How did you get in here?" she asked Yang. She looked him right in the eye. That, or Mom liked talking to bedside throw rugs.

"Mom, you can—see him?"

"Yes." She sounded dubious about having that privilege.

Out on the fire escape, Donahue whinnied. Mom made her way to the window like a sleepwalker and peeped through the blinds. "I see that—that black horse out there, too." She turned from the window and gazed off into the middle distance. "I seem to be seeing a lot of things, lately." Blinking her eyes, she behaved as if someone had just roused her from a dream. "T'ing, Timothy, I hate to interrupt your little visit, but I need to get my bathrobe out of the closet. He said I need to take a bath. I tried arguing with him, but it's no good. He is the expert, in these matters. Will you excuse me?" She floated over to the closet and got the robe.

"Mom, what are you talking ab—?"

The bedroom door crashed open. A blocky shape like a brown haystack filled the frame. " 'Ey! What's all the holdup? I get the water nice an' hot, you waste time. You think hot water grows on trees, woman? You come! I don't got forever." Grumbling, it stalked away.

"My *bannik*," Mom said, still in that spooky, detached tone. "I was on the couch, reading *The Hunt for Red October*, when he appeared. He's Russian, too, just like my grandparents; isn't that funny? And he says I need a bath." She started unbuttoning her blouse as she wafted out of the room. Yang slavered out loud and T'ing had to sit on him to keep him from following her.

I hurried after Mom, catching up with her halfway across the livingroom. "Who—*what* is that thing?" I held her fast by one arm; she just kept unbuttoning her blouse one-handed.

"I told you, dear." She sounded so reasonable it was scary. "He's my bannik; the *domovoy* in charge of the bathhouse. In our case, the bathroom, but he says he doesn't mind the change."

"*Right*, you told me. Only what did you tell me? What's a domovoy? And don't tell me it's a bannik."

A little of Mom's old grit came back. She yanked her arm free and did everything but brush Tim-cooties off it. "Don't get fresh with me, Tim; you're in enough trouble. A bannik is a bathroom domovoy, and the *domoviye*—that's the plural, dear," she added informatively—"the domoviye are old Slavic spirits who take care of this and that around the house and farm. That's what my *baba* used to tell me, anyway. You know, sort of like the brownies."

I tried to keep a cool head. "Mom, as far as you were ever concerned, brownies are either cookies or the caterpillar stage of Girl Scouts. Every single fairy tale you ever read me, from as far back as I can remember, you always ended with, 'And they lived happily ever after but of course *we* know there's no such things as fairies,' all in one breath. Now you're talking like you leap into the tub any time one of these domovoys snaps his fingers; if he's got fingers."

"*Domoviye*," Mom corrected me. "The plural is *domoviye*. But I do believe it's one bannik, two banniks." She managed a weird smile. "Not that he'd ever stand for two banniks under one roof, even if we had more than a single bathroom. Indoor plumbing is quite a help to him, and he was just delighted when he found all those boxes of bubble bath under the sink. I've been taking far too many showers, these days. You've got to take time to stop and smell the Calgon Bouquet.''

She sounded so *happy*! A lot of hostages develop starched-on smiles, too. If her eyes wouldn't have had that cornered bunny look, I might have believed that she'd found Nirvana in a bottle of Jean Naté After-Bath Splash.

I decided to cut to the chase, and strode ahead of her into the bathroom. The mirror was all steamed up, the tub brimming over with perfumed bubbles. Perched on the sink, with his fat rump in the basin, Mom's bannik swung his furry legs back and forth as he hummed to himself. My skin crawled when I recognized the tune: "Rubber Ducky."

He noticed me and stopped the music. " 'Ey, kid! Where's you mama? I get the tub all ready, put in good stuff, make her smell nice, hot water, go the whole nine *versts*. So she's where?"

I tried to look threatening. The bannik had arms thick as telephone poles and a mouthful of teeth to give piranhas pause. I decided to trade down and try to appear commanding instead. "Who are you and what are you doing here?"

"Who? Me? Ilya Mikulovich, at your service." He bounced off the sink and rolled up to me. Without warning he grabbed my left ear and yanked, sticking his bulbous nose halfway down the nape of my neck. "Hmm, you don't wash back here. Grow potatoes instead? You need a bath. Get in tub."

"I don't need a bath," I said through clenched teeth. "Now let go of my ear and—"

"Kids, *pah*! What they know?" With no further ado, Ilya hoisted me over his head and plopped me down, clothes and all, into the foaming tub. "Now *wash*." He had no trouble being both threatening and commanding.

"Tim!" Mom stood in the doorway, caught midway between alarm and helpless laughter. I wiped gobs of bubbles from my eyes and lifted one dripping sneaker over the edge of the tub.

"Think maybe you could've waited until I stripped?" I asked the beaming bannik.

"Is no need. Wash clothes, wash body, all same time. Very economical. This is my own thought I have just now, spur of the moment. Not bad, 'ey?" He looked ready to receive a medal.

I climbed out of the tub. He threw me back in. I picked up a washcloth and made a big deal of scrubbing behind my ears, after which Ilya grudgingly allowed me to haul my sodden self onto the bathmat. As I watched the water trickle down my body and puddle all over the floor, I fully realized the messy implications of a "leakage."

"Okay! Is now your turn, woman." Ilya was trying to chivy Mom into the vacant bathtub when the doorbell rang. The bannik made a face. "Is some things never change. The minute you try get into nice hot tub, is always something comes to interrupt you: doorbell, telephone, Fax machine, Cossacks, all same."

"I'll get it," I grumbled, dripping my way from the bathroom to the front door.

"Tim?" Mrs. Kaplan eyed me uneasily. "Is—is T'ing still here?"

I decided not to say, *Yeah, in the bedroom.* Mothers get most of their aerobic exercise by jumping to conclusions. Instead I said, "Sure, Mrs. Kaplan. I'll call her," and I did. Ours is a small apartment, but Mrs. Kaplan wouldn't know how small, or from which room T'ing was emerging. Hey, let her think it's the den or something!

T'ing heard me and came a-running, as expected. I also expected my good buddy, Yang the Mongolian Noel Coward, to come with her. I wasn't disappointed. Next on the ol' expectation list was for Mrs. Kaplan to see him, just as my mom had done, and realize that poor, innocent Timothy Desmond was not the wild man she so wrongfully mistrusted with her daughter. Rather I was the victim of extraordinary circumstances— Yang among them—and richly deserving of more second chances than postwar Japan. I only hoped she wouldn't faint.

This did not happen. She saw T'ing; she looked right through Yang. "I was just passing by and I thought we could check out another one of those backup photographers for Daniela's wedding, dear," she chirped at her daughter. It was a lighthearted chirp, in direct contrast to the disquieted stare she never once took off me. She literally backed out of the apartment, an iron hold on her baby's wrist, still jabbering social pleasantries in my direction. Some people think if you talk nonstop to a rabid dog, he won't bite.

"I'll see you in school tomorrow, Tim!" T'ing called as her mother made good their escape. Yang waved bye-bye over Mrs. Kaplan's head.

"She didn't see him," I told no one in particular.

"A possibility whose clinical frequency of occurrence has not escaped these peepers, my good chum." I smelled tingly tobacco smoke before I saw Master Runyon. He was seated behind me, on the convertible sofa. He had shucked the "Phantom" T-shirt for full biker gear—all leather, naturally. It was like seeing one of Hell's Munchkins. Hobson sat next to him, still in his butler's uniform. Every time I saw the little goblin I got the sensation that he'd been born wearing those stuffy threads. Rounding out the group on the sofa was Teleri, in a skimpy set of black lace and leather duds that would have made Madonna blush and Cher turn green with envy.

Mom came out of the bathroom in her robe. "Tim, was that the doorbe—? Oh, hello." She regarded the trio on our sofa with a deep, lobotomized calm. "I didn't know we had more guests, Tim. Why don't you offer your friends some milk and cookies?" Donahue whinnied again. "And oatmeal," Mom added. "I'll be in the tub, if anyone wants me."

11

Domestic Spirits, Bottled in Bond

I DON'T KNOW how I got through that night. By the time it was over, the only consoling thought I had to anchor me to sanity was : *At least The Powers That Be never ask to see your PSAT scores on college entrance applications*. Small comfort. The Powers That Be would also probably sign me up for double shifts with Mr. Izanagi, O joy, O rapture. While Mom took a three and a half-hour bath, I tried to do my homework with Teleri at my elbow, Master Runyon rooting through the closets and making snide remarks about my taste in shoes, and Hobson gliding around the apartment in a tidying frenzy. I don't know how he did it, but the little goblin managed to work himself into a frenzy that was—no lie—sedate. It was like watching Jaws ravage the Eastern seaboard under the influence of Quaaludes, only instead of devouring beach bunnies, Hobson scarfed dust bunnies.

Teleri sat on the dining room table that served as my desk. She made all sorts of helpful hints.

"Milord, if ye'd rather not study those great, dreary books, could be as I might be willing to write ye an excusal, on the grounds that ye've little need t' do homework."

I looked up from my Chemistry text, sore tempted. "And why might that be?"

The banshee shrugged her luscious shoulders. "Why, 'tis patent plain ye'll soon be dead, and what need have the deceased of all that alchimical pother?"

"If it's all the same to you, I'll pother on." It was weird, having something in the offing I wanted to avoid more than Chem homework. I plunged back into the exciting world of molal solutions with a willing heart.

Teleri was not convinced. "Have it as ye've a mind to, milord. I'm but a servant o' the Desmond line. Don't bother listening to anything *I* might have to say; oh, no. 'Tis always ye men as know better about everything, until ye come a cropper. Then it's glad ye be t' have a faithful banshee at yer side, ready and able t' keen ye over the borders of rest eternal. Well, I'm not asking fer any thanks, and it's no thanks I'll be getting until it's too late, but *I* don't mind. *I* know when I'm not—"

I slammed the textbook shut. "Teleri, is it in the cards that I'm supposed to be nagged to death?"

She sniffed delicately. "If I'd be knowing how death must come fer ye, milord, I'd not be wasting me time loitering about this poor excuse fer a bothy. There's better things awaiting me, once I've got the last o' the Desmonds tucked safe beneath the sod."

"Oh?" I couldn't keep a nasty note of skepticism out of my voice. "What kind of 'better things'? Tinkerbell going to retire and give you the castle-lighting concession at Disneyworld?"

"The sauce!" Teleri crossed her long, lithe legs—no easy play in a skirt that tight—and sat up taller. "*I'm* going to be a star!" she announced.

My guffaws were loud enough to fetch both Master Runyon and Hobson from their several tasks.

"What, might I inquire, is the cause of this unseemly brouhaha?" the luchorpan asked.

Teleri leaped from the table straight into his arms. She had to double over to cry on his shoulder, but she managed. "That ungrateful brat's the matter, Master Runyon, and no mistake!" Her accusing finger pointed right at me and shook with her sobs. "Scornful, he is, and venom-tongued enough t' doubt aloud as I'm to be the lyric sensation ye promised."

Master Runyon patted her on the back, or tried to. I gave him the benefit of the doubt when he could reach no higher than my banshee's leather-clad rump. "There, there, doll. If you are to burst upon the entertainment scene as brilliantly as I envision, you must not permit the uninformed salvos of a base mug such as him to deter you from your chosen career."

I rested my head in one hand wearily. "Don't tell me. You promised you'd make her into a big rock 'n' roll star as soon as she got done burying me."

Master Runyon scowled. "That, my thick-skulled friend, is all you know about it. Rock 'n' roll? Every chuckleheaded refugee from a nightmare takes refuge in said cultural dump. Pretty soon you will not be able to swing the proverbial cat onstage at a rock concert without the unfortunate puss smacking headfirst into your choice of boogiemen, zombies, trolls, or roadies of the undead. *My* client will not soil her delectable vocal chords by association with the riffraff connected with yon Dutch Elm blighted branch of Euterpe's pet saplings. *I* intend for her to commit what our Gallic brethren might term your common or garden *succès du scandale*—meaning a hit of truly boffola proportions—in a field altogether more worthy of the doll's talents."

"Opera?" I was awestruck.

Hobson set a cup of tea down at my elbow. "Commercials," he murmured.

I snarfed badly, spraying Tetley all over my textbook. The unruffled Hobson pounded me on the back, much to Teleri's pique.

"Madam, the amount he inhaled was quite insufficient to cause asphyxiation, I assure you," Hobson said smoothly. He wiped up the mess and brought me a fresh cuppa.

"Commercials. Maybe I am going to die; now I've heard it all." I snickered. "A banshee doing voice-overs for floor wax and mouthwash."

"Not," Master Runyon was quick to point out, "in the same commercial."

"And you're her agent?"

The luchorpan made a self-effacing gesture. "Ever since I came through the barrier and got my bearings, I have managed to familiarize and endear myself to local showbiz moguldom. Having made so many useful connections in the field, it would be a most regrettable circumstance to waste same. Also, I am becoming fed up with half-sole jobs."

"From shoebiz to showbiz. Why don't you slither into the bathroom and chat up Ilya Mikulovich? I bet you could get the bannik work as a stand-in for the Ty-D-Bowl man."

Master Runyon looked hurt. "Your ignorance is superseded only by your aptitude for being a jerk."

"*Gosh*, I'm sorry. The joy of learning that Teleri wants me to hurry up and die so she can sell dog food must've overwhelmed me."

Hobson materialized with a plate of Oreos. "Sir, if I may be so bold, might I point out the ancient truth that sarcasm is always wasted on Irish spirits.''

While Master Runyon made more soothing agent-noises at Teleri, I got my first chance to really look at the butler-cum-goblin. "You're not Irish," I said, picking up a cookie.

"No, sir. I do not claim the privilege."

"What are you, then?"

"I am the humble descendant of a long line of British hobgoblins, an honorable breed with roots deep in the soil of Cheshire. There was the usual diversification within the family—a number of brownies, some Billy Blinds, and of course Uncle Caliban." A cloud settled over Hobson's already morose features. "We do not like to speak of Uncle Caliban. He *traveled*.''

Hobson uttered these last two words the same way a Victorian spinster would speak of a relation who drank. Intrigued, I urged him to tell me more.

The goblin clucked a deprecating tongue over memories of his madcap kin, but you could tell he enjoyed raking up the old scandal. "A good goblin has no need to go gallivanting more than a stone's throw from his native hearth and heath; that is what my dear mama always said. Uncle Caliban, though . . . He said travel was broadening, educational, enriching"— Hobson lowered his voice—*"progressive.''*

I did my best to commiserate with Hobson over such wild and wacky notions as had possessed his black sheep uncle.

"I knew you would understand, sir." The gratitude in his huge red eyes was heart-rending. "I marked you for a kindred soul from the moment we met. If it is any consolation, you may know that I shall be most fearfully distraught upon your predicted demise."

"I'd really rather not have you dwell on that, if you don't mind. So, what became of your uncle?"

"Oh, he *would* travel, sir. He went to London to visit the Queen. The mouse was delicious, as he later told us, though one does not like to think of one's elders performing feline scutwork, even if it be beneath the royal chair of Great Eliza herself. London was the undoing of him. Took to giving himself undeserved airs after that comedic trifle premiered at the Globe. He would insist that Master Shakespeare owed him certain monetary considerations for the use of his name. He went so far as to cause that upstart scrivener to invoke the law, and you must know how dreadfully my kin regard the workings of your judiciary. When

Uncle Caliban therefore found himself without satisfaction or recourse, he went to the bad and turned boggart." Hobson hung his head.

"Changed his name to Humphrey?" I suggested.

My runty stab at humor earned me a reproving look from a master of the art. "A boggart, sir, is a purely vindictive domestic spirit whose deeds bring shame to honest goblins everywhere. Uncle Caliban was one of the worst. He ruined any number of butter-churnings and cheese-makings in the neighborhood, quite undermining the local esteem which my brownie kin had worked so hard to establish. We put up with his antics for nearly a century, but enough is enough. For the good of the family's reputation, I was chosen to conduct Uncle Caliban to the New World, where it was hoped the fresh air would set him right. It did not. And then—the ban."

"What ban?" I asked, my mouth sort of full. I was using my upper teeth to wedge open the Oreos, then licking the wafers clean of filling. Hobson averted his eyes in distaste.

"The ban, sir, that fell over this land soon after the late unpleasantness at Salem Village. It would appear that the supernatural having caused your antecedents no end of public embarrassment—through no fault of truly magical creatures, I might indicate—a strong subconscious consensus was reached. America simply could not countenance magic. The possibility for future humiliation of government officials and community figureheads was just too great. And so"—a voluminous sigh riffled Hobson's moustaches—"we were packed off, *portune* and *phouka*, to the Leeside."

I felt the old chill steal over my back. "Creepy place. But—I don't get it. How come Teleri could whisk me through a region that kept you and your kind imprisoned for so long? Did someone open a door for her or what?"

"There is no door to the Leeside, sir; no door leading *out*, at any rate. What we do have is a region contained by what you might like to call a net. As with all nets, certain things are small enough to pass through the mesh at any point, while others are not. Too, we now have the leakage site, but that permits escape at one point only along the boundaries."

"And where is that site?" I asked.

"You must forgive me, sir. The stress of emergence via so strait a way has the nasty property of causing one to forget details." The goblin would not have made a good used-car sales-man. His lies smelled worse than a jackal with the squits.

"Keep your secret," I told him.

"Pardon, sir?"

"I said, you don't have to tell me about the ins and outs of the Leeside if you're afraid I'll try forcing you back there. Not that I would, even if I had the power."

I thought I heard him say, "Don't you, sir?" just under his breath. Before I could be sure, Hobson spoke up briskly. "Entry is always easy for all, sir, regardless of qualification. *Facilis descensus Averni.* It wants a diminishing touch of mortality to obtain a similarly easy egress."

I snapped my fingers. "And Teleri was born mortal."

"Even so, sir. The taint remains sufficient." Seeing my offended reaction—mortality a *taint*?—Hobson added, "Surely you are not unaware of the saliently ichthyic aroma that likewise accompanies the young lady wherever she goes? That too is a mitigating element in her background: Nixie blood, or perchance some traffic with an enchanted salmon, such things have been known to happen in Ireland, quite unmistakable to one of my perceptions. Only a trace, mind—your Gaels have an honorable history of interbreeding with the otherworld—yet sufficient to make its presence known once the young lady crossed over the boundaries between fey and mortal."

I put down my half-gnawed Oreo. Them was fighting words. "Look, short, dark, and miserable, who made you the judge? The Irish were holding onto the light of learning while the English were doing their damndest to keep everybody bashed down past their eyebrows in the Dark Ages. Interbreeding with the otherworld, were we? You've got your nerve. Where do you get off making these stuffy pronouncements about my people?"

"Your people, sir? I was under the impression that your people were the Americans. The glory of the melting pot tradition and all that." Hobson's slow blink was like a shutter coming down on a pair of stoplights. "I meant no insult, sir. In the Old Country it was not considered rare or shameful for persons of the highest communal repute to admit some extramortal blood. Along the English coast we had more than our share of fisherfolk with selky ancestry. In France, the noble house of Lusignan was proud to own the fey Melusine as their foundress. Then of course you have your Greek heroes, scarce one of them without some otherworldly parentage in the cupboard, and ever so many others besides.''

Hobson's recitation took most of the wind out of my sails, but I still wasn't satisfied on a couple of points. "Let me get this straight: You're telling me that you and Uncle Caliban came over here from England—''

"Steerage-class on a supply ship bound for the Massachusetts Bay Colony; yes, sir.''

"—and Master Runyon did the same, only he came from Ireland?''

"At a later date than myself and my unfortunate uncle; indeed. As did the phouka Donahue, and a number of other—''

I waved off any further roll call of émigré ogres. "Now I'm going to guess, but is it a bet that Ilya snagged a steamer over here, too? And Yang?''

"I am not privy to the precise mode of transportation those gentlemen employed, sir, but one may safely assume they utilized the most efficient means available.''

"Ah-HA!" I shouted, leaping up from the table and scattering Oreos everywhere. I thrust a finger right at Hobson's quivering brown nose. "If you came over separately, why is a British critter like you hanging out with a gang of Irish sprites?''

"The Leeside makes strange bedfellows, sir. I trust you will not take that in the unseemly sense. Do not trouble yourself over our nationalities. Apart from a sorry inclination to palace intrigue, we of the otherworld have managed to avoid most of you mortals' taste for petty political squabbles. Mind you, there are instances—''

I wasn't about to let up on the cross-examination to hear him out. "If you and your uncle both got shut up in the Leeside, how come you're out and he's not?''

"I would not expect you to understand that such a circumstance is not only perfectly logical but a situation to be cherished rather than questioned, sir.''

I began to pace back and forth in front of the table, showing off for members of an invisible jury. Where was a law school talent scout when I needed one? "Why use mortal transport? Why didn't you and the rest just tank up on fairy dust and *poof* over here? If you're so supernatural, why travel steerage?''

"I am not in the habit of *poofing*, sir.'' Hobson emitted another one of his gale-force sighs. "A little knowledge is indeed perilous, it appears. If you will excuse me—'' He bowed and glided off to the sofa, where Master Runyon was engaged in animated conversation with a still-sniffling Teleri.

I don't know what Hobson said to them. If his discreet murmur got any discreeter it would be totally inaudible. I just saw Teleri look worried. Master Runyon, though, brightened right up. His mouth was a blur as he went into blarney overdrive. Little by little, my banshee's brow uncreased. She nodded dubiously and the grinning luchorpan pounded Hobson on the back, then gave him the old thumbs-up sign.

The little goblin returned to me. "It has been arranged, sir."

"What has?"

"Walk this way, sir." With nary another word, he headed for the kitchen.

Our kitchen is like thousands of others in the Greater New York area—or any other metropolitan territory where real estate is pre-mined gold. You can have appliances in it, or people, but not both. When I want a good science-fiction book, I just pick up one of these magazines showing suburban kitchens that still have room for pets and a personal computer.

Even though Hobson hardly came up to my belt buckle, the two of us in the kitchen made for a tight fit, especially when he insisted we both stand in front of the stove. "Turn on the oven if you would, sir," he drawled.

I complied, keeping one mistrustful eye on the goblin and one ear perked to catch the sound of the automatic ignition kicking in. "What temperature you want?"

"That is immaterial, sir."

"Come on, what do you—?" I cocked my head. There was no clicking, no reassuring *whoosh* of gas taking flame. I reached for the dial again, ready to turn it off before we had trouble.

"Do not do that, sir." Hobson's hands closed around my wrists. Automatically I struggled to break them free, but it was useless.

"Are you crazy? What are you doing?" I protested in vain. The goblin wouldn't let go. "This is *gas* we're dealing with. If it doesn't light and I don't turn it off, we could have an explo—" Ice closed up my windpipe. Maybe a big blast was Hobson's whole intent. It wasn't unthinkable. I'd grown a sight too familiar with the otherworldly, and you know what they say familiarity breeds. With his starchy stance and turgid personality, Hobson might not care for all the backtalk I'd been giving him.

And if I did go to my reward in a whole lot of different directions, Teleri would be free. Was that what the sofa conference had been about? Getting the banshee's blessing for my destruction?

"Hobson, please, don't do Teleri's dirty work for her!" I would have gotten down on my knees to grovel properly, but there wasn't room in the kitchen. "You'll be sorry for it some day! You'll—you'll be no better than your boggart uncle if you get me killed!"

"Killed, sir?" A wee twitch of one shaggy eyebrow betrayed Hobson's shock. With anyone else, you'd have heard their jaw hit the floor, but all I could hear was the low, constant, sinister hiss of escaping gas. "Killed?" He dropped his grip on one of my hands, but was too fast in getting my arm twisted up behind my back for me to do anything about escaping him. The pain forced me to my knees, room or no room.

"Killed; the idea." I glimpsed a matchbox in the goblin's free hand. Nimble brown fingers pulled out an old-fashioned wooden match with a tip all the colors of a summer sunset. For the fourth time I heard Hobson's dry, irritated comment, "Killed, indeed." His thumbnail flicked across the match-head.

With a roar, the kitchen flared into flames all around us.

12

Home Is Where the Hearth Is

THERE WAS DARKNESS behind the flame, darkness that went on forever. My mind dived deep into the night, and I felt as if unseen hands were peeling away first the layers of my clothing, then the layers of my self. Cold down past my bones, I fell through the darkness, too scared to scream.

Lightning scraped the night rawly bright. I saw the strike-line and heard the thunder as I woke to rain pattering over my face. I sat up suddenly and looked around, nothing but terror inside my head. The lightning struck again, and I couldn't recall a single comforting Science-class fact about it. All I knew was the fear.

They were afraid of it, too; they, the three small shapes huddled with me under the branches of the big tree. When the lightning bleached the sky, I could see their eyes, small and bright, and the shaggy outline of their rounded shoulders. My nostrils flared and quivered. Scent told me what sight confirmed: One of our kin was missing. One of our blood was out there, beyond the tree's temporary shelter.

I had no way of marking time. For me there was only *now* and *before*. When we heard the approaching footfalls, as the rain rolled away towards the distant hills, it was just another *now*.

Oh, no. Not just another one. A *now* to mark a new forever. She had come back to us, out of the storm, her sweet, familiar smell made stronger by the tang of smoke. Light danced at the end of her arm, the lightning perched like a hawk amid the tips of the dead branch she held. By signs and some few sounds, she made us break off other branches from our sheltering tree. Deadwood not too damp and bits of tufty grass were given to the light-hawk for its meat. She lowered its perch to touch the piled offerings, and it spread bright wings of warmth as it settled into the nest we had made.

From then on, the darkness could be kept at bay. The light-hawk sang a crackling song to us in gratitude for our care, and we served it the way many others after us would serve their gods: because there was something more in it for us. I stared into the flames, my kin beside me, and tasted the luxury of so many breaths drawn without fear. My mind relaxed, opening to thoughts I had never known before the fire came; *different* thoughts. Shapes leaped and spun and took alien wings in the fire. They were not like any living thing I saw by daylight, yet I knew they were alive.

In the warmth and the light that kept away the darkness, I made the signs to tell my family of the unearthly beings who lived within the belly of the flames. At first they hooted at me, but after a time . . . after a time . . . As we watched, as we let our dreams slip into the strange waters of imagination, one shape detached itself from its fiery home and took its place in our midst.

It was small, smaller than we, and more terrified of the night. We drew back from it, all of us except one. She crouched near— she, who had brought us the captured fire. Her eyes were very bright with something still more exciting than the burning branch she had brought us. There was a half-chewed root in her hand. She set it on the ground and nudged it nearer the new creature. It sought her eyes with its own—eyes colored like the flames. She made the signs to urge it on, the gentle motions and noises a mother uses to encourage her little one. A tiny brown hand, six-fingered, clawed like the big cats' paws, reached out tentatively and closed on the gift. No sound or sign of thanks was given, and in the next instant the creature scuttled back into the blaze.

When the day came, and I woke to blink sleepily at the embers, I found a hollowed gourd filled with the sweet miracle of the honeycomb, lying at my kinswoman's feet. I knew fear again, but this time it had changed; changed forever. The unknown was still a terror, only not so much so now that we had set down the first flimsy spar across the chasm separating our world from a greater one. I looked into the dying fire, and hurried to fetch it food.

The fire blazed and climbed from one night's darkness to the next. Rocks ringed it. Bowls of brass contained it. Flat stones slipped beneath it and sun-dried bricks supported it. But no matter where it burned, the fire brought its comfort, its serenity, its dancing shapes, and its fleeting insights to the otherworld. Years passed, and the vision into which Hobson had flung me washed over my eyes like a great river. I saw how every hearth gave birth to new generations of his kind—children of the flame. In the ring of firelight, men first took warmth, then courage, then imagination. Their tongues could form the sounds that became words, the words that became *once upon a time* as they tried to make their families share the wonder-tales they'd seen in the fire.

Sometimes the fire burned too high. I ran through streets of blazing houses, a child whimpering against my chest, as the monsters stepped out of the flames and strode like conquerors among us, devouring everything. I cowered against a crumbling plaster wall as the throat of a great mountain opened and the beast beneath spewed the fire of his rage against the sky. Tongues of burning rock drooled down the mountainside, ravenous. I dodged beneath my shield as naked oarsmen below me screamed, their bodies turned to torches by an unholy rain of Greek fire from our enemies' ships. The hawk had been too closely tamed by some, not tamed enough by others. I went about my business on the streets of Hiroshima as the sky became one final fire.

But they were always there. In the heart of every hearth, in the precious gift of a filled stomach and a moment of peace, in the soft glow of a single candle above an altar, I could sense the presence of something other than myself. I was not alone. I would never be alone, and no matter what shape the presence took, what mask it wore, this was the only thing that mattered.

"Did you see, sir?" Hobson's anxious voice was a lifeline that dragged me free of all the visions.

I was lying flat on my back in the kitchen, staring up into the goblin's scarlet eyes. My head felt full of sand. Hobson offered me a paw and did his part to get me on my feet.

I rooched my shoulders around, stiffer than if I'd spent a night camping on the sidewalk. "Yes," I said slowly. "I saw." I couldn't put more words than that around the awesome journey I had just taken.

Yes, I saw. Three words, big deal, but Hobson acted as if I'd given him just what he wanted for his birthday. "You *saw*, sir; of course you saw. I knew you would. And seeing all that, you cannot now deny that we never mean you any harm. You *do* see that as well, do you not, sir?" He was pleading with his eyes.

"I guess I do," I admitted. "Sort of. It's still kind of hard to think of Yang as not meaning any harm. The man is harm personified."

"To you, perhaps, sir. To his descendant, he is a loyal and ferocious guardian."

I was still half-lost in memories. "So that's where you came from."

"No, sir." Hobson chinned himself onto the stove top and flicked off the gas. "That is merely one of a number of traditions that has been handed down through the years within my family. I thought it might serve as well as any other explication you might require."

"What? Then why did you put me through all that when you don't even know for sure where—?"

"Might I inquire which you find more infallible, sir: Darwin or King James?" Hobson was again imperturbable. "The point is not so much how we first arrived as whether we shall be able to stay now that we have returned."

"Why shouldn't you stay? The Puritans are long gone, and if you've ever gotten a load of what's hot on the tubes or in the shops, you'd see that the otherworld's no embarrassment to anybody these days."

"Is it not, sir? I had not been so informed."

"Hobson, if I had a penny for every product with a unicorn or a dragon on it, I'd be rich."

"Monsters, properly speaking, sir. Hardly domestic spirits. Not our kind at all."

"What do you want for proof? People to believe in fairy gifts? They're halfway there. Just ask anyone who plays the lottery."

Hobson did not appreciate my brilliant talent for analogy. "You are pleased to be frivolous, sir. *You* are in no danger of being forced back into the Leeside lands by the authorities."

"What authorities? Who has the power to force you to leave?"

"Precisely, sir. Who does? Does anyone? If so, how shall we best avoid the person or persons in question?"

I sidled past Hobson to get to the refrigerator. "I don't see your problem. From what you've shown me, my folks have always gotten along with yours—almost always." A disturbing thought made me yank my head out of the fridge. "Uh . . .

except for the monsters. There wouldn't happen to be any monsters passed out through that leakage, would there?''

"If there were, sir, rest assured I would have heard from Uncle Caliban ere this. Milk, sir?'' Hobson beckoned with his fingers, and the milk drifted out of the fridge and poured itself into a glass that fluttered down from one of our cupboards. "Fortunately, the site of the leakage is very small; so small as to go unnoticed by our former companions in the cold lands. Far too small for any of them to pass through, I assure you.''

"Well, that's a relief.'' I sipped my milk, then recalled my manners. "Want some milk yourself?''

"Most kind, sir. In a saucer on the doorsill, if you wouldn't mind.''

I felt ridiculous, but I did it the way he wanted. The goblin hunkered down over his dish and lapped it clean, then dabbed his whiskers dry with an immaculate handkerchief. "Most refreshing, sir. Not up to the mark of what they used to put out for us in Cheshire, but eminently satisfactory.'' He drew a deep breath and let it out slowly. "The Leeside years have kindly allowed me to forget how sweet this world can be. A mercy; I would have missed it all the more poignantly.'' I was taken aback by how vulnerable the self-possessed Hobson suddenly looked. "It is good to be free.''

I don't know what took hold of me, but I set down my milk and clamped both hands on Hobson's shoulders. "You're right, it is; and you're going to stay free, if I have anything to do with it.''

His moustaches lifted with hope. "Indeed, sir? If it were not too great an imposition, might I have your word of honor on the subject?''

"May wha—?'' I chuckled. "Sure, for whatever good it'll do you. I give you my word of honor that no one is going to send you back—''

"I do beg pardon, sir, but when you say 'you,' might you specify that you intend the plural usage? I am not the only one in peril.''

Much as I hate having so-called adults treat me like a kid— you know, that constant Aw-ain't-he-cute attitude—I couldn't help going into the same obnoxious act with Hobson. Hey, power corrupts!

"Sure, why not?'' I almost patted him on the head. "I, Timothy Alfred Desmond, do hereby promise to do anything within my power to prevent the unlawful and/or unwilling return of any and all benign fugitives from the Leeside to the aforementioned region. Okay?''

"Honor, sir,'' Hobson prompted. "Some passing mention of your word of honor?''

"And to this I pledge my word of honor. *Now* is it good?''

"Excellent, sir.'' Hobson's moustaches were curled up into tight little spirals of whiskery joy. I actually got my first clear look at his teeth: razor-sharp, pointed, and the color of bronze. Frankly I liked him better when he drooped. "In return, in most heartfelt gratitude to you for undertaking so great a responsibility, I am for my part honor-bound to attach my domestic services to your household in perpetuity.'' He immediately fell to plucking lint nubbles off my sweater.

I didn't appreciate feeling like a berry bush. Doing my best to dodge the goblin's nimble brown fingers, I protested, "Hey, Hobson, you don't have to. Really. I'm on your side, sure, but it's not going to be a lot more than moral support; it can't be. I mean, if it gets down to cases, there's not all that much I can do to help. I'm not even a high-school graduate.''

"Perhaps not, sir,'' the goblin replied, still plucking away. "Yet what you are *not* has little bearing on what you *are*. We have always been glad of a Desmond or two to take our side in a quarrel, particularly one with your gifts.''

"Gifts? I don't have any—''

"I believe, sir, that this is yours.''

Hobson stopped delinting me. He lifted his hands and bowed his head. Balanced across the velvety palms a shaft of crystal no thicker than a willow twig sparkled. In its heart burned a fire that was twin and kin to all the flames that I had seen in my vision. My brain commanded my hands to stay rooted to my sides, but something deeper in me, closer to the heart, made my fingers close around the glittering wand and claim it for my own.

An earsplitting shriek turned my touch on the wand into a death-grip. Red light shot through the length of clear crystal, leaping in a modest burst of spangles from the tip. I spun around, holding the wand like a spatula.

Teleri held onto both sides of the kitchen doorway, her face chalky, her lungs filling with air for a second scream. Master Runyon clung to her arm. Neither one of them looked like your typical happy camper.

"Name of Nemed, Hobson!" my banshee gasped. "What evil have you done?"

"Leave it to those limeys to queer things," Master Runyon muttered.

"Evil, madam?" Hobson didn't so much as flutter an eyelash. "I prefer to call it job security." He regarded me with proprietary satisfaction. "Is that not correct, Dread and Puissant Champion of the Fey?"

"Huh?" said the Dread and Puissant fall guy.

13

Nice Work If You Can Get It

"CHAMPION OF THE Fey . . . I don't know, dear." Mom took a sip of her coffee. "I always expected that you'd come work with me here in McDonald's if you ever got a part-time job." She checked her watch to see how much more break-time she had left. She never used to do that. It made me feel about as skittish as she looked. I wasn't accustomed to my mom being anything but secure and in control.

"Madam, I assure you that the office is not lightly bestowed." Hobson was smooth and unobtrusive as a well-oiled hatpin piercing the brainstem. "Acting independently, I put him to the test. Not everyone who is offered a vision has the capability to *see* it. He saw. He is worthy to stand as our advocate on this side of the barricade. *Quod erat demonstrandum.*"

"An advocate isn't so bad, Mom." I hoped some fast talk would help her calm down. "It's just another word for lawyer. You wouldn't mind so much if I became a lawyer, would you?"

Mom continued crumbling her styrofoam coffee cup into tiny pieces. "Yes, dear. I'm sure it will be all right. I always did know you were talented, but . . . Champion?"

"Dread and Puissant Champion of the Fey." Teleri rapped out the title as if it tasted bitter. "There's a fine and toothsome mouthful fer a lorn, hardworking banshee to cram into the rhyme-scheme o' her dirge-making! At least now I've the notion of how the poor infant shall meet his doom."

"Doom?" Poor Mom looked even more rabbity. Her coffee cup was just a pile of white pellets.

Master Runyon laid his hand over hers. "You will have to

forgive Miss Teleri for an understandable confusion in terms. The doll is not the most precise of elocutionists. What she meant to say was, at least now she knows how he shall meet his *responsibilities*.''

"She said *doom* when she meant *responsibilities*?" Even in her strung-out state, Mom wasn't ready to buy that one right off the rack.

"A common error. A mere slip of the tongue. What our more educated linguists might refer to as a boner." Master Runyon smiled all the wider.

"Oh. Yes. Of course." Mom looked at me, and I saw the cry for help in her eyes. I couldn't do a thing to answer it; not then. Some Dread and Puissant Champion I was!

I rested both elbows on the table, trying to stake out a little territory. The booth was pretty crowded, though not everyone would see it that way. For instance, if Mrs. Kaplan would have waltzed in just then, she'd count three noses: mine, Mom's, and T'ing's. Let someone else try the tally and—

"God." Larry Perlmutter stopped dead in his tracks and stared at the nine of us.

Behind him, a bosomy brunette with a see-through body gave him a poke in the ribs. "Is this what I teach you? To take the Lord's name in vain?" She was dressed like a fugitive from a low-budget road company of *Fiddler on the Roof.* Even though she was semitransparent, there was nothing immaterial about how hard she slapped the side of his skull.

An elderly black couple at a nearby table only saw Larry jerk his head and tell the empty air to lay off him already. They changed tables. Fast.

"You, too?" I said wearily.

Larry rolled his eyes over his own personal misery, then surveyed my tablemates. It was pretty easy pairing up T'ing with her ancestor, who was doing something gross with his milkshake, but you couldn't tell the rest of the players without a scorecard. Explaining Donahue took some doing, especially since the phouka kept switching from his human to his horsey shape at irregular intervals. The frequent shape-shifts were more annoying than watching TV with a chronic channel-changer.

"You want to quit that?" I wasn't in the best of tempers. "You got the hiccups or what?"

The human Donahue blew his lips almost as noisily as his equine counterpart. "Is it a crime, then, to have one's salad the way it tastes best, yet also to want to drink through a straw? Try that with horse teeth, Dread One!'' His face stretched into a long, black muzzle as he took another mouthful of garden salad, no dressing, then shortened back so he could slurp up his diet Coke. This little exchange got me so peeved I forgot to ask Larry about his new girlfriend.

Mom's break was over. She and Ilya went back to work: she to a manager's varied chores, the bannik to moody mucking about with the dishwasher, for lack of something human to get into hot water. The rest of us stood up, ready to be on our way. Latecomer Larry offered to give lunch a miss and come along with T'ing and me; and the others. Always the others.

''What's this?'' Larry's new companion nabbed him by the ear and twisted. ''No lunch? Not eating your food? Children are starving in Smolensk, and you turn up your nose at a nice hot meal? The shame! Is this how your mother teaches you?'' She pulled his face nose-to-nose with her own, and in a voice that was pure, cold, nasty business asked, ''Do I have to do everything for you?''

I was wondering about the whens and hows of asking Larry if he really needed such a bossy girlfriend, when the lady pulled my friend's face even nearer to her own and—

''Near'' isn't the word. *Through* her own, yeah, that'll do. My eyes and mouth opened wide—and remember, it wasn't that easy to shock me anymore—while Larry's diaphanous date stepped right inside his skin and made herself at home.

''There.'' Larry's hands primly tugged down the hem of his baseball jacket. ''That's better.'' He sounded more self-confident with a new hand at the helm than when he'd flown solo.

It is *very* disconcerting to have your best friend look down his nose at you and say, ''Well? Are you going to give him something to eat, or were you brought up on the steppe?''

''*I* was brought up on the steppe!'' Yang volunteered.

''Shut up, honored grandfather,'' T'ing told him. She looked grim but resigned, like the parent of two-year-old triplets.

A quartet of Mohawked youths in the booth next to ours overheard her, caught the deadly look in her eye, took it all personally, and decided they would be happier elsewhere.

Yang the Alan Alda Impersonator was crushed. ''I think I liked it better when it was 'Yang, *bu*,' alla time,'' he confided in me.

''Mongols can't be choosers,'' I reminded him.

"Sir, if I might be so bold as to make a suggestion—?" Hobson was at my elbow. Hobson was *always* at my elbow. The little goblin took his obligations seriously, and his devotion to serving my domestic needs often got in Teleri's way. I think I'd noticed a growing resentment in my banshee's expression whenever she looked at Hobson. The arrangement was scarcely twenty-four hours old. I shuddered to think of how much suppressed wrath a banshee could successfully contain before something went flootch. The trouble was, I would be right in the middle of the flootching.

"Yes, Hobson?"

A lone wino thought I was talking to him, or that I was crazy, or both. He stuffed the remains of a burger into his coat pocket and hustled out the door.

"Sir, I trust that it has not escaped your notice that your friend has just been possessed."

I decided to lay off the cheap shot about Larry never having been a very prepossessing sort. "You trust right," I told him. "And after all the song and dance you gave me about domestic spirits being harmless, I've got to say this incident isn't doing your case a lick of good."

Hobson looked pained. "The entity occupying your friend's body intends him only good, sir."

"Why shouldn't I?" Larry's voice wasn't too deep to start with, but his tenant shot him up into the soprano range. "I only want the boychik to eat a decent meal. Is this so bad? Is this a crime? Is a McD.L.T. kosher?"

I told her it was not, but that such considerations never stopped Larry from onloading at least two, when the fit was on him. Tears spilled from Larry's eyes. "So, when he wants to, he eats *trayf* like there's no tomorrow, but when *I* ask him to have a little bite, he won't? You think I like to come back and possess an ingrate like this? Did I ask for my descendants to be picky eaters? I've got a choice? All I do is work and slave, trying to be a good dybbuk, and this is the thanks I—"

That was all Teleri needed to hear. She threw her arms around Larry and told him—I mean, her—that mortals were all alike, but when it came to being thankless scum, mortal *men* were more all alike than others. The dybbuk continued to sob as she caused Larry to pour out a flood of grievances.

We were now standing at ground zero of a blast zone of vacated tables. It didn't matter that there were twenty or more tray-bearing customers in search of seats; not one came any closer to our little gang than need be.

Then I noticed something peculiar: The empty tables were being filled. Little by little, one by one, people were edging into the seats around us. They were, as Teleri would put it, all alike. It didn't matter that some were young, some old, some well-dressed and some hardly dressed at all. A dozen variations on the theme of human skin and hair and eye color couldn't distract me from the one vital element they shared in common: Every last living one of them was dogged by one of the Fey.

T'ing noticed it too. I'll bet Larry would have, if his dybbuk had returned him to automatic pilot. Mom's McDonald's is pretty near Brooklyn College and the Nostrand Avenue subway stop, so it bags a big crowd. There wasn't a single familiar face in that mob of sprite-escorted customers, yet all of them gave me a tentative wave hello. A few even mumbled some kind of greeting. They recognized me as one of their own, a fellow sufferer. When they ticked off just how many of the Gentry I had on the payroll, a new respect came into their eyes. One of them—she looked like a college student—scurried over to clasp my hand before the long-nosed, chicken-footed critter sharing her fries shooed her back to her place.

"No harm, huh?" I was losing confidence in good old Hobson's recent assurances. "Look at those people. Circles under their eyes, haggard faces, nervous as a bunch of cats—Why do they all look so haunted, like they're on the run from a crime? Tell *me* their hearth-spirits don't have something to do with it!"

"But of course, sir." Hobson remained cool under fire. "It is exactly as you say. However, you would be making an incorrect assumption in assigning their current state of malaise to the direct intervention of their several attendant spirits."

Master Runyon puffed taffy-colored smoke from his unlit pipe. "I would be obliged to concur with mine learned comrade's thesaurus. It is not exclusively the fault of the various *wights*, *duendes*, *hinzelmänner*, *follets*, and—Oh, salutations, McGarrity! Long time, no sole—Nay, rather permit me to ascribe said shared condition of the heebie-jeebies to the fact that every mother's son (or father's daughter, so as not to overlook the dolls amongst them) is playing last-tag with the screaming meemies because he fears to be thought mad."

"He's right," T'ing said. "Just look at them. They're all scared, but they're not being frightened by the Fey. They feel the way I did when I thought I was the only one who could see Yang.''

''Can't they tell they're not alone?'' I asked. ''They see *our* little sewing circle as well as their own spirits. Should I go tell them that we can see theirs?''

Master Runyon detained me from my mission of mercy. ''I would be remiss if I did not point out that it is immaterial to yonder unfortunate gomers how many other people can likewise see spooks. This is, lest we forget, America. So long as there remains more than one other soul incapable of perceiving we otherworldly denizens, then that is witnesses aplenty with the potential for sending their pixified brethren to Chateau Rubberwalls.''

''That is America for you, sir,'' said Hobson. ''Individuality is all very well and good, so long as it is an individuality we can all agree on as acceptable.''

''I get it,'' I said. ''They're sure they're nuts, and if I tell them I see what they see, it only proves I'm nuts too.''

''Precisely, sir.'' Hobson's melancholy eyes touched every one of the Fey-ridden customers who had crept into our vicinity. ''Albeit whatever the world's opinion of your mental stability, they are not above taking some passing comfort from proximity to one who partakes of their woe.''

Master Runyon leaned against an invisible lamppost. ''Which is to elsewise put it: Misery loves company.''

T'ing's pitying glance swept the assembled Fey-ridden. I felt her arm steal through my own. ''Isn't there anything we can do to help them?'' she pleaded.

The old Tim would have said *no*. The old Tim would have blushed and pulled away from her. It's always more comfortable to keep the woman of your dreams *in* your dreams, where she can't make any sudden moves on you. There were times I missed the lovely and aloof T'ing Hau Kaplan of my idle fantasies. It was fun to daydream about dying in her arms while she cried over me and brushed flowers out of my hair. But now? Now my death wasn't such a way-out possibility, if I believed Teleri. Now there wasn't the safe distance of a daydream between us. Now she was real, she was here, and most frightening of all, she was drawing closer to me by the minute. Soon there might not be the thinnest veil of fantasy standing between us at all. I'd have to deal with her as she was, not as I'd ideally like to have her. The old Tim would have been scared witless by that situation.

The old Tim hadn't seen what I'd seen. He didn't know what I knew. I could have run away. Few people know that running away is a genetic trait. I got it from my father. He was real good at it.

I could have been like him.

"Tim?" T'ing was waiting for an answer.

"Oh, let the boy be!" Teleri made a disgusted sound through her nose. "If they've not the heart nor stomach to bear with what's their rightful heritage, then let them run scared, I say! There's naught to be done to help 'em."

"That," I said, "is what you think." I struck a Superman-rampant pose that would have embarrassed the hell out of Christopher Reeve. "The Gentry aren't the only ones who need someone fighting in their corner. Hey, making mortals feel uncomfortable is what got you Fair Folk shunted to the Leeside in the first place! Let's not go for a rerun. If the Dread and Puissant Champion of the Fey can't help his own people, who can? At least I'm going to try."

"Oh, Tim!" T'ing fell right into *my hero* mode. On her, it didn't look dippy. "You mean—?"

"Yes, T'ing." I took her into my arms. "We're going to make the world safe for daemonocracy."

14

Junior Achievement

"NOT *DEMONS*," I said, at my pedantic best with a fresh audience. *"Daemons."*

"There is a difference," T'ing put in.

"Demons, daemons, Dalmations, who cares?" Ms. Lenotre wrung her hands in despair. She was one of the prettiest teachers at Glenwood High, but the current situation had her frazzled down into a bundle of wisps, whimpers, and twitches. "If I don't find some way of dealing with this unspeakable fiend I am ruined. Ruined!"

"Ah, zat ees a fine way to speak of me, ees eet not? Yes? No?" My homeroom teacher's personal sprite huffed and puffed and looked ready to blow the house down; or in this case, the school. He was on the small side, but the efficient Hobson had been quick to tell me that the French spirits were the most insistent about size not being everything.

I tried playing the diplomat. "Please, please, no need for any outbursts. We're here to restore a little harmony between you and your—ah—hostess, that's all." I motioned for him to take the chair beside Ms. Lenotre's. He chose to mimic the chair instead. Of all the otherworldly critters I'd dealt with since assuming the Champion's mantle, shape-shifters made me the antsiest.

If felt bizarre to be in the teachers' lounge at Glenwood High, in the early, early hours before classes began (even before I was due for another one of those tooth-pulling sessions with Mr. Izanagi), yet there I sat, across a table from my homeroom teacher, and *I* was teaching *her*. Weird.

Ms. Lenotre shared the most common symptom of the Fey-ridden: She was jumpier than a frog on a griddle. The way her eyes kept darting toward the door, you knew she was prisoner to the thought of what would happen if any of her unpixified colleagues came in and caught her here, with us. I suppose I could have set her more at ease by telling her that she wasn't the only Glenwood faculty member who'd turned up this week with bogles under the bed, but I'd sworn confidentiality to all the other clients. Even if I didn't command her full attention, I had a job to do.

"You see, Ms. Lenotre, *daemon* just means a lesser super-natural being. The Greeks thought of them as sort of guardian angels, or sources of personal inspiration."

"Socrates had one," T'ing added helpfully.

Ms. Lenotre was not helped. "You know what they did to Socrates, Ms. Kaplan?"

I thought we could let that one go. "Now *demon*, that's just a corruption of *daemon*, only it picked up a bad rep when the Church came into serious power. You know, like in politics, first thing you do is smear the opposition. A daemon doesn't have to be an *evil* spirit."

The mock-chair made a loud whoopee-cushion sound at me.

"Yeah, well, *ta mère*," I told it.

For the first time, Ms. Lenotre smiled. "You have been doing your homework, Timothy; for a change. When I first heard the rumors about you, I didn't know what to believe. It was all too fantastic. But then, my life has suddenly taken a turn for the unbelievable. I thought it would be worth the chance, speaking to you about my . . . problem."

"*Problem?*" The chair burst its seams and became a bubbling cauldron. Noxious steam rose from a witch's brew of assorted tentacles à la king and made our eyes water. "You hear? You see? Zis wench, she ees not worzee of my favors. Eet would take a fool to stand for zis abuse. *Parfois*, I swear zat *ma mère* deed not raise any foolish *lutins*."

"Did you have this big a mouth on the Leeside, *frère* Jacques?" I asked it quietly.

One mention of the L-word and the cauldron froze in mid-bubble. It did a fast fade back to chair-shape; then the chair shrank itself into an ottoman. I didn't like using scare-tactics, but if it would make the motor-mouthed lutin any easier to deal with, I'd do it.

"I want one thing understood," I told the lutin. I didn't feel as stupid as you'd think, laying down the law to a piece of furniture. All those years of trying to convince Billy Klauser not to beat the crap out of me after school finally paid off. "I am *not* your enemy. I'm here—and so is T'ing—to help you."

The ball fringe on the ottoman rippled in scorn. "Help me, ees eet? I speet on your help! For centuries, we lutins have leeved weez mortals. Always eet ees ze same story: *We* are ze helpairs. We take care of ze animals, we do zis and zat around ze house. We only ask to be geeven some small beet of, how you say, privacee? But always, ze spies! You, *m'sieu*, you have not ze seengle drop of Franch blood een your meeserable body. Zerefore, you have not ze right to eentervene between me and zis woman—" I swear, I saw the ottoman *leer* at Ms. Lenotre. "You, *m'sieu*, are not Franch, not wanted, and a feelzee spy. I speet on—"

I opened my knapsack and laid the crystal wand on the table. A spectral pair of miniature dragons, red and orange, chased each other's tails up and down the length of the wand, vanishing in a burst of sparks. The ottoman went from green brocade upholstery to stark white gauze. Little tufts of stuffing dribbled out from beneath its blanched fringe.

"Ah . . . forgeeve me, Dread One. I was only makeeng a leetle small, how you say, zhoke?"

Ms. Lenotre's face was the same pasty color as the ottoman. "Timothy, where did you get that?"

"Probably the same place you picked up this lutin," I told her.

"What did you call it?"

"A lutin," I repeated. She wasn't the first of my clients to need more than a nodding introduction to the creatures that were suddenly sharing their roofs without splitting the rent. "Lutins are French domestic sprites. They like kids and animals, from what I've heard, but they're about as fickle as a well-lobbied senator. One minute they want to help you, the next minute they're playing tricks. And as you might have guessed, they're not too fond of what they call spies."

"But what have I done to deserve—?" A wisp of steam and a warning growl rose from the ottoman. "Why am I the lucky one?" Nice save, Ms. Lenotre.

"Because you're French."

"Timothy, I *teach* French; I was born in Newark." I caught

a whiff of teacherly condescension wafting back into her voice.
It was a good sign, an indication that Ms. Lenotre was no longer
so badly scared. She was resuming the role of authority and
things were returning to normal, which was just what we wanted.

"You were born in Newark, but your family wasn't." She
looked startled; I was on the money. "I'll admit, not everyone
with a last name like Lenotre has French roots, but the fact that
a French sprite latched onto you proves you must. Think."

She did. "Three of my grandparents came from Louisiana.
And we're supposed to have some cousins in Quebec—"

I spread my hands. "*Voilá*. You can't fool the Fey. They're
better than a tabloid journalist at rooting out your real family
background, and they only attach themselves to people who share
their origins."

Ms. Lenotre looked askance at the lutin. It had assumed the
appearance of a mischievous child. "And there's no way I can
. . . detach it?"

"Ms. Lenotre, maybe you won't want to."

That was T'ing's cue to break out the flip-charts. I segued into
the standard recitation of the advantages of having your own
personal daemon. Hey, look at what it did for Cinderella! For
starters, I emphasized the fact that most domestic sprites lived
for no other purpose than to lighten household chores. Payment?
A sip of milk, a bit of cake. Thanks? Never desired; actually,
to be avoided, on pain of alienating the sprite and losing his
goodwill and services.

Ms. Lenotre heard me out with rising interest. "You mean,
he might even change my Tartuffe's litterbox?"

"Willingly. Joyfully. Often. Ms. Lenotre, although you
weren't asked to join, you are now irrevocably one of the Gen-
trified."

"Or the esoterically enabled," T'ing said. "With perks and
privileges most unions only dream of getting for their members.
We want to help you learn to enjoy it."

She was hooked and gaffed, but not yet netted and in the boat.
"Timothy, it all sounds so perfect, it makes me wonder why I
ever thought of having this—lutin-thing—as a punishment.
There's just one more question I have to ask." I indicated that
she should fire away. She pointed to the crystal wand. "What
are you?"

That jerked me up hard. *What* was I? This, from the woman

who had given me a B-minus in French 101 just last year? You ask a human being *who* he is. You ask a monster *what*.

T'ing was in there before I could defend myself or attack Ms. Lenotre's prejudices. "He's a public relations representative, Ms. Lenotre," she said. A smooth smile lifted the corners of her mouth, a smile too much like Yang's when he recalled the good old days of rapine, pillage, and keeping overdue library books. "So am I. Mainstreaming is our business. You know you're not the only one who's been singled out by the Fey. More are turning up every day. Tim is simply doing his modest part to ease any resident-immigrant frictions. It's a new game, and he can teach you the rules. If you're happy, and your lutin is happy, then we're happy."

Ms. Lenotre continued to keep a weather eye on the lutin. "Well . . . it doesn't sound so bad when you think it over. I suppose I could adjust."

"Rule One," I said. "If he gives you any grief, send for me. *I'll* handle him." I patted the crystal wand and gave the lutin a smug look.

The lutin transformed itself on the spot into a white bunny-rabbit as big as a collie. Its whiskers trembled. Fat, Disneyesque tears trickled down its quivering nose. Big, pink, pathetic eyes stared at me, making me feel like a real candidate for the pooper-scooper. Ms. Lenotre couldn't restrain an exclamation of sympathy. She threw her arms around the bunny, nearly stroked its ears off, and implored it not to cry.

The lutin snapped back to human shape, and before Ms. Lenotre knew what was happening he got her in a hermetic liplock. Black fur sprouted all over the shape-shifter's body, relieved only by a wide, white stripe that ran from his head to the tip of his bushy tail.

"Ah, my leetle peegeon," he purred. "Zis ees more like eet. Yes? No?"

I covered my eyes. "Rule Two, Ms. Lenotre: Don't let him watch any more cartoons."

Ms. Lenotre was only the first that morning. It was a long, long day, made worse by the fact that those of my teachers who hadn't been tapped by a Leeside returnee all decided to get into a homework-assigning competition.

Ilya was alone in the apartment when I came home from school, lugging a burden of books and dragging a load of exhaustion. (I had new respect for game-show hosts. Keeping that vapid smile nailed to your face all day *hurts*.) The bannik was hunched up in the kitchen sink, glumly paging through a plumbing catalog. He brightened up at once when he saw me.

" 'Ey! You kid! Howzit going, 'ey?"

"Great," I said, deadpan. Sagging in places I'd never sagged before, I looked around the apartment. "Where is everyone?"

"Your mama, she—"

"I know she's at work. I mean *everyone*. Usually we're seven for breakfast, these days, but not even Hobson was here this morning. I had to get my own breakfast for the first time all week. Teleri's pulled a vanishing act, too. Isn't she afraid I'll croak behind her back, just to annoy her?" I was whining, I knew it, and I didn't care.

Ilya tsked. "Life is tough. You just wait little bit, I run you nice hot bath, yes?"

"No." His face fell. I amended my rejection. "Later, all right? I've had a busy day, and no chance to tackle any of my homework during study hall."

"Nice hot bath clears the mind," Ilya wheedled, clambering out of the sink. "Sharpens senses. Reduces unsightly cellulite. Also kills lice."

My brows rose. "Where did you hear about cellulite?"

The bannik shrugged. "In McDonald's, there is wisdom." Wistfully he added, "Your mama, she tells me to go home and wait for her here. Is too many hairballs in the restaurant dishwasher—either I shave or go home, she says. Shave!" He barked with bitter laughter. Well he might. The bannik was all beard and a couple of eyes. Start shaving that and he might not stop this side of visibility.

"I'll talk to her, Ilya." I must have sounded as beaten-down as I felt.

"Kid, you sad?" The faithful bannik contemplated me like a sympathetic toupee. "Hard work, being Dread and Puissant Champion of the Fey, yes?"

I flopped down on the sofa, feet up on the arm. "There are eight million *tomten, moerae, kami, ch'eng-huang*, and *kobolds* in the Naked City. I feel like I've made the personal acquaintance of every one of them today. On top of it all, it's Friday."

"So? Is T.G.I.F. Party down hardy. Bust loose. Shop until drop. Catch rockin' pneumonia, boogie-woogie blues. Take nice hot bath." Ilya was proud of himself. "Goodness, gracious, great balls of bearings."

"I gotta baby-sit the Mandels." I dumped my books on the table and hit the fridge.

I heard footsteps behind me as I grubbed through the refrigerator, searching for a snack. I thought it was Ilya, but the bannik's voice was never that sweet, or that vexed.

"A fine thing!" Teleri confronted me as I emerged from my search with a leftover chicken drumstick in my teeth. Master Runyon would hardly have known his protégée. She had abandoned the relentlessly hip dance-club clothes for a white cowled robe straight out of an Excalibur-aRt-Us movie. The hood was pulled up, completely overshadowing her face. I assumed that all that material was having some kind of dampening effect on her voice, because it was much, much softer than the norm; little more than a whisper, actually.

Less volume did nothing to mitigate the level of sarcasm in her words. "There he stands! The grand and glorious mantle of Champion resting upon his shoulders, and all he does with it is natter on, in company wi' that soot-haired slut, playing the matchmaker for mortals too chicken-livered to accept the services o' the Gentry without someone there to wet-nurse 'em alone!"

I took the drumstick out of my mouth and set it on the counter. "And how would you rather I spent my time? Before I die and you get to sing about whiter, brighter washloads, that is."

Her voice dropped to the borders of audibility as she sneered, "Perhaps ye'd spend it better if ye were more aware of where ye're needed more, and what it is that's expected of a hero."

"A *hero*?" Our so-called kitchen was narrow as some folks' minds, but Teleri's accusation set me to pacing back and forth in that miserable space. "That what you want from me? To be a hero out of one of your old Irish tales? A giant-killer? A dragon-slayer?"

She tucked her chin even deeper into the shadowed recesses of the cowl. "Better that, than what ye are."

"Yeah? Well, Flatbush is fresh out of giants and dragons, and anyway, I'd probably cut my own toes off if you handed me a sword. I'm doing what I can, okay? I'm re-teaching all those frightened people out there that you're not necessarily nuts if you can see more wonders than your neighbor. Want me to stop?

Want my folks to go back to being terrified of yours? I've got news for you: Fear breeds hate, and that's what got you banned.''

From deep within her cowl, Teleri whispered, ''Oh, there's no need to lesson me on hate, milord; none at all.''

She pulled the hood back. Her golden hair was gone, hacked off savagely at the roots. Her cheeks were scored with jagged, bloody tracks. She lifted her face to let me see the bodiless black claw that clung to her throat, half-strangling the voice out of her.

''Well, milord?'' she croaked in an awful parody of her former kittenish ways. Tears flowed as she gulped for air. ''Now might ye guess where a hero's needed more?''

15

Shadows

WE LEFT ILYA to keep house and explain my absence if Mom came home before I did. I checked my watch: Still more than a couple of hours until the Mandels were expecting me. For a moment, I thought it might be a good idea to give T'ing a call and tell her what had happened to Teleri. Ever since we'd begun the outreach program to our fellow Fey-touched mortals, it had become just natural to think of it as *our* project. T'ing worked by my side through it all. Part of me felt good about that, part was getting more than a little scared. Of what? I didn't have a name to lay to it, and *that* was the scariest part.

Better to deal with a fear I could handle. Someone, some*thing*, had hurt Teleri, and was still hurting her. If the black claw bit into her throat any deeper, could it possibly—?

Could you kill a banshee? Teleri had died once, as a mortal girl. Could her second life be as easily taken from her? I wanted to think that was impossible, but I had the icy feeling that *possible* was more likely the answer. Knowing that, I didn't want to think about it at all.

I had to. I didn't have any choice. Someone had to do something, and for want of a bigger, better, less foredoomed hero, I was tagged It.

When I dialed T'ing's number, Mrs. Kaplan told me that they were just going out the door to get T'ing to a final fitting for her bridesmaid's dress, any message? I considered asking Mrs. Kaplan to pass on a cautionary word to Yang about keeping his eyes closed in the ladies' changing room. Why bother? Yang would never peek; he'd ogle, drool, and make suggestive hand-signs, many of which needed an interpreter. Only T'ing might see him at his merry pranks, and she knew how to pull the choke-chain on her honored ancestor. One quick ''Yang, *bu*!'' and Mr. Congeniality usually stopped pursuing his vice of the moment. Either T'ing had some ineffable power, or the phrase just happened to tick him off enough to make him depart the premises in a huff. No sense adding to Mrs. Kaplan's case for my speedy admittance to Bellevue.

''Just tell her Tim called.'' I hung up and tossed the crystal wand into my gym bag. ''Let's go.'' Teleri nodded and again concealed her ruined beauty in the kindly shadows of her cowl.

She led and I followed. I asked no questions, afraid that if she paused to answer me, I would have to look at that ungodly claw that had wrung my banshee nearly silent. *Who could do something so cruel?* I asked myself. A second thought, more frightening than the first, came to torment me: *Who—what— could have the power to do so much to a creature of magic?*

We didn't fly through the cold Leeside lands or ride Donahue to our destination. The phouka was gone, along with Hobson and Master Runyon the luchorpan. Gone where? That was another question I was too cowardly to ask. If this was what had happened to Teleri, worse might have happened to them. If that were so, I couldn't stand to face it just yet.

We walked through streets I'd known all my life. In front of Bradley's News 'n' Chews I spied a couple of clones of the beefbrains who'd run afoul of Yang. One of them was hanging out solo, the other had a badass *barabao*—an elfin Venetian import, one of the Leeside's many self-styled gifts to the ladies— helping his master think up slimy things to yell at every passing skirt. A boy and his *lauru*—another hot-to-trot Italian sprite, cuter than the barabao, and a much snappier dresser—made kissy faces at Teleri as we passed the Napoli Pizzarama. A couple of *t'ien-wang*, the celestial door-guards, were engaged in a labor-management dispute with Tsao-Wang, god of the hearth, while three bewildered waiters looked on outside the Hong Kong Garden restaurant. As we went by the big picture window of the discount drug store, I saw inch-high *portunes* scurrying back and forth. Their old-man faces were awash with delight as they performed a multitude of services for their adopted host, though a pair of slackers in the ranks were having the time of their little lives going skateboarding on packs of Smith Brothers cough drops with a couple of rolls of Life Savers cobbled on for wheels.

There went the neighborhood.

I didn't slow down to see what sort of otherworldly activity Feidelstein's Kosher Delicatessen had attracted. I speeded up instead, dragging Teleri with me. Something was haunting Feidelstein's, all right. I didn't need to look. I already knew what it was—something worse than any dybbuk or daemon or dragon— and I'd escape it if I could.

I'll just go get us some cold cuts from Feidelstein's, Timmy, and when I get back we'll all go have us a picnic.

Sure you will, Dad. Sure.

So I ran away from a memory. Yes, Mr. Izanagi, I know you can't really do that. I wish to God you could.

At last we reached a street without stores, an old block where all the street-level "taxpayers" were boarded up, boards and walls alike sprayed with a tangle of obscene graffiti. A storefront church preached a faded message of love and welcome over its door, barred with a grinning iron grate. Broken glass sparkled in empty doorways. A discarded syringe crunched under my shoe. We were maybe three blocks away from the section I knew best, but in some cities three blocks takes you into a Leeside all your own. This one doesn't let its inhabitants escape that easily.

Teleri stopped. "This is the place, milord." She placed her hand over the black claw at her throat and tried to loosen its grip just a little; she failed. "Down there," she rasped, nodding her head.

We stood at the top of a short flight of concrete steps leading down to a dimly lit passageway between two old apartment buildings. You could call it a cross between an alley and a tunnel. It led from the street to the scabby rear of the buildings it undermined. One lousy yellow bulb cast sickly shadows over a row of brimming garbage cans and the closed door to the basement of the left-hand building. The stench was intense, and this was just October. I didn't want to imagine what it would smell like in the heat of August.

"How did it happen?" I clutched my gym bag tighter, feeling the sleek, faceted sides of the crystal wand through the rough cloth.

Teleri tried to tell me, but every word was painful. " 'Twas Hobson summoned us. Master Runyon and I, we were seeking out more o' those as the Fey had chosen. Just as ye'd bidden me, I was acting the mortal wench, wi' Master Runyon playing the decoy sprite, as if he had the haunting o' me." She coughed, and clutched at the claw. The metallic luster of its four vicious talons was dulled by Teleri's upwelling blood.

"No more." I slipped my arm around her waist and let her lean on me. "We'll get you free of *that* first and worry about how you got it after. Do you think they're still down there? The ones that did this to you."

My poor banshee could only nod weakly. Her slender hand rested on my chest, light and cold as an ice-rimed twig. I'm no Billy Klauser, but I could support her whole weight in the crook of my arm. Rage swelled in my belly, leaving no room for common sense. I was going to demand an accounting from whatever force, human or fey, that had hurt her so badly. Strong, steady heat emanated from the hidden wand. The warmth flared up with my anger and seared the canvas bag to ash. Bare crystal facets dug into my palm as Teleri and I descended the concrete stairs.

With every step we took, the wand gave off a stronger light. First it shone with the faint blue of shadows on fresh snow, then deepened to a sea-wave green. We passed the row of garbage cans, stood beneath the squalid yellow bulb. Splinters of yellow shivered the wand's emerald depths, dashed small starbursts of true gold from the core of the crystal.

"Here, milord." Teleri's voice had dropped so low it was a whisper's hungry ghost. The brighter my wand burned, the colder I felt her skin grow. We stood before the battered metal door, its surface of shiny black enamel chipped so that the old coat of sickly dull green paint beneath stood out like patches of mold. There was no handle, no hinges, no sign that this huge slab of steel was ever meant to be an entry or escape route except for the fact that it was different from the rough cement walls flanking it.

I touched the wand's tip to the center of the door. A circle of light a foot across rippled out from the crystal, but nothing else happened: no sparks, no blast, no hissing sound of metal puddling away incredibly into steam, nothing. I might as well have poked at the damned thing with a Boy Scout flashlight.

"For his court . . . it wants more." Feebly Teleri stretched out her palm to me. Puzzled, but not knowing what I needed to ask, I passed the crystal wand into her keeping.

Her face looked horrible in the watery light cast up from below. She folded both hands around the wand and held it tenderly against her breast like a lady holding a single lily in an old, old picture book. The tip of the wand nearly brushed the black talon set in the banshee's throat, and I thought I saw the claws shrivel back just a little from all possibility of such contact.

Then she changed the angle of the wand very slightly, the tip now resting in the small indentation at the base of her throat, and she began to sing.

It wasn't any kind of wailing that rose from the banshee's throat, no keening for the dead or the soon to die. Although her words were all in a language I didn't understand, their melody wove a spell of meaning that penetrated my mind and made all words unnecessary. Light was in her singing, and a love for life that has the strength and courage to wait until the darkness passes. Sorrow wove a second thread, and yearning spun a third. Everything that made the world a treasure—even the knowledge that it was not a treasure to keep forever—all of that was in the banshee's song.

At first I didn't notice the drop of blood seeping up around the tip of the wand. Only when the drop grew too heavy, and left a slowly sliding trail of scarlet down between Teleri's breasts, only then I blinked myself aware of what she had done.

"Teleri!" I snatched the wand from her and saw the raw, red wound cut by the crystal.

She took an unsteady step away from me, a weak smile on her lips. "Nay, milord, 'tis nought, and 'tis most freely given. So it must be. Go on. Now ye've the means of entry, if ye've the will to use it." She gestured at the bloodstained wand in my hand. "Sometimes what's cleanly's not always welcome."

I moved like a puppet, horrified by the pain Teleri had inflicted on herself, as if she wasn't already carrying more than enough suffering from the black claw's grip. The wand swayed of its own power, seeking the black door. My hand didn't guide it, it guided my hand. I felt the jar as crystal touched metal. I heard the groan as metal swung away on invisible hinges, back into a greater darkness. I felt Teleri lurch into me, holding onto my shirt, her feet barely dragging after as I carried both of us across the threshold into whatever waited beyond. The wand was a pure white beacon, a sword-shaped beam of light leading us on.

I had taken maybe four, maybe five steps forward when a loud clang behind us told me that the grim door had swung itself back into place. The wand outlined our faces with a pale radiance, Teleri's drying blood the only mark to alter its perfect light. It shed just sufficient brightness for me to see a few feet ahead of us. We walked over cement slabs, about what you'd expect to find in the basement of any apartment building. The wand's beam bobbed over several rusty, crumpled cans of Coca-Cola, some wadded-up newspapers, a torn brown paper bag that leaked eggshells, fruit peelings, old bones, and coffee grinds. I saw nothing weirder than six bundles of *National Geographic* magazines tied up with pink ribbon and stacked against a wall.

"Teleri," I whispered. "Teleri, are you sure we're in the right place? You're positive this is where—?"

Something heavy fell on my shoulder. Teleri's ruined hair brushed my cheek as her head lolled against me. She was unconscious, a dead weight in my arms. For a heart-stopping instant, I was afraid she was gone. I sat down cross-legged on the dank floor, cradling her in my lap, the wand set to one side. The palm of my hand was colder than a stone when I held it near her lips and no warmth of breath touched it.

"It's OK, man." An encouraging murmur brushed past my ear, setting every hair at the back of my neck on end. "Hey, really, you can trust me. They don't breathe anyhow. Not the way we do. Here." The wand rose up on its own, landed in my slack hand with a hearty slap. "You try holding *this* near her mouth and you'll see."

I did. A mist formed between the banshee's parted lips and the nearest facet of the crystal. Granules like specks of snow solidified in the smoke, forming a perfect miniature of Teleri the way I'd first seen her that night in the Mandel's apartment. The little image danced and laughed, twirled through the figures of a dance to music I couldn't hear. Oh, God, she looked so *happy*!

"See?" The quiet voice nearby came again. It had a disturbingly familiar sound to it. "What'd I tell you?"

"Who are you?" I shouted, forcing all my fear to sound like anger. "What do you want?"

"Hey! Take it easy, man. You mean you can't see—? Oh. Oh, yeah, right, I bet that's it. *Hey*!" This time he shouted so loud my ears rang. "Hey, you guys, howzabout a little light, huh? We saving money or what?"

A circle of clustered candles flared up from golden stands all around us. Neil Fitzsimmons, my good buddy from the Rawbone Kings, crouched at my side. He looked different. Green velvet tunics with yellow silk capes suited him. He still had his jeans and Air Jordans on, though, and that Rolex.

"Hi." He didn't sound too sure about it. When he smiled,

the big black circles under his eyes vanished for an instant. Nothing could hide the clayey color of his face.

"Jesus Christ, Neil, what the hell are you doing—?"

"Welcome." A second voice, deep as an empty well and about as inviting, echoed over my shoulder. This guy sounded sure; of everything. I turned my head.

Cloth of gold can really be tacky if you spread too much of it around. When you add a couple of iridescent scaly throws with the dragons' wings still attached, you know you're not dealing with a class act. Toss the whole mess over the body of a turquoise Thunderbird convertible, perch a few naked nymphs on the hood, and I guarantee you are no way in the presence of Mr. Goodtaste.

Of course with all those elfin swordsmen backing him up in rows five deep, I wasn't going to be the one to tell the king of fashion understatement that brown wingtips don't go with a Junior Astronaut aluminum foil jumpsuit.

"Welcome," he said again. His words came out clipped and toothy. "Dread and Puissant Champion of the Fey, our house is yours. We have been expecting you, rather. Ain't that so, gels?"

"Cor!" exclaimed one of the nymphs, and tittered.

"Lummy!" cried the other, and jounced.

"Ow!" squealed a third, and with more presence of mind than her sisters, grabbed the dangling foxtail on the Thunderbird's antenna and gave it a hearty yank.

The front grillwork dropped like a drawbridge, and Master Runyon and Donahue in human guise came tumbling out almost on top of me.

I did a quick tally and came up one short. "Where's Hobson?" I demanded.

"Here I am, sir." He stepped around the right front fender of the car and knelt. I knew right off he wasn't getting down on his knees for me.

"Here he is, my lord Palamon, just as I promised." The goblin raised his large, sad eyes to the nymph-encumbered fellow who was in the driver's seat in more ways than one.

"Oh, I say. Goody." He snapped his fingers and a fourth nymph jiggled up with what looked like one of those *piña coladas* they serve in hollowed-out pineapple shells.

A little paper parasol looks really silly when it's sticking out of the top of a severed head.

16

New Kids Under the Block

I LOOKED UP from the silvered scroll and saw Hobson standing in the doorway of my prison cell. "Out," I told him. The little goblin did not obey. I wasn't really expecting him to. For all his jabber about attaching his domestic services to my household in perpetuity, his recent actions had made it plenty clear that now and always, he served a different master.

He wouldn't go, but I could take myself away from him, in a way. I went back to studying the scroll on the slant-top desk before me. It wasn't very absorbing reading—your basic chronicle of life among the highborn elfin court, *Dallas* with dragons—but it was all I had.

The desk itself, like most of the furniture in my cell, was made of precious metals, exotic woods, and semiprecious stones. The walls around me groaned with the weight of fine tapestries and embroidered silk hangings. The "less is more" dictum did not apply. This wasn't your usual run of Sing Sing suite. Stone walls do not a prison make, etcetera, but the flip-side of that quotation says that all the interior decoration in the otherworld don't make a cell any less of a cell.

I finished reading the scroll and used the gilt-clasped velvet strap to girdle it shut again. Hobson still haunted the doorway as I replaced my reading matter in its ebony wall slot and took down the next scroll over. This one was written in violet and saffron ink on white parchment thin as butterfly wings, wound around blue jade rollers. The moment I had the beginning of the roll laid out flat on the aventurine desktop and touched the first character with my fingers, every alien squiggle on the page writhed like a pin-pierced worm until the words resolved themselves into understandable English. I'd touch-translated fifteen or so similar scrolls since my incarceration, and I still thought it was the neatest trick since Velcro. Too bad it couldn't work for me on one of Mr. Richter's Spanish tests.

"Mr. Desmond, sir." Hobson had floated from the doorway to crowd my personal space. He stood close enough for the stiffer bristles of his moustache to prickle my elbow through the fabric of my shirt. I counted to ten and jerked my arm back hard. I was aiming for his Adam's apple—unless the Fey call it Puck's persimmon—but the little groaner dodged. "Mr. Desmond, sir, I have come upon a twofold business. You will find it to your advantage if you would hear me out."

I swept the scroll from the desktop. It bounced over the agate and carnelian tiles, unspooling like a runaway roll of toilet paper. Hobson gasped in shock, and before he could draw breath to say a word, I seized him by the throat and shook him hard.

"Listen, you traitor, I'll *throw* you out before I hear another peep from you. I don't know what you're playing at. I do know you're the reason why Teleri's been hurt, why I'm locked up, why Donahue and Master Runyon—your *friend* Master Runyon—why they're all prisoners down here." Hobson's shiny shoes left the floor as I hoisted him by the collar, then slung him away. He skidded over the slick floor and plowed into the painted footboard of my griffin-shaped bed. The monster's amber eyes blinked and the gold-leaf beak creaked open in cranky wooden protest.

Hobson got to his feet in judicious installments. He kept a guarded look fixed on me, as if he expected another onslaught any moment. Upright at last, he brushed invisible dust from his sleeves. "Thank you very much, sir." His voice had all the effervescence of a puddle of thirty-weight. As fast as he could, without actually breaking into a trot, he removed himself from the room. No bolt slid home on the far side of the door, and there was no sound of heavy chains being drawn into place across the wood. There wasn't even the tiny *snick* of a padlock's hasp, but the door was securely locked for all that.

I knew just how securely. You see, my cell door opened fine for anyone, coming or going, including me. The trouble kicked in when you stepped through. For all of them—Hobson, the elfin guards who'd first marched me down here, the genial brownie-turnkey who looked after my needs—the door opened onto the hallway along which I'd come. If I peered out through the ample eye-level grillwork, I could see dressed sandstone walls hung with large paintings and adorned with a slowly rusting collection of outlandish weapons. If I slid my fingers through the handle and pressed down on the latch-tongue, the bolt drew back with a well-bred *click*. If I pulled the door open, the hinges made no sound, the airy corridor beckoned, and no guards clanked their spears together to prevent my departure.

If I took a single step over the threshold, the corridor blanked away and I stood in the dark heart of the Leeside.

It didn't take more than three or four repeated experiments before my common sense convinced my doubting brain that *yes*, this was happening and *no*, we *knew* it wasn't possible according to the laws of the physical universe. However, since Lord Palamon's express philosophy was *Sod The Physical Universe* (I'd caught a glimpse of it, worked very prettily in cross-stitch on a wet T-shirt one of his household nymphs was almost wearing), it was better to play the game by house rules, logical or not.

Every one of my experimental escapes ended by me taking a hasty giant-step backwards and having the cell and the corridor reappear around me. I never went so far as to dare more than a pace forward. I wasn't all that certain I'd be able to get back to the safety of my prison if I did. My brain and my common sense might disagree about what was and wasn't possible, but they concurred in their dislike of the Leeside.

I glared at my cell door for a while, then wound up the blue jade scroll and brought it back to the desk. I returned to my reading.

"I say, you weren't very kind to poor old Hobby, were you?" A skinny hand lousy with garish rings drummed jerkily on the exposed parchment. Under the touch of those pointy white fingertips, English words twisted themselves inside-out into a mazy written tongue where every few characters or so a spot of firefly light glowed up from the page. I didn't have far to twist my head if I wanted to come eye-to-eye with Lord Palamon.

Eye-to-eye was a hard hand to play. Eye-to-teeth was easier. His narrow lips concealed a set of horsey choppers that made me think of Chiclets, of sugar lumps, of very small refrigerator doors, and hiding something about as cold.

I tried treating him to the same freeze-out I'd used on Hobson, but Lord Palamon lacked his servant's tolerance for low-grade insults. Black talons like those that had grasped poor Teleri's throat sprang from his fingertips and shredded the parchment I read, making the table beneath scream.

"Where were you bred, boy? Never taught to answer a civil question, what?"

I pushed myself away from the desk and stood. Lord Palamon was not that much taller than I, but with legs so long and slender he seemed to overtop me by several inches. He'd put aside the Reynolds Wrap leisure suit in favor of the solid Hollywood Middle Ages look. Purple velvet sleeves drowning in ermine tails the size of badgers weighed down his arms. Beneath his robe was a floor-length tunic, cloth-of-gold spruced up with emeralds, rubies, and sapphires, and on his head a diadem that looked like it had been carved from a single diamond.

I looked down at his feet. "Nice Reeboks."

"I say! Do you like them?" Lord Palamon retracted his talons, then pointed his toes, showing off. "Bit of a steal, actually. Haw!" He beckoned, and my griffin-bed came crawling dutifully. Gathering up his cumbersome robes, he flung himself onto the downy mattress and struck a languid pose. "Read any good scrolls lately?"

"Nothing but fairy tales. I'm waiting for the movie. I figure they'll get Danny DeVito to play you."

Lord Palamon winced. "You're acting quite the silly ass, you realize," he told me. "Bearing grudges against the Fey—well! Bally waste of time, that. Your time, to be exact. Unless you've your heart set on toddling off into the fairylands and giving the whole aging business a miss, you'll never manage. Be stone dead before most of us even notice you're irked. What's the good of a snit if no one pays it any mind? And what *did* you expect of poor old Hobby, after all? Loyalty to you above me, his natural lord? Independent thought? Ethics first, feudal obligations second? Haw! Want his uncle Caliban for that line of Bolshie rubbish, you would. Not that you'd want Uncle Caliban for much, once you'd taken a good look at him. It's a strong-bellied man can face a boggart before brekkies."

"If Hobson works for you, what was he doing hanging out with Master Runyon? Or are they both your boys?"

Lord Palamon clucked like a prize Leghorn. "Dear me. Not even the whisper of an honorific, let alone my proper titles. America *is* everything Cousin Fantod said it would be, curse her for understating the case. 'Bunghole of civilization' doesn't begin to cover matters sufficiently, does it now?" A crest of green fire reared up from the elfin lord's blond widow's peak and from there ran all the way down his spine. From between newly sprouted fangs he informed me, "You will addreth me by my proper title, you gutterthnipe. That'th *Lord* Palamon, Thupreme Theigneur of the Elvenfolk and Motht Rethpected—" He yanked the fangs just before I bit through my fingers. I had three digits wedged between my teeth in an effort to keep from laughing. "—*Most Respected* Commander in Chief of the Fey. *There!* Which means I not only outrank you, and deserve at least a *sir* when being addressed, but that *you*, you miserable young whelp, are working for *me*."

I straddled my chair backwards and tilted it back like a rearing horse, though the carved ivory legs complained. "I quit. Drop dead. Sir."

I'm not stupid. I knew what I was doing.

All right, who am I kidding? I was playing a bluff the best I could, taking a chance based on some pretty shaky logic. If Teleri had the power to zap me into a toad and call up a drooly horror, how much stronger was Lord Palamon's magic if he'd had the power to harm Teleri? That was one side of the balance. On the other was the fact that the man himself had come to have speaks with me. Oh, he'd sent Hobson in first, but he could've sent in one of those armed-to-the-teeth Tinkerbell-on-steroids types to teach me manners after I gave Hobson the boot. He hadn't. He'd come himself. I rated.

How highly? I was about to find out.

His fiery spinal ridge spluttered out amid trails of sooty smoke and flurries of ash. Lord Palamon's face went the color of liverwurst. Happy elves do not resemble delicatessen. I was screwed. I wondered whether I'd get a nice funeral, or just wind up pinned to a dissecting board back at Glenwood High.

Then Lord Palamon took a deep breath, and his normal color returned. "You are a fighter after all, sir. I rejoice. Raw, perhaps. Undisciplined, assuredly, but we have always found it easier to impart manners to a man of spirit than to teach pluck to a—a—What the deuce is the word I'm after? Means an utterly wet weed?"

"Wimp, sir?" I was so happy to be breathing that I threw in the courtesy title as a sop.

"Haw! Just so. Demme, but you Yanks do have a way with words. Wimp. Excellent." He dithered on. It was mindless, but I'm afraid I share that fine American fascination for really *good* upper-crust British accents. No matter how inane the words, we love to listen to the melody, which is why there'll always be an England, and an American market for all the wot's-all-this-then costume-drama television they care to export.

Eventually Lord Palamon returned to the point, in much the same way as Odysseus got back home to Ithaca. "Here," he said, reaching into his sleeve and tossing a long, leather-wrapped package onto the desktop. "Fancy you'll be wanting this."

I undid the knotted strand of seed pearls binding the package. My crystal wand sparkled up at me. The last I'd seen of it was in the hands of one of Lord Palamon's beefier nymphs. I'd surrendered it, not willingly but prudently. There were just too many of the elf-lord's troops present, Lord Palamon was holding hostages, and I had no idea of the wand's range or full capabilities. No sooner had I turned it over than four more nymphs in the *Playboy* idea of nurses' uniforms jiggled over and took Teleri from my arms. When I tried to object, the view was cut off by a phalanx of elves who looked like they shopped exclusively at House O' Hides 'n' Spikes. (You ever wonder how many studs, rings, and assorted piercing hardware you can fit on a pair of pointed ears?)

I looked from the wand to the elf-lord. "You're giving it back to me?" He clucked again. "Sir," I added.

"Dear fella, of course we are! And we're all frightfully sorry we had to take this route with you, but we had no choice. I must insist, you're not to blame Hobby. He had his duty to do, and he did it." Lord Palamon sat up a little straighter at the word *duty*. Somewhere just outside my cell door, the strains of "Rule, Britannia" were being played very poignantly on a plastic kazoo.

"Yes, his duty, less than which no self-respecting British bogle can be expected to perform. Name the champion, all very well, but *test* the champion—Haw! Another kettle of fish entirely, that. Sticky wicket. Bit of a rum go. Hard cheese if the bounder toddles. Bad form, what? Dashed—" He was off again.

"Lord Palamon," I said, "cut to the chase."

I passed my cup. "And that business with the Leeside appearing whenever I stepped out of my cell—That was also part of the test?"

Lord Palamon nodded. "Not the real Leeside, don'tcha know. Only a view of it. Wouldn't touch the genuine article on a bet, even if I could. They shan't see old Palamon back there any time soon, you may lay to that. Excellent showing you made, Timmy, old thing. *May* I call you Timmy?''

''No.''

''You may call me Pal, if you like.''

''Uh-uh.''

''Right, then. As I was saying, absolutely top-hole spunk you showed, going into the dark lands time after time. There's courage!''

''What courage? I only took one step out the cell door,'' I protested. ''And I came right back.''

''Well, 'course you did. It was the bally Leeside! We want a hero, not a damn fool.''

Teleri poured the tea. It was the color of transmission fluid and smelled of hyacinths. ''One lump or two, milord?'' She looked like a miniature wedding cake in froth after froth of white lace. All marks of her recent ordeal were gone.

I sniffed the tea suspiciously as a cat at an unfamiliar litterbox.

''Oh, go on, then.'' Teleri's pretty hand fluttered under my nose. ''Drink up, milord. 'Tisn't poisoned, nor like to keep ye from ever returning to the upper world. I'd be keening me poor heart out fer yer approaching demise, else.''

''Haw! 'Course not.'' Lord Palamon slurped his cuppa noisily, violet eyes aglow. He had shucked the road-company Camelot threads for a crisp cricket uniform, with simple mink kneepads and a modest golden bat, diamonds imbedded only in the handle. Such restraint wasn't like him. Maybe he was trying to impress me. ''We don't want our Dread and Puissant fella muckin' about down here, where he's not likely to do anyone a bit o' good. Wanted up *there*, he is.'' Disconcertingly, the elf-lord pointed sideways when he said that.

We sat on a patch of lawn so green and velvety it might have topped a very expensive pool table. In the distance, pearly punts sailed along a sparkling river, and the sky above was a pastel parfait. You could put on five pounds just gazing at the sugar-candy clouds.

I put the tea down untasted and frowned at my banshee. ''You were never hurt at all.'' I made it sound as if Teleri had let me down.

She whammed the silver teapot down so hard, the lid flew back and a bewildered, long-tailed rodent went for an unscheduled flight through the atmosphere of Faerie. ''Whisht! Is that all ye know of it? Was it in me skin ye were, to speak with such authority o' the pain?''

"Look, I know this whole thing was a setup from the word *go*. Lord Palamon told me you couldn't tell about how brave I'd be in a crisis just by asking, so you put me to the test. It was a very real-looking test, that's all.''

"There was naught o' that in what I suffered. Real enough, all the pain, and well-remembered.'' She shot Lord Palamon a black look. "There's some as doubt me thespian talents, and claim I couldn't act me way out of a paper bag. Rather than take me word fer how well I could convince ye to follow me here below, *some* folk felt the need to make it *real*.''

My laugh crackled like an empty nutshell. "*Real*. Sure it was. Illusions are your people's biggest stock in trade.'' (I said *illusions*; I wanted to say *lies*.)

Teleri reached for a cream bun in a threatening manner. Only Lord Palamon's timely intervention prevented me from learning whether my banshee had watched enough Three Stooges movies to get the full deadly use out of pastry missiles.

"I say, Timmy old top, if it's our bally hearts on a platter you're after, I'm afraid you'll be going off disappointed. Our ways aren't your ways, that's all. Desperate times, old thing, desperate measures. Elfland expects every manikin will do his duty.'' The unseen kazoo accompaniment was back, this time playing "Jerusalem.'' I plucked up the tablecloth and found Hobson crouched beneath, puffing into the instrument. I dropped the cloth back over him. "For what lies ahead,'' the elf-lord concluded, "we cannot merely rely upon the good intentions of our mortal brethren.''

"So now we're brothers.''

Lord Palamon huffed. "Indeed. You needn't sound so sarcastic about it, sir. There's been more than one incident of interbreeding between the Fey and you wandless wallahs. Isn't your own family example enough?''

Teleri blushed and dimpled. " 'Tis not really kin to the young Desmond I be, milord Palamon. And the nixie blood that's mingled with my own—A lass can't be blamed fer her grandma's wee slip. They tell as the full moon shining on the Shannon's sweet waters has led more than a few honest girls astray. Not all of their descent are forced to smell like salmon.''

"Salmon? Haw!'' Lord Palamon slapped his thigh. "That's a good 'un, missy. Think I meant you? I'm not Supreme Seigneur of the Elvenfolk for nothing. I keep straight who's been dabblin' in whose drawers, beggin' your pardon. It's bloodlines that'll bring the war, and it's bloodlines we'll need to save us.''

"War?" I asked. I didn't feel so good.

" 'Course, war! Think we'd have gone to all this fuss just to ask you round to sip a friendly saucer? War, right enough, and likely it's begun already, up there." Lord Palamon stood and came around the table to thump me heartily on the back. "Time for a bit o' the old loin-girding, Dread and Puissant, old boy. Time to prove the promise of your blood. Time to do your pater proud."

"Pater . . ." Even without a lick of Latin, I'd heard that word before. I knew what it meant. "My—father?"

"Oh, didn't I mention?" Lord Palamon snapped his fingers and a flap tore free of the cotton-candy sky. The blast of the Leeside roared through.

In a dark wood of evil trees, I saw a man in mail and wool and leather. The naked sword in his hand was heavy. Dirt and dried blood smeared his face. A slim and fair-haired elf floated a little way before him on the path, the fey's dim luminance the only light among so many shadows.

This way, my lord. It cannot be much further.

The man stumbled and leaned against a tree. *You've been saying that forever. I've had enough. Fight your own damned battles. I want to go home.*

That was what my father said: *I want to go home.*

I leaped from my chair, but the tear in the sky was only an illusion. I grasped air, and fell sobbing back to earth.

17

Feudal Attraction

NEIL CAME INTO the empty nursery pretty quietly for a guy his size. I sat on the floor amid a scattering of strange toys, all made of priceless materials, all exquisitely contrived. One and all, the marvelous playthings had been left as if dropped in mid-game. Not a single elfin child was anywhere to be seen. When Lord Palamon told me I'd have plenty of thinking time alone in here, he wasn't kidding. If he hadn't called this room the nursery straight out, I wouldn't have had a clue. The toys might have passed for a grownup fey's prized miniature collection. (Lord Palamon himself liked to acquire beer cans.) The only wall décor was a mirror in a garnet-studded frame. What was I expecting? A mural of pudgy pink unicorns? In the back of my mind, buried under all the raw revelation of what the lord of Faerie had shown me of my dad's fate, I wondered what had become of the children of the Fey.

Neil knelt beside me just as I figured out how to make the tiny amber knight attack the opal-armored giant. I didn't quite have the hang of it. The knight's hatpin sword slashed empty air until the giant's turquoise mace bashed him flat.

"At least you know he's alive," Neil said.

"Who?" The giant was strutting around in a little circle, waving his mace, jaw flapping in silent challenge.

"Whaddaya mean, 'who'? Your old man! All these years, you think he's maybe dead or something, and you finally find out that—"

I pinched the giant's mace between thumb and forefinger. The mechanical manikin made several attempts to wrench it free. I didn't let him. I was the stronger.

"I finally find out that these creatures have been holding him captive all the years I thought he'd run out on Mom and me. Why'd they do it? I'll bet he didn't want to stay, only they forced him to. Lord Palamon called him their hero. He said how well Dad did with a sword, how quickly they could train him. Like he was a dog! They didn't ask his consent to be the Fey's pet mortal swordsman. They just took him away from us." I snapped off the tip of the turquoise club.

"Lord Palamon tells me I've got as much skill with magic as a mortal can hope to have. Hobson smelled it right away, and gave me the champion's wand. Now they say they want me to help them. They *claim* I've got a choice. What kind of choice? They've got my dad. He's still trapped in the Leeside, fighting the battles they left behind, while they lounge around out here and enjoy sunlight and breezes and flowers. They're the only ones who know that awful place well enough to help me find him again, and even if I do, God knows if I'll be able to get him out. So I'm the Dread and Puissant Champion of the Fey, and I'm supposed to risk my life for the same bunch that stole my Dad from me."

Neil gave me a sheepish smile. "Hey! At least you got a career."

I picked up the victorious giant and hurled it against the far wall. It smashed the painted glass of the mirror.

"Seven seconds bad luck," Neil said.

"You mean seven years."

"Not down here. Time and space, man, they don't mean shit to the Fey. See that corner of the room? The one with the building blocks? Straight up from there you got Milwaukee. That corner by the door, if you got the way to find the path out, it'll leave you in Pasadena. Take the right route through that wall with the mirror you just totaled and I'm pretty sure you hit Waco. Third corner buys you St. Louis; that wall with the door takes you to Motown, and the fourth corner—" He hesitated. "Well, who needs Poughkeepsie?" He stood up and strolled the perimeter of the playroom. "I always wanted to travel."

"The way you look, your first stop should be the Mayo Clinic. Jeez, Neil, what are you doing here? You another one of their prisoners?"

"Me, a prisoner?" He looked genuinely surprised by the

thought. "Naaaah. You think anyone can hold a Rawbone King if he don't want to be held?"

"How long has it been since you got a little sunlight?"

He shrugged. "Who knows?" He checked that fat Rolex of his. "Like it? 'Sa present from Andraste. She says she set this sucker to Faerie Standard Flextime for me, but you got me what that means in human time." A goofy smile took over his face. "I'm not bitching. So I miss a year or two up there, big deal! What'd I leave behind? I'd like to see my old man try knocking me around now! And if I ever do go back, I'm taking Andraste with me. He tries to lay one finger on me, she'll bite it off to the shoulder. What a woman!"

"Sweeeeet." Honey dripped off the word, webbed the whole room with unwholesome stickiness. The air beside Neil thickened and clotted gray. Pale green hands parted the folds of a hooded cloak as soft as smoke, and featureless white eyes stared at me.

I would have called her blind, if not for the eerie feeling that her pupilless, unirised eyes were watching me more intently than any owl ever studied a field mouse, and with about the same motive. She seemed unaware of Neil, though he took her into his arms at once and stroked the lustrous fall of straight bronze hair that plunged all the way to her naked feet. She shook herself free of his clasp, and her cloak fell open to show that she was bare beneath it.

Slowly she approached, with hands outstretched as if to feel her way. Her nostrils flared and her lips were parted. Did she also scent and taste the proper path to take? Abandoned toys lay strewn at random over the polished goldstone floor. She never stumbled, and her toes never even brushed a single one.

"Deeeear Neil, to speeeak of me so kindly," she said as she wove her way nearer to me. "Sweeeeet love, what a surprise. You never told me he had come." Some of her words were stretched unnaturally long, drawn thin and sickly sweet as strands of taffy. She mewed them with the insinuating appeal of a hungry kitten. "So we own the threeeee at last: Hero, bard, and mage; man of the sword, the song, the spell. Nevermore the Leeeeside's blast may seeeek to claim the Fey."

I scrambled off the floor and away from her. She swung her milky gaze after me. "Ohhhhh. Shy, is heeee? Yet brave enough to serve and stand with our lord. Such valor as you seldom seeeeee deserves reward." She opened her arms to me, and her skin glowed like the throat of a white lily. A wash of snowy blue swirled in her eyes, and I found myself following the swirl of color against stark white. She seemed to float nearer, though she hadn't taken a single step. I was the one who was drawing closer to her tantalizing embrace.

A moan of anguish rushed into my ears. "Get away from her, motherfucker! She's mine!" Pain burst across my jaw. I staggered back in time to miss Neil's other fist as he swung at me wildly. The crystal wand slipped from my belt into my fingers as smoothly and naturally as if it were a dog I'd whistled for. Teleri's blood still blackened the tip, which crawled with a glowworm's nest of orange and blue fires. Every drop of anger in me, fresh as well as old, condensed into a stream of power that flowed with terrible strength from my heart into the shining conduit of crystal. It only wanted a word, a thought, to send destruction knifing through Neil's panting body.

"Peace!" Teleri was an explosion of white and gold, erupting out of the broken mirror's garnet frame. Green eyes bright with wrath, wearing just her rage to keep her warm, my banshee stood spread-eagled between Neil and me, her powers thrumming through the air around her like an organ's deepest note.

Neil and I both stood there, looking about as stupid as we felt. "Hey, he was tryin' to take her away from me!" Neil's fists stayed up as he jerked his head in Andraste's direction. "Nobody messes with my woman."

Andraste's giggle was shrill and nerve-fraying.

"Take *her* from *you*, is it?" Teleri slapped Neil's hands down as if he were an overly aggressive kindergartener. Her small fingers next closed tightly on his chin and forced his head up. "Faith, the bloodless sight o' yer own sorry phiz in the mirror'd be wakening enough fer a sensible man. Haven't ye the brains of porridge, lad? Or will ye let the *lhiannan sidhe* drain ye dry of blood as well as poetry?"

"Teleriiiii, you haven't the right to come betweeeen what's mine and meeee." Andraste whined worse than the Mandel kids in chorus, but she didn't make any violent follow-up moves, and Teleri silenced her with a single glare.

"The curse o' piddlin' public house rhymsters and cheap parlor poetasters be all yer lot, ye blood-guzzling trollop! If ye'd kept yerself satisfied wi' the one, I might've let ye go yer ways fer a time. But no, ye needs must turn greedygut, and lure me poor young lord into yer toils, when the lad hasn't the sense that's in yer larger rocks.''

''Hey!'' was about all the grievance I got to lodge.

''—and how'd ye like it were I to tell Lord Palamon that ye came near to havin' our bard and mage both be the deaths o' each other ere we'd had fair use o' them?''

Andraste scrunched herself up smaller and smaller inside her gray cloak. ''Neeeeeil,'' she mewed, making tiny mouse-paw motions for him to save her. He lunged for her, but Teleri was there, sidestepping neatly between them and thrusting him easily back, as if he were weightless. As if the two fey were the only ones there, Teleri focused all her ire on Andraste.

''Away, away, ye bottomless craw! 'Tis yer own greed that accuses ye, and frees yer prey. He's quit o' ye, and the next peep I hear from ye'll be the warrant that brings ye before Lord Palamon's justice!''

Andraste dwindled like a guttering candle flame. Her legs and arms folded themselves beneath her cloak, and her whole body curled in on itself until there was only a pinwheel of steely mist at Teleri's feet. The banshee gave a satisfied snort, and the mist too blew away.

''There,'' Teleri said. ''That's done.''

I grabbed her by one arm, Neil by the other. Both of us shouted ''What *was* that?'' in such perfect unison that you'd think we were working up an act.

My banshee looked demure, if that's a possibility when you're buck naked. ''And didn't I tell ye? Ah, Neil, me love, 'tis truly the luck o' the Irish that blesses ye. It's not every man escapes the *lhiannan sidhe* this side o' the grave. Horrid clever, she is, and ravenous as fire. She'll take a fancy to a likely lad—though always one as has a touch o' the poet—and make him hers. But woe to the boy whom the fairy mistress claims! Her love will drain him o' strength, and her passion will bleed him o' poetry, and her hunger will empty him o' heartsblood until it's any man's guess as to which o' her feedings kills him at last.''

Neil listened to all this with the look of a man who has just come out of a round-the-clock marathon of playing Super Mario Brothers. I was pretty poleaxed myself.

''Poets?'' I blurted. ''She only feeds on poets? Then what the hell was she doing chowing down on *him*?''

Teleri patted my cheek. ''Broad-minded as a royal magistrate, aren't ye? And did ye ever imagine that poetry might fold her wings in any nest she pleases?''

I tried to recall any clues from the past that might hint at Neil's lyric gifts. Nothing. Even his attempts at obscene boys' room graffiti were illiterate. If poetry had set up housekeeping in Neil's soul, I hoped the Muse had lodged a complaint with HUD.

Still, the *lhiannan sidhe* must know her customers.

"Say something poetic," I instructed Neil.

"OK." He bit his lip in concentration, then declaimed: "There once was a man from Racine—"

Teleri beamed all through that one, then asked for and got as an encore the one about the man from Nantucket. Neil forgot his lost love-leech under my banshee's one-fey assault of appreciation and applause. I learned more than I really needed to know about the bishop of Balham, the barmaid at Yale, and the unvirtuous young lady from Smith before I got a word in edgewise.

"You call *that* poetry? You call *him* a bard? Those are nothing but a bunch of crummy limericks!"

"A fine old town, Limerick," Teleri said coldly. "And one as I've been proud to name me home. Or is it slipped yer mind, it's done?"

Oops. Teleri of Limerick. Of course. Silly of me. I tried to work up a graceful apology before Neil could segue into anything about a young man named Tucker.

Then we heard the crying.

I thought it was maybe Andraste, still hanging around invisibly where she wasn't wanted. The whimpering was high enough, and calculatedly pathetic. Neil's already drained face lost more color at the sound, leaving him looking like an AWOL client of the city morgue.

"Where's that coming from?" he gasped. "Where is she?"

"Hush!" Teleri placed her fingers over his lips. " 'Tis not the *lhiannan sidhe*." She cocked her head, harking to the sound of weeping. If anyone's an expert on sorrow, it's a banshee. Suddenly resolute, she snapped to attention. Latching onto my hand, she marched me across the room to the shattered mirror.

"There." She pointed at one specific garnet in the frame. "That's where this one's being kept. Faith, and a merry dance he must've led the child-tenders, to merit so great a penitence."

I peered closely at the gem she indicated. It was a big, faceted garnet about the size of a blueberry muffin. Teleri was right:

The crying came from this stone. I squinted out a closer look and thought I spied a darker shape moving behind the facets. I had questions to ask, but Teleri had only orders to give.

"Go on, then!" She dealt me a healthy shove of encouragement. "Free the poor babe! Or is it that ye've a fondness fer hearing infants weep with heartbreak?"

"How do I—? Oh." I raised the wand, looked at it, at the mirror frame, at Teleri. "Is this going to need some blood to work?"

"Just . . . do . . . it."

"I'll try." I took a deep breath for no sensible reason other than it seemed you had to do *something* as a warm-up to sorcery. I made a big deal out of aiming the tip of the wand dead on the center of the facet facing me. "All right, here we go, on the count of five. One . . . two . . . three—"

"*Do* it, ye great turnip!" Teleri whopped me between the shoulder blades with enough force to dislodge last week's dinner. I squawked and jabbed the stone. There was a soft *chink* as crystal struck garnet, then a most satisfyingly loud and impressive explosion, complete with crimson smoke and gold fireworks.

When the smoke cleared, Blake Mandel sat cross-legged on the nursery floor, wiping his nose on his sleeve. I hunkered down to comfort him and he sandbagged me with a stuffed chimera.

"I wanna go *home*, butthead!" he shrieked.

I rubbed the side of my head and looked up at Teleri. "Toad?" I suggested, hefting the wand. "Lizard? Vice-President?"

"Cute kid," said Neil. "For a changeling."

18

Mister Ogre's Neighborhood

I SAT AT my place at the elfin council table and tried to concentrate on the matter at hand. I'll admit that next to Blake Mandel's recent captivity, and all that its abrupt termination had revealed to us, my problems seemed kind of small. Still I couldn't help wondering how things were going back in the real world with Mom and T'ing and my probably-shot-to-blazes-by-now academic career. It would've been nice if I could've called home and told them everything was all right, more or less. But did AT&T run lines this far out from reality and, if so, would it still count as a local call? I sighed and said a silent prayer that Lord Palamon would get on with business, so that maybe I could get home sometime this century.

You know what *fat chance* means?

"I cannot be expected to conduct a council of war under these circumstances." Lord Palamon slapped his jodhpurs sharply with an ivory-handled riding crop and stalked back and forth the length of the conference table. "Changelings present at what is of necessity the very acme, the utter tiptop of complete and absolute strategic secrecy. Why, the idea!" He waggled the crop at Blake Mandel, who had hauled himself onto the tabletop uninvited and was spitting on a pile of official-looking documents to see if he could get the ink to run.

"Here, now! I say! Cease! Desist, you little stoat! Egad, I think foul scorn that any mortal brat dare invade the paperwork of my realm. Off with you, you miscreant reptile!" The Commander in Chief of the Fey let off little gusts of steam, like a maniacal plum pudding, and popped his monocle. It clattered onto the teakwood board, where Blake pounced upon it and promptly stuck it up his nose. When it wouldn't fit all the way, he threw it back at Lord Palamon.

"Get it out of here." The elfin lord didn't mean the monocle. He spoke in that terribly *controlled* sort of voice, a tone that clearly articulates: *Please do not force me to kill you quite as messily and painfully as I would prefer, because I haven't the time right now to make a proper job of it and I'd really rather change clothes first.* "Remove it from my sight. Return it to the nursery immediately and secure it posthaste."

"No one touches the kid." I laid my wand on the table and rose from my place. "The only place Blake's going is home." I wasn't loud, but I too knew how to make my voice communicate more than the words I uttered. Right then I was telling Lord Palamon that it is very bad luck for a ruling sovereign to alienate any potential allies on the eve of war.

"Home?" Lord Palamon's lips wobbled. "Well, dash it, of course the little bugger can go home. Right away. Instanter. Chop-chop. Half a tick. Before you can say—"

"Jack Robinson." I thought I'd save him the trouble. "He's still here."

"Yessss." Lord Palamon nibbled the leather loop at the tip of his crop thoughtfully. "So he is."

I wished the table were not so wide, so that I might reach across it and give the elfin lord a solid thwack upside the head with my wand. Maybe that would jumpstart him. I glanced to either side of me, where Neil and Teleri stood, playing the roles of my retainers. They looked pretty fed up with Lord Palamon's bluff and jolly brand of incompetence, too. A little farther to my right, Master Runyon sat astride Donahue, the better to be able to see what was going on aboveboard. Lord Palamon had ordered only one chair for our side of the table, and that was mine.

There were plenty of other chairs, all on his side. These resembled a fleet of Santa Claus's surplus department-store thrones, every one occupied by an aristocratic fey. They were of both sexes, of varying sizes and degrees of beauty, but all were sumptuously dressed. Like their lord, they had access to untold stores of fine fabrics, furs, and jewels. Again like Lord Palamon—or else in diplomatic homage to him—collectively they had about as much taste as a bowl of diluted water. One sight of their beaded, brocaded, gold-laced and spangle-dripping outfits would have given Mr. ''Ten Best-Dressed List'' Blackwell a seizure of gout.

Lord Palamon's siege was vacant. He preferred to pace. Atop the carved and jewel-encrusted backrest, between the paper parasol and the stick-on Garfield doll, Hobson crouched like a constipated owl. He kept looking at me, misery in his eyes. I continued to ignore him.

''It's not as simple as all that,'' Lord Palamon was saying. ''Changelings, don'tcha know. Ceremony to be undertaken first. Parental consent and cooperation to be obtained.''

I regarded Blake, who was trying to write dirty words on the state documents with earwax. I wondered whether Yang would take on an apprentice if we ever got Blake back home. ''You mean we have to get his parents to agree to the tradeback?'' I forced myself to smile confidently.

''Oh, absolutely, Timmy, old love. Can't do without it. Parents have to participate, *quid pro quo*. Brewery of eggshells gambit, what? Have your mortal fellas stir up a few of the old cacklefruit empties in a walloping great pan of water, put it on the cooker where the changeling can see, wait for the sprite to ask what's all this then and tell 'im that you're brewing eggshells. Haw! Sends 'em clear crackers, it does. Mad as a mandrake. 'Two hundred years old I be,' they cry, 'and I never did see the like!' Well! Coming right out and owning up to their proper age like that jolly well puts the kibosh on the whole arrangement. Can't have a two-hundred-year-old fey watching Sesame Street all the bally day. Not the done thing. All off. Whoops, home the changelings come to me and it's back into his rightful basket for the mortal pup we swopped.''

Lord Palamon scratched his head with the riding crop, setting his leather aviator-helmet askew. ''You'd think after all these years of stewing shells, the changelings would catch wise by now. Some never learn, I fancy. Tsk.'' His teeth blazed forth in a dazzling display. ''Still, regs is regs. No eggshells, no scarpering off for him.'' He gestured at Blake with the crop. Blake nipped the little leather loop clean off and spat it out at Lord Palamon's feet.

''I wanna go *home*!'' He threw himself backwards on the table and had a fist-flinging, heel-drumming, earsplitting, state-of-the-art tantrum.

''Of course,'' said Lord Palamon, while his peers gazed on in stricken fascination, ''I have always stood foursquare on the side of reform over hollow tradition. The boy wants to go home, home the boy goes, and the sooner the better." He tried to capture Blake's attention. "Yoo-hoo. Laddie-boy. You're quite free to go. Don't let me detain you. Consider yourself at liberty. Ahem. Am I making myself heard? I say, young-feller-me-lad, king's X, bags I yield, truce! *You can bloody well sod off for home!*"

Blake's tantrum stopped. He sat up and gave Lord Palamon an angelic smile. "Gosh, thanks, dickhead."

"Harrrumph. You're entirely welcome, you animate turd." The amenities seen to, Lord Palamon looked to his counselors. "We'll just have to find another safe-house topside for—Lord Hogbane, refresh my memory, there's a duck; who've we got occupying this little pimple's place on the surface?"

A crabbed and wizened older elf took out a shining folio and commenced turning pages. He looked as if he belonged at the North Pole, checking who'd been naughty or nice. "Ah, yes, m'lud. Here we are. That would be young Throckmorton, Hazelberry's nipper."

"Oh, dear." Lord Palamon looked troubled. "He won't be an easy one to lodge elsewhere. Foul temper, our Throcky's got."

I was astounded. I remembered the fake Blake Mandel, a child capable of giving the Care Bears diabetes. If he was an example of foul temper among the children of Faerie, I hoped I never met any of their sweet young things. I could feel my teeth rotting out of my gums at the thought.

"Jesus Christ, looka the size of that book," Neil said. He leaned across the table, craning his neck like a brontosaurus as he tried to steal an upside-down peek inside. Lord Hogbane censured him with a single grimace and slammed the volume shut in a spray of glitter.

Now I was interested. "How many changelings have you placed on the surface, anyhow?"

Lord Palamon rolled his eyes innocently at the ceiling, where a row of drowsing brownies hung headfirst from the rafters like so many fuzzy hams. (The parasol attached to the elf-lord's chair was not merely tacky but served a useful purpose during epidemics of Grimm's Revenge.)

"Ohhh, couldn't say, actually. Not with anything like precision." He pooched out his cheek with his tongue. "Our sphere of influence is still so limited. We've barely inched away from the initial leakage site. Much as we'd like to put some serious distance between ourselves and it, that is not a present possibility. Regs, don'tcha know. Arcane gravitational response field and all that rubbish. Not as if we had so many tots to farm out to begin with. Too little time since the first exodus from the cold lands to work up a really thumping population of—''

"One hundred forty-eight," said Lord Hogbane from behind the ledger. "Sixty-one percent in Brooklyn, twenty-three in Queens, eleven in Manhattan, and the remaining nine percent in''—he squinted at the page—''Massapequa. Wherever that is.''

Neil nudged me. "That don't add up."

"Never mind," I murmured back. "I don't think sixty-one percent of one hundred forty-eight is a whole number anyway."

"You mean they maybe switched *fractions* of kids?"

"I just mean elves piss on real numbers." Aloud I said, "One hundred forty-eight changelings, huh?" I whistled. "So that's why your nursery's bare. Where are you keeping the mortal kids you swapped them for?"

"Dear me, no need to put that edge in your voice, sir. The tykes are quite safe and happy, I assure you."

"They are *not*!" Blake shrilled. "That jerkface has all of us locked up in a whole buncha cruddy rocks all over this stoopid place!"

"A temporary measure," Lord Palamon said between his teeth. "Purely a precaution, for the dear lambs' own sakes."

I tried to look knowledgeable and compassionate, like a TV doctor. "Driving you nuts, were they?"

"Bonkers," Lord Palamon confessed. "Stark raving. *This* one alone''—he jabbed a finger at Blake, but yanked it back just in time—''could teach blue ruin to a boggart." He sighed. "All we wanted was a nice, safe place for our children to wait out the war, tucked up snug among you mortals."

"I hate to break this to you," I told him, "but life with my people isn't all that safe for kids, even when they're two hundred years old. Do these changelings of yours have any serious powers?"

Lord Palamon chuckled. "Rather not. Ever so amusing to watch the precious moppets stumble through their first enchantments. Most of them have the hang of your basic come-and-go spells—else how would they ever manage to get home again if their hosts drum up the old eggshell bit, eh?—but anything beyond that . . . tchah! I don't imagine the wee mites would be

half so charming if they weren't that helpless. It don't last forever, more's the pity. Three hundred years blink by and—
whoosh!—adolescent swine, every last one of 'em."

"Helpless is not a safe thing to be."

"Oh, bosh! All children are. That's what adults are for, to
look out for the little snivelers, help them along, protect them,
don'tcha know."

He hadn't been back in the outer world all that long. Maybe
he didn't know.

"Not all adults," I said, and I told him about the stories in
the paper. A child from our neighborhood gone missing who
didn't come back, not as a changeling, not as itself. Another
gone, and the hands of the police as empty as the arms of its
parents. A clue discovered that only led to despair, not to any
culprit. A mother pushing her shopping cart through the super-
market and bursting into bitter tears when she forgot and turned
into the baby-food aisle. I saw her and thought she was crazy. I
went home and told my mother about the funny thing I'd seen.
She showed me a day-old newspaper, with the same woman's
grief-stricken face in a grainy photograph. *Fourth Victim Vanishes.*

Lord Palamon's mouth was a straight line. "Abominable. Incredible. Sirrah, I do not presume to guess at your motives for
telling me so great a falsehood, but I advise you to reconsider
any repetition of the same. Adults who would prey on the helpless young? The infants of their own breed?" He made a loud
noise of disgust. "And you say *we* spin fairy tales!"

"It's the truth." It wasn't a truth for any human being to be
proud of.

His Lordship's eyes grew keen. "Perhaps. Or perhaps it is
only a ploy of yours to persuade us to remove our children from
your midst. If so, it will not wash. We have them safe now, far
from here, where our foes will never think of looking for them."

"Real nice. And what will your foes do when they come hunting your kids and only find the mortals you grabbed in exchange?"

"Oh, not a hair's worth of harm. You must believe me."

"Why should I? How should I know what sort of monsters
your enemies are?"

"But they're *not* monsters, old thing. Gad, the thought!" Lord
Palamon shuddered. "Monsters, ugh. Left all that well behind
us when we wriggled free of the Leeside, we did. Portal's too

demmed small to pass even the middling horrors. The only enemies we've got to face are fey, like ourselves.''

I was horrified. "That's what you want my help for? To fight your civil war?''

"Nothing civil about it, ducks. *Your* war, too, or will be. Too many years locked up in the Leeside, and a Supreme Sovereign's subjects think all rules are off once they break free. Nasty, democratic atmosphere gets into everything, pops tradition into a cocked hat. No sense of *duty* anymore. No respect for the greater glory of a world-spanning Elfland. No selfless devotion to the noble schemes of Empire that must unite all Faerie under the strict though enlightened guidance of a sole leader whose dearest wish is merely to bring the benefits of firm governance to the benighted—''

"Bolt up, you imperial windbag,'' said Lord Hogbane. Cries of *hear, hear*! and a lone, pitiable *shame*! came from the assembled elves. While Lord Palamon stood gulping air like a stranded halibut, the elder states-elf proceeded: "When we first came to this country, it was in the suite of a single people. Since then, so many others have come, from so many different lands, all bringing their household spirits with them. The same ban on magic that exiled us to the Leeside also thrust away the foreign sprites. We banded together in the cold lands, for mutual protection, and acknowledged Lord Palamon as our leader.''

" 'Course they did.'' The elf-lord preened. "Supernatural superiority will out every time.''

"It was the only way to make him shut up,'' Lord Hogbane confided, loud enough for Lord Palamon to hear. "And it kept him out of the way. Every time there were important decisions to be made, we sent him off to open a phouka-traders' fair or judge a nectar-brewing competition or something.''

Lord Palamon stalked away to kick the wall for a while.

"All that changed when the portal was discovered. By ones and twos we squeezed our way through into the outer world again. Once on this side of the barricade, and the Guardians' watchful eye avoided, we thought to return to the old ways. It could not be so. Too much had changed. Too many differing peoples had come to live in this land.''

Neil got hostile. "You got something against the American way?''

Lord Hogbane observed him narrowly. "You are, I believe, what is called a Rawbone King, are you not?''

"Yeah. So?"

"And you are perhaps familiar with another group of similarly organized youths who call themselves the Hellbloods?"

Neil's jaw tensed. "Fucking bastards. They tried to take over some of our turf last May, we gave them plenty to take home and remember."

"Turf. Territory. Only room for one master, or group of same, on each separate enclosure thereof. Am I correct?"

"Huh?"

"You don't share turf," I translated.

"Oh. I getcha. You bet your ass we don't."

Lord Hogbane had a cold, small smile. "Neither do we."

19

The Mutts of War

IN THE PASSAGEWAY between worlds Teleri and I stood face to face. A little farther along the upward path, Neil held Blake Mandel by the hand, both of them waiting patiently. That is, Blake waited patiently only after Neil appealed to his better nature. Neil has a way with kids, much the same way a Marine topkick has with new recruits, only he doesn't need to yell up their noses to get his point across. He just speaks softly and points out how much larger his body parts are when compared to the kid's. Then he flexes things. Trust me, the still, small voice of conscience has nothing on the swift, sudden wedgie of retribution as promised by Neil Fitzsimmons.

I wasn't worrying about the effects that the Rawbone King Mary Poppins was having on Blake's tender psyche. What Teleri had just told me took all my attention.

"You're not coming back with me?" I couldn't believe it. "Why not?"

Her lips curved up, but her eyes stayed sad. "Fine talk fer one who couldn't wait to be shut o' me constant attendance. Changed yer mind, have ye?"

"Maybe." I took her hand, making believe it was an accidental gesture. She didn't object. "Maybe I just got used to having you around all the time, telling me I'm about to buy the farm."

"Is that the way of it, then?" She had acquired a red-and-black silk kimono in Lord Palamon's court, with the leering face of a dragon picked out in real emeralds on the back. From out of the dragon's mouth came a crewel-work word-balloon containing the words DON'T WORRY, BE HAPPY in that cheesy lettering style that tries to make English words look like Chinese characters. The dragon was making the Hawaiian "Hang loose" sign with its claws. It didn't matter. Teleri could wear Lord Palamon's favorite Groucho nose and glasses; she'd still be beautiful.

My hand tightened over hers. I was through pretending. "Why can't you come? Even if you were one of Lord Palamon's subjects, you heard that he's nothing but a figurehead. You don't even owe him lip-service loyalty. You came over here directly from Ireland; you never shared the Leeside exile with the rest of them. You're free! You can do whatever you want!"

"So I can." She lowered her eyes and waited for me to understand.

I refused. "There is a war waiting for us up there. I believe it, and I've got no way to tell how bad it'll be by the time we get back topside. Neil and I are the only two free to intervene; we can't take the time to bring my dad through from the Leeside now, even if we knew how. Suppose we need a swordsman?"

"I'm no swordsman, Tim," she said softly.

"Suppose we fail because we didn't have enough help?"

"A man o' fine words and a man o' the wand will be match enough fer what's awaiting ye. Ye've little need o' me."

"Words! What's Neil going to do? Recite dirty limericks until the enemy cracks up? And this wand—I don't really know how to use it. I needed you to make it work for me at the gateway to Lord Palamon's realm. I'm no magician, but you—you're magic." My voice caught. "I need you."

Teleri smiled wanly. "Once I was as mortal as ye be. When the time came, I took to the enchantments well enough. Ye'll do the same. Magic's not out of reach as most folks this side the water'd have ye think. Magic's in yer blood, if ye're yer father's son. And 'tisn't such a wild war as Lord Palamon'd preach it, the great blowhard. He mere wants an excuse to strut in that rank awful new uniform o' his. I've seen it. 'Tis enough to put Jenny Greenteeth off her feed." She patted my hand. "Ye'll be fine."

Why wouldn't she *see*? "But suppose for once, Lord Palamon's right? Suppose this *is* a war, Teleri! Suppose—I took a big gulp of the cool, damp tunnel air. "Suppose I die."

Still avoiding my eyes, she said, "Then I will mourn, as is the banshee's duty."

I dropped her hand and lifted both of mine, as if I wanted to offer up all my incredulity. "Days, *weeks* of dogging me everywhere, just so you'll be on the spot with your dirge when I die, and *now* you want a vacation? What if you miss your big chance? What if I'm dead and gone before you even tune up your pipes? You're supposed to *warn* me of my death, not show up ten minutes too late and say, 'Oops. Better luck next time.' Banshees don't get to do encores!"

That made her look up. Her face was wet. "Oh, me dear, me dearest lord, can ye not hear the foolish words yer own mouth utters? Speaking as if ye see naught but death ahead, and ye longing fer the dark sight o' it."

"Well, why not?" I tried treating it like a joke, for her sake. "Ever since we met, my death's been your favorite topic of conversation. Let's see, how does that go again? 'Woe and wurra-wurra to the Desmond! Sorrow and general bogusness attend the house of Des—' "

"Will ye hush?" She clapped her hand to my mouth. "Oh, wicked the luck ye'll bring upon yer head with such gabble." She took her hand away, but the ghost of its gentle touch haunted my lips. "As bad as the luck I came nigh bringing ye with me thoughtlessness. A man who dreams he's foredoomed dances too near the edge o' the grave. In war, that's a caper ye seldom may cut twice. Magic awaits ye above, milord, and I've no way to know if it will be the killing kind. I'd not have ye dare more than ye'd do otherwise, if ye'd had better counsel. All I know is that ye must not have sight o' me anymore if ye're to live and prosper."

"Teleri, that doesn't make sense!" Her sorrow and her determination to leave me had twisted me up inside. "What's the big deal if you're with me or not?"

"Merely this, tradition's teaching that I forgot, to me shame: The banshee wails fer those of her clan as are bound to die, but *only appears when the death is near*! Ah, Tim, and can't ye see it? Sight o' me should've come within a breath o' yer death! And did it?"

"Uh—"

"Weeks have passed since first I bewailed ye, and still ye live."

"Look, I'm sorry if I—"

"Ye think ye're to die when ye're naught o' the sort! Tim, forgive me if ye can, but know it's truth I'm telling: *I made a damned mistake!*"

I went wide-eyed and pulled as far back from her as the tunnel would let me. "Heck of a glitch, lady," was all I could get out of my mouth.

The tears were really pouring from her eyes, though never a sob or a sniffle. Teleri might have screwed up once with indiscriminate wailing, but damned if she was about to make the same mistake twice. "When I was sent from Erin, a lightheart, foolish thing I was. Naught in me head but moss and merriment, and a heart overfull with the excitement of sailing over to the New World." More bright drops spilled down her cheeks. "Ye're not the first Desmond this wicked world has known."

I wasn't. I recalled Great-grandma Katherine's book of pictures. There had been so many Desmond boys! "You mean, you were sent over to mourn the death of a different Desmond?" She nodded. "Except you got distracted by other things, and by the time you got around to taking care of business, I was the only male Desmond you could find?"

She hung her head. "Time! What did a heedless creature such as meself know or care for mortal time?" She wiped her lashes with the drooping sleeves of her kimono. "Ye do already know how the time slipped from me."

"That girl you had the nice long chat with." I nodded. "Bridey Murphy. Right."

"Dust," Teleri sighed. "Safe enough she was, while in the compass o' the rath's magic still clinging to me, but once she stepped beyond—Like them as enter into the fairy halls and dream they pass but a night's feasting, only to come back to a surface world a century the older. Poor Bridey. I'm sure that's what befell her."

"Wait." I grabbed both her hands this time and squeezed hard, as if the strength of my grip could influence the shape of what she was telling me. "Time among the Fey is different, right?"

"That it is."

"So you mean, when we go back up there it might be—later than we think?" I pointed up the passageway, where Neil was telling Blake about how life is no fun if you can't sit down anymore.

She stopped crying. A thoughtful look came over her. "Now, there's a question. So much is different on this side o' the water, yet every fey tradition claims . . . Hmm. Lugh love me, I'm a liar if I say I know."

"Oh, great." I slumped against the tunnel wall. "Wonderful. So for all I know, the minute we take one step back into the real world, Neil and I crumble into itty-bitty piles of vacuum-cleaner stuffing and Blake toddles off to collect Social Security."

"Well, milord," Teleri said with an optimistic little smile, "if that's so, at least ye'll have me there to keen the dirge all proper fer ye."

"Gosh, that's a load off my mind." I trudged up the passageway, Teleri chirping merrily behind me. The thought of my possible future as a Dracula-hit-by-dawn impressionist kind of distracted me from the fact that my banshee made no more mention of staying back in Lord Palamon's domain.

Part of me was glad. I knew I didn't want to lose her. I didn't realize how important she was to me until I saw her with that black claw at her throat. What did it matter if that had been one of Lord Palamon's ploys? It woke me up. Like I said, I needed her. I wanted her near, and not only when I was about to die.

Why? Hard to say. Hey, give me a break, I still guess half the time on multiple-choice tests. All I had were a bunch of raw feelings, not the labels to put on them. I had one idea, but— Naaah. Couldn't be. In love with a lady of the Fey? Me? Uh-uh. It would never work out. We were from two different worlds; literally. She was over three centuries old, while I didn't even have my learner's permit yet. What's more, I was pretty sure she didn't count as a Catholic anymore.

And then there was T'ing. Wasn't I the kid who used to clog up his free brain-space with fantasies of the lovely and aloof Ms. Kaplan? Yeah, dreams about her and me and springtime and flowers and—

That was before Teleri. That was before Yang. That was before the two of us teamed up to play diplomacy on behalf of the returning Fey. You don't have fantasies about your business partner. You don't moon over someone who's gone from *cute* to *capable*. You don't waste time dreaming about a girl who's become about as mysterious and elusive as the inside of your locker. How can you get all slush-skulled romantic over someone you *know*?

Damn T'ing anyway; she'd gone human on me. She couldn't be content just staying a distant vision of unearthly loveliness and inexplicable attraction. She had to turn into a person. But you've still got to dream, and that was where Teleri came in. She was the one I loved.

Glad I got that straight.

Only . . . if a century had passed above, I wondered whether T'ing had ever missed me.

"Wait here," I told Neil and Blake.

"I wanna go *ho*—!" A cautionary throat-slitting motion from Neil, and Blake silenced himself in mid-yawp. "Well, I do," the child sulked.

Home. The next step I took would tell whether any of us could hope to go home again. The portal to the surface world revealed precious little to tell where we'd come out. Brooklyn, right, and Flatbush, definitely—that much had been guaranteed by Lord Hogbane when he set us on the upward path. We couldn't just backtrack and go out by the same gateway that Teleri and I had entered. The paths to and from Lord Palamon's realm are one-way only. The best the Fey could do was listen to the destination we ideally wanted, and aim us at the nearest thing to our desires.

Through the muzzy golden outline of the doorway I saw a glass showcase full of layer cakes and assorted cookies. The gorgeous smells wafting in confirmed that we were about to exit into a bakery. I could see a mirror behind the counter, but nothing else on the wall. A calendar would have helped. Bakeries don't tend to give away any hints as to their age. Okay, so maybe the bakeshop of today has "Low Cholesterol" markers jabbed into everything, and by the year 3050 they'll have signs saying "Today's Special, Radioactive Crullers!" but heavy calories are basically transcultural and timeless. Mars needs strudel. I'd have to take the chance.

"Milord, I could steal through and learn how much time's flown," Teleri offered, clinging to my back.

"No." I wet my lips and rolled the crystal wand between my palms nervously. "I think it'll be all right. Lord Palamon's counselors wanted our help with this war. It wouldn't be smart for them to make us late for it."

"If it is a war," Teleri said.

I nodded and stepped through. All kinds of nothing happened. I mean, I didn't crumble to ashes. I checked out the shop; it looked empty, even though daylight streamed in through the big front window. I read the backwards lettering and learned I'd come out inside the GOLDEN ROSE BAKESHOP, FRED KLAUSER, PROP. Lord Hogbane had come through for us better than I'd hoped. The Golden Rose was right in my neighborhood. Why was it so quiet? Maybe it was Sunday. All the better; Neil could jimmy the lock, or I could zap it with my wand, and we'd all get out nice and quiet.

I turned to beckon the others through.

Then Billy Klauser's mother stood up from where she'd been cowering behind the showcase, and screamed, "My God, Tim, where did you come from? Never mind. Hide! Duck! Run for your life!"

"Huh?" I said, with my usual intelligence.

A seven-layer chocolate cake struck me full in the face. *Phouka lover!* sneered a disembodied voice. *Bannik's boy!* another taunted. *Yah! Your mother does it for poltersprites!*

A second missile walloped me from the right, and a third from portside. Something sticky trickled down my neck. I touched it, and my hand came away dripping red.

I tasted it. Cherry pie.

No doubt about it: This was war.

20

Tough Cookies

"FOOD FIGHT! FOOD fight!" Blake crowed with glee and dived into the showcase for more ammunition. The kid was a dead shot with a Charlotte Russe, a veritable ninja of the black-and-white cookie discs of death. His first free throw took out the kobold who'd splatted me with the cherry pie; his second left a grogan spitting banana cream.

Neil and Teleri and I lay low, the three of us shoulder-to-shoulder in protective formation around Mrs. Klauser. This was harder to do than it sounds, since all of us were cowering behind the bakeshop counter, out of harm's way.

"Jesus!" Neil rooted a glob of blueberry filling out of his ear. "How come you didn't see alla this shit flyin' around before you told us to come on through, Tim?"

"Young man, your language . . ." Mrs. Klauser might be besieged, but she wasn't about to be morally compromised. Only the sheer size of her baby boy Billy kept the locker-room gang from snickering every time he exclaimed, "Gosh all hemlock, I just broke my fudging finger in gym!"

It was pretty plain where Billy got his heft. You could tell how many years Mrs. Klauser had been in the bakery business by running a tape measure around her upper arm and counting the inches. Where other women have hands, she had muscular Ping-Pong paddles. When she didn't like your language, you cleaned up your act before she cleaned your clock.

"Uh, gee, Mrs. Klauser, I'm sorry." Neil looked contrite. You don't get to be a living Rawbone King without knowing when to retreat. "I just wanted to know how long this fu—funny situation has been going on."

"It was a standoff until you showed up," Mrs. Klauser told us. "They came in just as Walter and I were opening up the store."

"Walter?" Last I heard, Billy's dad was named Fred.

"I thought they were friends of his, until they started talking." She shuddered, and on a woman her size, it was a seismic event. "Such threats! Such vicious names! Such *language*! I was frightened; I hid. Walter stood up to them. He told them to clear out, that this was his place, that they had no right to me or Fred. 'That's what you think, babka-breath,' one of them said. He—he had a Bavarian cream pie in his hands. He looked like it wasn't the first time he'd used one. Walter grabbed a pecan coffeecake from the counter. Like I said, a standoff, but when you came in so abruptly like that—" Her brows knit. "Where *did* you come from, Tim?"

I glanced at Blake. "Baby-sitting." I could've used a mouthful of butter right then, just to see if it would've melted. From the dubious look Mrs. Klauser gave me, my chin probably would have been dribbling yellow grease.

Whether or not she bought my story, she had bigger matters bidding for her attention. So did we all. Beyond the barricade, on the side of the store with all the custom-order cake catalogs and accessories, our foes kept winking in and out of sight. Every time one of them appeared, it was armed with another payload of pastry. The walls dripped meringue, the floor was a mine field of smashed stollen.

I popped up from behind the counter a couple of times, like a prairie dog with a death-wish. This was my hour! This was where I showed myself to be worthy of the honorable title and mystic weapon Lord Palamon's minion Hobson had bestowed on me. My wand was leveled and ready, lacking only a target. I waited for the next appearance of an enemy. There came the flash of a red cap and the scent of chocolate. I swung the wand in on my mark and concentrated all my power.

The world went black-forest cake.

"Tasty," Neil said, scooping my face free.

I stared at the turncoat crystal wand. "Nothing happened. Not one sweet fucking-a thing!" I shook the wand roughly, as if it were a clogged pen.

"Timothy . . ." Mrs. Klauser admonished.

The Dread and Puissant Champion of the Fey apologized for being a potty-mouth.

Blake scraped a double fistful of chocolate-cherry goo from my cheek and let fly. A loud *splosh* followed by a string of Teutonic cuss words lofted back over the barricade. Teleri patted the child's head and passed him an angel food cake, which he rejected in favor of the more aerodynamically sound properties of a tray of cinnamon rolls.

"My store! My store!" Mrs. Klauser moaned.

"Ma'am, how'd all this get started?" Neil asked. "I mean, before we came in. You got any idea what brought these creeps?"

Billy's mother shrugged helplessly. "How should I know? Things have been—oh dear, you're going to think I'm crazy, but such weird things have been happening to—no, I mean *visiting* us lately."

"Things like them?" Neil jerked his thumb at the gang of sprites-gone-bad on the far side of the counter. The battle was heating up; the little people were blinking in and out of sight faster than a lightning bug on amphetamines.

Mrs. Klauser nodded. "Yes, but just one: Walter. I found him in here one Saturday morning a couple of weeks ago, when I came to open up the shop. I thought I must be dreaming. I'd never seen a human being so *small*, not even a dwarf. He was sitting on the counter, his hat in his lap, as if he were waiting for a job interview. I told myself I must be imagining things. How could he have gotten into a locked store without setting off our burglar alarm? Then he saw me, bounced off the counter, made the funniest stiff little bow, and handed me—Wait a moment."

She crawled on hands and knees to just below the cash register and hit the NO SALE button blind. The drawer popped open and she fumbled under the cash tray while beset by a hail of pound cakes that were true to their name. At last she found what she wanted, slammed the drawer shut, and crawled back to give me a small ivory calling-card.

WALTER VON EISENDORF

Hinzelmänn for Hire
Valhalla Venusburg Brooklyn
Der Hinzelmensch ist was er isst.

"Ah!" Teleri read the card over my shoulder and sounded very knowing. "Good fortune's yer lot, madam, to have attracted the help o' one o' the hinzelmänner. Wonderful good workers they be, and ever willing to see to yer chores fer ye." A slab of gingerbread whacked the wall behind her, sprinkling Teleri's hair with spicy shrapnel. "This isn't like 'em at all," she said, fidgeting with the crumbs that had trickled down the back of her kimono.

"No, it's not," Mrs. Klauser agreed. "As soon as Fred came in and saw the little man too, I knew for sure I wasn't nuts. By that time, Walter had whipped on an apron and was turning out the most delectable cakes either of us ever tasted. There goes one now." She sighed as a gorgeous Linzertorte gooshed its life out against the showcase.

"So, like, where's this Walter now?" Neil asked. He grabbed a fistful of donuts and chucked them into No Man's Land. "He run out on you when things got nasty?"

"No, no. I wish he had!" Mrs. Klauser's face was pinched with misery. She gestured toward the other side of the counter. "He's out there. He's doing his best to protect me, but I'm so afraid that they might—" Her voice cracked. Her blunt fingers dug into my forearm. "Tim, it's not Walter's fault! He's risking himself for no reason! He didn't know the truth about me when he came here. All he said was, 'Frau Klauser? That is a nice German name. It is very important for me to work for those my family has always served. It can not be otherwise.' " Her hands were very cold. "He was so emphatic about our name. I know I should have told him all about me, but—but I was afraid he'd be insulted and find another place. We couldn't lose him! If you'd have just one taste of his *Pfeffernusse* you'd understand."

The way the food was flying, it was only a matter of time until one of those famous *Pfeffernusse* found me. Blake got off several rounds of solid macaroon mayhem, giving a whole new dimension to the phrase "toss one's cookies."

"I'll do what I can, Mrs. Klauser." I sounded confident, which was more than I felt. I gave the wand another angry shake, hoping for some reaction. *Nada.* I tapped it on the floor a few times; no fire, no spark, not even an anemic glow.

Very well, then; alone. I inched my eyes just barely over the edge of the counter, spying out the enemy. It was hard to get a head-count of the opposition when they wouldn't stay still or visible. I remembered the kobold—a squat, thick-bodied creature with a serious case of the uglies—and the grogan that Blake had beaned. The only reason I knew they were a kobold and a grogan respectively was that Teleri had told me.

"—and usually not an atomy o' ill-will in either one of 'em, milord. Yer grogan's famed fer helping the farm folk in the Scots highlands, and yer kobold might do the wee bit o' mischief now and again, but 'tis mere high spirits. Whatever can have possessed 'em to bear such a wicked grudge against an innocent hinzelmänn?"

What indeed?

It didn't help that I knew two of the players' names. That didn't make them any less hostile, or any easier to keep tabs on. Once I spied the flicker of a pristine white apron, tied over the paunch of a tiny man. This, I assumed, was the hinzelmänn Walter. He stayed just long enough to lob a three-tiered wedding cake into the opposite camp. A tall, elegant lady wrapped in purest white from head to sandaled foot countered with an unfrosted cake the size and weight of a small manhole cover. She had an accurate eye; the missile clipped Walter in the temple, sending the hinzelmänn staggering. With howls of triumph, the kobold, the grogan, and a hayseedy sprite I hadn't seen before all went visible at once. They leaped on poor Walter. Every one of them was armed with one of those Christmas fruitcakes people use for doorstops. They'd kill him.

I couldn't allow that. I'd given a promise of help to Hobson. Even if he had no honor, that didn't mean I had to sink to his level. Maybe if I showed Lord Palamon's council how well I kept my pledge, maybe they'd hurry up and redeem theirs: my dad's rescue. So what if my wand didn't work? Did that mean I was under any less obligation to the Fey? And I could still use it to clobber some sense into any number of elfin skulls. I leaped over the counter. "Stop! Drop those fruitcakes! Halt, in the name of the—WHOA!"

I stepped squarely into a dollop of coconut custard and skidded right down the strike zone. Walter's assailants were too startled to wink out, or to get out of my way. Fruitcake hit the deck with the *crump* of mortar shells. I plowed straight into the lady in white, who screamed, "How *dare* you, you utter swine!" She gave me a mighty shove, ricocheting me backwards into the kobold. He only came up to my knees, so I tumbled over him and rolled full tilt through all the assorted yuck on the bakeshop floor until I hit the Special Orders section. Little plastic brides and grooms took unscheduled honeymoon flights. Ring-binders full of cake dècor patterns showered down on me. When it was all over, I lay on my back with my feet covered in sugar candy roses, my head resting on a *minyan* of marzipan bar-mitzvah boys, and my mind wondering where in hell my wand had got to.

That's the way it is in the aftermath of really big disasters. You fixate on the most trivial things and tend to ignore the—Oh. Did I mention the big wedding-cake knife the grogan was holding at my throat? My oversight.

"Dinna move," he grated, "any o' ye, else he's fooked good an' proper."

Teleri, Neil, and Mrs. Klauser had all surged to their feet when I vaulted the counter, ready to back me up. Now they saw that backing down was in order. Blake had a brace of eclairs in his hands, the pins pulled, but a sharp command from Neil made him drop them. I had to tilt my head backwards to see them, so I got an upside-down view of the general surrender. Blake stuck his tongue out at me. Obviously I only lived to spoil a kid's good time.

I saw my wand sticking out of a monumental panettone just beyond my reach. I wasn't fool enough to try grabbing it, not with the blade-wielding grogan crouched above me. The knife he held was the size of a small sword, usually rented out to weddings where the cake was bigger than the newlyweds' first apartment. The grogan was another of your teensy sprites, so it took both hands for him to handle that slicer. Different as day and night we mortals may be from the Fey, but there's at least one thing we both react equally piggily to: power. His sun-browned face crinkled with vile exultation until he could have been one of the California Raisins playing Mr. Hyde. "Aye, that's it, ye huge, galumphing bastards. Dinna move, I say."

The lady in white prissily picked her way around the various clumps of collapsed patisserie to prod me with her sandal. "Get up."

The grogan protested. "Och, now, missy, if he gets up, how'm I to keep the lad mindful? I canna reach that high."

A twisty, cold smile perked up the lady's thin lips. "You'll be able to reach just high enough, Jimmy."

Comprehension smoothed half the wrinkles from the grogan's face as I stood up and he saw exactly what he was going to have me by. "Aye, missy, that's so, isn't it?" His teeth flashed the same color as the knife, both a damn sight closer to my body than really comfortable.

"Now." The lady folded her arms and turned to the others. The kobold chuckled merrily, a roly-poly teapot creature, and rubbed his hands together in anticipation. The other, more rustic-looking critter did a victory jig until the lady chilled him with a look. "If you are *quite* done cutting the fool, Umberto? Really, these *salvanelli*. Such yokels." She raised her brows. "Now we will settle this dispute once and for all."

There was a horrible finality in the way she said that. Mrs. Klauser outweighed the lady by two quarterbacks and a short-stop, but she trembled.

The hinzelmänn took up a protective position right in front of Billy's mother. "You will not touch her," he snapped at the lady. "You will depart and leave us in peace." His plump jowls were tense, his cupcake of a chin thrust forward pugnaciously. Though his once-spotless apron was now a smear of assorted frostings, he looked ready to fight on in Mrs. Klauser's defense.

I cleared my throat. "Just what exactly seems to be the trouble here?"

The lady gave me a shot of strychnine with her eyes. "You will speak when spoken to, *boy*. What we discuss is none of your business."

"The heck it's not! Do you know who I—?" The grogan shifted the knife a significant distance. I clammed.

"Dread and Puissant Champion o' the Fey, he is!" Teleri spoke up proudly on my behalf. She flicked her custard-blobbed hair away from her face and treated the lady to a look of scorn. "I may not know yer face, madam, but I can smell the Leeside clinging to yer garments. Were ye so in love with the foul place that ye'd have us all sent back there? Such ye'll do, and worse— a curse on yer vinegar puss!—if ye hinder our champion any further."

"Champion!" The lady did not exactly *spit*, but the sentiment was there. "A fine showing we'll make with such as this on our side! Oh no, my girl, we'll have none of your Lord Palamon's half-brained measures here. Now we're free, after all the bitter centuries, and free we shall remain!"

"Not without help," Teleri countered grimly.

The lady was pleased to laugh. "From *him*? You might require such, pathetic little airy fairy ragamuffin that you are, but my

followers and I do not. We are competent enough to help ourselves more than sufficiently.''

Custard notwithstanding, Teleri's hair began to crackle. The
hotter her green eyes kindled, the more apprehensive the grogan
grew, until he gave a nervous twitch that I didn't like one bit.

''You wanna watch it with that knife, fella?''

One corner of his mouth jerked up. ''Sorry, laddie, but 'tis a
heavy blade and there's no escaping gravity. Ye canna change
the laws o' physics.''

I was more worried about him inadvertently changing my vocal range.

My banshee was speaking again, menace swelling by the second in her voice. ''A fool Lord Palamon may be, and a grand
and glorious mistress o' every magic *ye* may be, but that never
stopped these mortals ye so despise from banishing ye and all
yer playmates to the cold lands. Tied to 'em, we be, with a cord
whose nature we may never know. All of us, fey and mortal,
dangle from either end of it over a fearsome dark. 'Tis a worse
fool than Lord Palamon who tries to shred that cord fer a whim.''

The lady stood even stiffer, until she resembled a fluted column. ''Who are you, that you presume to preach prudence to
Vesta? Must the goddess of hearth and home endure such im-
pudence?''

''Oh, *scheiss*, she's talking about herself in the *verdammte*
third person again!'' the kobold grunted. ''She gets like that,
there's no reasoning with her.''

''Goddess, is it?'' Teleri was markedly unmoved by the revelation. ''Sure, and don't half the kickshaw nymphs in Lord
Palamon's court call themselves the same? Had I a penny for
every out-o'-work Astarte I've known, I could buy me that darling wee suburban rath just beyant Dublin.''

''*We* are no nymph. *We* ward the hearth-fires of holy Roma
Mater herself.''

''Third person plural,'' the kobold rumbled. ''*Ficke.*''

'' 'Tisn't in Rome ye be now, madam, and far from any temple built to yer worship's honor, or yer honor's worship, as ye
prefer.'' Teleri assumed a businesslike air. ''If it were elsewise,
would ye be mollocking about with this roughneck crew, bick-
ering over yon poor manikin's right to serve where he likes? 'Tis
the vocation of all spirits of hearth and home to ally themselves
in service to compatible mortals. Walter's done so; why perse-
cute him?''

"Because he has no right whatsoever to be serving under this roof!" Vesta's scowl was an even match for Teleri's. "And *she* cannot deny that!" The hearth-goddess jabbed a finger at Mrs. Klauser.

Billy's mother broke down. "It's true, it's true!"

"What?" Walter was stricken, his face paler than the streaks of vanilla frosting on his cheeks. "*Gnädige Frau,* how can you say this? Behold! Is your name not Klauser? A fine name for one of my kindred to serve! In the Old Country, my ancestors always—"

"This isn't the Old Country, dear." Mrs. Klauser knelt to speak to him eye-to-eye. "And Klauser is just my married name.

"*Ja,* this I know, but what does that signify? I am still a good *Deutsche* sprite, and you are of the same descent I—"

"No." Mrs. Klauser's confession was hurting her as much as Walter. "Only one-quarter *Deutsch*—I mean, German-American."

The kobold uttered a yelp of pleasure.

"My mother's parents were Italian and Scots—"

Umberto the *salvanel* and Jimmy the grogan gave three cheers.

"—and my father's mother was—I'm not sure, I *think* she may have been Italian too, but—"

"Roman." Vesta's mouth was small and hard as a nailhead.

Neil loosed a sarcastic laugh. "Hey, come on, lady! How dumb you think we are? Nobody ain't *Roman* no more; not the way you mean. Jesus! Alla them old-time Romans got run over in the chariot races before the volcano blew, y'know? Right after the slaves revolted for Easter." (My learned colleague got most of his classical history from watching old epic movies.) "We weren't born yesterday."

Vesta smirked. "Neither was I. You will have to take my word for it on matters of blood, boy. It is the nature of the otherworldly to scent out those mortals most akin to us." She wiggled her nose at Neil. "Hmm. Predominantly Irish, with all other ancestry reduced to traces too small to be worth any competing sprite's attention."

Neil blushed. He must have been recalling the very special otherworldly attentions he had attracted from the very Irish *lhiannan sidhe.*

Vesta folded her hands across her tightly bound bosom and spoke to me. "So you see, O last and least of champions, *nil tam difficile est quin quaerendo investigari possiet.* And having found what we sought in this lady here—that is to say, a mortal whose blood is compatible with our own several heritages—we intend to remain here and serve her. *Whether she wants it or not!* As for this creature''—she stared down her nose at Walter—''*vae victis*. The rest of you can clear out with him.''

''You have not the right!'' Walter shook his fists at the lady. ''I will return! I will claim what is mine! So easily you do not displace a hinzelmänn!''

I tried making nice. ''Look, Vesta, if all your party wants is a mortal to serve, we've got a whole country full of them. No matter what you read in the *New Yorker*, some people live west of the Hudson.''

''They may,'' she replied. ''We cannot.'' And the goddess began to weep.

It was perhaps not the optimum moment for Blake to get bored enough to whop the displaced divinity right in the face with a prune Danish.

21

Child's Play

"DON'T KILL HIM," I said. "Please?"

Vesta scraped dark brown mush out of her eyes and mumbled something ominous in Latin. Since I know about as much Latin as Neil knows Sanskrit, anything the goddess uttered sounded ominous to me.

"He's only a little kid! Okay, a brat, but you can't kill him for that!" In appreciation of my heroic pleas on his behalf, Blake called me an asshole.

"Oh, can't I." Vesta intended that as a statement. On reflection, she said, "No, I don't suppose I can. Harming a child is unthinkable, even a junior gargoyle like this." She sniffed delicately in Blake's direction. "As I thought. Pure Vandal, with perhaps a smattering of Hun."

Blake pushed his nostrils up with two fingers and made pig-noises at her. Vesta got that disturbing little smile on her face.

"Child, has anyone ever told you about Circe? She had such a *way* with males. Shall I demonstrate?"

"NO!" I would have lunged, but Jimmy the grogan was still holding the knife on me where it counted. All I could do was intervene verbally. For all the good it would do. "Please, leave the kid alone. He can't help how he's acting. He just wants to go home."

"Home . . ." Vesta softened somewhat at mention of her sacred stomping grounds. "The question is: Does his home want him?"

"If they knew he was missing, they would."

"Indeed?" She glanced at Blake, who was nonchalantly trying to scoop up another handful of ammo. Neil let him get it up to chest level before he seized Blake's hand and mashed the goo into the kid's own shirtfront. Vesta listened attentively to Blake's ensuing tirade. "Fascinating. One would hardly think that this whelp's absence would be difficult to notice. The peace and quiet he left behind must be deafening."

"His parents don't know he's gone because Lord Palamon's people put a changeling in his place," I explained.

Vesta's eyebrows went up so high she reminded me of Larry Perlmutter in his Mr. Spock mode. "Trading elfin children for *this*? I always said Palamon was a few *ova* short of a *duodecim*. Why would he—?"

"Because of you," I said. "You and all the rest out there like you and the stupid turf war you've got going. The Fey aren't so crazy to get their hands on kids like Blake, they just want their own children out of the way when the shi"—I caught Mrs. Klauser's frown—"when the shirt hits the fantasy. That's why we're here: To stop your in-fighting so the changelings can leave and the human children return to their real parents."

"The fighting will stop," Vesta said. "*After* we have sorted matters out to our own satisfaction."

"What makes you think you'll have time for that? Or that we humans will stand for having our world become your battlefield?"

The goddess smirked. "If you are the best advocate humankind has to offer on this side of the barricade, what makes *you* think you mortals can prevent us from doing as we like?" She said *mortals* like it was something you scrape off the bottom of your shoe.

"The Leeside," I replied simply. It was mighty satisfying to watch the goddess go a little gray. "And our power to open it. Why did we shunt all of you into the Leeside before? Because you made us mortals *uncomfortable*. It felt better not to believe in you, so we made it the social norm to laugh at anything supernatural. Only kids believe in fairy tales; kids and weirdos. So all the kids in a hurry to be grownups quit believing as soon as they caught on. Nice going. You cut the children off from magic once, and you're about to do it again."

Vesta pooh-poohed the idea, but she was still a bit nervous. "We domestic spirits are scarcely the stuff of nightmares. We earn our keep, pull our own weight, and pay our way. We *add* to mortal comfort, boy!"

"Yeah? How comfy does Mrs. Klauser look right now?"

Vesta's smug expression drained away as she really studied Billy's mother. While the truth was sinking in, I continued: "You're fighting over mortals. Why? Why *can't* you spread out into fresh territory? What is it, the old can't-cross-running-water bit? So go *under*! Neil, tell her about the passageways down in Lord Palamon's realm."

The goddess raised her hand imperiously. "There is no need to tell us. We are aware of all such thoroughfares. As supreme divinity of the hearth and home, we were present during the initial settlement of New Faerie and witness to the discovery of the web paths."

"Ficke," the kobold growled. "Any more *we's* show up and the pompous bitch will have to let out her girdle."

If the kobold had some smarts, he would have kept his sentiments to himself. The hint of a scowl flicked over Vesta's face, the only sign that she'd overheard the kobold, but it was enough to make me inch a little farther away from the malcontent.

For the moment, however, Vesta went on as if nothing had been said. "We were likewise present when it was learned that any path leading beyond a certain compass of surface territory was useless to us. Thus far and no farther from our point of escape might we tread. We might not learn what cause so hindered us; we might but theorize. The lingering pull of the Lee-side? The tardy attentiveness of the Guardians to our flight? Some enchantment in our midst, a malicious spell cast by one powerful and treacherous enough to turn against his own kind?" Her smile was wan. "Your guess is as good as mine."

"I wouldn't waste time guessing," I told her. "I'd do something about it."

She's a virgin, Teleri whispered into my mind. *Been one for millennia. That's why that laugh o' hers has such a wicked brittle edge, I fancy.*

"You think I'm funny, huh?" I crossed my arms—slowly, so as not to alarm Jimmy.

Vesta thumbed aside a few mirthful tears, taking the last of the prune Danish with them. "Oh, infinitely so, boy. Ah, sweet Jupiter Liber, I haven't enjoyed such a laugh in ages! Jimmy, put down the blade. We must reward those who jest for our pleasure."

" 'We,' " the kobold snarled. " 'Us.' Getting too *verdammte* crowded in here for me. I want my work, curse it! I want a roof over my head and a mortal creature to dwell with and a sip of milk at dusk and dawn for my troubles. Is that too much to ask?"

I saw that flicker of irritation pass over the goddess's classic features again, so I thanked her effusively for calling off the grogan and moved as far from the kobold as I could. He continued grousing, oblivious to the sound of thin ice breaking up underfoot.

"I'm glad you find me amusing. Why don't you try to find me useful, too?" I asked.

"Useful?" Vesta echoed. "How? In your role as champion, perhaps?" She gave a deprecating wave of the hand. "Can you open the web paths? Can you give us the fresh territory we need?"

"I can try."

"*Try!* This is no light matter, boy; this is our survival! A domestic spirit who does not serve becomes embittered. As helpmates of the hearth were we summoned from the dark, and without service we shrivel up, turning to the shadows within us. All the good we have to share with you festers without use! We devour ourselves."

Her eyes were stark with remembrance. "In the cold lands, boy, before we fought free, there were many of our kind who soured. In the dark places, monsters dwell, and worse than monsters. Can you know how it pained us to watch our kin surrender to the dark, give themselves willingly to be transformed into that which we most hate and fear? Spirits of warmth and creation, makers and menders, turned into wraiths of black, wanton destruction. From desperation, boy! Because they saw no solution, no escape, no end. And now that we are free of the cold lands, it well may all begin again. Don't you see?" She seized my arms and shouted in my face: *"We* must *serve, or we perish!"*

She was breathing hard when she let me go. I was kind of winded myself. "Now speak to me of your usefulness, boy." She sounded lost and weary. "Tell me, make me believe, prove your power. I would so dearly love to hope. Once upon a time, in the dark places, I did see a mortal champion. I know they are not mythic creatures. I watched him save a fluff-brained *lar* named Julia Drusilla from a particularly vicious lamia. In the ages when I ruled in Roma, I saw better swordsmen, but never one with so much heart." Her cool gray eyes gazed into the past. "We are in his debt."

"Are you, now?" Teleri stormed forward. "Then pay a middling of it in courtesy's coin to the swordsman's son."

Vesta looked unwilling to believe that Teleri meant me. "You?
You are the son of Great Hern?"

"*A*hern," I said. "Timothy Ahern Desmond. I'm his son,
Timothy Alfred."

The lines of incredulity remained tight across the goddess's
high brow. "Where is your sword, then, swordman's son?"

"There." I pointed to my wand, still stuck upright in the
panettone. "May I have it back now?"

That tickled her. "That toy? What a pretty trifle."

"It's not a trifle." I was very calm. "It's at least the equal of
any sword." *If I only knew what to do with the damned thing,* I
thought, but I wasn't going to let Vesta know that. "*May* I?"

"Of course." The goddess yawned. "Jimmy, toss the boy his
plaything, will you?"

The grogan scampered across the floor to obey, but when he
tried to pick up the wand, it wouldn't budge. He tried one hand,
then two, then both hands with feet braced against the fruit-filled
cake, all to the same effect: Zero.

"What are you playing at?" Vesta tapped her foot. "Here!
Umberto, you fetch it."

The salvanel danced over to mock the grogan's failure, only
to go down in similar defeat. When the goddess assigned the
task to the kobold, it was the same story. Walter the hinzelmänn
put in his oar without being asked, then organized the four small
sprites into a tug-o'-war chain with Jimmy as anchor, gripping
the wand like death. It was as if the faceted crystal shaft had
driven roots into the core of the world.

"Beggin' yer pardon, missy, but I dinna think we ought to
keep at it this way," Jimmy appealed to Vesta as the elfin chain
hauled away. "The crystal canna take much more o' this."

"The crystal can take fools better than I." Vesta strode up to
the recalcitrant wand, bowling over her minions as she went.
"My strength is as the strength of ten because my heart is pure."
She wrapped both hands around the wand and yanked.

She missed her grip, lost her footing, and fell on her keister
in a pile of chocolate ganache.

I strolled into the batter's box. " 'Scuse me." Three fingers
were all I used to pinch the crystal tip. There was a happy ending
hovering somewhere overhead, and I wanted it to be just as
spectacular as possible. When you wish for the sword in the

stone and have to make do with the wand in the panettone, you've got to add your own touch of showmanship. Of course, if the wand refused to come out for me, too, I was going to look like a jackass.

I pulled carefully. The wand gave. I pulled harder. The wand was free, that simply. No angelic choirs or shafts of pearly light, but at least I didn't pitch over backwards. I turned a sigh of relief into a self-confident grin and offered the downed goddess my free hand.

Vesta's mouth gaped so wide she might have been posing for a fountain. Rather than getting up, she knelt and placed her hands in mine. "Forgive my presumption, lord. By this token I see that you are truly Great Hern's kin. As such, I give you my allegiance, I acknowledge your right as Dread and Puissant Champion of the Fey, and I recognize all arbitration you may effect as binding upon me and mine. How may I serve?"

"Ha!" the kobold crowed. "Now the puffed-up trull is first person singular! Good, it is good! Yes, very—"

The goddess's head swerved around like a snake's. Blue flames from the home-fire's heart lanced from her eyes and engulfed the kobold. When the sparks fell to ash, all I could see was a prettily painted box with an elaborate latch standing in his place. Blake—who had never heard of leaving well enough alone—crept near and poked the latch. The lid flew back, and out sprang a jumping jack with the kobold's ugly features frozen in wood forever.

Vesta lifted a calculatedly sweet face to me. "I'm very good with children, too," she said.

The sign over the door said "Agency." That was all. The boards were off the windows, which sparkled as if they'd been washed *and* waxed. The alley gateway to Lord Palamon's realm was within spitting distance, which in this neighborhood was a very common unit of measure. I was just going out the front door with Blake when a plump, dark-eyed man hustled up and introduced himself as the pastor of the storefront church next door to the Agency.

"An employment agency?" he asked, looking hopeful. "There are many in my congregation who—"

"No." I hated to disappoint him. "Not exactly."

"Then what? Something governmental?"

"In a way." I disliked hedging, but I didn't think he was quite ready for the truth. Maybe he'd get fed up with my no-answers and go away. Maybe Blake would tilt his head back and whine about how he wanted to go *home*.

No luck. For once in his miserable existence, Blake was the picture of angelic patience. The little snot.

"A talent agency, perhaps? I have a daughter who sings a little."

When there is no escape, surrender. I held the door open and bowed him inside.

Bright lights and sleek surfaces leaped out at us. If you walked in off the street in midtown Manhattan, in the Century City section of L.A., in the swankier parts of Dallas, Chicago, Atlanta, or Washington, D.C., you'd see much the same sort of ultra-glossy office-spread. Lean, clean lines of Italian design furniture glittered under state-of-the-art track lighting. Potted palms looked happier in their brushed silvertone containers than they'd ever been on the beach at Waikiki. Carpet the color and softness of a pureblood smoke Persian cat purred underfoot. A dozen top-of-the-line P.C. stations were ably manned by nymphs dressed like a year's worth of *Cosmopolitan* cover girls.

The preacherman stared. I could tell, just as surely as if his skull were glass, that he was figuring out square footage and the laws of probability. He knew that all the "taxpayer" stores on this block had about the same amount of floor space. He also knew it wasn't near enough to accommodate twelve desks, a luxurious waiting area, plus a supervisor's station *and* have anything behind the big door at the rear with the GENERAL MANAGER golden plaque on it.

He looked to me for sanity. I shrugged. Blake sniggered.

Before he could bolt, Master Runyon spotted us. The luchorpan held down the supervisor's post—only fair, since it was his traditional pot o' gold we'd skimmed to provide the security deposit, six months' rent, and furnishing for the Agency property. He stood up at his desk and hallooed, spilling the stenographic nymph off his lap with a little squeal and a lot of thigh-flash.

"Greetings and salutations, my friends." The luchorpan shook us all by the hand effusively, even though he'd just bid me farewell less than five minutes before and Blake's paws were stickier than August asphalt. "And to what do we owe the honor of your custom? No, do not inform me of this. Permit me to hazard a guess. The gentleman who accompanies you is—what?—

Hispanic, unless I misperceive myself. You are in luck, sir." He pounced on his desktop Rolodex. "We have just acquired the services of one Luisa Dolores Aguirre de Salazar y Montoya, a *duende* of the highest repute with an excellent set of pins." He punched a button on his intercom. "Yo! Donahue! Pray commend me to Miss Luisa and tell the doll to toddle in here posthaste."

"Duende?" Now my comrade really looked like a man of the cloth, if the cloth were bleached linen.

"Don't worry," I comforted him. "You'll like her. Duendes are compulsive neatniks. You could use a little maintenance help at the church, couldn't you?" I tossed in the clincher: "For free?"

"Yes, but—Certainly, but—Free would be nice, but—What is a—?"

"Reverend"—I wasn't sure what his proper title was, but he wasn't objecting—"you're not crazy; you're *select*. If not, then when you came in here with me you'd only have seen an empty store with maybe a pile of cardboard boxes in one corner and a busted-up chair in the other. You wouldn't even have been able to read the Agency sign."

The big door in the back opened and Luisa came out. Like all duendes, she was small and dark; she was also very beautiful. She gave the reverend her most dazzling smile.

"Encantada, honrado señor." Her ghostly skirts fluttered up as she curtsied.

"Igualmente," he replied, absently. To me he whispered, "I'm—I'm supposed to be seeing her, too?"

Teleri popped up from behind a ficus tree in the reception area. "No doubt about it. No charge, either. Just put out a little milk every night, the occasional saucer of gruel, and ye'll have years o' trouble-free service. Or return the sprite and any unused portion o' her powers to any Agency outlet fer a full refund." She clapped her hands onto his shoulders and steered him out, the duende floating after. "Thank ye fer patronizing. Have a nice day."

"Very good, Teleri." I gave her a short round of applause. "You'll get that advertising gig, no problem."

She rounded on me angrily. "None o' yer cheek, milord! 'Twas merest luck we had a suitable sprite on call who'd be compatible with yon gentleman ye dragged in. Meantime, yer own proper chores want seeing to! *Him* fer one." She pointed at Blake, who fired off a volley of underarm fart noises at the banshee.

The intercom on Runyon's desk buzzed like a hornet with heat rash. *Is the Dread and Puissant Champion of the Fey still out there?*

Runyon depressed his SPEAK button. "It would appear so, to the casual yet accurate observer, boss-lady."

Well, you tell him that when we send someone out on an assignment, we expect them to do it! We are presently up to our gluteus maximus *in human children awaiting repatriation, they are none of them sufficiently housebroken to our taste, and we have yet to find a satisfactory jobber of empty eggshells in the NYNEX Yellow Pages. What is more—*

"I'll go in and explain," I told Master Runyon softly while our esteemed general manager took another deep breath. I nimbly edged past the gaudy box blocking the big door.

Not nimbly enough. The latch went *spang* and out popped the leering kobold. "Ms. Vesta is in conference. Please take a seat. She will be with you shortly. That is not our department. The check is in the mail. You are not on Ms. Vesta's schedule for today. Would you mind coming back tomorrow? Ms. Vesta is on a business trip. Are you sure that is how you spell your name? We have no record of your call. One of Ms. Vesta's assistants will get back to you on that as soon as—"

The receptionist-in-a-box was still jabbering on as I opened the office door.

22

I Go, Ego, We Go, Libido, Rah!

VESTA'S OFFICE LOOKED like a cross between a day-care center and the monkey house. Small beings—many of them debatably human—sprawled, crawled, hung, swung, rocked and rolled on every available surface of the room and its contents. At the core of Chaos Central, Vesta's desk was an isle of blessed calm. This the goddess had achieved by virtue of surrounding it with a ring of impenetrable flame. She wore a pinstripe charcoal business suit and for want of Yorick's skull, sat contemplating the empty aspirin bottle in her hand.

" 'Keep out of reach of children,' " she read aloud. "Excellent advice." She slammed the bottle down, popping the child-proof cap skyward. "Well, what do *you* want?"

"I just wanted to let you know that I'll—" Two miniature bacchantes ran straight for me, shrieking. At the last minute, they dived between my legs. Their aim was almost perfect.

"You were saying?" The goddess waited for me to come out of my fetal crouch of agony.

"Just that as soon as I take Blake home and let my mom know where I've been, I'll be right back with extra help for you. The Agency will have all these little—*Get away from me, you!*—darlings safe in the bosom of their respective families within forty-eight hours, tops."

The fires around the desk burned lower. "Forty-eight hours are approximately forty-*nine* hours too long for me. When next I see Lord Palamon, I shall hang him up to twist in the wind from a meat hook by his pointy little elfin brain. He didn't *have* to release these juvenile basilisks into our keeping until *after* we'd retrieved his changeling brats!''

''He must've figured we wanted to have the real kids right on hand when we effected the swaps,'' I said, with no credibility whatsoever. One look into the goddess's eyes told me she shared my real theory—that Lord Palamon couldn't wait to be shut of the small mortals. ''Could be he figured you wouldn't mind, seeing how you like children so much.''

''Like children? *Ego?*'' Vesta had a laugh hollow as a Richard Nixon Sings! concert hall. She leaned towards me over the flames and said, ''Why do you think I've always been so big on virginity?''

With a wild, exultant whoop, Blake plunged into the general riot. I tried to call him back to my side, but no one had ever trained the little thug to anything less than the choke-chain. Mrs. Emmeline Mandel and Dr. Spock would have much to answer for on the Judgment Day. Child abuse is just as wrong whether given or received.

Vesta watched the kids' antics grimly. ''The family hearth, *our* purview, has always been a place of sacred harmony. I fail to see how—*Touch my autographed krater of the rape of Persephone and you die, you midget minotaur!*—how returning these infants to their parents will ensure the domestic tranquility.''

''They're not all that bad,'' I lied. ''What you need here is a little organization.''

''That's what you said when you had us establish this whole Agency setup,'' the goddess grumped. ''Lord Palamon promptly used it as a dumping ground for these knee-high Neros.'' The ring of flame shrank to a sullen sizzle.

''The first step in successful organization is the enlistment of appropriately skilled personnel.'' I reached across the smoke for her telephone. ''Trust me.''

''All right, shoats!'' Yang lashed his sword into the edge of Vesta's desk to make sure he had the children's full attention. ''Now you listen! You play nice games, Uncle Yang doesn't kill you. You give me any crap, we play kick-the-severed-heads. *Your* heads! Got that?''

The children nodded. You could see their adorable tousled heads bob up and down in unison, like a row of underaged Rockettes.

''Hey!'' Uncle Yang took out Vesta's Boston fern with a swift backhand swing of the blade. Fronds showered the floor. "You just nod? You think I can hear the rocks rattle in your worthless skulls? I ask a question, you give an answer! Got that?"

"Yes, sir." Over two dozen throats, but a single voice.

"That's 'Yes, O Honored Uncle Yang, Most Endearing and Affectionate of Care-givers!' "

Quite a mouthful for the Sesame Street set. They did try. Yang was not pleased with the results. He stalked into their midst, sword point tracing random patterns on the air inches from his small charges' faces.

"We will make it easy. 'Yes, O Honored and Beloved Uncle Yang the Superb.' Can you say 'Uncle Yang the Superb'?" His sword homed in on Blake Mandel's nose. "I think you can."

"Yes, O Honored and Beloved Uncle Yang the Superb," Blake rattled off, letter-perfect.

"Good." Yang sheathed the blade and turned to Vesta. "Now where's the fucking milk and cookies?"

T'ing was leafing through a back issue of *Unnatural Geographic* when I joined her in the Agency waiting area. She dog-eared a photo-spread on "Stalking the Wily Insurance Underwriter" before greeting me.

"It says it's impossible to make them breed in captivity and that they'll probably be extinct within thirteen years," she said. "Of course it's an old magazine."

"Hello to you, too." I wondered why she was looking at that stupid magazine and not at me.

"Hello doesn't cut it, Tim." She folded her hands over the magazine in her lap. "Where have you been?"

"Making friends. Influencing people. Getting into the odd food fight. Didn't Neil tell you when he walked you over here?"

"He told me plenty." She still wouldn't look up. "Neil's a pretty good eavesdropper, but he'd make a lousy spy. He hears more than you think, then spills it all to anyone who asks." Now she did lift her face. "I hear you're in love."

"Who, me?" How nice to know that despite my empty title, useless weapon, and nonexistent honors as Dread and Etcetera, I hadn't lost my gift for sparkling repartee.

"At least she's not a *lhiannan sidhe*. He told me about them, too. There'll be something left of you afterwards . . . if it doesn't work out." A funny, sad smile tugged at the corner of her mouth. "That's silly of me. Why shouldn't it work out? There've been other mortal men who went off into the Faerie lands with their lovers. Endless life, endless youth, someone as beautiful as Teleri to love you—why wouldn't you make that choice? What can the ordinary world offer you that's even close to competing?'' She patted my hand. ''Only do me one favor before you take off for good, okay? You be the one to tell your mother you're going.''

''Mom! I tried to call her but setting up this Agency's bitten off most of my time. What's been left, either I'm asleep, walking dead, or she wasn't home to answer the phone. Is she all right?''

''Yeah. I guess so.'' T'ing made a helpless gesture. ''I tried my best. She called me the day you vanished, you know. Because I was so close to you.'' Again, that twitch of the lips that called up an echoing ache inside me. ''It's hard to tell someone who's that upset that they can calm down, everything's going to be fine, your son will come back tomorrow for sure. Then tomorrow keeps coming, but you don't come back. What can I say to her? She keeps calling me every day, and every day I keep telling her more lies.''

The pang went deeper in me than any I'd felt before. ''How long—how long have I been away?''

''Daniela gets married a week from this Sunday.''

''God.''

T'ing's older sister was having an early December wedding. October had just been spilling over into November when I entered Lord Palamon's realm.

''What did Mom do?'' I demanded. ''She ever call the cops?''

''We told her not to—Yang and Ilya and I. We all figured you must be on some sort of vital mission connected with the Return. The important thing was patience, we told her, and figuring out some way to cover for you at school.''

''School!'' I slapped my forehead. ''I've been gone almost a month. How did you manage—?''

''We asked your mother to help us with that. It was good for her, a distraction. She''—I thought I heard T'ing's voice catch—''really missed you.''

I wanted to ask, *Was she the only one?* but I'm still a big coward. It was safer asking, ''What you tried—it worked?''

''You got lucky, Tim.'' She was back to staring at the closed magazine. ''Most of your teachers are—like us. They can see the daemons. You're passing everything but Spanish, and we got Yang to turn in a special note from your mother, asking to have you dropped from the course. My honored ancestor tried, but Mr. Richter just couldn't see him.'' She sighed. ''He looked so cute in your Mets jacket, too.''

''*Yang* has been taking my place?'' I made a mental note to have my wardrobe fumigated. ''How? He doesn't even look like me!''

''He shaved.''

There was a flash of the old T'ing's genuine smile. ''Ms. Alexinsky says she never heard Hamlet's relationship with Ophelia interpreted like *that* before. I think she wrote 'earthy but interesting' on the written report. You also got your first A in gym class. Billy Klauser won't be bothering you again, either. I think you owe some thanks to Yang, Master of the Knotted Wet Towel of Disfigurement. Still, you may have to hide out from Brooke, Ashley, Heather, Megan, Summer, Kirsten, and Jennifer. Tiffany, on the other hand, thought it was kind of cute the way you came right out and said you wanted her to warm your yurt. She thinks it's a kind of low-calorie yogurt.''

I sank onto the squishy black leather sofa beside her. So this was how it felt to be a changeling. ''I am doomed. I am dog meat at school.''

''That's another thing: Yang made a few—mmmh—innovative suggestions in the cafeteria. About alternative sources of protein. On the walls. In meat loaf gravy. Mr. Alden wants a group-meeting with you and the school nutritionist in his office next Tuesday.''

I doubled over, arms protecting my head from any further assault. ''I'm ruined! I am absolutely done with having any chance at a normal life! I have been looted, sacked, and pillaged out of existence by your wacko ancestor.'' I straightened up and jabbed a finger at T'ing. ''I'm holding you personally responsible for it when I get rejected from Princeton.''

''Princeton?''

''Hell, yes!''

''I thought that after you took care of the changelings you were going to go . . . away.''

I reached for her hand, but stopped. What I had to say was serious, and I didn't want the touch of her distracting me. What a weird sensation, actually to *know* what I wanted. Not what someone else decided, not what my friends or my family or all the slick-paged and shiny-screened media oracles preached I was *supposed* to want; just me.

"I'm not going anywhere. This is where I belong, T'ing," I said. "Right up here on the surface, warts and all. I want a real life—real doesn't have to mean boring. I want to get back to Glenwood High—if Yang's left any of it standing—and get through the rest of this year, and the next, and then get into Princeton if I'm lucky, Vassar if I'm not."

Her laugh sounded plenty real enough; wonderful. "What are you going to do? Put 'Dread and Puissant Champion of the Fey' down on your application under Extra-Curricular Activities?"

"Turn 'em all into toads if they don't like it." I winked at her.

"So you're really going to stay." She said it softly, her eyes aglow. I couldn't remember the last time I'd seen her so happy. Suddenly she was touched by the old magic—the simple, unspectacular, mortal enchantment that had let my dreams turn her into something more exquisite, more wonderful than any lady of the Fey. "You don't want to be with Teleri?"

I started to clasp her hands again. That was all the old Tim would have had the guts to do, especially out where a dozen giggling nymphs could see. Then the still, small voice of total lunacy in my head yelled, *Go for it, fool!* and I put my arms around her the way I'd always dreamed of doing and I took a deep breath and I thought I smelled apple blossoms and I opened my mouth and I said:

"Naaahhhh."

Still the ol' sweet talker. But I kissed her. It wasn't anything like the way I'd imagined it. No lights flashed, no naked cupids dumped rose petals on my head, nobody cued the hidden fifty-six-piece string ensemble. No one punched up the laugh-track either, so I guess I'm not a total jerk.

A pair of excellently rounded knees presented themselves for my inspection. A nymph in an orange lambsuede minisuit and blaring purple silk blouse loomed over me. "Dread and Puissant Champion of the Fey?" she asked from behind a crinkly sheet of paper that didn't do a thing to hide her giggles.

"Yeah?" I was too giddy with happiness to demand a little respect from the rank and file.

The paper knifed under my nose. "Fax for you, bwana." She skittered away on four-inch red spike heels.

I checked out the message. "Uh-oh. It looks like the restoration of Blake Mandel to his original keepers is going to have to wait."

"Problem?" T'ing was back in her efficient partner mode. At the first hint of merry hell in the offing, she went straight from tenderness to troubleshooter. The transformation no longer jarred me. If the happy ending needed a dragon or two to be slain, I was grateful that the princess in my story knew one end of the sword *and* the dragon from another.

Maybe she'd be able to figure out how to upload the wand, while we were at it.

To more pressing matters first, however:

"Big trouble," I said, crumpling the paper. "Call Neil. Go to Master Runyon's desk and ask him if anyone's available to help out. Ask Vesta if she can spare Yang."

"What is it, Tim? A battle?"

"It's worse than a battle, T'ing. It's war."

23

All Washed Up

"Somebody—" Donahue panted as he galloped. "Somebody—and I'm mentionin' no names, mind!—somebody is getting—a wee sight—too many saucers o' milk—fer one wi' a crupper—t' size o' County Kerry t' start wi'."

"I take that remark from whence it comes," Master Runyon countered. "Certain equine parties should not cast the first aspersion as to personal heft. I have seen a higher class of nags running in the fifth at the Acme Glue Works."

Donahue snorted angrily, puffs of orange smoke blooming from his nostrils and baby lightnings making a Jacob's ladder of his tail.

"I *said* we should've taken the Flatbush Avenue bus!" T'ing clung to the irate phouka's mane, terrified by the speed, the critter's temper, and the unnaturally crowded riding conditions. Stretch limos were one thing, stretch horses another. The poor girl just wasn't used to barreling through the streets of Brooklyn astride a black steed whose back conveniently elo-o-o-o-ongated to accommodate all riders. At last count, Donahue was carrying six, plus a little old lady who had flagged him down and ridden with us for eight blocks, under the impression that we were going to Coney Island. She was pretty peeved when Master Runyon told her that the cross-town phouka doesn't issue transfers.

"Hold on," I told T'ing. "We're almost there."

"So we are," Donahue put in. " 'Tis a foul violent field o' war awaitin' us. I can smell the stench o' burnin' flesh already."

"Whose flesh?" T'ing asked, her fingers snarling themselves deeper into the phouka's midnight mane.

"Someone Irish." Teleri set her mouth grimly. "Or partways Irish, at least. I feel a keening coming on."

We rounded a corner on two legs, passing Miracle Slim's Genuine Goat Bar-B-Q. Donahue flared his nostrils and rolled up the whites of his eyes as we charged through the tangy veils of smoke drifting from the eatery.

I leaned past T'ing to hiss in the phouka's flattened ear, "Was *that* the burning flesh you smelled?"

Horses can't shrug while galloping—if they ever can—but Donahue managed to communicate the sentiment that lies behind all shrugs. "Whisht! Leastways 'twasn't I who claimed t' goats was Irish."

Teleri's arms tightened around my waist. I was riding the phouka sandwiched in between her and T'ing, both ladies riding barelegged and barefoot—Teleri from force of habit, T'ing because she'd lost her shoes when Donahue leaped over a gridlocked taxi. In circumstances other than a war-call, it would have been paradise.

"Mock as ye will," the banshee said, her mouth a razor-straight line. "There's wicked doings on the wind, and the flutter o' the raven's dark wing over us. Mistaken I've been ere this, milord, but there's that in me bones as knows the truth o' harsh death approaching. The banshee kindred may only wail over those o' their own clan, but we've all the power to sense when the Shade draws near to any man. Or woman."

"Teleri, you—"

"Stop! Oh, Donahue, fer love o' Dana, *stop*!"

My cries for an explanation were ignored. At Teleri's urgent command the phouka skidded to a sudden stop in front of a self-serve laundry. Neil was riding caboose, with Master Runyon wedged between himself and Yang. At this unscheduled halt, Neil jerked forward so hard that the luchorpan was squeezed from his seat with the force of a well-spat watermelon seed. On the recoil, Neil pitched off Donahue's rump into the gutter. Yang kept his seat the best of the bunch, which was only natural for a Mongol horseman, though he yowled to high heaven over the injustice of it all when Teleri slipped from her place before him and went running into the Ford Suds-O-Mat.

"Come back!" he shouted. "We were almost having sex!"

"What the hell—?" I muttered, slinging my leg off of Donahue's back and racing after the fugitive banshee. The smell of hot, damp, soapy air hit me like a wall as I bolted into the laundromat. The sound of the banshee's wail pierced my belly as I stood gasping.

Doom untold and dole unreckoned fly round the towers of Desmond! Heartache and foul loss attend the green-topped rath of Desmond! Wail, wail for the brave souls who pass, marching into the endless night! Ill the day and evil the hour that ever saw the birth of heroes doomed to die this day!

Teleri crouched on her knees, hands cradling her face as she pressed it to the cold linoleum floor. Her bright hair flowed over her shoulders, the ends trailing through snowy scatterings of spilled detergent. Her whole slim body shook as she rocked back and forth at the feet of a solitary lady.

The lady saw me and shifted the cigarette she was smoking from one corner of her mouth to the other. "What's with the chick, man?" Hazel eyes glinted at me from behind wire-rimmed glasses. A beaded headband plastered down shiny brown bangs, helped keep waist-length straight hair out of her face. She balanced a pink plastic laundry basket on one hip. "Bad trip or what?"

"Uh . . ." I bent to help Teleri, bemused by how matter-of-factly this lady was taking the scene. Sure, in the past several weeks a lot of people had gotten used to seeing sprites, but how many would react so coolly to having a banshee in full-throated mourning wail come zooming in off the street and throw herself at their feet? "She's upset about something," I finally said.

"Shit, I knew that." The lady hoisted the hem of her paisley granny dress and scratched her unshaven leg. She flipped open the lid of one of the washing machines and dumped in a packet of soap, then started loading it from the pink basket. "It's me." She whipped out a white shirt. Its bosom was thick with dark red blood.

"Ah, Tim, why did ye need follow me in here? Don't be looking at it!" Teleri clawed for me, tried to make me avert my eyes. "Curses drag ye down, Rowan o' Kinsale!" she screamed at the tranquil laundress. "What black fate brought ye here from Eire, to haunt us with yer ill-wishing?"

"Bitch," Rowan replied evenly. "This is a free country. I got as much right to emigrate as you. Nobody told you to hassle my scene. So, like, feel free to get out of my face any time." She took out another blood-stained shirt and dropped it into the washer, then smiled at me. "We were, like, rath buddies back home. Little bimbo never could stand it for anyone but herself to have a career. Can you dig it?''

I watched her as she cleaned out the lint trap. "You know, for an Irish spirit, you talk so—so—''

'' 'Murrican?'' Rowan put on a burlesque John Wayne accent. "Hey, man, I'm supernatural, not stupid. The minute I set foot on this soil, I got the message: Forget what you were; be what we'd like you to be. White bread goes down soooo much smoother. So I, like, played the game and did my job and no one hassled me. Wasn't any of my own kind around to tell me any different.''

Of course not. They were all still trapped in the Leeside—*not* the fate of a creature as adaptable as Rowan.

"Don't look at her more, Tim," Teleri begged me. '' 'Tis true what Rowan o' Kinsale says—the *bean nighe* never lie. I knew her of old in Eire. Oh, fer love o' all dear t' ye, flee while ye may, milord! Think only o' the battle awaiting us—the war it well may be by this—and let us begone.''

Rowan crammed three bloody beach towels and a similarly sanguine pair of ski pants into the tub. "Put a sock in it, Teleri," she rumbled, measuring Clorox. "You know as well as I do that he wouldn't even be able to see me if he wasn't supposed to.'' She dumped in the bleach and rummaged through the laundry basket. "Wanna check if there's anything in here got your name on it, man?''

That was the last thing I wanted to do, but I found myself taking a step toward her anyway. Teleri stiff-armed me back. "Ye needn't, milord; ye *mustn't*. There's ways on ways of turning aside the evil tidings that the *bean nighe* brings, if ye've the strength and the power.''

I knew that name—*bean nighe*, the female fey who, like the banshee, predicts death. The old tales say that her way is to wait by a fording-place in a stream and wash the clothes of those about to die. If you recognize your own garments among the *bean nighe*'s washing, you know you're doomed, and if the clothes you spy are stained with blood, your death will be a violent one.

"Teleri, you are, like, *so* full of shit. If he's got an appointment with me, he'll keep it. Mellow out." The *bean nighe* tossed a handful of balled-up socks into the machine, all of them spattered with gore. While she worked, she sang "The Yellow Submarine.''

"A malediction seize the hour that brought ye here," the banshee said between gritted teeth.

"Oh wow, you on some kind of power trip? I mean, maybe you set out for America before me, but I sure got here before you. The home team wondered what happened to you, so I was the one volunteered to find out." Rowan adjusted the cycle and temperature controls on the machine. "I hopped the puddle in the sixties." She flashed me the peace sign. "Part of the big Brit invasion, can you dig it? Didn't find Teleri till now, but hey! I found peace and love and sunshine and flowers and rock 'n' roll. And one Christmas Eve I found some dude who said he was just in town for the night, helping his boss-man make some deliveries." She closed her eyes, enjoying the memory. "Boy, could *he* deliver. Far-out buns, but those ears—I could never have a meaningful relationship with a Trekkie, you know? Their idea of being politically aware is telling the Klingons from the Romulans, okay? I'm a Maoist myself." She looked proud of it. "I was at Woodstock, baby." She shook out a pair of boxer shorts. Blood made a Rorschach blot on the white cotton. I pulled the front of my jeans forward and casually checked whether I was still wearing my Jockey briefs.

The *bean nighe* tsk-tsked over the stained unmentionables, then gave them a spritz of Spray 'n' Wash before dropping them into the basket with the rest. In a sadder voice she added, "Altamont, too. And Kent State." She slammed the washer lid shut. "Spare change, man? Got any quarters?"

Teleri was hauling at my arm hard enough to dislocate it. "Oh, milord, I beg ye, come away! We've work to do! To have seen the *bean nighe*'s bad, but if ye linger, ye run the peril o' marking yer own clothes among her load."

I wriggled out of the banshee's grasp and approached the fey washerwoman. Common sense told me to listen to Teleri, but a strange attraction emanated from Rowan's plump, placid body. It's human nature to poke sticks through the bars of a tiger's cage, to open the package with the label DON'T!, to want to know what lies behind the last dark door. My own fool curiosity combined with the *bean nighe*'s own peculiar power to make me gravitate nearer and nearer to what might be my undoing.

"Mind if I look?" The croaking of my own voice surprised me.

"Hey, man, help yourself. I offered, and you've got free will. That's the way we've always played this gig." Rowan's look was amused and pitying. "You really want to know? You're not afraid?"

I reached up inside the sleeve of my jacket and took out the crystal wand. After picking off some of the lint, I laid it down on top of the washer, next to the *bean nighe*'s bottle of Downy fabric softener. "I'm Timothy Desmond, Dread and Puissant Champion of the Fey. I think being brave goes with the job."

"No shit." She studied me hard while ashes from her cigarette drifted down over the tumble of clothes still in her basket. Then, without a word, she took out a pink sports shirt. The tiny, embroidered alligator on the left breast had a tiny embroidered arrow piercing its skull. A trail of crimson droplets dribbled down. She smoothed out the collar so that I could read the laundry mark there, plain as plain:

DESMOND.

"The *bean nighe* aren't into lies," she said. "And Teleri always was too damn good at her job. If this wasn't supposed to be, she never would have been drawn in here to find me." A hand thick with poison rings and Indian bangles patted my arm. "War is not healthy for Dread and Puissant Champions and other living things." She tilted up the washer lid and tossed in the pink shirt. "Sure you don't got any quarters, man?"

"Tim?" T'ing called to me from the sunlit street outside. "Tim, we've got to get going. What are you and Teleri doing in there"—she peered into the Ford Suds-O-Mat—"all by yourselves?"

Rowan fanned her hands, not even about to try explaining the self-evident. She blew four small smoke rings that spun themselves into silvery quarters that fell into her palm. I looked to Teleri, but the banshee just shook her head. Sight of the *bean nighe* was not for everyone.

"Nothing," I shouted back. "Teleri just—"

"I was having to powder me nose," my banshee announced, steering me forcefully out of the laundry. Behind us, I heard a coin-slide being pushed in and released, then the gush of a filling washer.

24

All's Faerie in Love and War

SOME WARS GET all the good names, the names that really
sound like they mean business: The Hundred Years' War! The
Thirty Years' War! The Crusades! The War to End All Wars!
The War After the War to End All Wars Didn't! All of them
grand, splendid names that say: Here is the glory of battle, here
is conflict on the sweeping, epic scale, here is the victory worth
winning, the death so romantic you'd have to be an awful wet
blanket to whine about being the one to die it.

Here is a war to take *seriously*.

On the other hand, there's the War of Jenkin's Ear and—my
personal favorite—the War of Richard Izanagi's Sweet *Okole*.

"There! In there!" A young woman in jeans and a Whale
Watch sweatshirt ran straight up to Donahue before the phouka
could come to a complete halt. She grabbed for the absent reins
and wound up yanking his mane. The phouka's eyes burned red,
but you could tell such exhibitions were very small potatoes to
this lady. She was waving madly at something behind her. While
the others clambered off Donahue's back, I stayed up to get a
better view.

It was quite a scene. In the middle of a row of reclaimed
brownstones stood one whose façade had been repainted with
malice aforethought. No one who wasn't packing a grudge
against all sighted humanity could come up with that shade of
green and deliberately slather it all over the exterior of a house.
The door was painted sky-blue, with a fluffy herd of *trompe
l'oeil* clouds that wouldn't fool an astigmatic mole. Above the
portal hung a sign showing a cute, pudgy panda sharing a sun-

flower with a cute, pudgy kid. The center of the sunflower was a blobby rendition of the globe, and arching above this tableau of trans-species would-you-like-a-flower-gimme-a-donation airport hustling was the message: ANANDA PANDA WHOLLY CHILD NURSERY SCHOOL.

All of which I saw floating on thin air about five feet above the building's foundation. You could see straight through to the back yard, where a bunch of kids and a handful of adults tried to keep a wooden swing-set between them and the airborne school. Plumbing trailed beneath the hovering brownstone like lead-pipe guts. Lightning flashed from the painted clouds on the front door. The cute, pudgy panda on the sign grew a set of saber-tooth tiger fangs while I watched, and commenced eyeing the cute, pudgy kid meaningly. Atop the roof, a replica of King Kong made entirely of Lego blocks stomped back and forth, beating its chest. The building reverberated with a sound like a garbage disposal trying to pass a Buick. Yellow goop bubbled from every window, some of it solidifying into shrieking faces. Horrible enough, but to add to the horror, the faces were all recognizable cartoon characters. The Damnation of Faust is as nothing next to the Damnation of Elmer Fudd.

Even I knew that this was going to do a number on real estate values.

I jumped from Donahue's back and joined my comrades, who surrounded the hysterical woman. Yang was the only one smiling. He would.

"It all happened so suddenly," the woman gasped. "Most of the children were playing outside in the back yard, thank God. Brittany and I were in my office, waiting for her father. Mr. Carlysle, there, was with us." She indicated a big man who stood about six feet away, on the sidewalk where we'd congregated. He looked ill at ease in his dark suit and drab tie, even taking into account the current level of pandemonium. "He'd come by to pick up his niece—family emergency. I was just about to let him go into the back yard to get her when Mr. Izanagi came in."

My guidance counselor's name jerked my eyes wide open. I *thought* that Ananda Panda rang a bell.

"Starchild!" I snapped my fingers. "Moonfree!"

The lady looked at me warily. "You—knew our late furry earthpartners?"

"The dead hamsters, right? Sure. And I know Mr. Izanagi, too. Where is he?"

"In there." Frost twinkled on her every word. I guess I wasn't speaking with proper respect for the dearly deep-sixed varmints. The teacher pointed in the direction of the transformed building.

"Still? But you got out. Why didn't he?"

"They let us go—me, Mr. Carlysle, Brittany. *He's* the only one they want." She didn't envy Mr. Izanagi his popularity one bit.

The big man, Carlysle, came to join us. "Look, I'm in a hurry; I've got places to be. What's going on here? I'm supposed to pick up my niece and—"

He reached for the lady's shoulder. Yang's broad fingers closed delicately around the man's wrist. "I'm sorry. All our operators are busy. Please stay on the line and the next available operator will take your call." The Mongol showed me his teeth. "See? Don't tell me Yang never learns nothing new!"

Carlysle pulled away from Yang, grumbling something about uppity firemen that made no sense to me at all; not just then.

I was still trying to pinpoint what had turned the Ananda Panda school into the ultimate in performance art. "You said *they* let you go. Who are *they*?" I asked the harried teacher.

She looked me right in the eye. "You come riding up here on *that*"—she meant Donahue—"and ask who *they* are? I didn't take names, if that's what you mean, but there are about seven of them, and they all want a piece of the action."

"*Seven?*" This was far and away worse than Mrs. Klauser's case. "Are you sure?"

I was not making any points by questioning the lady's information. "Perhaps you don't know," she said in a way that implied I was lucky to know which end to put my jeans on. "Mr. Izanagi is Hawaiian."

"Oh, God." I knew what that meant, all right. There was a kid from Hawaii in my freshman Social Studies class. He liked to call himself a "poi dog"—what we'd call a Heinz Fifty-Seven Varieties pooch; you know, mega-mutt. He counted German, Chinese, Filipino, Samoan, Portuguese, and Irish folk in his immediate ancestry. If the continental U.S. is a melting pot of nations, Hawaii is a top-of-the-line Cuisinart, with more than half a dozen European cultures blending right in with the same number of Pacific peoples, the native Hawaiians, and any space invaders lucky enough to land there, for all I know.

This speaks highly of Hawaii's warm welcome to all comers, but it spells nightmare when you count the warring, turf-hungry Fey from all the different bloods Mr. Izanagi had in him. My guidance counselor was a one-man United Nations of Faerie. I dreaded what I was going to find inside that building. If I found the way to get *into* the building, in the first place. "So what happened? Why did Mr. Izanagi have to come here in the middle of the day anyhow? Brittany do a job on another rodent?"

"There have been no more—incidents." The glaciers moved south. "We are *very* pleased to say that Brittany has come to take full responsibility for her share of the planet. *She* exhibits no reactionary post-Linnaean prejudices concerning our less highly placed brethren in the Great Chain of Being."

It struck me that some of the links in this Great Chain could stand a little tightening.

"In fact," the lady went on, "we asked Mr. Izanagi to pick up his daughter because the dear child read her 'Elegy Upon a Favorite Snail-Darter Snared in a Set of Plastic Six-Pack Rings' and was emotionally overcome." She wiped away a tear or two of her own. "Such a wonderful change in her ecological consciousness."

I looked at T'ing. T'ing looked at me. Brittany Izanagi was a living legend at Glenwood High, an urban myth after the fashion of the exploding poodle in the microwave oven and the severed head in the abandoned hatbox. There was no need to guess the true cause behind this miraculous transformation, and the answer was *not* oat bran.

Another changeling.

"Go on," I directed. "Mr. Izanagi came in; then what?"

"Then—" She spread her hands. "Then chaos."

"Accurate," piped a sweet voice behind me, "but hardly specific." I looked over one shoulder and saw Brittany Izanagi. "Greetings, lord."

I turned around and squatted down to her level. "I see you know who I am."

"As you know me, more or less." Amazing how pretty the little girl's face looked when it wasn't contorted by a tantrum. "You have met my father, Lord Palamon."

"Ah." I got down on one knee. "Sorry. I didn't realize I was in the presence of royalty."

"Brittany!" The nursery school teacher was flabbergasted. *"You?"*

Old, old eyes in a young face toned down the teacher's shrill astonishment. "Really, Ms. Five Bear, considering the intensity of Fey occupation among the Ananda Panda faculty, you should hardly be surprised." The elf-lord's daughter took me aside. "All of them. Not a single one unchosen."

"I sort of suspected that," I replied. A very firm suspicion when our motley crew rode up on phouka-back and the lady ran *at* us, not *away*.

"We like to think of it as spirit-world validation of our holistic pedagogic philosophy," Ms. Five Bear said demurely.

"*We* like to think of it as any port in a storm," Brittany whispered. Aloud she added, "Ms. Five Bear herself was in the care of an especially industrious *tomte*, for a while, until she made the mistake of renting a video of *The Seventh Seal*."

"So?"

"The tomten are *Swedish* sprites, lord." The changeling sounded just like any small child forced to put up with adult thickheadedness. "You know how melancholy they can get. Screening a Bergman out where a tomte could see it—You might as well forget about getting any more work out of him for the next decade, and that's only until he works through all of his futility-of-life meditations. Ironic detachment will take him even longer, and somber resignation—"

"I'm sure it will," I said. "But Five Bear doesn't sound all that Nordic."

"I was born Lucia Bergstrom, okay?" the lady under discussion snarled. "So my tomte mopes; so sue me. Now can we drop it and *do* something about the nursery school from Hell?"

Gee, Toto, I don't think we're being holistic anymore.

"You still didn't tell me how you all got out."

"If I knew, I'd tell. One minute, I was asking the gentlemen if they'd like some ginseng tea, the next I saw those—those—"

"Poltersprites," Brittany said with the bored detachment of a normal child going through her multiplication tables. "Kami, domoviye, drakes, brownies, *menehune*, and wights."

"—*things* come storming through the door. Before I could say a word, they jumped poor Mr. Izanagi, and when I tried to grab him—" She stopped explaining. There was no explanation she could give. "We were here, on the street, and the school was just the way you see it."

I beckoned Teleri and the gang into a huddle. "Can they do that? Just *vip*, and transport humans somewhere else?"

"One spirit alone of those Her Highness mentioned should not have so grand a power," the banshee murmured. "Together, though, with all their several small magics joined, there's little knowing how mighty an enchantment they could command."

"Any guesses?"

A pessimistic banshee is a sobering sight. "This much I'll tell ye, milord: Since we've arrived, I've tried and tried on the quiet to whisk myself up to one of yon windows, in hopes of bringing ye some intelligence of the ruckus inside."

"That would be helpful."

"So it would, if it were still possible." She shook her head. "I failed. Their concert o' powers bars the use o' our own. The Fey inside stand as one against any further invasions."

"Fucking trade unions," said Yang.

Master Runyon offered a sliver of hope. "I should like to point out to you that such a concerted harmonic combination of powers is as rare and fleeting as a chorine's affections. Very seldom are the Fey of different stripes able to agree for any length of time. If we were to practice a form of very second-story work indeed, thereby obtaining ingress to the premises, we might then be on the spot to sow discord among them, sabotage cooperation, and in general toss a monkey wrench into the works."

"And kick butt," Yang suggested. T'ing gave him a noogie.

"I'm with the barbarian," Neil said. "Only one question." He tilted his head back to observe our goal. "How do we get up there?"

"I really appreciate this, Mr. Carlysle," I said. The big man clasped my hand reluctantly and started up the five feet of non-existent stairs leading to the actual front steps of the Ananda Panda school. Everyone else fell into place in a human chain behind us.

"I just want to get going," he grunted. When the man was willing to communicate with us at all, it was like collecting on a long-begrudged debt. *Not* exactly voted Most Sociable, was our Mr. Carlysle, and not exactly on the same wavelength as the rest of us.

"He thinks you're firemen and that this is a drill," Ms. Five Bear/Bergstrom whispered. "When the creatures seized Mr. Izanagi and flashed us out of the school, he came away with a perfect recollection of walking out in orderly fashion under his own power. He can't *see*—you know—"—she nodded at Yang,

Teleri, and Master Runyon—"as they really are." She confided this to me before we began our assault on the floating brownstone.

"And what does he make of Donahue, there?" I thumbed to the phouka, who was blissfully submitting to the caresses of the elfin "Brittany," like any earthly horse spoiled rotten by an adoring little girl.

"Fire truck."

"Oh." I pondered this information. "He looks pretty strong, maybe we can get him to help us get into the building, give us a leg up, something like that. You know, appeal to his sense of public spirit."

Ms. Five Bear looked doubtful. "I wonder if he's got one. When we were speaking in my office before, waiting for his niece Melissa to come in from free-play period, he seemed so— empty. He talked about picking her up like she was an extra bottle of milk. I tried to call Melissa's mother and double-check about him, but there was no answer. There *is* a Mr. Peter Carlysle listed in the child's file as someone to call in case of anything." Her frown deepened. "I wish I'd have met him before this; he's hard to talk to, and a crisis isn't the best time to get to know someone. He's so *impatient*! I can understand him being in a hurry if there's a family emergency, but he never once volunteered any specifics about what sort of emergency it is."

"He's not the chatty kind." I dismissed the teacher's doubts too flippantly. "First we have to get your school back to normal, then you can sort out this guy's family problems." I studied the airborne school and rubbed my chin. "If he doesn't see fey things as they are, I wonder how he's seeing *this*."

I found out when I asked him. "Different?" Mr. Carlysle repeated my question. "What do you mean? Why should I see anything different?" He tapped his wristwatch crystal. "Is this drill going to take much longer? The building's evacuated. Can't the children go back inside?"

I temporized. "Not really. Ms. Five Bear, here, tells me that somebody may still be in there—a visitor who doesn't know the correct fire-drill procedure. We can't sound the official all-clear until we get the premises totally vacated."

"Well, *vacate* them. If that visitor's still inside, what are you doing just standing around? Go get him *out*. I'm in a hurry. I've got to get my niece and get going."

Brittany sidled up to us. "Who is your niece?" she asked in that angelic changeling voice.

Soft and sweet as it was, the sound startled Mr. Carlysle badly. He seemed to hesitate. I put it down to the shock of having a child speak up so boldly to a total stranger, especially what with all the cautions kids get taught these days. "Melissa Torrigiano," he said.

"You mean Lissie?" Brittany inquired.

"Yeah." He came near to making the answer sound like another question.

Lord Palamon's daughter wrinkled her nose. "You sure?"

That was a weird question, even for a changeling. Mr. Carlysle ignored it and spoke to me instead. "Look, can I maybe do something here to help get this operation moving?"

I smiled. "I was hoping you'd say that."

Disbelief is a wonderful thing. It's got the power to strike ordinary mortals selectively deaf and blind. Compared to it, simple faith in things not stamped Unconditionally Approved and Sanctified by Modern Science is like the first fragilely blooming snowdrop of March next to an August stand of crabgrass, or a butterfly compared to a musk ox.

Still, if you want to climb a set of stairs that's no longer there, it helps to have a deaf, blind, crabgrass-eating musk ox on your team who *refuses* to see things as they are. That was how we all climbed up to where the actual front steps began, by holding onto Mr. Carlysle's imagination disability. Donahue watched our ascent from the street. Seeing a supposed fire truck accompany us might have been too much for even Mr. Carlysle's stolid mind.

"Lot of steps to this school," Mr. Carlysle mumbled as we trod on nothingness. "Seems like more than the other buildings. That's weird."

"Zoning, man," Neil told him. "Totally warped zoning regs, you know?" The Rawbone King had a touch of the poet in him after all, or just a healthy gift of the blarney. His explanation didn't make sense, but it invoked the great god Bureaucracy, which never does. Mr. Carlysle accepted it; it was mumbo jumbo, but it was *his* tribe's mumbo jumbo. One man's UFO is another man's angelic visitor is a third guy's swamp gas.

He didn't even crab when we insisted on having him go first, all of us holding hands. (I was counting on Mr. Carlysle's rock-hard pragmatism being conducted through the whole team by physical contact, sort of like electricity. Surprise! It worked.)

We just called it Section XXII-A, Paragraph Three, Sub-paragraph 805-g (See Footnote) of the New York City Interim Fire Code. Regulations. Rules. Rigmarole. Procedures. Laws and Orders. Abracadabra.

The sky-clad door wasn't locked. Once inside the school, we didn't need to hold onto our mundane human talisman. I asked Ms. Five Bear to lead the way to her office. I figured the invading sprites were holed up there, dickering over who had the best claim to Mr. Izanagi's hide.

"I can take you!" Brittany chirped. She'd insisted on coming with us. It seemed like a good idea at the time. If I couldn't command the compliance of the renegade sprites by flashing my totally nonfunctional wand, perhaps they'd pay some heed to the daughter of their nominal lord.

Anyhow, the elfin princess threatened to hold her breath until her face turned blue if I made her stay behind.

Now she raced through the school halls and up the interior staircase, curls flying. On the second floor she gestured at the door all the way at the end of the corridor. Multicolored flashes of light burned behind the frosted glass panel. The thunder of drums shook tiles loose from the floor which, once free, took off like a squadron of fighter jets. They looped, soared, and dived through the air until blasts of raw energy lasered through the keyhole and shattered them.

Along the walls, the kids' tempera paintings of happy bears and roly-poly kitties turned into a hideous gaggle of green ta-rantulas as big as hassocks. They rushed us, buzzsaw teeth snapping. For the first time, I found a use for my Champion's wand. When I bashed it down on one of those man-eating divots, the beastie stayed bashed. Yang whomped all he could, his sword dripping what looked like mint-flavored gel toothpaste. Master Runyon's golden shoemaker's hammer did for some more. Teleri and T'ing had no weapons, but they managed to cooperate, grabbing opposing legs on the same monster and playing Snap the Wishbone; nauseating to watch, but effective. I decided I never wanted to have both of them angry at me at the same time. Neil went into a Bruce Lee crouch and made a jackass of him-self, stomping the crawlers while shrieking, "You killed my brother, insidious villain. Now you die!" He kept his mouth moving after he stopped talking. If there's a future for kung-fu movie mimics, the boy is set for life.

Ms. Five Bear screamed at the spiders that she was their earth-sister who came in peace. One of them bit her in the ankle. The lady got *mad*. "Go share someone else's planet, you miserable hairballs!" she shouted, taking off one shoe and dishing out some hefty grief on their arachnid heads.

Mr. Carlysle took Brittany's hand and stepped out of the path of the shaggy terrors, grumping something about writing a letter to the Fire Commissioner to amend Sub-paragraph 805-g. He and the changeling child disappeared into one of the empty classrooms as the rest of us finished off the giant spiders and reached the office door.

An abrupt, uneasy calm settled over the hall. There were no more odd sights or sounds, as if we had bought a truce by reducing the green tarantulas to gummy coleslaw. It was quiet; *too* quiet; so quiet you could hear an old World War II movie how-quiet-was-it cliché drop. I gingerly touched the doorknob with the spider-gooped tip of my wand. When nothing went *kaplooie!* I ventured my hand. The knob turned easily and I opened the door.

"—worked through your anger very thoroughly, Oki-Tsu-Hiko-*sama*. Now, don't you feel better?" Mr. Izanagi leaned on one corner of Ms. Five Bear's desk twiddling a pencil. On the floor at his feet, seven sprites of markedly distinct appearance sat in a loose semicircle.

"*Hai.*" The little figure in a gorgeous silk kimono tucked his hands into the trailing sleeves and bowed deeply.

"*Arigato,* Izanagi-*sama.*" He dashed a few beads of sweat from his high brow. Four explosions of magenta fire went up where the droplets hit the floor. "In future, I shall strive to rechannel all hostile feelings toward Boris-*sama.*"

A domovoy who looked close kin to Mom's bannik made a series of deprecating noises. "Bah, is no need! Come, *tovarisch* Oki, we forgive, we forget, we are all brothers here, *da*?" He enfolded the exquisitely dressed Japanese spirit in a hairy hug.

Mr. Izanagi was in hog heaven. "Isn't that wonderful, group? Say, why don't we all try to get in touch with these good feelings? Group hug, everyone!" As I watched, the seven assorted Fey and my guidance counselor fell into a mass snuggle. One broke away, sobbing.

"My last master, in Devonshire! Left 'is jacket in t' pantry by accident an' I takes it for a gift o' clothing. Never do stay where they give us brownies gifts o' clothes, we don't. Left before I give 'im t' chance t' explain things. Now 'tis dead an' gone 'e be, these many years, an' 'tis too late t' tell 'im as I'm sorry.'' He wept into his shaggy paws while a fiery drake in Louis XIV finery and a noise-making poltersprite with lederhosen and a boom-box tried to comfort him.

"Oh, that's good, Wat, that's very, very good." Mr. Izanagi got down on his knees with them. "Let it all out, work *through* your grief, come to terms with your browniehood. Group, can we help Wat out, here?"

Then he looked up and saw me and my contingent goggling through the open door. "Tim, this is a *closed* encounter group meeting. These people have a *lot* of unresolved cathexes to deal with. I am not expecting to see you again until Wednesday, at school. This time please try to confront your unresolved Oedipal tendencies by some means other than threatening to stick certain portions of my anatomy into the pencil sharpener."

"Happened when I was being you. Stupid goat-bugger called me *paranoid*," Yang seethed in my ear. "I think he's out to get me."

"Yes, Mr. Izanagi," I said, backing out and shoving everyone else along with me. "Sorry, Mr. Izanagi. Uh—Just one thing. Would your group members mind—um—coming to terms with the architectural trauma they've got going here?"

"Put down the building!" Yang barked over my shoulder. "And cut the horseshit!"

A dark brown sprite in lei and tapa-cloth loinwrap toddled up to the Mongol. "Chee, brah, you get one pilau mout'. You like beef o' wot? No make li' dat. We fix 'um, yeah?" As he spoke, I felt the school settle gently earthward. Our collective sigh of relief made him smile. "Some good, eh? Laydah." He waved us off with a hang-loose hand sign.

"Thank you, Kimo," Mr. Izanagi said. "Now, group—" He was getting back to playing shrink to the preshrunk and we were pulling out of the room when the telephone rang. Mr. Izanagi answered it.

"Oh, Ms. Five Bear?" he called, hand over the mouthpiece. "It's for you. A Mr. Peter Carlysle. He says he's been delayed a couple of hours at work, so he won't be picking up Melissa Torrigiano for her grandmother's birthday party until—"

That was when we heard the scream.

25

With a Single Step

NEIL WAS THE first to reach the closed classroom door. He tried the knob and found it locked just as the rest of us came bowling into him. While we sorted ourselves out, I could hear the interweaving fragments of two distinct conversations, one from back in Ms. Five Bear's office, the other from inside the locked room.

"—Carlysle told one of the men he works with to call you earlier, Ms. Five Bear. Didn't he—?"

"—*know* you're not Lissie's uncle! You're no kin to her at all! We can tell. We recognize what's in the blood. You don't have—"

"—me that phone! Mr. Carlysle? This is Ms. Five Bear. What does this man you work with look like? Is he big? Tall? Do you know where he is right—?"

"*Quiet!* You're a nice little girl, so you just calm down and I'll give you something—"

Yang squirmed free of the pileup and eyed the lock significantly. Sword drawn, he pulled back his leg and kicked the lockplate with all his strength. The jamb groaned, and a crack showed. He gave it another bash. Long splinters starred out around the metal.

"Don't sweat it, man. Allow me." Neil insinuated himself between Yang and the door, inhaled deeply through his nose, let out a lunatic yell, and whirled into a mule-kick that tore the bolt free of the surrounding wood. The door flew open as Neil collapsed onto Teleri's shoulder. "Oh, shit, that hurts. Son of a *bitch*, that's the last time I try that. I think I broke my ankle."

He looked into the room and saw the false Carlysle holding Brittany fast by one twisted arm.

"On the other hand"—Neil's eyes narrowed—"I think maybe I'll break somebody else's neck."

We strode in, shoulder to shoulder. I felt our cold loathing of the man like an armored shell around us. I wondered whether he could see it. I hoped he could.

How was he seeing us? As New York firefighters gone mad? I don't think so. Sometimes you don't need the powers of Faerie to give you the true Sight. Illusions can't survive the fires of hate and fear, not even one man's illusion of a comforting "reality" that lets monsters walk among us as if they're human beings.

He backed away from us slowly, still holding onto the changeling Brittany. He had her pulled in front of him, a living shield, even though none of us had firearms. Lord Palamon's daughter whimpered. Elfin or mortal, a child is still just a child. When you steal away the one thing her world is built on—that all grownups, kin or not, care enough to keep her safe from harm—you've committed the crime. Abuse and murder are only bloody-minded afterthoughts.

Even children can fight back, though. I saw pulses of bright panic emanating from her, warping the air around her and the monster. Under my breath, in my mind, I urged her to call up some measure of magic to turn against him. All I saw was her fear. In the instant of any assault, so many adults freeze like headlight-taken deer, forgetting every glib scenario for self-defense they ever made while reading crime reports in the papers. *Oh, that would never happen to me. I'd scream. I'd run. I'd do thus-and-so. I wouldn't be a helpless victim.* But when the time comes, everything flees but fear. Did I expect better of a baby, even if her father was the lord of all Faerie?

"Let her go." Yang stood at my right hand. His voice scraped the blade's edge over naked skin.

Neil darted out to my left. He grabbed a heavy wooden yardstick from the chalkboard and broke it over one knee. He jabbed the jagged end through the air like a spear-point. "You heard the man. Let her go."

Teleri and Master Runyon flanked Yang. The luchorpan beat a dead-march with his hammer in the palm of his hand. The banshee's eyes shone with icy intent, and her face was sharp and pale. I clutched my wand so hard that the facets cut into the skin. A warm hand closed over mine, a grip full of alien strength.

The cool crystal warmed. T'ing elbowed Yang aside to take her rightful place beside me.

"Let her go. It's over for you," she said. She spoke so quietly to him that it startled me. Her warmth overrode the chill of hatred weighing down the air, pierced the wall of ice that was driving him from us. She took a step forward, letting go of my hand and the wand, stretching out her own in a coaxing gesture to the monster. Though he could see she carried no weapon, he cringed at her approach, dragging Brittany with him.

"Please," T'ing said, coming on. "You know you have no choice. It's over."

His tongue rasped over his dry lips. His free hand plunged into one pocket. A wickedly long and slender blade flashed from his fist. He laid it against the elf-child's cheek. "Leave me alone." The words seemed to come out of the last pit of darkness. Shadows seeped into the throbbing rings of light around the child, and the sob of wild winds bled through the silence of the room.

He backed away from us. Behind him, the classroom wall melted from pale blue to stormy gray. Plaster ran in fat white tears, bricks rippled open into a gateway. Beyond, bare-branched trees tore color from a roiling sky. The monster cast a quick glance over one shoulder and saw what waited to receive him. His eyes shone, welcoming the drear land, and he retreated faster.

Every step he took nearer the gate brought its own awful transformation. Brittany's tear-streaked face fined down to the fragile bones of the Fey. Her eyes bloomed, huge and haunted in a face grown luminous as a pearl. She was casting off her human semblance, returning to her true form. Though every other thing about her changed, her terror remained to twist and sour her elfin beauty. She stumbled, and the monster's knife-blade licked her skin. Its touch traced a line of livid blue that puckered into a worm-track scar.

He changed as well, her captor, though perhaps he never knew it. The constricting business suit he wore so awkwardly sagged from his body, the fabric belling out in the blast from the gray lands. Cloth ripped to tatters, tatters shredded into the coarse hairs of a shaggy coat covering his crouching body from neck to feet. Another step backwards, and his shoes touched the encroaching ground of the other place. Leather moaned, then vanished as moon-white talons sliced through, digging a sure grip into the gritty earth. He felt beneath his feet the cold soil of his spirit's true home, and he laughed. We saw the sharpness of his teeth. Triumphant in power, he flung the knife from him scornfully. It was a poor second to his claws.

I looked to my companions. One and all, we stood aghast at what had invaded our own world. Fear thrust hate aside to hold us by the heart, unable to move. I saw Teleri's lips form the word: *Leeside*. I recalled what I'd been told of how easy it was for any, fey or mortal, to enter there, but as for coming out again—

When you're a child, frightened, all you can think of is *away*! *Get away*! You never ask if you're escaping a bad situation for a worse. The haloed energy of the changeling's panic-stricken magic was fading as the monster dragged her with him deeper into the cold lands. She had opened the gateway, but he had sensed the kindred spirits awaiting him beyond. She felt her mistake too late, and screamed.

"Let me go! Let me go! I want my father!"

But they had passed the gateway. Darkness irised in around them, and the night devoured the sound of her voice as the passageway began to close.

"Come on!" My own cry clapped against my ears. I was running across the classroom floor, never looking back to see if anyone would follow me. The gateway to the Leeside lands was dwindling, the child-stealer racing off with his captive in tow. No second thoughts for me, no time. I saw a closing gateway, and I was damned if it was going to shut me out. I flung my arms across my face and leaped—

—and landed rolling on rough, dank ground, with dry weeds raking my face. I lost momentum rather suddenly when I rammed the roots of a huge oak tree. Sere leaves rustled in the branches, crunched under my hands and feet as I stood up and brushed dirt from the seat of my pants.

Hey, man, don't hassle it. It all comes out in the wash. A long-haired phantom in a granny gown drifted past me, bearing a plastic hamper full of soiled clothes. The apparition of the *bean nighe* Rowan o' Kinsale floated away down an alley of winter-stripped birches. I followed with my eyes until she was a match-flame wisp of white that disappeared in the distance.

I looked down and saw that I was now wearing the same pink sports shirt the *bean nighe* had been washing earlier. There was no blood on it; not yet.

"Pink isn't your color, Tim."

I whirled, straining my eyes to find the speaker. There was no sun to see by in the Leeside lands, only the stark, selfish light of an overcast winter's day.

"Here I am." T'ing sat with knees drawn up to her chest, her back resting against the oak. She gave me a halfhearted wave. "At least you're not done up like a total idiot." She stood, the better to show off the gorgeously embroidered silk robes and elaborately jeweled hairstyle that her passage into the Leeside had bought her. "I should count my blessings," she said, tottering up to me on delicate, cramping shoes. "They didn't bind my feet."

"Are you the only one who came through with me?"

She glanced around the stricken grove. "Looks like. Can you blame them?"

Yes, I could. For the first time I understood Mom's angry lectures about how everyone at work and at home always expected *her* to pick up their messes for them. Where was Neil, with his big-deal-streetfighter reputation? Where was Yang the Allegedly Dauntless Scourge? Where was Master Runyon, with his smooth line of talk? Where—this hurt worst—where was Teleri? Cowards. Cowards all. Damn it, how dare they cling to their fear and leave me alone with mine?

I'm not very good at hiding my feelings, especially the bad ones. T'ing must have read the bitterness in my face. She was too sharp to try talking me out of it. She just leaned on my arm and said, "If you help me revamp these stupid clothes into something I can *move* in, we can get going before the trail's cold."

"You'd think," I said a little while later, teeth clenched. "You'd honestly think this dumb hunk of rock would be good for *something*." I sawed at the excess fabric of T'ing's regal robes with the edge of my crystal wand, to no purpose. "Ow!"

"Cut yourself again?" T'ing stopped tying back her sleeves to look down at me solicitously.

I sucked the blood from the fleshy bridge between my left thumb and forefinger. "It's sharp enough for this, but it won't slice the cloth." I held up the wand and glared at it. "For two cents, I'd throw it away."

"Never mind, I'll just tuck up the length into my sash or something. Let's move." T'ing took off her dainty slippers and pitched them into a tall stand of feathery weeds.

"Ouch," said a martyred voice.

I went on the alert instantly, aiming the wand at the stir among the weeds. "Who's there? Come on out! Show yourself!"

The dry stalks rustled and parted before the majestic nose and twin moustache cataracts of the goblin Hobson. "Good day," he intoned in just the manner to assure you that it wasn't nor would it ever be.

My mouth tightened. "What are you doing here?"

"My duty."

"Oh, yes. I know all about your *duty*." My sarcasm made no visible impression on him.

"I do not believe you are as fully aware of it as you flatter yourself to be, milord," Hobson replied evenly.

"Yeah? Try me. You've come to bring Lord Palamon's daughter back, right?"

"Lord Palamon's—" In an instant, the goblin's expression went from melancholy resignation to appalled astonishment. "But—but my lady Eleziane is safe. I myself saw to the exchange. You must be mistaken, milord; you *must*."

Poor Hobson looked so undone that I felt a pang of the old fondness for the little goblin come stealing back into my heart. He was still jabbering about how we had to be wrong, when T'ing knelt beside him and delicately brought him the news.

"Oh! This is dreadful, dreadful!" He wrung his hands so vigorously that his twiggy fingers got tangled in his moustache. "Not even the Leeside still holds monsters to touch this mortal spawn. With these eyes I have seen the bloody-muzzled lamia lick her kittens tenderly, and the dragon go without his share of the prey so that his hatchlings might be fed. Yet you humans— Oh, it doesn't bear thinking of."

"Don't worry, Hobson." I found myself wanting to ease his mind, all thought of his earlier betrayal gone. "T'ing and I will help you rescue her. That's why we came through to the Leeside."

"I am well apprised of that, milord," Hobson snapped. His helpless sorrow blinked away, replaced by hard determination that would brook no nonsense. "I have been observing you at a distance for some time, concerned only with your welfare. You may believe that or not; it is immaterial. My *duty*, which you so scorn, may be to Lord Palamon first, but I did not swear myself into your service nor name you Champion lightly. Precedence, sir! Allegiance, too, must acknowledge priorities. Having discharged my *duty* to Lord Palamon, I have ever since devoted myself exclusively to clandestine attendance upon your person."

"Tap my phone, too?" I couldn't resist another dig.

Hobson tugged the lapels of his butler's uniform primly. "If I acted in secret, it was because I knew you found my presence distasteful. I have revealed myself to you now only because you issued a direct command to that effect. If you wish, I will remove myself from your sight."

"Leave me alone?"

"That, sir, I shall most emphatically *not* do."

"Not even if I give you another of those direct commands?"

"Sir, I swore myself into your service, and—"

"Well, swear yourself out!" I shouted, gesturing with the wand like I was some manic orchestra conductor. My grudge against him reasserted itself. "We don't need you."

He remained unruffled. "That may be so, milord. Now as ever, it is my folk who need you. I serve Lord Palamon, but my true vocation lies in the service of a chosen human: yourself. Indeed, by aiding you in the recovery of my sovereign's child, I shall be performing the highest of services for you and all your fellow mortals besides."

"Which is?" The goblin's unusual self-confidence brought out my direst skepticism.

"Milord, if you commanded as much power and as little restraint as Lord Palamon and someone stole *your* child, how might you react?"

He asked the question so guilelessly, letting each word sink in. It brought a score of possible outcomes to my mind. All shared the starting point of an elf-lord's revenge, and all contained absolutely nothing remotely like a pleasant ending. The damage an angry Lord Palamon and his folk could do to humankind was phenomenal. The spirits of hearth and home were small, but anyone can tell you it's the little things that can really get you.

"I see," I managed to say. "Does—does Lord Palamon know his daughter's been taken yet?"

"Not yet, milord."

T'ing took my hand, offered her other to Hobson. "Let's make it so he never needs to know."

Hobson's tufty brows rose. I witnessed the impossible: the lifting of the corners of his mouth into a chummy smile. He accepted her handclasp readily. "My poor services are at your disposal, milord, milady."

Not for the first time, I contemplated the ineffective symbol of my highflown title. "Your poor services can do a heck of a lot more than mine."

He cocked his head. "Ah, yes. The Dread and Puissant Champion's wand of office. That quite reminds me." The goblin dipped his fingers into the several pockets of his uniform. A slip of pale blue paper glimmered in the barren Leeside light.

"What is—?" I unfolded it and read:

WUNDA-WAND!
Astound Your Friends! Confound Your Foes!
Solid-State Capability and Reliability
For the Mage Who Knows
Assembled in U.S.A. from parts mfrd. in Tir na nOc
(Some Disrobing Required)

"The directions, milord," intoned the little goblin. He dug into another pocket and his clenched hand came out glowing like a rainbow. "And the batteries."

26

Professional Courtesy

THE COTTAGE NESTLED in a little glade, its door overhung with blue-black ivy, the small herb garden a tangled puzzle of unwholesome-looking weeds. The tug of the crystal wand was unquestionable, its dull orange glow flaring yellow the closer we came to the crooked green door.

Was it my imagination, or had that door been a little more to the *right* when I first spotted it?

"In there?" I paused at the edge of the wildwood. The crystal wand had gone from fractious to user-friendly too quickly for me to trust its directives completely. I looked to Hobson for confirmation. The goblin knew the territory, or should know it after all those years trapped in the cold lands. "Whose house is that?"

Hobson pondered the question. "I fear that this purlieu lies far from my own accustomed haunts, milord. We domestic spirits inhabited the more thickly settled portions of the Leeside. Strength in numbers, and all that. This bijou abode is far too cozy to shelter monsters"—he shuddered; we had glimpsed more than a few uncanny shadows on our way here—"yet too isolated for it to belong to one of my breed."

A scrawny rook cawed from the ridgepole, then keeled over and slid down the mossy tiles, dead. On the slats of an old rain barrel up against the side of the house, turkey-tail fungus stirred as a greeny-gray tentacle whipped out, lassoed the feathered corpse, and reeled it in. Loud slurpings and crunchings came from the barrel. If this was Hobson's idea of cozy, I didn't want to see his interpretation of a handyman's special.

"Milord, if the wand indicates that this should be our path, we ought to heed it," Hobson urged. "You *have* committed to memory the proper spells for converting it from tracking device to offensive weapon, just in case?"

"Oh, yeah, sure." I lied. I had the instruction sheet wadded up into a small, damp ball in my jeans pocket. I'd read through it; once. Every time I thought about it, my stomach turned over.

I am no good at following directions. If Teleri hadn't totaled my chances at the PSAT exams, I probably would have done it to myself. Mind you, that's with plain, simple, *English-written* directions. The how-to sheet for the wand was scrawled in high-tech thee-thou-ese. I got as far as "Forbear ye, under penalty of ye most stringent banns, to impinge ye devices of a most arcane and aweful power into ye bodye of ye wande, lest perforce ye summon forth forces against which ye wot not ye means to con-trolle." (All that, and I *think* it means "Don't overload the cir-cuits.") The only reason the wand worked now was that Hobson had booted it for me, asking if I understood. I just watched and nodded and smiled and acted like it was the simplest thing in the world. He kept telling me it was.

Maybe I could find a way to make him convert the wand from tracker to smacker when the time came. Meanwhile I'd devote myself to earnest prayer that I'd never need to use the crystal for anything but peaceful purposes.

My prayers would *not* be answered if there was something nasty lurking in that cottage.

"Uh—Let's not rush into anything here," I suggested as Hob-son started marching out of the woods. "Why don't we just *ease* up to the place, take a peek in the window, see if the wand's got it right?"

Hobson took umbrage. "Milord, are you questioning the workmanship of your wand? It's not as if it were one of those shoddy foreign jobs, a *thyrsus*, or some such trash."

T'ing couldn't have stepped in more promptly to smooth Hob-son's ruffled fur than if I'd cued her. "I think Tim's right. Noth-ing against the wand, Hobson, but if the beast is in there with Lord Palamon's child, we'd better not startle him. Who knows what he'd do then?"

The goblin's eyes grew moist with distress. "By no means, milady. Oh, certainly not! If any harm should come to Lady Eleziane—" His voice caught.

"None will." T'ing was wonderful. "Not if we're careful."

We crept up on the cottage as a ground fog came inching out of the trees on the far side of the glen. I shivered. There was as little way of keeping track of earthly time while in the Leeside as when in Lord Palamon's realm. I didn't know how long we'd been in the gray lands, but I did know I'd felt cold from the first. The chill of the Leeside had a way of sneaking under your skin, leaving you with the conviction that you'd never be warm again.

"Do you see a window?" I whispered to T'ing.

"Hard to tell," she replied. "The walls are so low and the roof hangs over so much, there might be one hidden under the eaves. Say, wasn't the door over on *that* side of—? Oh, never mind. We'll have to get closer. How's the wand?"

"Still pulling." That was the truth. The crystal shaft had gone from pale amber to the color of champagne, and its vibrations left my palm tingling. It wanted the cottage, it wanted *in* the cottage, and it wanted it *now*.

A four-paned square of ochre glass high up one wall glimmered with jack-o'-lantern light. I volunteered to play the spy, balancing on a stack of logs as I chinned myself over the grimy sill. Through the pocks and air bubbles and ripples in the thick panes, I made out the fire-backed silhouettes of a sturdy table and four chairs, three of them occupied. A hearthside bench supported four additional—people? It was impossible to see the inhabitants as more than vague bulks. There was the rumble of talk, a snatch or two of song, and the heavy thunk of earthenware mugs knocking together. It all seemed very festive until you remembered all the stories of trolls, giants, and plain human outlaws throwing themselves a post-massacre party.

The wand was burning blue-white now. I thought I'd better stick it into my belt before one of the revelers inside caught sight of such a bright beacon in the window.

Remember what I said about never getting warm again? I was wrong. My wand was plenty warm. Magic or mundane, it answered the rule that where there's light, there's heat; lots of it. I felt the fire right through my pants and leaped up, yowling. The logs decided to go somewhere else. They rolled out from under my scrabbling feet as I tumbled backwards onto T'ing and Hobson.

"Get it out! Get it out!" I shouted, flapping my hands desperately as I groped for the wand. When you catch fire, they teach you to stop, drop, and roll until you smother the flames.

It doesn't work when you've got a mystic branding iron down your pants.

"If I may, milord." Hobson extricated himself from our impromptu huddle with deferential grace, then did the same for the wand.

Now I knew how the lion felt after Androcles pulled the thorn from its paw. I gabbled a stream of thanks, which washed over the impassive Hobson and left no trace.

"If you are quite done, milord?" He handed me the wand.

An axe-blade of light fell between us. A door now stood ajar where only a window had been before. "Is this what the blood's come down to, then?" A hearty voice boomed boldly out into the fog, defying all the mean-souled chill the Leeside could create. "Faith! And I thought ye said he'd been called fer a hero, sweetheart. A fine hero, as goes creepin' round the houses o' honest wizards like a common burglar. Are ye that, then, Timothy Alfred Desmond? Are ye a common hooligan, t' yer family's shame?"

Two beefy hands scooped me up and held me high, as if I were a child again. I saw a ruddy, joyous, open face that I'd seen only once before, and that time in gritty sepia tones in an old photograph album.

"Un—uncle?" It couldn't be, not even for me, and I was getting into the habit of impossibilities. "Uncle Seamus?"

The man roared like a walrus, firelit whiskers shaking with laughter. "*Great*-uncle to ye, I be, ye young rascal, and could be I'm that proud o' it, from the tales some have been tellin' me. Ah, but there's no trust t' be put in the poets. What's not moonshine's madness."

An outraged cry came from inside the cottage. "Bull*shit* it is, man!" I could name that tune in three notes: Neil Fitzsimmons. He appeared behind my great-uncle Seamus—Seamus the "fairy friend" who had vanished from his kinfolk's knowledge so many years ago, presumed dead—and looked ready to break some heads. "I told you guys everything like it is, okay? You're in so thick with the Fey, *you* go ask 'em who their Dread and Puissant Champion is, huh? Go calling *me* no liar. Hey! You put Tim down when I'm talking to you!"

"T' be sure, t' be sure." Seamus lowered me to the ground. I was fairly unnerved by the manhandling I'd just gotten at the hands of my long-gone ancestor, but that was just a minor upset next to the successive traumas I got as first Neil, then Yang, then

Master Runyon, and finally Teleri came to crowd the cottage doorway.

"What took you so long?" Yang demanded. He glowered at T'ing. "You and my beloved granddaughter been having sex?"

"This is grave, Tim." Uncle Seamus rested his elbow on the table and took a long drink of beer. "Very grave."

"We know. Can you help us?"

He leaned back in his chair and studied the bare-beamed ceiling. Bunches of strange herbs hung drying there, some glass flasks in red and blue and green, and several stuffed beasties that looked like the Hades Highway road-kill. Behind him, by the fire, the owner of the cottage fussed over a steaming cauldron and mumbled to himself in German. He wore a frowsty set of wizard's robes, thick with astronomical symbols and speckled with dandruff. Over the mantelpiece, between an autographed first edition of the *Fairfax Daemonologia* and an Elvis Presley bourbon decanter, hung his diploma: Iohannes Faust, Ph.D.

The brew in the cauldron kept bubbling over and swamping the fire. The wizard was constantly obliged to add dry fuel and use a crystal wand that was great-granddaddy to mine to rekindle it every few minutes. He was aided by a hideous, bow-legged, hip-high manikin with a face like a walnut meat and a werewolf's fanged under-bite. Hobson kept his back turned to Dr. Faust's assistant, his brown cheeks flushed with shame. No wonder. I could still hear the raucous greeting the little goblin had received from him:

"Arrh! Hobsie, there ye be at last! Coom gi' yer Ooncle Caliban oon wee whifsy, do!"

God knows what a *whifsy* is, but Hobson gave his black sheep uncle neither whifsy, reply, nor time of day. The boggart shrugged and went about his chores.

My friends and colleagues had dragged the fireside bench up to the table. Everyone except T'ing and me had a fat mug of beer. It didn't do any good reminding Neil he wasn't old enough to drink legally. No one checks your ID in the Leeside. Neil reasoned that if you're old enough to avoid being chomped, rended, bashed, or blood-drained by the legendary monsters still trapped in the gray lands, you've earned the right to down a few cold ones.

Waiting for Uncle Seamus to answer made me antsy enough

to regret being so strait-laced about surface-world rules. My mouth was dry and getting drier. "Uncle Seamus—?"

"Half a minute, lad, I'm ponderin'. Ye say yon wand brought ye here, and so it must've been t' some purpose. T' find yer friends as followed ye, that's it. It's nothin' t' do wi' me. Be on yer way, follow it yet. 'Tis a better guide fer ye than ever I'll be."

Suddenly I understood something about my great-uncle; something none too pleasant. "You're afraid to come with us."

His mug struck the tabletop like a mallet, splashing foam. "And am I? Not wi'out cause! I left yer world behind me when I passed into Faerie. Safe wrapped in their magic, I was glad t' go wherever they ventured, and when the cruel blind eyes o' mortal men refused t' see the Gentry more, I followed me truest friends into exile."

He eyed the contents of his mug sadly. "Now the ban is broken. Now they're gone t' seek th' sun, and dance 'neath th' moon, and never a backward glance. Where does that leave me?" Tears trickled over his laugh-wrinkled cheeks. "I loved 'em, Tim. I loved 'em all truer than ever I loved a mortal soul, and here's the payment fer all my loving."

I patted his huge hands. "You can come back with us, Uncle Seamus. I know Mom won't mind; we're family. Maybe we're not as pretty as the Fey, and we don't give as good parties, but we'll always stick by you. Come home."

"Home . . ." Seamus' sigh ended in a groan. "There's the full measure o' what I've forfeited. Years have rolled over th' earth. Time waits fer me on th' far side o' th' portal, ready t' rend me into dust if I set foot over. Ye've mounted a hunt, young Timothy! Who's t' say where th' quarry may run? He's mortal yet, fer all he's a monster, and mortals may leave the Leeside lands wherever the pull o' their lives is strongest. We want no special gateway! What's t' become o' me if the chase turns hot, and the prey leaps free o' the dark lands, and I run after him, unheeding?" He shook his head sadly. "If I'm afraid to die, 'tis only fer having had so many years t' contemplate death's full meaning."

Uncle Seamus rose from the table. I thought I saw sorrow in his eyes as he gazed at me. His touch was surprisingly gentle when he took one point of my shirt collar between his fingers. "I see as ye've a fear or two o' yer own t' contemplate, lad. I've an eye fer what's been part o' *her* washin'." He took a deep breath. "And still ye go, huntin' down what may be yer own doom?"

I folded my hands over the crystal wand. "I have to take the chance. I can't let him get away with this. A child's in danger."

"So there is, Tim." Uncle Seamus walked to the cottage door, which had now moved itself near the fireplace. A curved bull's horn banded with silver hung there, suspended from a rusty nail by a cord of braided blue leather. Uncle Seamus took it down and opened the door. He blew three short blasts into the gloom, and one long, wailing cry.

"There," he said, coming back to me. "That'll do it."

"Do what?"

"Why, be fetchin' ye th' help I'm too much th' craven t' give ye. Ha! Hark t' that, now." He cupped his ear and smiled. "Never a call come t' him yet but that he answered it timely. A hero's heart, true t' th' blood. Ye've a right t' be proud o' him there, and he o' you."

A fearful suspicion gathered in my heart. My chest grew heavy, as if the rolling fog outside were pouring into me like lead. A knock sounded at the door, a special rapping pattern I had heard before, too long ago. Hobson's uncle Caliban toddled across the room to answer it, but I got there first.

"Please." The boggart growled at me, but he stood aside. I pulled the latchstring and let the door swing back by its own weight.

His sword was sheathed, his boots were dirty. I couldn't tell the last time he'd had a bath, or shaved, or combed his hair. There was a deep weariness in his eyes, and fighting that a clear, ready gaze. He stared at me for a time that held all the years that had been stolen from us.

Then my father threw his arms around me and wept.

27

Crystal Visions

WHAT A HUNTING pack we were, barging through the trees, snapping more dry twigs underfoot than a passel of B-flick Nazi spies. Only Teleri and my father managed to move without alerting the immediate world—she because she'd opted to float along, he thanks to his dear-earned woodcraft. They led us, with the rest of the order of march left pretty much to individual talents. If you could keep up, you were in the fore; if not, too bad.

My wand had been benched, stuck in my back pocket after Hobson "talked me through" the process for taking it out of tracking mode. It wasn't necessary anymore, not with my father's sharp eye for a trail and my banshee right there to give him heavy moral support.

My banshee? I no longer held sole title. This little jaunt into the gray lands had turned into a treasure hunt for Teleri. Imagine how she felt, family banshee to the last of this branch of the Desmond clan, and suddenly there are *two* additional Desmonds for her to cherish. Granted, one of them is an eternal prisoner of the Leeside, by his own choice, but there won't be any trouble at all about bringing the other one back to the surface world. Dad would age some when we emerged, but he'd be far from crumbling to dust like Uncle Seamus.

"There." Dad pointed at a prickly stand of blackberry bushes. A scrap of fine white linen flapped from a thorn. He motioned for me to join him as he studied the embroidered clue. "Torn from a cuff, judging by this handwork."

I nodded. I had no idea how he could tell, but these were the most words he'd addressed to me since our reunion and I didn't want to lose them.

He touched the bramble from which he'd picked the cloth. "The right height for a child's sleeve. We're getting nearer." He broke into the easy jog-trot of a seasoned forest runner, without bothering to ask whether we could keep up with him.

Teleri had no problem, and Master Runyon's short legs were astonishingly powerful. Neil had the practice—he'd be the first to tell you how many miles he'd logged running away from the scene of the crime, the cops, rival gangs, and his old man's heavy hand—but as for the rest of us . . .

T'ing's robe worked itself loose from her belt and tripped her. She fell full-length in the powdery dry crushed leaves. Her cry fetched the front-runners back and gave poor, winded Hobson the chance to catch up. I was right there.

"You okay?" I tried to pick her up, but she didn't need me. This was getting to be a trend.

Dad didn't give her the chance to answer. In his hunter's leathers he stood above us in silent reproof. "You're ill-dressed for what we have to do," he told her.

"This wasn't my choice," T'ing answered. She didn't raise her voice, but I could tell she wasn't in the mood for a lecture, no matter how short. "It happened to me when Tim and I jumped through the portal. Fashions haven't changed *this* much."

"I see." Dad got down with us and examined T'ing's courtly dress. "Something like that happened to me when I first came over." His lips curved up, but his eyes were wistful. "I was just going to the corner for a newspaper—"

"And the deli," I put in. "You said you were going to get us some cold cuts and we'd have a picnic."

"Did I?" He gave me a vague look. He hadn't been talking to me. "Anyhow, I heard a cry for help. If I would've been a normal person, I'd have run the other way—to 'get help,' you know." T'ing had all his attention. "I didn't. I followed the call, and suddenly I was *here*." His eyes took in the whole grim panorama of the cold lands in a way that described their inescapability far better than words. "Here, dressed like this, and carrying a sword." He patted the scabbard at his waist.

"Were you afraid, Mr. Desmond?" T'ing wasn't annoyed with him anymore.

My father's eyes followed visions only he could see. "Funny to be called 'Mr. Desmond' again. The Fey didn't think too much of my given name—not glamorous enough for someone chosen to protect them, the conceited little bastards—so they took my middle name and altered it to suit them. Great Hern, they called me, after a legendary hunter-hero. I never thought of myself as much one or the other. The most I had to hunt up was the last copy of the Sunday *Times*." When he looked at her, he was like a man who suddenly realizes he's lost something. It hurt that he wasn't looking at me that way.

"Afraid . . ." he echoed. "I decided to be afraid after I did what I could to help whoever was still screaming. Such a big voice for such a little spirit! The monster chasing it was little, too, thank God. I should've had my head examined; I didn't know what I was going to fight, or how to fight it. I was lucky I knew which end of the sword to grab. I just knew that something had to be done. In the end, all I had to do was wave it around and holler enough to spook the ugly. Then I had lunch." He turned to me. "You were right about the cold cuts, Tim."

"So that was the first." A deeper chill than the cold lands ever spawned encased me. "And after?"

"After"—he was looking at T'ing again—"after, there were other calls, always others. I learned how to handle my sword before I got myself killed. I learned the ways of the land. I met your great-uncle here, and the doctor, when he was in residence. I think I would've gone crazy for someone human to talk to, otherwise. Our family have always had close links with the Fey, but friendship isn't family."

I knew it wasn't; better than he did, I knew. "You could've come home." I hadn't wanted the charge to come out so abruptly or sound so hard. I never intended to accuse him of a crime I couldn't fully put into words. "Any time you wanted, you could've left. You didn't have to wait for the Leeside to spring a leak. Humans can come and go as we please from the cold lands." My voice rose scornfully. "Or didn't you know?"

"I knew." It was nearly impossible to hear him with his face turned from me like that. "Uncle Seamus told me that soon after we first met. And the good doctor's comings and goings between Leeside and Outside are legendary."

"Then why didn't you leave?" I didn't care how many horrors I roused with my shout. "Why did you stay here? Why didn't you come back to us? Why didn't you come *home*?"

My father drew his blade and carefully cut off T'ing's finery to just below her knees. "There. Now you'll have it easier, miss.'' He helped her up and set out on the trail again, with no further words for any of us.

I stood there, my whole body taut, my throat too strangled with rage to let any sound escape. Why didn't he answer me? Damn it, he *owed* me that much—an answer, an explanation, an apology for everything he'd stolen from Mom and me by staying here. And for what? To nursemaid a bunch of imaginary creatures no sensible person wastes time thinking of? To protect the gentler dreams from the crueler ones? What kind of a man wastes his life fighting to defend dreams?

Why? Why had he made that choice? Why, when he had food to bring home and shelter to provide and all the little errands of daily life to take up his time? Why, when he had a warm, safe place to be where he could shut the door behind him and not have to think about the cold that lay beyond, or the beings who couldn't escape the cold?

''Tim—'' T'ing's smooth fingers undid the knot my fist had become. ''If we don't hurry, we'll lose them.''

For a minute, I wanted to say, *Good! Let them go! What's the worst that can happen? Lord Palamon's child dies, big deal. The monster's got a tally of other missing kids already; what's one more? Hey, she's scared? She needs someone? She wants her father? Well, she's not the only one! That's how it goes. Live on the surface-world, live tough. It's no business of mine.*

I couldn't. Every time I tried to force out the words, they snagged on my heart. *What's one more?* One too many. *It's no business of mine.* That's a lie.

My suffering is no justification for another child to endure the same. My imperfect life doesn't give me the right to wish worse on anyone else.

I drew my wand and cupped it in both hands. Hobson wasn't there to activate it for me. He had gone puffing on ahead, desperate to keep up with the group. At rest, unlit, the wand was still beautiful. Even in the dim light I could see my reflection along one facet. I never knew I looked that old.

Tim . . . My father's image spoke to me out of the depths of the stone. I almost dropped the wand. *No!* the image cried out. *Please wait; hear me. Listen to what I am too ashamed to say any other way than this. I am only a swordsman, but still—I've learned a little magic after all these years. The doctor is a fine teacher; you'll see. Hear me. Please, son. I've faced monsters here, and all those battles never took a tenth of the guts I need to say this, to speak to my own child.*

T'ing stepped behind me and saw the small face captive in the crystal. "Tim, what's your father doing—?"

"Sshhh." I wanted to hear. I brought the wand nearer to my eyes.

You heard what I said before, Tim? About being afraid only after I'd played the hero?

"Go on," I said hoarsely.

You were right; I could have come home any time I chose. Why didn't I? Because I was afraid; the hero, afraid. After all the fighting was done, after the Fey found their way free of the Leeside, when all that was left in this terrible realm were monsters and worse and I really wasn't needed any longer, I found the thought of going home more frightening than any dragon. How would I explain my absence to you and your mother? If I didn't love the two of you so much, it wouldn't have been so hard. What could I say that would be enough to heal the hurts? 'Hello, I was needed elsewhere so I forgot you needed me, too'? 'They called me a hero, gave me a legend, filled their children's eyes with worship every time they spoke my name'? 'I'm back now, so let's go on from here as if nothing happened'? No matter what I'd say, it would still come out sounding as if I'd taken the two people I love best and sacrificed their happiness in the name of my own damned pride.

"Dad . . ." My breath fogged the shining crystal for an instant. "Dad, it's all right. It will be. I think I—I think I understand."

The image was blurring, its contours running like a face reflected in a rain-streaked window. *What can you understand?* The voice was a wind-rustled husk. *That your father hasn't even got the courage to tell you this face to face? That you're the son of a coward?*

"Tim, the others—" T'ing was tugging at my sleeve. "We have to catch up to them."

"In a minute!" I jerked away, still staring into the crystal. My father's face began to fade, retreating into the wand's core. I couldn't tell whether he could hear, but I had to say it: "I do understand." The image was no more than a flake of flame. "And I love you."

The flake froze, shimmered. The breath of my words blew it gently into light that flowed the length of the wand. Radiant with a glow too rare to come from any source pure science could reduce to crisp equations, its fires sang to me. I heard them in my soul, in the place where you recognize the right thing to do, even if it's the crazy thing.

That's nothing special. Lots of people see the flame, hear the song, recognize what's crazy-right.

Doing it, though, no matter what you lose along the way . . . that's for heroes.

28

The Gift

"THERE HE IS; there!" Teleri clutched my father's shoulder, anchoring her floating body to his.

"Shh. I see." Dad squinted into the outlandish brightness that backlit the monster and his small prisoner. All of us shaded our eyes. After the unrelieved dimness of the cold lands, we faced a boundless sky that dazzled like the curve of a sunstruck shield.

Whatever hand had set the boundaries and formed the substance of the Leeside, in this place it had drawn a scene unlike any other. The gray lands stopped short at the edge of a perilous cliff. There was no horizon, only light, pure and blinding. I wondered what I would see if I could crawl to the brink of the abyss and look down. A weird, attractive force was pulling at me as I crouched in hiding with the rest in a thicket of trees. I drew my wand and felt the drag more strongly, even though it was no longer supposed to be tracking the monster.

Hobson noticed. "Milord will be thinking of home." He saw that I didn't understand him, so he elaborated. "The desire is often enough for a mortal to depart the Leeside at any point. However, you are most likely to emerge where the call of your surface life is strongest."

"I see. So that means I wouldn't pop up cross-town. There's a relief."

"Indeed, milord. Quite convenient, particularly as so few of our visitors here carry sufficient omnibus fare. And to further the principle of attraction, your departure would include any and all of those Fey in your company."

"Does that mean Neil would come out near his place?"

Hobson raised his brows. "In view of the gentleman's avowed distaste for his current domestic situation, I would think not. In dealing with a group of mortals—purely a theoretic situation for myself before this—I would assume that the strongest desire would be dominant. But of course"—he dropped his eyes modestly—"I am no physicist."

Neil poked me, ending the discussion. "What're we waiting for?" he whispered. "We've got him trapped. There's nowhere he can go."

"That's just it," I replied. "Nowhere but over the edge. He'd take her with him."

"So what do we do? Just stand here with a finger up our nose?" He glanced at the wand. "That stick good for anything besides carry-on baggage? Can't you use it on him somehow?"

"Remember what a *big* help it was in Mrs. Klauser's bakery, bright boy?" I wanted to do more than lurk, too, and I didn't appreciate Neil prodding me.

"What I remember is you pulling it outa that hunk of cake when no one else could. That *means* something, man. And you call me 'bright boy' all snotty like that again and you're gonna be trying your luck pulling it outa somewhere the sun don't shine."

My father spoke: "We're at the very limits of the Leeside. I've never come this far and I don't know what lies beyond. If we're going to rescue the child, some of us will have to distract him long enough for others to get her away. Above all, we don't want him to panic." We all agreed, and fell back to plan specifics.

A little while later, I lay on my stomach in the tall grasses and watched tensely as T'ing went gliding out of the scrubby growth to the monster's right. She had volunteered to play the lure. I tried to object, but when I caught the dangerous spark in her eye, I decided I'd save time and grief by retreating. The lady was resolved. She held her head high, the elaborate arrangement of braids and tresses still pretty much in place. The hem of her gown was hacked short, but the sleeves still trailed nicely when she undid the knots. As she walked, she softly crooned an Oriental melody—Near Oriental; "Hava Nagila" was the best she could call to mind under pressure.

The monster heard her, then saw her. His head jerked up, his whole body stiffened. He crouched very near the precipice, clutching the elf-child's arm. The lady Eleziane no longer screamed or cried. You need a hope of salvation if you're going to call for help, and she had given up hoping. She didn't even look up when T'ing appeared.

T'ing didn't try to get too close. She stopped far enough away from him to keep him calm, near enough to keep him distracted. She ran through her song a couple of times, then started talking. It was like before, in the school, when she'd been the only one to try coaxing him instead of commanding. He regarded her suspiciously, but I saw his grip on Eleziane shift from her arm to the tattered fabric of her sleeve.

I was down in the weeds to the monster's left, with Hobson beside me. Neil hung back among the trees, waiting for Dad to cue him. Yang skulked there as well, ready to make a shrieking, sword-waving dash if need be. Master Runyon was the Mongol's backup force of one.

My father had maneuvered cautiously around through the scanty trees to the monster's right, where he and Teleri could keep a close watch on T'ing. I couldn't see them from where I lay; I wished I could.

I could see T'ing, though. I could hear her, too. She was speaking softly to the beast—empty, frivolous words intended only to fill a silence. I longed for the certainty of knowing how his mind was translating all this. For a man who looked at a phouka and saw a fire truck, how had he dealt with the Leeside, the courtly Chinese lady, his own repulsive transformation?

I shouldn't have wasted my time worrying. A soul dead enough to prey on the young will never see itself as it is. Wherever the monster *thought* he was, that was the only place he could be, reality be damned. His imagination shriveled up and died the minute you asked him to envision the pain or pleasure of anyone but himself. The borders of his universe stopped at his skin.

As I watched, I saw him begin to relax. Soon he was smiling, his fangs reflecting small flashes from the wall of light. He began to respond to T'ing's casual chatter. Neil stepped from his place, strolling across the open ground, hailing T'ing as if this were a chance meeting. The monster flinched, but not so badly as before. If he recognized Neil or T'ing from the nursery school, he didn't show it. God alone knew what was going on inside that creature's mind. Maybe he saw himself as in a museum, a park, some other wide-open public place where a lady could strike up a friendly conversation and another guy could just innocently happen by. Could be.

Neil was still a distance off when the beast beckoned T'ing to come closer. I heard him speak about the child with him—his niece, he explained. Did T'ing want to say hello to the little girl? By all means. She was a shy thing, but please, please come closer. He let go of the child's sleeve, the better to motion T'ing near.

I saw the vicious smile twist across his face. His talons plunged into the dry Leeside soil and tore loose a jagged stone. He laughed as he struck her, blood springing from the gash across her cheek. She toppled towards the cliffside, Eleziane whimpering and trying to creep away.

Yang's battle cry shattered the air. He wasn't waiting for orders now, and he wasn't the only one. Master Runyon sprinted after him, whirling his shoemaker's hammer in golden circles overhead. Neil froze a moment, then broke into a run, shouting curses. Dad and Teleri burst from cover, the banshee a howling streak of burning hair, my father charging with naked sword.

"Hobson!" I gasped. He anticipated me. Already he was up and running, unarmed but determined. I sprang to my feet, feeling the wand's pull growing stronger as I raced over the dead grass.

The monster heard us and laughed. He knew where he was and what he was. If that knowledge didn't horrify him, it was only because he had no shame. Deliberately he watched us come on, gauging the distance, gloating because he knew it would be too much for us to cover before he finished what he had begun. The stone in his paw was sticky and red. He raised it for another blow—

—and shrieked with fury and frustration when he saw T'ing staggering away with Eleziane in her arms. The blow had dazed her too much to run, but she managed to stumble towards my father and Teleri.

The beast reached her first. He seized Eleziane by the hair and pulled the elf-child's head back until her throat was bared. T'ing fought him as best she could, twisting so that her body was between him and the child. I could hear his eerie chuckle above the sound of battle cries and pounding feet and my own panting breath. I knew that we would be in time to save either T'ing or Eleziane, but never both.

Then I heard words rising from my chest, words I didn't know I knew. Something blazed in my hand. A winged wind streamed from the crystal facets and lifted my feet from the ground. I no longer ran, but flew with the breath of magic under me. I pierced the air between like an arrow and shouted for joy as I struck the beast away.

Momentum; it does the darndest things.

Right over the edge, the two of us, straight down into a gulf of light that sealed everything else from view. There was a roaring all around me, but all I could see was the monster. He clung to me with both paws. The more I flailed at him, the closer he clung, until I felt the cool, inescapable sensation of his talons slipping through my shirt and deep into the flesh beneath. I remember smelling the stench of his breath, seeing the unhealthy yellow of his eyes and thinking, *I wonder if his claws are long enough to reach my heart?*

The light spun on and down forever. Blood trickled over my chest, a sluggish, sleepy flow. I still held onto the wand, but it had gone back to being useless. It hung by my side as, little by little, I felt the strength drain from me. The monster's clutching claws no longer dug so painfully deep. He was going away, and I could sleep. Even the rank heat of his breath was fading to a memory. Instead, my head was giddy with apple blossoms.

Impact made me grunt, but didn't hurt at all. Far away, I heard a metallic screech, a thud, and a babbling of many voices that ebbed to a pleasant murmur.

"Tim! *Tim!*" One voice stabbed through the haze.

Oh. Wasn't that nice. T'ing had come to take her old place in my fantasies. It was very comfortable, resting with my head in her lap. But really, she was going to have to do something about her hair if she wanted to be asked back into my dreams. It was all tousled, and her face—! Would it hurt her to wash off a little of that dried blood?

All right, I'd allow the blood, but the tears just had to go. They were making her face all streaky, and I knew for a fact that a running nose wasn't part of my original script for this scene.

"He's dying."

Who was she talking to? Hey! You're supposed to be paying attention to me, T'ing! Whose fantasy is it, anyway? I'll put up with a few editorial nips and tucks, but my by-God-freaking poetic integrity isn't going to stand for all this noise!

Listen: There it went again. Someone besides T'ing was sobbing. If I turned my head I could just see—

Teleri? My banshee *crying*? "What kind of a gyp is this?" I had a right to complain. "Where's all that 'Woe and wurra-wurra' shit now that I need it?" She only covered her face and sobbed louder, rocking back and forth on her knees.

Something hard pressed against my chest. Deft fingers folded my hands over a cold crystal rod. "I have failed him." Hobson's voice cracked. "If I had served him better, he had not come to this. The Fey have lost their Champion, but I have lost a good and kindly master."

Now I saw the faces gazing down at me. What were all of them doing here? Two's company, guys. Romeo and Juliet checked out without witnesses. Heathcliff and Kathy didn't work with an audience.

Hobson's long moustache was dewy. He turned from me to speak to someone outside the ring of faces. "Milady, will you allow this to be? Is there nothing you can do?"

Neil and Master Runyon stepped to either side. The lady Ele-ziane, small and lovely as a budding rose, came to lean over me and place her hands on my chest to either side of the crystal. Her childish face was strained with effort. A penetrating vitality pulsed from her body to mine, only to drain away in the answering beating of my heart. She sucked in deep, shuddering breaths between clenched teeth, and screwed her eyes shut against the weird, pebbly light of the place where I lay.

"It isn't working." T'ing's voice went high. "Why isn't it working?"

"Leave her 'lone." I was mumbling badly. Would anyone hear? Damn, no one ever paid attention to me. " 'S only a kid. Been through 'lot. Le'er be."

Eleziane's eyes opened, her shoulders dropped. "I cannot mend what is torn so badly. Too much was sheared away as they fell through the portal. I can piece together the fabric, but I cannot weave the web for the piecing."

It was quiet, then. I let my eyes close. I was too tired to go on. Pretty soon the dream would end, and I would have to go back to classes and homework and T'ing Hau Kaplan not knowing I was alive. Too bad. This was one of the best farewell scenes I'd called up yet, even if it needed an "Occupancy by More Than Two Star-Crossed Lovers Is Unlawful" sign.

"I can give you your web, my lady." Where had I heard that voice before? Everything sounded all cottony. Layers of foam separated me from the rest of the world. I couldn't even feel T'ing's arms around me anymore. No, wait, there they were;

stronger than before. She was lifting me from the ground. She smelled of leather and sun and a heady fragrance that was part of lost Sunday afternoons and nearly forgotten good-night kisses.

"Tim . . ."

I opened my eyes and found myself cradled against my father's chest. The crystal wand was balanced between us, one tip above my heart, the other resting over his. I caught sight of Lord Palamon's daughter, watching us anxiously. "You are sure, Great Hern?" she asked.

My father nodded. "Just give me time to say goodbye before you begin."

"Yes." It was the most awestruck of whispers.

"Tim, can you hear me?" I blinked, then nodded. "Good. Listen. There's a lot you'll have to forget, but one thing I want you to remember: What you truly give for love, you never can regret." His lips brushed my forehead. Then he spoke to Eleziane: "All right."

Her little hand closed on the wand. White energy surged through it, pain that wrenched me more awake than I wanted to be. The beating of my heart rippled outward, pounding me like an earthquake. My whole body shook in time to the unrelenting rhythm. My father's body pulsed too, to a different beat. Beat against beat, the throbs that jolted us intensified until I thought the world was one huge heart.

Gradually I became aware of a subtle change. My father's body no longer kept its own tempo, but pulsed in phase with mine. All at once, there were no boundaries of self and self, no separate skins. Outlines blurred. A new layer of living flesh fell easily into place over the part of me that the beast's claws had torn. The pressure of the crystal wand against my heart grew heavier. I thought I felt a cool breath on my lips, a whisper in my ear that said, *No regret. Gladly given, my son.*

Far away as the moon, near as my blood, a piercingly sweet voice was wailing, *Woe, ever woe, for the passing of the Desmond!*

29

Dismember of the Wedding

TELERI'S KEENING HAD barely died away when the lady Eleziane asked, "When are we?"

"Don't you mean *where*, dear?" T'ing insisted on treating the
elfin child as if she were an ordinary kid. The funny thing was,
I think Eleziane rather liked it.

"No, I know *where* we are already. I want to know *when*. My
father will be worried if I've gone missing too long, but he's
willing to make allowances for the time-slippage if I tell him
I've been in a different realm."

"You got a curfew, kid?" Neil sympathized.

I sat up on the cold tile floor. Baggy wool breeches made me
itch like mad. Leather creaked and chain mail jingled. "Never
mind *where* or *when* we are. I want to know *what*." I gestured
with what I *thought* was an empty hand. The sword I held told
me otherwise.

Hobson was right there to relieve me of it. It was the oddest
blade I'd ever seen—not that I'm the big authority on swords,
but I don't believe too many of them are honed steel edging a
core of glittering crystal. "Do you recall nothing, milord?" he
inquired.

"I don't know. I—" I checked to see if my head was still
attached. "We were in the Leeside, chasing the kidnapper. He
hit T'ing, I jumped him, we fought, there was a cliff, we fell—"
I looked around at my comrades. "What *did* happen? Why am
I dressed like this? What happened to my wand?"

"I am certain you will recall it all in time, milord." Hobson
helped me up and solicitously buffed my armor. "Passage to or

from the Leeside will on occasion take certain sartorial liberties.''

''I'll say,'' T'ing commented. She was still in her ravaged silk finery.

''Your wand, milord,'' said Hobson, proffering me the sword hilt on the crook of his arm. ''I hope you will find it more utile in its present form. If not, I shall see to the matter of effecting a refund or exchange personally.''

''And what happened—what happened to the monster?''

Hobson bowed me over to the only window in the room. I had to push aside several bleach bottles and a couple of brooms before I could look out. I saw a busy street arched by a small overpass. A crowd had gathered around a produce truck. The police were there, one of them speaking reassuringly to the jittery driver.

''He's telling him to take it easy.'' Eleziane was at my elbow, ears perked. ''There are lots of witnesses, and they all say that the man just jumped from the overpass deliberately, right into the path of the truck. If the driver couldn't stop in time, you can't blame him for a suicide.'' She lifted her eyes to me; they held happiness again. ''I owe you my life, lord.''

''Don't mention it.'' For some reason I couldn't remember just then, I didn't want to think about life-debts. I took her hand and faced the others. ''So we've come through. The worst is over. Now we've just to get back to—T'ing, what are you doing? Shut that door. We don't even know where we are, yet, and there's some neighborhoods I don't want to get caught in dressed like this.''

T'ing came away from the door to our cramped, pungent haven. She looked sick. ''The worst hasn't even begun. Do you know *where* we are, Tim?''

''Look, that's what I want to find—''

''Or *when*?''

''I think that was Eleziane's question; right, sweetheart?'' The elf-child smiled at me.

T'ing wasn't smiling. ''*Where* we are is in a maintenance closet at Rosemont Manor, *when* we are is my sister's wedding day, and *what* we are is dead dogs the minute my mother—who I just saw walking down the hall out there!—catches us.''

''Your *mother*?'' I pushed T'ing aside, opened the door a crack, and peered out. There, backed by flocked blue velvet wallpaper and trussed into a dress to match, stood Mrs. Kaplan.

I shut the door as noiselessly as I could. "You're missing and she's still having the wedding?"

"The wedding date wasn't that far off when we went into the Leeside. When you looked out, did you see the skinny woman going arm-in-arm with my mother? Well, that's Cousin Sophie. My bet is that Mama called her first and said she was thinking about postponing the wedding until I turned up. That's when she gave my mother the fifty-buck lecture about teenage pranks, sibling rivalry, Daniela's broken heart, and the show must go on. Mama probably gave in out of sheer exhaustion before Sophie could go on to her why-did-you-have-to-adopt-it's-just-borrowing-trouble sermon."

I was amazed. "You *know* all this?"

"I know Mama and I know the effect Cousin Sophie's nagging has on her. I also know that Sophie's son Nathan's being bar-mitzvahed next month and *nothing* had better try upstaging that production, up to and including Armageddon." She folded her arms. "We have to get out of here. We just have to wait until the whole wedding's over and make a break for it." She leaned against the doorjamb, prepared to stand vigil.

"Wedding?" Yang brightened. "Out there? With food? Drink? Doe-eyed women of incredible complaisance and not much brains?"

"If Sophie's daughter Jillian made it back from Club Med in time"—T'ing wasn't really taking Yang's questions seriously—"yes."

"*Yeah!*" With a whoop intended to stampede yaks, Yang the Overly Sociable leaped forward feet first and kicked open the closet door.

"Save us all!" Teleri exclaimed. "He's run mad!"

"Oh, I dunno. I could use a little party-time myself." Neil sauntered out of the closet after his good buddy. We heard the shrieks a little later.

"Ooooh, that sounds like *fun!*" Eleziane bounced up and down eagerly. "Can we go, huh, can we, huh, can we go to the party, huh, *pleeeeeeeease*?" All the high-court training of Faerie took a quick back seat to every whining, whimpering, wheedling technique she'd picked up during her changeling stint as Brittany Izanagi. She held onto my arm with both hands and tried to see which way it would unscrew faster. "Pretty, pretty please with sugar on it, huh?"

"No, we can't," I snapped. I had a headache with a promising future.

"I *wanna* go! I *wanna*!" Eleziane stopped bouncing and started shin-kicking. "I hate you! You're mean! You never let me have any fun!"

"Is it any fun to be *alive*, you little termite?"

It was no good reminding the child of her life-debt. Kids are kids, and they've all got the memory capacity of furniture. Unless you count grudges; *those* they remember.

"I . . . wanna . . . GOOOOOOO!"

Footsteps pounded down the hall outside. Voices were raised in panic. Master Runyon liked the sound of it and slipped through the door. I slammed and locked it after him.

"Nobody else is going *anywhere*! I mean it." I swept the room with my sword for emphasis.

Hobson cringed. "Milord, I assure you that I have no desire to go out *there*. Such a pother. This is just like what happened the last time I took Uncle Caliban anywhere."

Eleziane disagreed. She filled her lungs and let it all out at a decibel level found solely on construction sites.

Someone outside was saying, "Listen! That sounds like a child."

Someone else harrumphed, "And after they had the nerve to tell us we couldn't bring our little Chelsea. *Well!*"

"Never mind your little Chelsea, that child sounds like she's in trouble." The doorknob rattled. "It's locked!"

"*I* wouldn't mind locking myself in somewhere safe. Did you *see* those awful people who just came in? Did you ever in your life witness such behavior? And this is just the pre-ceremony reception! Have you any *idea* what the big one with the weird hair and whiskers is doing with the wheel of Brie?"

"I'm getting the fire axe."

When disaster threatens, the wise man makes his move. Mine was to drop to my knees in front of Eleziane and gibber. "Honey, sweetie, darling, you wanna go to the party? Okay, you can go to the party. Just one eentsy little thing, okay? For Timmy? One bitsy favor for nice Uncle Dread and Puissant Champion of the Fey?"

She eyed me cautiously. "What?"

It was a lovely wedding. T'ing's bridesmaid's dress fit so beautifully that Daniela forgave her for being late. When Mrs. Kap-

Ian tried to get a straight answer out of her younger daughter about where she'd been, the bride simply snapped, "Mama, did you every think you might be happier if you didn't know *everything* your kids have been doing?" That must have struck a chord, because Mrs. Kaplan left T'ing alone for the rest of the wedding.

She grounded her for a month afterwards, though.

Mrs. Kaplan complimented me on my tux. I guess she figured that I wouldn't have gone to the expense of renting a monkey suit if she hadn't invited me to the wedding; she must've forgotten, that's all. I did look sharp, and she further commended me for having gone the whole nine yards to rent a Fred Astaire cane, too. Too bad the coat-check girl at Rosemont Manor cut herself when she didn't hold it by the pommel like I showed her.

I could see T'ing's mother mentally going over the guest list every time she caught sight of one of our crowd. First came doubt, followed by concentration, puzzlement, and finally the rationalization that we wouldn't be dressed for the affair if we weren't supposed to be there, and the really bad ones had to be from the groom's side anyway.

Master Runyon liked his pearl-gray suit just fine, but he was really ecstatic over the shoes, especially the free set of lifts. He and Teleri struck up a wonderful acquaintance with T'ing's Uncle Ed, the Luggage King. My gorgeously gowned banshee took me aside later to confide happily that her luchorpan agent had all but gotten Uncle Ed's signature on a contract naming Teleri of Limerick the official Luggage King Spokesprincess. " 'Tis only local access cable ads I'll be doing," she twittered, "but 'tis a start."

Over by the punch bowl, Yang played baby-tender to Eleziane. Clothes make the Mongol. He was a splendid sight in an outfit straight out of the Liberace Memorial Design collection. (He had found the white satin dinner jacket he started with to be a shade too conservative.) Like the rest of us, he owed his garb to the elf-princess's magic. Eleziane hadn't wanted to cooperate, but what little girl can resist the chance to play dress-up with a bunch of giant Barbie and Ken dolls? Lord Palamon's daughter had done us proud.

She was now doing Yang even prouder, acting as curly-haired, adorable bait for every single woman in the room. The Mongol horseman simply stood there, giving out permission for the ladies to coo over the child and taking in a collection of phone numbers.

I passed by in time to hear Cousin Jillian tell him he didn't look Jewish.

"I'm not," said Yang. "But that could change. You like sex?"

I left while she was telling him about Club Med, and went to find a pay phone so I could call home.

Epilogue

Uncle Caliban moped around the little cottage snugged in the heart of the Leeside. Nothing was *fun* anymore since Great Hern's passing. Seamus no longer joked or sang rude songs, and the doctor himself had taken to making more and more frequent trips to the outer world. He never would take Caliban with him, no matter how devotedly the boggart served him.

It wasn't fair! Caliban stuck his lip out as far as it would go, until he cut it on his belt buckle. He stomped out of the cottage to take out his bad temper on the trees.

He was just mashing the fifth sapling to splinters with his tusks when he felt the breeze. It was like no wind he'd ever sensed blowing over the chill Leeside lands before. It was warm, and comforting, and it smelled wonderful!

It smelled like food, very *tasty* food. The boggart had little brain, but more than ample stomach. He snuffled after the delicious aroma until he found himself standing before the obscure little snag in the fabric of the Leeside.

It was a painful fit. For a while, he considered retreat. No smell, however toothsome, was worth all this discomfort. He tried to wriggle backwards the way he had come, but he couldn't. It was go forward or go hang. The boggart dug in with his huge, filthy feet and gave himself one last push—

He was through. The smell was even stronger here. He only paused long enough to thumb his nose at the raveled hole that had allowed him to escape, then he scampered off to track down whatever smelled so good, and kill it, and eat it.

He was no longer on the premises when a wandering *oni* happened upon the hole. The horned blue demon scratched his mounded belly philosophically as he tried to determine whether it was his karma to fit through such a niggardly opening. The mouth-watering wind caressed his flat nose and his decision was made.

"What has karma done for me lately?" he asked the world, and dived for the hole. It took hard labor, but he managed to win through. The *oni* had a reputation for getting the job done as well as for devouring unwitting victims.

And he'd hardly stretched the hole. Not a bit. Not so that you could notice. It wasn't *that* much bigger now, was it?

Not at all.